Rosie Thomas

The Potter's House

HARPER

Harper
HarperCollins*Publishers*
1 London Bridge Street
London SE1 9GF

www.harpercollins.co.uk

First published in Great Britain by
Random House 2001

This edition published by *Harper* 2015

13

A catalogue record for this book
is available from the British Library

ISBN: 978-0-00-756322-7

Set in Sabon by FMG using Atomik ePublisher from Easypress

Printed and bound in Great Britain by
Clays Ltd, St Ives plc

MIX
Paper from
responsible sources
FSC **FSC C007454**
www.fsc.org

FSC is a non-profit international organisation established
to promote the responsible management of the world's forests.
Products carrying the FSC label are independently certified
to assure consumers that they come from forests that are managed
to meet the social, economic and ecological needs
of present and future generations.

Find out more about HarperCollins and the environment at
www.harpercollins.co.uk/green

The Potter's House

Rosie Thomas is the author of a number of celebrated novels, including the bestselling *The Kashmir Shawl*. A keen traveller, she has climbed in the Alps and the Himalayas, competed in the Peking to Paris car rally and trekked in the footsteps of Shackleton in South Georgia. She lives in London.

By the same author:

For Theo

ONE

The first time I saw the woman who later ran off with my husband she was giving directions to two removals men. They were struggling to lift a sofa round an awkward bend in the communal stairs and I was waiting to pass.

There were two flats per floor in Dunollie Mansions and this was evidently the new owner of the one directly above ours. Old widowed Mrs Bobinski had lived up there for twenty years in a fug of simmering soup fumes and mothballs, and then she died in hospital after a very brief illness and her heirs put the flat up for sale. It was on the market for months, partly because mansion flats like ours were no longer fashionable, if they ever had been, but mostly because the two nephews were asking too much money for it. I had heard from the Frasers on the top floor that the place was finally sold, but no one had any idea who our new neighbour would be.

'Some nice, unremarkable couple just like us,' Graham Fraser cheerfully assumed.

'And us,' I added, more thoughtfully.

I stood to one side to let the woman and her puffing retinue pass by. She was walking upstairs backwards and would have collided with me if I hadn't put out my hand to steer her away. She wheeled round at once.

'God, sorry. Can't even look where I'm going. Hang on a sec.' The last words were called down to the two young men. The one on the lower end hitched his shoulder under the padded arm and stared up in sweaty disbelief.

'Don't worry about us. We've got all day, Col, haven't we?'

Ignoring him, she introduced herself to me. 'I'm Lisa Kirk. Just moving in, number seven.'

'Let your end down, Col.'

'Right you are.'

I told the woman my name and pointed to our door. She was younger by far than anyone else currently living in the flats. I would have put her age at twenty-three, although I learned later that she was actually twenty-seven. Fifteen years or so younger them me. She had fair hair with blonde streaks and a soft leather rucksack slung over one shoulder. Even her combat pants had obviously come from somewhere expensive and fashionable, well away from the firing line. She looked as if she ought to be moving into a loft in Clerkenwell or a pastel-fronted little place in Notting Hill, not a flat in a stuffy red-brick block in a Kensington backwater.

'If you need a cup of sugar. Or maybe gin ...' I said.

'Thanks,' she answered and smiled. An attractive smile. 'You come and have a drink with me when I've got the glasses unpacked. Tell me what I should do with the place.'

I flattened myself against the wall as Col and his counterpart hoisted the sofa again. They laboured past me, with Lisa Kirk leading the way. I went out to post my letters and to the greengrocer's down the side street to buy vegetables for dinner, then walked slowly back into the building.

The shallow stairs and the bare landings in Dunollie

2

Mansions were kept clean and swept, and blown light bulbs always promptly replaced by Derek the caretaker who lived in the basement. There was a mahogany table to the left of the front door above which communal notices were posted, about things like holiday refuse collection, temporary interruptions to the water supply or work on the old-fashioned but effective central heating system. There was a faint scent of Derek's floor polish and an even fainter whiff of disinfectant, and occasionally the rattle of the lift door grille followed by the hum of the machinery. It was a quiet, unflashy place.

I always liked the two solid doors on each landing, facing each other at a slight angle on either side of the stairwell, and the ornate brass door furniture worn with polishing, and the diamond panes of leaded glass on either side of the central panel. The hallways within were dark and would have been claustrophobic if the ceilings were not so high, but the rooms opening off them were bright and well-proportioned, especially the corner drawing rooms with their bay windows looking in two directions. From the top flats there was a view of the dome of the Albert Hall and a landscape of rooftops and chimneys, but in summertime our windows, lower down, framed nothing but the leafy plane trees out in the street. When there was a breeze the leaf patterns moved on the floor and furniture. Even in winter the bare branches made a screen against the walls and windows across the wide street.

I liked the sense of enclosure. And the well-ordered, dull and unimaginative sheer *safety* of everything.

It was not a background against which you could, for example, imagine anyone running amok. No one could chop through the three-inch thickness of the front doors. The walls and floors were solid too, and no murmur of the outside world ever penetrated. We all lived there in our separate castles, friendly enough and with Derek to sweep up: the Frasers on the top floor, and Mark and Gerard the gay couple who lived opposite Mrs Bobinski's, and Peter and me, and the rest. But separate. There were no children in the block. The flats weren't quite big enough for families. It was a place for small dogs, like Mark's and Gerard's schnauzer, and childless regret, like mine.

It was a few days before I saw Lisa Kirk again. I told Peter about her that evening, when he came home from work. I remember him sitting in the armchair against the Chinese yellow wall of the drawing room, with a drink on the stool beside him. It was September, and the leaves of the plane trees were just beginning to brown and crisp around the margins.

'How old?' he asked and I told him – underestimating by about four years as it later turned out.

'Oh, God. It will be techno music at all hours and impossible parties, and people running up and down the stairs. We should operate on a co-op system, like the Americans. Nobody admitted unless approved by the committee.'

Peter affected fogeyishness, sometimes. It was one of the ways he tried to look after me, by pretending to be staider and more reliable and conservative than he really was. It was one of those unspoken contracts that long-standing couples make, knowing their partner's needs and histories. In fact, he was a tolerant man, with a remarkable capacity to overlook other people's foibles and most of the irritations generated by them.

'We'll see,' I said, because there was nothing else to say, and moved on to the other snippets of the day's news. I wasn't working, then, and it was sometimes difficult to think of anything at all to relate. Lisa Kirk's arrival was a welcome new topic.

When I met her for the second time we were both coming in with Safeway carrier bags, at the end of a damp afternoon with the smell of autumn thick under the plane trees.

She rested her bags on the stairs beyond our front door and looked down at me.

'Come up and have a cup of tea. Have you got time?'

A commodity in abundant supply, as it happened. I pushed my own shopping into our hallway and followed her up, curious to see and know more.

Old Mrs Bobinski's decor was mostly still in place: Regency striped wallpaper with darker rectangles outlined in grime where murky pictures had once hung, fluted wooden pelmets, central light fittings hideous in gilt and smoked glass. Against this backdrop Lisa had partially arranged her modishly beaten-up brown leather sofa, CD tower and two tall glass urns filled with coiled snakes of twinkling little lights.

'It's all a bit of a tip.' She sighed. 'I haven't had time to think, let alone get anything done to it. I needed to move quickly after I split with Baz. And I really liked this place. Lofts are a bit done-that and Dunollie Mansions is so ...'

She eyed me, transparently wondering which word to use in order not to offend me. '... Neutral,' she concluded. 'You know. I reckoned you could do anything here, make it into anything you wanted, without it being a *statement*.'

'Really?'

I felt a twitch of dismay. This refuge, my safe haven, was about to teeter out on to some cutting edge of style. I didn't want it to be invaded or to have its sagging face lifted.

'If I ever get *time*. Come in the kitchen, I'll make us some tea.'

There was the same schizophrenia in there. A maplewood butcher's block on wheels, an espresso machine and Philippe Starck knick-knacks disposed against Mrs Bobinski's yellow Formica, and one of those American refrigerators with an ice dispenser in the front, finished in pillar-box red. This monster fitted into none of the available spaces and hummed in the corner of the room next to the door like a TARDIS waiting to dematerialise. I found myself touching the polished metal handle, wondering where I would end up if I stepped inside and let it take me along.

'Are you hungry?' Lisa was asking, watching my hand hovering. 'I'm afraid there's not a lot in there, I'm not much of a kitchen person really, it's just that we bought it jointly and I didn't want Baz to end up with it. He only used it to keep those little vodka or champagne bottles in, you know, from when everyone used to stand at parties drinking through straws. But I've just got some stuff from the supermarket if you'd like …'

'No. I'm not hungry.' I withdrew my hand. 'But I would like a cup of tea.'

She went on chattering and rummaging in cupboards for cups and tea bags.

'Raspberry? Lemon and ginger? Peppermint?'

Gooseberry and leek. Tamarillo. Artichoke leaf.

'Or there's some ordinary.'

'Ordinary would be good, thanks.'

When she opened the door of the TARDIS to take out the milk, I saw that it was empty except for a bottle of champagne and one of those pre-mixed packets of artful salad. We settled ourselves on a pair of steel-and-leather chairs at opposite sides of the kitchen table. Lisa lifted her cup, smiling at me again. She had grey eyes, neat features and lovely skin that seemed to have light shining through it like tissue paper stretched over a spotlight tube. I felt tired and colourless, and touched with envy. There was no point in envying youth, I reminded myself. It was a fact, vivid but perishable. You might as well be jealous of oranges.

'Here's to new neighbours,' she said.

We drank to each other and then Lisa hitched her chin at our surroundings.

'What do you think I should do with it?'

'You could paint it all white.'

She gave this suggestion careful consideration, as if it was the most imaginative proposal she had ever heard.

'Could do, yes.' And then, with an abrupt switch of focus, 'Are you married?'

I told her that I was and for how long, and that we had no children.

Lisa fixed her gaze on mine.

'Do you mind not having children?'

'I have learned to live with it.'

She stood up from the table and went to lean against one of the cupboards, and the TARDIS began a low humming as if preparing to relocate. When she moved, the curved wings of her shoulder blades shifted beneath her T-shirt and poignant knobs of bone showed under the skin at the nape of her neck. Her hair was pinned up today with a butterfly clip. She stood not quite looking at me, hesitating, and I waited for what she wanted to say. It was warm in the kitchen; Derek had this week fired up the big central heating boiler. We were snug in here. The heat and the hum of the refrigerator and the sense of enclosure that Dunollie Mansions always gave bred an impression of intimacy, as though Lisa and I were old friends who had momentarily lapsed into thoughtful silence.

'I suppose that's what you do. Learn to live with things, I mean. I wish I was any good at it. *Can* you learn?'

I shifted on my leather-and-steel perch. At once Lisa moved forward and poured more tea. She didn't want me to leave yet, because she needed someone to talk to. I was a good choice, after all. I had gradually become someone who listened, rather than a creature who went out and did things.

I thought that Lisa Kirk was probably lonely. And that her loneliness might last as long as a nanosecond, before the next Baz came along.

'Learn? I don't know. It was just a lazy figure of speech. You accept what you are dealt, or you kick against it. The end result's probably no different anyway.'

While she considered this Lisa groped on the floor beside her seat and found her handbag. She took out a packet of Silk Cut and lit one while I looked at the bag. It was made of chartreuse suede and shaped like a pineapple or maybe a hand grenade.

'Like it? It's my design. I make handbags, my own company. I'm opening a shop in Walton Street soon. We're called Bag Shot.'

I had seen the name, possibly in a *Vogue* spread of witty accessories.

'I do like it,' I said truthfully. I was impressed. I would too readily have dismissed Lisa as merely a trust-fund babe or daddy's girl, and now it turned out that she was a designer and a businesswoman.

She tipped the bag upside down and a heap of keys and lipsticks and ticket stubs fell out.

'Here,' she said and gave it to me.

I examined the cunning fastening of the hood and the bottle-green silk lining. The little golden label stitched to the inside said 'Bag Shot by Lisa Kirk'.

'It's beautiful. You can't just give it to me.'

'Yes I can, I want to. God. Anyway, we were saying about learning to live with things, only it's without in my case. Baz was my business partner, you know, he was the one who knew about start-ups and leases and money, and I just drew pictures of bloody handbags and chose stuff to get them made up in. We lived together as well, obviously. Ever since I was twenty-one. Work and play, me and Baz. And then it fell apart, like a piece of machinery suddenly worn out. He met a woman at a party, I was yakking and drinking but all the time I was really just across the room, frozen, watching them fall for each other like they were in a movie. And then, once that had happened, it got really difficult to go on working together, and ... so.' She spread out her hand, taking in the kitchen and the red refrigerator and ourselves, sitting facing each other across the table.

'I see,' I said. We sat in silence for a minute.

'Baz's new girlfriend is pregnant.'

'Oh. When did all this happen?'

'They met four months ago.'

'That was quick.'

'It was, wasn't it?'

I clasped and unclasped the lid of the bag. 'You know, you'll find someone else. More quickly than you think, probably. I'm sure everyone tells you that. And you can find a new business partner too although that may be a bit more difficult. The requirements are more stringent.'

She smiled at that.

'Maybe I won't find anyone, on the other hand. I feel pretty useless.'

I told her what she probably expected to hear, that you don't get your stuff featured in *Vogue* or fix yourself up in mansion flats in Kensington at her age if you are anything less them talented and able. We drank some more tea and talked a little about how Baz and she had worked together, and then about the flat and her plans to transform it once, as she put it, the shop was able to run itself around the block. She showed me round the rest of it and I saw that her bed – as narrow as a child's – was in the little second bedroom that Peter and I used as an occasional spare room, and in the main bedroom with its good light was her drawing board, with big cork panels pinned with scraps of fabric and sketches and pages torn from magazines resting against the walls alongside it.

I thought of our tidy rooms below, static and silent at this time of day, and the way this web of Lisa's uncertainty and tentativeness and peering into the future was exactly superimposed on them, not just on Mrs Bobinski's. It made me feel as stiff as our decor.

We returned to the kitchen. Lisa picked up the bag and put it into my hands.

'Thank you,' I said.

She came with me to the front door and I looked through the diamond glass panels at the swimmy, distorted view of the hallway.

'Would you like to have had children?' she asked, with her hand on the latch.

I knew that she was only asking for whatever my answer might reflect on her own situation, on the baby her ex-lover was expecting that she believed should have been hers.

'You'll have a baby,' I said as gently as I could. 'You've got all the time in the world.'

'But would you?' she persisted, with the tactlessness of self-absorption.

I am used to deflecting these thoughts, but still I saw the pictures now, the queasy procession framed and frozen by the camera shutter, *click*, all the way back into history, *click* and *click*.

'No.'

Her hand had dropped back to her side so I opened the door myself and stepped out into the hallway. We exchanged unspecific invitations to have a drink, or drop round for a kitchen supper. And then I went downstairs to the close air of our own flat where the supermarket carrier bags were waiting for me to attend to them.

Peter sat in his usual chair, with a whisky at his elbow. He had had a reasonable day, he said. Busy, and the Petersens people were a bunch of amateurs who couldn't run a tap, let alone a software licensing programme, but nothing really to complain about.

'And you?'

He looked across at me, arching his eyebrows behind the fine metal ovals of his spectacle rims. I told him about having tea with Lisa Kirk, and showed him the chartreuse hand grenade.

He examined it, inside and out.

'Bit extreme, isn't it? Do women really buy this sort of stuff?'

'Yes, I think so. They probably pay about two hundred quid for it. She runs her own business and is about to open a shop.'

He puckered his lips in a soundless whistle, interested now. Peter was a management consultant, with expertise I couldn't even guess at. He read and wrote reports in a language as impenetrable to me as Mandarin, and he too had a company, on the comfortable earnings from which we lived our sedate life in Dunollie Mansions. 'Chalk and cheese,' my mother said before we married, which was also not long before her early death from ovarian cancer. (My father and she separated when I was about twelve, and he married again and acquired a second family to which he and his new wife swiftly added. The Steps and Halves, my mother and I called them.)

Chalk and cheese Peter and I may have been, but we were determined to have each other. We were introduced by a photographer I knew who gave a drunken Christmas party in his studio, to which Peter was brought along more or less on a whim by the photographer's agent. I remember looking across the room, through a sea of outlandish people who didn't at the time *look* outlandish to me, and seeing his well-cut suit and the lights flickering off the shields of his glasses. He was the one who looked out of place in that company of Mapplethorpe boys and six-foot women. After a little

11

while the photographer's agent brought him across and introduced us.

'Cary Flint, Peter Stafford.'

I remember that we talked about our fellow guests and a new book of our host's pictures, and a Matisse exhibition we had both recently seen in the South of France. I had to work hard to sustain this cocktail party standard of chat. I was very thin at the time and taking a lot of pills, and felt speedy and mad. I was disconcerted by the way this man tilted his head towards me so as not to miss a word of my insane gabble, and I also saw the way that his hair fell forward over his temples and the mildness of his eyes behind his glasses, and my knees almost buckled with lust for him. The party was reaching its crescendo. Two boys were exchanging tongues under the ribs of the spiral staircase that also sheltered Peter and me. A procession of other models' legs filed up and down past our ears and I noticed that he never even glanced at all this thigh and buttock because his eyes were fixed on me. I began to speak more slowly, although I had to shout over the noise, and all the time he watched my mouth with minute attention. Blood hummed in my ears, drowning the crashing music.

At last Peter took my glass out of my hand and put it down, reaching past the intertwined boys to do so.

'Shall we leave now?' he asked.

Outside, the cold air hit me in the face. My tiny party dress also exposed a length of bare leg and my coat didn't cover much more.

Peter wrapped a protective arm round my shoulders.

'It isn't far to my car.'

I couldn't even remember whether I had come in my car, let alone where I might have parked it. That was how I was in those days.

Peter's turned out to be low, two-seater, quite old and with an interior of creased leather and glowing wood. I learned later that it was a Jaguar XK140. He always loved old cars and kept a series of them on which he bestowed almost as much affection as he did on me. He took me that night to a French restaurant in Notting Hill, old-fashioned but good, and made me eat whitebait and steak. I drew the line at pudding, although he wanted to order one for me. I hadn't eaten a pudding or a slice of cake since I was fifteen.

Over the first course I confessed what I believed it was only fair for him to know from the beginning. If, in fact, there was actually going to be anything further, if this start didn't turn out also to be the ending. There had been a few evenings of that sort, lately.

'I am afraid that I am mad. Known fact. Crazy. Completely barking.'

He chewed his food, reflecting briefly on this idiotic announcement.

'I think I will be the judge of that,' Peter Stafford answered.

I ate as much as I could of my steak and vegetables, without making much of a dent in the portion, and all the time I could think of nothing but how soon we might be able to go to bed together. When he was finally convinced that I wasn't going to eat tarte Tatin or chocolate soufflé, Peter shepherded me back to the Jaguar and drove me to his flat in Bayswater.

We kissed for the first time under the overhead light in the hallway. In his sitting room, standing beside the floor-to-ceiling bookshelves, I reached around to the zip on the back of my dress and undid it. Slowly, I let the folds drop to the carpet. I was naked underneath except for my pants. He covered my breasts with his hands.

I kicked off one high-heeled shoe and then the other. Barefoot, I was closer to his height. He took my hand and led me into his bedroom, and closed the door behind us.

13

When he took off the last garment he knelt over me and looked.

'Oh God, oh God,' he breathed. After a beat of fear I realised that it was in pleasure and admiration, not dismay. I put my arms round his neck and pulled him down on top of me.

When we made love, Peter Stafford made me feel three-dimensional.

I forgot the jut of my hips and my overlong and protuberant spinal column, and the dull grate of bone. In his arms I became languorous and creamy and *fat*.

Afterwards he held me against him, warming me with his solid flesh.

'Cary, Cary. Be still,' he ordered and I knew that he didn't mean just now, under the crisp covers of his bed, but in my life. No more spinning around and gobbling pills. No more talking nonsense or drinking or dementia.

'I asked Cecil to bring me over to you,' he said. Cecil was the photographer's agent. 'I didn't think you would even speak to me, but I made him do it just the same.'

'I would have come to you, if you hadn't.' Maybe I would have done, too.

That was a Thursday evening. I had a job the next day, but I called in sick. It was the first time I had ever done such a thing and my booker was astonished. Peter called his office too. We stayed in bed for the whole of Friday and for the weekend that followed it, except for when we got up to forage for something to eat and drink. I padded around wearing one of his shirts because I had nothing with me but my party dress and we fed each other cold chicken legs or buttered toast.

'Good,' he approved.

Another time when we were quietly lying together and

14

watching raindrops on the window glass he asked, 'Why did you say you were mad? Except for the job you do and the people you do it with you seem exceptionally sane to me.'

I fended him off. 'No real reason. Drink, nerves, babble. Or I suppose that if someone were to look at you and then at me, they might put you in the sane category and me in the other. Just as a matter of relativity.'

'Because of the way we look, relatively?'

Without his glasses Peter's eyes were soft, with creases at the corners. His forehead and the faint lines hooking together his mouth and nose and the curve of his lips were already dear to me. I touched them, stroking the skin with the flat of my thumbs.

'No. Nothing to do with that. It's history.'

'What history?'

'Tell me yours first.'

He held me so that my chin rested in the hollow of his shoulder. I closed my eyes and listened while he described his childhood. He was the middle one of three boys, children of a City solicitor and a career mother. They lived in a good house in Hampshire and the brothers played cricket in the garden and sailed dinghies, and went to a suitable public school and then on to appropriate universities.

'Not very interesting, you see,' Peter said.

'It is to me. Where are your brothers now?'

He told me that they were both lawyers and both married, and made a joke about it being such a conservative family that his own minute deviations from this norm were regarded as acts of rebellion.

'No wife, you mean?'

'No law, no wife. But I have had a couple of girlfriends. I'm quite normal, you know.'

I did know already, but I wanted to know more about his background because he was so safe and rational, the living equivalent of the scent of clean laundry. Everything about Peter Stafford, past and present, was a magnet to me.

Probably after that we started to make love again and so his original question to me was forgotten. I avoided talking about my own history that time, although eventually, of course, I did confess it to him.

In any case, within three months Peter and I were married.

He asked me once or twice if I had seen our new neighbour again, and I told him no. Then I met Lisa parking her car as I was coming back from a walk in Hyde Park. We talked for a minute or two, and on impulse I asked her if she would like to come and have dinner with us the following week. To my surprise she accepted. She was lonelier than I had calculated and Baz had not yet been replaced.

Lisa rang the doorbell late, well after all the other guests had arrived. Peter answered the door and I heard him introducing himself and then Lisa's laughing response before he shepherded her into the drawing room. She was wearing a short, slippery red dress with a little pink cardigan shrugged over it, and red suede shoes. Our guests collectively sat upright, our old friends Clive and Sally Marr and Mark and Gerard from upstairs, and the visiting American woman associate of Peter's, and the young portrait painter and his girlfriend whom I had invited in an attempt to span the age gap between Lisa and the rest of us. Her arrival was like a shaft of daylight coming into the nighttime gathering.

I saw her looking around at the room that was identical in shape and size, and yet so different from hers.

'Your flat is very smart,' she said, after we had greeted each other.

'Is it?'

'Definitely.'

16

I introduced her to the others and as she moved around I saw that what she brought with her wasn't exactly light, but warmth. Aside from her youth and her prettiness, she had genuine heat that thawed the formality of the occasion. Clive Marr unwound his long arms and legs from their self-protective embrace and shook her hand, and Jessy the American woman smilingly made room for her on the sofa. I hitched my black woollen sleeves round my wrists. I was glad that Lisa Kirk was entirely natural and at ease, and that she didn't need her hostess's protection. My hands were cold, so I went closer to the fire and warmed them.

The evening took off. Clive told a funny story I had never heard before about his days as a houseman under an autocratic consultant who thought his inveterate stutter was an affectation. 'D-d-d-iverticulitis, Dr Marr?' he mimicked, embedding his own impediment within the fearsome doctor's voice with surgical precision.

Everyone laughed including Lisa, and Clive looked boyish with pleasure.

Dan Cruickshank the portrait painter gossiped indiscreetly about the royal princess who was currently sitting for him, and Mark and Gerard leaned forward greedily to catch the details. From across the room Peter smiled at me, his eyes creasing behind his glasses. I smiled back, buckling my mouth into a curve against a sense of alarm that I didn't yet recognise.

We went into the next room to eat. The candles reflected tapering ovals of light off glass and polished wood. Lisa studied Peter's pictures, a pair of splashy Hodgkins and a small Bacon. She had taken off her little pink cardigan and her shoulders were bare except for thin straps. Her skin was pale and the candlelight seemed to strike off it, breaking and intensifying into painterly slashes of green and peach and yellow so that I narrowed my eyes to make it recombine, wondering if I had already had too much to drink.

'Lisa, would you like to sit here?'

Peter drew out the chair next to his. I took the other end of the table, between Gerard and Dan. The talk and laughter swelled and I sliced and spooned food on to plates and watched it disappear. After long years of conditioning myself, I didn't any longer care much about eating. But I had plenty of time at my disposal to prepare meals like this one and cooking was still one of my pleasures.

At my end of the table Dan and Sally and Jessy were talking about portraiture. Peter had wanted Dan to paint me and we had met originally to talk about the project. I had hedged and demurred, because I didn't want to sit and be scrutinised so closely, and in the end the idea had come to nothing. But we had remained friends with Dan and therefore also the current one of his series of girlfriends.

'I would still like her to sit for me, but I don't think I can persuade her,' Dan was saying.

'You should keep trying,' Gerard advised.

Lisa had been deep in conversation with Peter. Her attentiveness to him made her seem taut as a stretched bow with the arrow in the notch and ready to fly. But now she turned her head. Our eyes met and locked.

'It would be a wonderful picture. When I first saw Cary I was almost too afraid to speak to her.'

'Why is that?' I asked, in spite of myself.

'Because of the way you look.'

There seemed to be a shift in air pressure, as in the seconds before the sound of an approaching tube train becomes audible. *The way you look*. When I was much younger I possessed an outlandish kind of beauty. I was six feet tall, with a smooth face that make-up artists could paint over with a hundred other faces. I used my appearance to earn money as a photographic model. But I was past forty now and what was left of my extreme looks had been for a long time more

18

an affliction than a blessing because they were at odds with what I felt inside. It was like having always to wear a mask, only it was also a mask that age kept on distorting.

'I remember that you talked quite a lot, in fact,' I said, recalling the confidences about Baz and his new girlfriend and the pregnancy.

There was that change in air pressure again, a movement of the atmosphere that made you suck in a breath to reinflate your lungs. In the sudden silence that was broken only by the clink of cutlery I realised that the new atmospheric component was hostility. It had replaced the oxygen.

Lisa and I were still looking at each other, the glance twisting between us like razor wire. Peter sat in his place at the head of our table, his eyes still mild behind his glasses, maybe unaware of the arrow pointed at him. But I think he did feel the tension of the bowstring. This was about him. Lisa Kirk believed that she had spotted Baz's replacement.

'Oh yes, once I knew you,' Lisa said softly.

My body went stiff. That this child should think she knew me on the basis of a couple of encounters, when I had devoted so much and so many years of effort to concealing everything. Everyone in the room, it seemed, immediately began talking very loudly about the first thing that came into their heads.

Mark adjusted the already perfect folds of his turned-back shirt cuffs. He had smooth wrists, lightly tanned from the latest trip to Kerala. And then he reached out to touch Lisa's handbag that was lying next to her plate.

'I read somewhere that women's bags actually represent an intimate portion of their anatomy. Do you think there's any truth in that, Lisa?'

Dear Mark, kind and vicious in the same breath. Tonight's little bag was in the shape of a pink satin heart, sequinned and beaded, and certainly quite anatomical if you chose to look at it that way.

19

'If it is true, I'm in the right business, aren't I?' She smiled. 'Even if it is only a representation. Dealing in a commodity that is so constant and yet so sought after.'

Lisa was utterly self-possessed. I had the sudden certainty that nothing would deflect her and nothing would disconcert her. She wore her youth and sureness and desirability like armour plating.

Peter's American associate was giggling at this risqué turn in the conversation, and Lisa lifted up the bag and gave it to her to examine.

'What do you think, Jessy?'

'It's certainly pretty enough.'

'Thank you.'

I slid out of my chair and began to collect up the plates from my end of the table, moving very deliberately and with a smile nailed to my face.

The evening came to an end eventually. Lisa rested her fingers gently and briefly on my forearm as she kissed me goodnight and then gave exactly the same attention to Peter.

When Peter and I were left on our own we stacked the plates in the kitchen, blew out the candles, retreated to our bedroom as we had done so many times before. I lay very still in our bed and he put his arms round me, which made me conscious of how brittle I felt.

I wasn't ageing well, I thought. Now that I no longer had it, I wanted my weird beauty back again. I wasn't a model, I had failed to become an actress – which had been my subsequent intention. Another strange choice for a woman who doesn't like to be looked at. Much uneventful time had elapsed and I didn't know what I was any longer. Except that I was Peter Stafford's wife and a resident of Dunollie Mansions, for now.

'Catherine, what's wrong?'

He doesn't often call me by my full name.

'Nothing. Did you enjoy the evening?'

He shifted a little on his hip, considering, and I felt the warmth of his breath on my face.

'Yes. I think it went quite well. Clive was in good form.'

Tenderness towards him spread beneath my breast-bone like heartburn. Peter always considered his judgements, and tried to be fair and objective. How had we lived together for so long and been so different, in our chalk and cheese way?

Lying in the dark I found myself thinking of the night we met and fell in love, standing under the ribs of a spiral staircase while a procession of models went up and down past our heads. Lisa Kirk told me about watching her Baz falling in love at a party in just the same way and I was sure I had witnessed the same flash of lightning tonight, between Lisa and my husband, even though I didn't think they had exchanged a word in private or even an unwitnessed glance. The three scenes made a bright little triptych in my mind's eye.

I moved an inch closer to Peter and kissed his closed mouth. At the same time I lifted and crooked my upper knee. One of those signals that long-time couples read so well. He put his hand over my ribcage and splayed the fingers over the bones, as if he was fingering piano keys.

'I love you,' I told him, which was the truth.

'And I you,' he answered politely. 'And I worry about you.'

I didn't press him to explain the dimensions of his anxiety. 'What did you think of Lisa Kirk?'

'I liked her.'

'I thought you would.'

I exhaled and his fingers moved again.

We made love, a little awkwardly, as if there were a sheet between us.

After that, it was only a matter of time.

TWO

Every day of each season on the island of Halemni had its own perfection, but to Olivia Georgiadis autumn was the best time of all.

The heat of summer was contained in the brazen midday, while the chill mornings and evenings gave a taste of the coming winter. There was a smell of woodsmoke and burning pitch as the fishermen overhauled the boats, and the houses and tavernas around the harbour wall lost their wide-eyed summer expressions as shutters were nailed in place. The last of the holidaymakers were carried away on ferries and hydrofoils towards Rhodes, or distant Athens, and their flights to Munich or Stockholm or Gatwick. There was a collective sense of relief at the season's end as the little community prepared to turn inwards.

Olivia was thinking about autumn and other things, as she made her way down the hill to her house. Her two boys were running ahead of her, their brown legs twinkling in the sunshine as they leapt the rocks. Olivia walked more slowly, with empty baskets in both hands. She had been to take cake and flasks of coffee to her guests who were at their easels in the shelter of a band of stunted trees near the top of the hill.

'There's Pappy!'

Georgi, the older child, balanced on a cone of rock and pointed. His brother Theo immediately ran up and pushed him sideways. Georgi toppled off and Theo leapt on to the rock pinnacle in his place.

'I am the leader,' he crowed.

'Mummy, Mum, did you see what Theo did?'

The two of them spoke a mixture of Greek and English that Olivia and Xan always enjoyed. Xan's Greek mother was less admiring.

'They sound nothing like little Greek boys. They sound like nothing on earth,' Meroula Georgiadis complained.

'Take it in turns,' Olivia told them automatically.

She dismissed the thought of her mother-in-law and watched her husband walking back along the harbour wall instead. He was looking over the turquoise water, past the moored caiques and the smoking tar barrel, but she could see the way the wind blew his hair into a crest, just as it did with Georgi's. Her heart's rhythm altered for a second or two as it always did when she caught sight of Xan after a separation, even if it had only lasted for an hour.

'Come on, Theo,' Georgi yelled, opting to ignore the rock dispute. He ran away downhill and his brother scrambled after him. Theo was only five, the younger by two and a half years, but he was impulsive and imaginative where Georgi was calm and cautious. Olivia began to run after them, with the empty raffia bags flapping against her legs. The low mounds of wild sage and spiny burnet alternated with outcrops of bare limestone and she skipped from one safe footing to the next, unconsciously copying her sons.

The old houses in Megalo Chorio, the principal settlement on the island, were whitewashed cubes with door and window frames painted bright blue or green. They lined the harbour wall and the sides of the one street that led away from the

23

sea. On the village outskirts, a few metres back from the sickle curve of the beach, was a row of new concrete boxes, half of them unfinished with thickets of rusty metal sprouting from the flat roofs. These were the apartments and studios rented by the tourists in summer, those who didn't stay with the Georgiadises or in private houses or one of the two tavernas with rooms in the main street. The new buildings were an eyesore but Olivia had taught herself not to look at them. The tourists brought money to Halemni, they needed somewhere to sleep, so it was necessary to have such places.

The Georgiadis house stood at the back of the village, forming the short side of a rough cobbled square dominated by a huge fig tree. Across the square Taverna Irini faced a tiny church with a rounded blue dome. The fourth side was open and gave a wide view of the bay and water skittishly silvered by the sunlight. The house had originally belonged to the island's potter, but the local craftsman had lost the competition against cheap imported plates and dishes, and had retired to the west side of the island. Xan and Olivia had bought the house and its outbuildings ten years before, when they decided to make their lives here where Xan had been born. Before that Olivia had travelled so far and for so long that she believed to settle in one place, with Xan, would be as close to heaven as she could ever come.

And in many ways the belief had been justified. She would have argued with anyone that every idyll must have a flaw, in order for it to be recognisably an idyll. Xan came along the street just as Olivia and the boys reached the front door. He was a big man, black-haired and black-eyed. He put his hands against the oak of the door lintel and made an arch of his body. The boys ran underneath, shouting with noisy competition.

The house was washed pale-blue, like a reflection of the early morning sky. It had two storeys with shuttered windows and small iron balconies at the upper ones. The rooms were small and not very convenient, but the outbuildings were ideal. Xan had converted them into a row of modest studios, and it was these that housed Olivia's summer guests. They were English, like Olivia herself, mostly middle-aged or retired, and they came to Halemni to paint.

Olivia and Xan made a living out of the painting holidays, just, which put them in about the same financial position as everyone else on Halemni. And they had the winters to themselves, when the wind worried at the shutters and salt spray caked the harbour stones.

Olivia stooped and tried to pass the same way as the boys, but Xan caught her by the hips.

'Hello, *yia sou.*'

They kissed briefly, smiling into each other's mouths.

'Everybody happy?' Xan meant the guests up on the hill, peering across their easels at the view of the village and the coast of Turkey like smoke on the skyline. This fortnight's guests had been a more than usually demanding group. They complained about the cold at night and about the mid-afternoon heat.

'For five minutes, at least. Chris is up there.'

Tuition was provided by Christopher Cruickshank, a good teacher and a talented watercolourist in his own right. Olivia cooked and hosted evening parties, and led walks if anyone wanted to explore the island.

Xan's contribution was largely his geniality. It was one of the reasons why the English couples came back year after year and recommended the Georgiadises to their friends. Xan took them on boat trips and grilled fish on a driftwood fire, and teased them about English weather and their native reticence, or anything else except their ability as painters. In the remainder of the time he fixed damaged ballcocks and repaired the generator, and did whatever other running repairs were needed.

Xan grinned. Nothing more needed to be said. It was the last day of the last booking and tomorrow the hydrofoil would take them all away.

'Pappy, look. It's a war,' Georgi called.

Xan put his arm round his wife's shoulders and they squeezed through the doorway together. The boys had perched at the big scrubbed table in the kitchen, knees and feet bundled up anyhow on the chairs, and were drawing on big sheets of coarse paper. Georgi's picture was of aeroplanes looping and smashing in mid-air. Tiny men spilled out of them with triangular parachutes sprouting from their backs. Xan put his head on one side to study it. He thought how sturdy and alert and busy his sons were. This was all Olivia's doing.

When he first met her she always had her eyes and her attention fixed on the next place. But then, to his amazement, when they fell in love she quickly agreed to come home with him to Halemni. She had fitted in here as easily as if she had been born in a house overlooking the bay. They married and the boys were born, and it was as if she had turned herself inside out, like a leather glove reversing to its silk lining, the wanderer turned into the anchor. Olivia became the best mother he could have imagined and the little household revolved around her steady sun.

'Why did you give up your glamorous life to come and be poor with me on this rocky island?' he used to ask her, when it still seemed remarkable to him. 'Even if you had done enough travelling you could have gone back to England, to your family and your friends.'

It was true, Olivia acknowledged. Her parents were there, and all her friends from school and university, and a couple of sort-of boyfriends she hadn't missed much while she was away. It was the ordinary network of a normal life and she had broken out of it in the first place because she didn't

26

want to be defined by it. Most particularly, she didn't want to live like her mother and father had lived.

'I came here with you because I loved you more than anything or anyone else in the world. I still do. And I stay here because I am so happy,' she told him.

It was the truth. When she put her arms round Xan she felt how solid he was and rooted in his own ground like a great tree. By comparison England seemed a pale place, and her parents' and friends' lives defined by too many compromises to do with more money and less love.

'Is that what bullets look like?' Xan asked the boy. Dots and dashes like Morse code radiated from the wings and nose cones.

'It's *light beams*,' Georgi said witheringly.

'I see, okay, of course. The light fighters. What's yours, Theo?'

Big stripes and thick crayon patches. 'Heaven,' he said. 'For Christopher.'

Theo's tongue stuck out between his teeth as he worked. He gave the painter's name the full Greek pronunciation.

'Lucky old Christo.'

'They've been drawing all morning,' Olivia said. She had unlatched herself reluctantly from Xan and was unpacking the baskets, smoothing sheets of tinfoil and replacing them in a drawer.

Nothing was wasted here. Halemni had only small pockets of fertile ground. Everything that the islanders couldn't grow or make themselves came in by boat from nearby islands or the mainland. Every sheet of paper and tube of paint and square of sandwich wrapping that the Georgiadises used was counted, and not just because of the scarcity but because there was not enough money to permit waste. Like most of the islanders they lived by a rule of frugality so entrenched that they rarely even noticed it. The children drew on the backs of the guests' discarded sketches and when there was none of that paper they used the insides of cardboard cartons. They considered themselves rich in other things.

Xan sat down at the table. Olivia went into the stone larder that led off the kitchen and brought out a bowl of tomatoes, a chunk of goat's cheese and a dish of yoghurt and put them on the table. Xan stretched a lazy arm and took a loaf of bread out of a basket near the big old sink. Olivia baked their bread and grew the tomatoes in her vegetable garden behind the house. The goat's cheese came from a farmer inland and the oil from their neighbour Yannis who had the island's best and biggest olive grove.

'Put your drawings away now,' Xan told his sons. 'And pull your chairs straight.' He broke off a hunk of bread and bit hungrily at it as he passed the remainder to the table. Like his own father, Xan believed in do as I say, not do as I do. The boys did as they were told, lining their seats up opposite their parents' places and turning their faces to the food. They had the same straight noses and thick eyebrows as their father.

Olivia sliced bread and handed the bowls, and for a minute there was silence as her men ate. Before her marriage she would not have considered it but it came to her naturally, now, to look after their needs first. She smiled to herself, thinking that some of Meroula's ways had rubbed off on her. Xan saw the smile. She caught him looking at her over the boys' heads and the heat that flashed between them made her fidget on her seat and push the hair away from her damp cheeks.

The children were given bowls of yoghurt with a spoonful of honey dribbled in the centre. Theo stirred his into a sepia whirlpool, while Georgi dipped his spoon carefully into the glistening puddle and ate it with slow, sucking noises before licking up the plain outskirts.

28

It didn't take long to eat the meal and no one made any comment about it. The food was what they ate almost every midday. As soon as the boys had finished they squirmed on their chairs until Xan nodded them permission to go and they ran outside. At once Olivia was on her feet, clearing the plates and storing the leftovers. Xan went to the stove to heat a pot of thick coffee. This was his job.

'Who was there?' Olivia asked.

'Yannis,' Xan's fingers made a little tilting gesture next to his mouth. Yannis liked to start early on the raki, and lately did not stop until the day's end. Olivia lifted one shoulder in a shrug of exasperation, mostly on behalf of Yannis's wife.

'There' was the kafeneion down on the harbour, where Xan had just been. It was a dingy place with no tablecloths or taped music or candles in bottles, and deliberately so because these things attracted the tourists. It was where the island men gathered to talk and play backgammon, in the late mornings after the fishing and before the afternoon's full heat, in the golden in-between seasons of spring and autumn. In high summer the village and the beaches belonged to the invaders and in the winter everyone kept more to their houses.

'No one else?'

Megalo Chorio was a small community and the Georgiadises knew everyone. The small details of who had been where and what they had said were common currency, handed on like folk remedies. Xan mentioned a couple of names and Olivia nodded as she worked. They didn't need to enlarge on anything for each other. She manhandled a metal pie dish into the big oven and slammed the door on it, standing up with her face slightly flushed from the blast of heat.

'Coffee here,' Xan said. They rested their buttocks against the scrubbed table, heads level and thighs just touching, and gratefully drank. Apart from in bed, they did not have many minutes alone together.

A thin line of sunlight striped the floor and Olivia watched it as it thickened. The window faced west and this signal of the sun meant that the afternoon had begun and the guests would be back soon for their late lunch. After a morning's painting they were ready for food and siestas. She sighed as she put her cup aside and Xan tipped his chin against her shoulder.

'One more day,' he said.

'Come on. I don't think of it like that.'

'Yes you do.'

'Well. Maybe at the very end of the season I do. But I'll be looking forward to them again by the time May comes around.'

It was true. This was the rhythm they lived by and she was happy with it, because of its regularity and simplicity. When she was travelling there had been no such rhythms.

The telephone rang. Xan made an impatient noise and reached out but Olivia beat him to it. She tried to field the business calls from the booking agents in England and from guests, because Xan could be abrupt and if there were messages to be passed on he often forgot them. In any case, she knew who this caller was. Olivia's mother usually rang on Friday afternoons, when her husband had gone upstairs with the newspaper after lunch.

'Mum? Hello. Yes, of course I'm here. Yes, we're all fine. Busy, you know, but it is the last day of the season. And you? How is he?'

'He' was Olivia's father. All the time she was growing up he had been a dangerously unpredictable figure, someone to be propitiated by her mother and herself. Now that she was an adult and the two of them were old, the roles were almost reversed. Denis had become the propitiator and Maddie the one who was impatient. Olivia hunched her shoulder to hold the receiver at her ear, listening to her mother's news of the week.

She was used to this compact exchange. For twelve years between the ages of twenty-one and thirty-three Olivia had moved from place to place, taking photographs and selling them to travel magazines and picture libraries whenever she could, and doing casual jobs when she could not. She kept in touch with people by means of postcards and occasional calls, and she was happy enough with this arm's-length contact.

Until she met Xan Georgiadis, when everything changed.

'Anyway, Mum, I'm glad you've had some sun at last even if the garden's parched. And have you heard from Max?'

Max was Olivia's brother, younger by two years. As children they had been allies within the controlled zone of their family life, and he was still closer to her than anyone else in the world except her husband and children. But Max lived in Sydney now with his wife and daughters, and regular telephone calls were too expensive for Olivia. She relied on her mother for weekly news and waited eagerly for Max's less frequent calls to Halemni. You should get e-mail, her brother had told her, but he might as well have suggested getting a Learjet.

There were voices across the little courtyard that separated the studios from the main house. The guests were back.

'Mum, I've got to go. They need lunch. Yes, I will. And you too. Speak next week.'

'How is she?' Xan asked absently. There was the long table to be laid for lunch outside, and food to be placed on it. Meroula was part of the fabric of their everyday lives but Maddie was remote, more of a concept than a real presence. Olivia felt guilty about this, but there was no solution to it.

'She's fine.'

Christopher Cruickshank put his head round the door. 'We're back.' He had a thin face almost bisected by a hank of fine hair. When he was painting he wore the hair pushed back under a decomposing straw hat.

Olivia was already taking the big tray of spinach pie out of the oven.

'Welcome,' Xan laughed.

'Is everything ready for tonight?' Christopher asked. There was a kid to be spit-roasted, the centrepiece of the last night's party.

'I think so,' Olivia said, running through in her mind what needed to be done. 'You will light the fire in good time?' She asked Xan this question every two weeks throughout the summer season.

'I will.'

There was no moon that night and the sky held only a faint afterglow that made it seem a blue-black hollow ball pitted with stars. The sea was black and calm for late in the season. Inky wavelets slapped the harbour wall and whispered into the shingle on the village beach. Xan had hung lanterns in the branches of a tamarisk tree, and there were candles all down the long table under the *avli*, the pergola with its vine shading. The kid had been roasted and carved and eaten, and the fire of driftwood had shrunk to a powdery crimson core, and now the English voices were louder and less careful.

Olivia looked down the table. The double line of faces was reddened by the sun and wine. It was always a good moment, when the inhibitions finally broke up. It was just a shame that it almost always took until the very last night. These people had chosen to spend their precious holidays here and they had brought their paintings and sketches to be admired and commented upon, and so given oblique insights into their lives. They stirred a wash of affection in her and she knew that she would miss them all through the winter. She would look forward to the first rash of floppy sunhats in the sharp early summer sunshine.

And it was always like this, she remembered. It could have

been any of the years since they had begun here. Each season's beginning and end made her feel the same, eagerly anticipatory or affectionate and pleasurably melancholy.

This was the tissue of happiness, she thought. Phases repeated themselves, and accretions of memory and pleasure built up, and you could dip down through the layers and examine them, like tree rings or sandstone deposits. The awareness of permanence on Halemni weighted her limbs, making her feel dizzy and voluptuous with satisfaction. She loved their life here and the people she shared it with. Looking down the table again, she even loved knife-faced Christine Darby and her pompous husband, who had complained about the beds and the food, and Christopher's eccentric teaching methods.

Xan moved into the lantern light beside her, removing empty wine bottles and putting a full bottle of Metaxas in their place.

'None for you,' he teased with his mouth close to her hair, meaning that he could see she had drunk enough.

'Oh, go on. Just one. You never know what it might lead to, if you're lucky,' she whispered back.

Later there was dancing. Christopher played the guitar and the English couples swayed and jigged under the branches of the tree, and then draped arms over one another's shoulders and pointed their toes in a wobbly imitation of Xan, at the end of the line, when he led the Greek dance. He was a supple, stately dancer and the guests looked like a row of jerky puppets as they tried to follow his steps.

Olivia was like the maypole in the middle with two ribbons twisting around her.

'I can't,' she protested. 'My legs don't work at this time of night.'

'Legs like yours don't need to,' Brian Darby murmured in the knowledge that his wife was out of earshot.

And at the same moment at the far end of the line it was Mrs Darby who spotted the bear-like man shambling at the rim of the lantern light. She crooked her elbow gaily to indicate that he should join in.

At once he lurched towards her and locked both arms round her neck to stop himself from falling flat on his face. As soon as she got the full blast of his breath Mrs Darby changed her mind about the invitation to dance. She tried to shake him off and pull herself away, but the line of dancers reeled the two of them along like fish on a hook. All the other guests thought it was a joke and shouted encouragement, then hooted with laughter as their legs tangled. The man pressed his stubbled face closer, trying for a kiss, and the woman screamed. A little bullet of shock discharged itself into the atmosphere.

Xan had already disentangled himself from the staggering bodies. He ran to pull the man off.

'Oh, bollocks,' Christopher muttered and flicked his cigarette past the tamarisk tree before going to help.

'Yannis, Yannis,' Xan shouted.

Christine Darby was pinned on her back by an inert body. Her arms and legs flailed helplessly. Xan hauled the man up by his shirt, exposing a thick mahogany-brown torso matted with black hair. The man muttered thickly as Christopher added his efforts to Xan's. Together they propped him back on his feet while Mrs Darby gave a series of thin shrieks.

Olivia knelt over her.

'It's all right. He won't hurt you, he's just drunk.'

Brian Darby came out of the knot of onlookers, only a second or two belatedly, with his fists jerking like a wound-up toy. He took a cocky swing at the mumbling Yannis and missed the side of his head, and Yannis made a surprisingly swift counter-swing that did not miss. There was a soft smack as his massive hand connected with the other man's nose. Darby fell like a sack into the arms of two other guests as Xan and Christopher pinned Yannis's arms behind his back. Xan put two fingers in his mouth and whistled.

Olivia swung from Mrs Darby to the woman's husband, who had been lowered by his supporters into the nearest chair. The man's nose was bleeding. A carmine stream ran down his chin and dripped on his mint-green Lacoste shirt. She caught the flow with the nearest screwed-up paper napkin and tipped his head back. His mouth flapped open and shut as he gasped like a landed codfish.

'Here,' she called over her shoulder to Christine who was now vertical again. 'Hold this while I get some ice.'

Out of the shadows across the square a little posse of men came running to Xan's whistle. They man-handled Yannis's now unprotesting bulk out of the light and towed it away.

Xan wiped the flat of his hands down the sides of his jeans and dropped his shoulders.

'Okay, everyone. Drama over now. Let me see how it seems, Brian.'

Olivia came back with ice cubes from the kitchen fridge.

'Bloody well assaulted me,' Mr Darby puffed. His nose, when Olivia manipulated it, appeared not to be broken. 'I want to report him.'

'Of course you do, I understand that. I'm so sorry this happened. But he's been drinking, you know. Yannis and his wife have been friends of mine for many years, they have had some troubles …'

Xan was soothing. His big warm hands turned the man's chin from side to side as he explored for signs of further damage. Olivia put her arm round Christine's shoulders. The other guests murmured in a circle, telling each other exactly what had happened, enjoying the excitement. Darby had not been an especially well-liked group member.

Christopher had followed the village men and their cargo but he slipped back now and gave Xan a tranquil nod. Evidently Yannis had been made safe for the night.

'I want to call the police.'

Xan pressed the ice pack over the bridge of the man's nose.

Mrs Darby seemed fully recovered. She squeezed Olivia's hand and let go of it, then peered down into the upturned dish of her husband's face, with no sign of appetite.

'You punched him first, in fact.'

'He assaulted you. What should I do, shake hands with him?'

'I don't think he meant to …'

'I'm certain he didn't,' Xan said. 'He's the gentlest of men, normally.'

Brian pushed aside the ice pack and forged to his feet. The bleeding had stopped, but there was a rusty patch on his chin and a crust in the groove beneath his nose.

'I know what's right,' he bellowed. 'Whose side are you all on?'

Xan and Olivia were shoulder to shoulder, with Christopher under the tamarisk branches a yard away. At the same moment two of the men who had led Yannis away rematerialised at the outer rim of the lantern light. The mein looked around. 'I see. Stick together, you island people, don't you? Suppose you have to, in a place this size. Marry each other's sisters. Or your own.'

'Brian …'

He cut his wife short. 'I'm going to wash my face, then I'm going to bed.'

After he had gone Christine said, 'I'm sorry.' She looked embarrassed and unhappy.

'It was Yannis's fault. But he meant no harm, I can promise you.'

She followed her husband, out of sight around the blue wall of the house to the studios.

Xan picked up the brandy bottle. 'I'm so sorry about all that. Would anyone like another drink?'

But it was clear that the party was over. Olivia glanced up at the shutters of her sons' room. If either of them had been woken by the raised voices, they might be afraid.

'I'm just going to see ...' She whispered to Xan.

The room was faintly barred with light that came through the cracks in the shutters. It was scented with skin and damp, sweaty heads. Georgi was sleeping on his back with one arm flung above his head but Theo's bed was empty.

The bedsheets were rumpled, still slightly warm. She knelt on the splintery floorboards and looked under the bed, but there were only a few clumps of dust and a plastic toy soldier. The one cupboard was empty except for clothes and toys. She whirled round, soundlessly for Georgi's sake. The window was open but the shutters were securely latched behind it. Outside in the corridor there was darkness and only the light from downstairs throwing a dim glow that just reached the top of the stairs. The door to her bedroom stood ajar; the white bedcover was stretched smooth, the curtain that hung across an alcove to make a wardrobe revealed nothing but clothes when she drew it aside. Theo was not in here either.

Olivia fled to the last door on the upper floor.

The door stood open. This was a little boxroom, with one tiny window looking away from the sea. It had been Olivia's darkroom, or that was the original idea when she and Xan had first bought the house. But she took very few photographs now: there was too little spare time. It was used mostly as storage space for art supplies. She stepped into the thick darkness and immediately she knew that Theo was here.

Carefully she knelt down and stretched out her hand. Her fingers connected with a warm curve of pyjamaed body. She gave a sharp exhalation of relief and patted him, quickly exploring the small shape. He was fast asleep, curled up on the floor between the door and the wall. He had been sleep-walking again, had found their bed empty and had wandered on in search of his mother and father.

Olivia crouched down, breathing unarticulated snatches of gratitude and relief. She scooped the child into her arms and held him against her, one hand cupping the back of his head. Then she trod back to his bedroom and laid him down under the covers. She sat for a few minutes on the floor beside the bed, listening to his easy sleep and breathing in the smell of him. A yard away Georgi gave a small sigh and turned over. They were fast asleep, both of them. She stood up and hovered for a minute longer. Theo had always been a light sleeper, troubled by nightmares that were the dark side of his vivid imagination. He didn't yet have the words to express his ideas and the frustration came out as tantrums or clashes with his brother, or in his sleepwalking. She didn't know why this frightened her so much.

Max and she had been the same, she was thinking, only she had been the volatile one and Max had obediently followed where she led. He climbed the garden walls after her and dug burrows to hide in, and stole penny sweets from the corner shop under her direction. They made their own world of hierarchies and escape routes, clothing them from the dressing-up box and living outside what they didn't yet understand to be their parents' compromises.

It was the better way round, the way her own children were. The older, more circumspect one restrained the younger one just enough for safety, but was lit up by his anarchy. Olivia bent down and kissed each of them again, made warm and heavy by the absolute weight of her love for them. A sense that she was too fortunate, that she couldn't hope for this perfection to continue, scraped at the margin of her mind. She pushed it away from her, out of the room and into the darkness where the sea rubbed over the shingle beach. She closed the door of the bedroom and went downstairs again.

Outside under the tamarisk tree the candle lanterns had been blown out and the fire spread into a grey mat of ashes. The trestle table had been cleared of the last cups and glasses and the white cloth bundled into a ball. Xan and Christopher had moved quickly. There was no sign of any of the guests. She picked the cloth up in her arms and went inside with it.

The two men were in the kitchen. Xan was scraping and stacking plates, and Christopher was cradling a brandy glass against his thin chest and leaning against the stone side of the old bread oven.

'Theo's been sleepwalking again. I found him asleep on the floor in the darkroom.'

Xan came to her and took the ball of tablecloth out of her arms. He threw it into the corner and put his arms on her shoulders.

'Is he all right?'

'I put him back into his bed. He seems all right, he never woke up, but I'm worried about him. Why does he keep doing this?'

It was perhaps the sixth time in three months.

Xan said, 'Children do it. You worry too much.'

Christopher drained the two fingers of brandy left in his glass and put it down amidst the clutter of dirty crockery on the wooden drainer.

'I'll be off. I'll be up in the morning to wave them off, of course.'

'Goodnight, Chris. Thanks for your help.'

'Nothing to it. Pity Yannis didn't sock him a bit harder.'

When they were alone Xan put his arms round her again. 'Let's leave this. Come to bed.'

Olivia rested her forehead against his. They were the same height.

'Yes.'

They had no curtains anywhere in the house and in their own bedroom they left the shutters open at night. They had to get up early and it was easy to wake up with the light creeping across the room. Olivia lay with her husband's arms round her and her chin in the hollow of his shoulder. It was the best moment of the day, this, when they exchanged their last thoughts, the words becoming disconnected as they drifted towards sleep.

'It must be worse than being dead,' Xan breathed.

'What?'

'To live in a marriage like that. Those people, the Darbys. They look at each other as if they wish they were.'

'You can't tell. You can only guess what other people are like inside their marriages. You only know your own.'

'You can tell,' he insisted, stubborn as his mother.

'It doesn't matter. Why are we talking about the bloody Darbys? This is all that matters. I'm worried about Theo.'

'Don't be. He only walks in his sleep, like children do. I don't know why you worry so much.'

Olivia tilted in his arms, looking into the room's blackness and at the faintly paler suggestion of the window.

'Maybe because I'm happy. Because I am afraid to lose it.'

However hard she tried to banish it there seemed to be a whisper of threat here in the room with them, a whisper that was nothing to do with the problem of Meroula or the worry about money or guests or the business.

Xan laughed. It was a sound deep in his chest and she felt the vibration as he pulled her closer. He didn't share her fears.

'You were once so brave. My lone traveller, afraid of nothing in the world.'

He often teased her about this, that she had come to Halemni to be a wife and mother after having seen everything there was to see and done everything else there was to do.

'It isn't fear, exactly. I don't want anything to change and yet the boys change all the time, and I suppose anxiety comes out of that.'

'You can't stop change,' he murmured. Xan was sleepy, but he still ran his hand over the curve of her ribs, into the hollow of her waist and up the swell of her hips. Olivia breathed out and lay back. It was late and they had to be up very early, but it made no difference when he wanted her, as he did now. It hadn't changed since the first time he saw her and wanted her, in Bangkok by the monsoon-swollen river. She was a thin, crop-haired, pale giantess then, all dangling legs and arms, among the tiny smooth Thais.

'Don't worry, I love you,' he muttered as his hand slid between her thighs.

Christopher Cruickshank had walked down to the beach. He sat on the shingle now, smoking a last cigarette with his back to the lapping water. The beach beds had all been taken into storage for the winter.

Only one or two lights showed in the tiers of houses. Left to itself, Megalo Chorio went to bed early. The tip of his cigarette glowed as Christopher gazed upwards. Immediately above the Georgiadises' house was the dark hump of the little hill where he had taken the guests for their last morning's painting. Beyond and behind that was a paler glimmer against the black sky. This was the limestone cliff, crowned by a ruined castle of the Knights of St John, that dominated Halemni bay and the beach and the harbour. And perched in the saddle of hillside that rose up to the bluff were outlines too square to be natural rock forms. Although they were all but invisible in the darkness, Christopher knew the shapes and the scenery so well that his mind's eye supplied the image as clearly as if it had been bathed in sunshine. These were the ruined houses of Arhea Chorio, the old village. It had been abandoned a generation ago, when families moved down to the coast away from the hill farms to the tavernas and beach stands. Now the roofless houses disintegrated slowly into the heaps of stone from which they had been built.

Christopher liked the old village. When he had a free afternoon he would climb up there to spend an hour reading or sketching among the stones, with only the lizards and an occasional basking snake for company. Very few of the summer tourists ever bothered to make the hot scramble up there and for weeks at a time he was the only visitor. Now, as he smoked, he kept his eyes fixed on the ruins, or the view of them that his inner eye supplied. He felt an uneasiness at his back, coming off the water like a winter fog, and it was more comfortable to look up the hill at the old houses.

When he had finished his cigarette he threw the butt over his shoulder into the sea. He played with the idea of smoking another, but he was cold and the invisible fog breathed around him. He scrambled to his feet instead and crunched up the shingle. He rented a room in the main street and his bed was waiting for him.

It had been a long day, the end of a long season. He would stay on Halemni maybe another week, or two weeks, and then he would head north again for the winter.

THREE

I am in Turkey, sitting on the sea coast and staring westwards.

I have almost forgotten why I am here, if there ever was a particular reason for coming. It doesn't matter anyway. One place is much like another for the time being.

This is a skeleton of a hotel, pasted over with white concrete skin so that it looks smooth but brittle. There are big blind windows and flimsy balconies like pouches under a drunkard's eyes.

I sleep as much as I can, in my hotel bedroom, behind closed curtains. And when I can no longer sleep I sit on the balcony under the shade of a parasol. Even though it is late in the season I don't like the sun to touch my skin and my pale eyes water in so much harsh white light. I keep my sunglasses in place and try to read, and the time slowly passes.

I can't pinpoint exactly when Dunollie Mansions stopped feeling like a refuge and became instead a place that I wanted to get away from. It was probably not very long after the dinner when Peter met Lisa Kirk for the first time.

He was busy in the weeks immediately after that night, working on a job that demanded longer hours and even more concentration than usual. He stayed late at the office, and seemed tired and distracted when he did come home. I should have interpreted the signs at once and spoken out about them, but the potential for that kind of conversation seemed already lost. Instead I tried hard to be less demanding, as if that might win his approval again. I embarked on some redecoration in the flat, and discussed colours and finishes with the painters. I went out looking for fabrics and spent time putting together colour boards for Peter's approval.

'Very nice,' he said, pressing the rim of his glasses against the bridge of his nose with the tip of his finger, an indication of stress that I had learned to recognise long ago.

'You like the green, then?'

'Yes, if you do.'

I didn't care about the green and I knew that he didn't either.

Once or twice I had a cup of tea upstairs with Lisa in her flat.

There was no reason to refuse her invitations, nothing I could have identified except the thin squeak of hostility between us, and I was ready to think that that might be a product of my imagination, the murmur of my own madness. Peter apparently didn't hear the sound, although he always had done so up until now and been able to take the right reassuring steps. He was too busy, or maybe he was simply tired of listening out for it.

Lisa didn't choose to come again to my flat, Peter's and mine, although I always invited her. We went upstairs instead.

Each time I saw her she seemed younger and warmer and more bursting with life. There were signs that she was making a home of Dunollie Mansions, but they were fairly limited ones – an armchair of steel and cowhide stood in the living room, with its paper and corrugated wrapping only partly removed; a patch of wall in the dark hallway had been experimentally striped with different paint colours.

'What do you think?' Lisa waved a hand as we passed on the way to the kitchen.

'Pink?'

'You're right. Too sugary. Much.' And then a sigh. 'I'll never have time to get this place together.'

We drank tea, sitting next to the big red refrigerator.

'What's happening about Baz and the girlfriend?'

She shrugged. 'Idyll of delight, I suppose. I don't care. Fuck 'em.'

Fuck my husband.

Was she doing it then, or did that come later?

There is someone at the door. Room service, with some meal I have ordered and will not eat.

The waiter is the one who always comes, day or night. He never seems to go off duty. When he takes the trays away he looks under the dish covers and sees that I have barely touched the food, and he sighs in reproach. He is very young, perhaps only fifteen or sixteen.

He puts the latest tray down on the low table, and makes a big show of displaying the food and unfurling the napkin for me.

'Is good,' he cajoles, 'is very nice.'

I smile at him.

'It looks delicious.'

'I close the blinds?'

The light is fading over the sea. The sky is mushroom pink and the water is the same colour as the inside of an oyster shell.

'No, leave them open. I like to look at the night.'

'You need something else maybe?'

45

He hovers protectively and I am touched by his concern for me.

'No, thank you.'

We wish each other goodnight.

The plan, if it was ever as conscious as that on my part, was for Selina and me to take this holiday together, a late-season two weeks on the Turkish coast in a pretty resort called Branc. Selina is an expert on hotels and she promises me that this one is good – Swiss-owned and run, but with a proper local feel to it.

'The pool will be clean, the food close enough to authentic but without poisoning you.'

'Why Turkey, Selina?'

She shrugged. 'Why not? It's fashionable. I've been every-where else.'

Selina is currently between husbands. She has had three, or maybe four. I have known her since our modelling days and we have always kept in touch. It was her idea for us to make the trip.

'Two women on their own, darling? Free and independent? We will have a fine time. You get out of London and you'll feel better, believe me.'

I agreed that we should go. It was autumn again in London, the time last year that Lisa Kirk arrived, and she and Peter had now been living together for five months. I had started to wonder how much longer it would be before she was pregnant. The child Peter had always wanted.

I didn't look forward to the holiday with much enthusiasm. When I thought about it at all I imagined it would be like the holidays my mother and I took together, after my father left us and went off to the Steps and Halves. Two women consoling each other, solicitous about sun cream and making sure that the other was comfortable, but still locked inside themselves with separate, clamorous voices in their ears. Maybe my mother would put it differently, if she were here, but I can still see the white triangle of her face and the misery in her eyes. Nothing I did ever rubbed it out for long. Of course not.

I probably do Selina a major injustice. We might well have had a wild time together, sitting on bar stools and drinking lurid cocktails, and then tripping off to discos to enjoy the startled attentions of the local Lotharios, in the absence of any younger prey, like a pair of giraffes displaced from the herd and yapped around by hyenas. The comparison would have drawn one of Selina's yelps of laughter, before she flicked her lighter to another Marlboro.

In any case, she developed appendicitis four days before we were due to leave. I could have cancelled, but I had somehow got used to the idea of going to Turkey. I was even relieved at the thought of being able to do it alone, and not to have to keep up the pretence of being cheerful and energetic.

And so here I am.

I think about Peter, of course.

I prefer to remember the early days, when we were first married, when he used to drive us off to the country for weekends. We would go to little hotels in Suffolk or Devon, and lie in bed late and then take unambitious walks before coming back for tea, and drinks, and dinner. He was always trying to make me eat, and my evasions became a joke and then a kind of game between us.

'Scone, darling? With some home-made jam and clotted cream?'

'Just the cucumber, out of the sandwich, thank you.'

Peter belonged to the National Trust, for God's sake. Not even my mother was a member. I thought this was funny and delightful, and if we didn't go for a walk we would look up some local great house or ruined castle in the book and drive in the Jaguar to see it. I remember the smell of warm leather seats and brake fluid.

All of this felt very adult and secure, after the way I had been living – on and off planes, in and out of clothes and studios and hotel bedrooms, with men around me and in me whom I didn't like or trust. Whereas I loved Peter and I trusted him absolutely, and he had the knack of making me feel loved in return. His love balanced out my guilt: it didn't take it away, nothing could do that, it just counterweighted it and allowed me to function while still carrying the old burden around with me.

Peter had a conventional exterior, which he enjoyed cultivating, and inside this there was a quirky and clever man unlike anyone I had ever met before. I adored his cleverness, and the way he could weigh up people and problems quickly, and act on his observations and deductions. He was decisive where I was tentative, and generous where I was suspicious.

He was also the most sensuous man I had ever known. He loved food and fine wine and beautiful old cars, and pictures and made-to-measure suits and sex. He was the best lover. In bed, as I noticed the very first time, when he took off the shields of his spectacles there was the different soft face of an alternative, exotic Peter who belonged to me alone. I liked to smooth away the creases hooking his mouth with my thumbs. The stroking stretched the thin skin of his lips into a secret smile.

The food on the tray has gone cold. I prod at it a little, then cover the plates up again and slide the whole lot outside the door.

The sky is dark now. I stand at the window and look out at the line of lamps that line the hotel garden, and their broken reflection in the sea. After three days of gazing at it I am familiar with the view. The beach, with a row of beach beds and yellow mattresses under jaunty yellow parasols, now furled for the night, lies just beyond the garden wall. There is the water and a rim of tarnished silver where it meets the sand. Across the water are the donkey-brown humps of some nameless islands in the Greek Dodecanese. Nameless to me, that is – I asked my waiter their names, by sign language, and he rattled off something unintelligible with a dismissive shrug. There is no love lost between these people and the Greeks.

I am surprised by how close the islands lie to the Turkish mainland. Selina would probably have known. Selina would have maps and guidebooks, whereas I, of course, do not. That would be Peter's role.

Always, I come back to him and how crippled I seem to be without him. And it is exactly because of this infirmity that he is no longer here. At some point – it must have been one day, maybe even one hour, or during the course of one single conversation – the fine balance tipped again, this time coming down against me. My needs from him became greater than his pleasure in me. I was too much to look after. Or maybe we just knew each other too well and the function buttons became worn with too much pressing so the connections didn't work properly. Is that what always happens, with long-term partnerships?

Whatever you like. I don't know.

I can't go on feeling crippled by Peter's absence or by the things that happened long before I met him, that much I do know after my days alone in this white hotel.

It ought to be possible to rub out history. To start again with a clean piece of paper, to write on it with a fresh and optimistic hand. That's what I am doing here – making sense of what has happened and needing to work out what shape my life will take from now on. Selina's absence means that I have to face the definitions and decisions alone and therefore properly.

So I have come out of my room. It is the fourth day and I have ventured down to the beach. With the full complement of yellow beach towels and robes and tubes of cream and magazines and paperback novels, of course. I have arranged all this and myself under a parasol, and I am flipping through *Vogue* when a shadow falls across the sand beside me. I look up to see my waiter, with a tray balanced on his shoulder. His shabby black shoes look incongruous so close to the lazy waves.

'Madam, you come to the sun. I am happy. I bring you water and Italian coffee.'

There is a bottle of mineral water, and a *cappuccino* complete with chocolate powder.

'Thank you.'

We smile at each other and he carefully arranges the drinks on the little table under the parasol.

'What is your name?' I ask him and he flushes a little. His skin is downy, hardly darkened with hair except on his top lip. He is probably even younger than I estimated.

'Jim,' he says. With a hard 'J' sound that sounds quite un-Turkish.

'Like *Jules et Jim*?' I ask fatuously.

'I am not sure. But is a good name.'

'Very good,' I agree. Jim begins to back away, with the tray hanging flat by his side, and then hesitates. 'An Inglis man is here. In Branc. Maybe you go for a boat ride?'

I must look desperate, or desperately miserable, or both. However, an English man is the last thing I am looking for.

Very firmly I say, 'Thank you for thinking of it, but I don't want to meet anyone here. No one at all, Jim.' And I put the magazine up in front of my face to shut out the threat.

'Okay. Good morning,' he says and crunches away up the sand to the garden wall. I know I have been rude and that he is offended.

When I was first married I thought I might become an actress. Because of the way I looked then and some of the people I knew, I was given small – tiny – roles in a couple of films, but I wasn't any good at it. And if I wound up hating the scrutiny of the photographer's lens, I hated the film cameras even more. After a year or so I stopped trying and it was a relief. I didn't have to earn money, because Peter provided for us both. I didn't have to do anything except be married to Peter and have a family.

I have always had an ambivalent attitude to my body. Its length and skinniness enabled me to earn a living, but I hated the way people stared. I knew that they were only looking at it, and not into me in order to judge what they saw within, but the knowledge didn't lessen my discomfort.

Peter used to say that they were looking because I was beautiful and I should be glad.

'Plenty of women', he said, 'would change places with you.'

Up until then, at least, the legs and arms and breasts and backside had done what I wanted them to do. They moved for the camera and showed off whatever garment I was being paid to parade.

But I couldn't get pregnant.

Not properly pregnant, so the baby stayed inside and grew. I had two miscarriages, very quickly, but the doctors were still optimistic and reassuring.

'Don't worry, it happens. You'll have your family soon.'

Peter took me home and fed me and held me in his arms at night.

Then there was an ectopic pregnancy that ruptured one

51

of the Fallopian tubes. This time there was anxiety. My chances of conceiving were diminished by fifty per cent. I was too thin, they told me, I was anxious and tense and probably depressed. All these things counted against us in our efforts to have a baby. I must relax.

Peter took me away on holiday, to Italy.

Soon I was pregnant yet again and it seemed that this time it might take. I got to four months and we told our friends and dared a celebration. But I miscarried again, in hospital, a sixteen-week boy. It was the last time. The last time I was even able to conceive.

I did hate my body after that, with a cold anger that made me want to mutilate myself. I needed a scapegoat and I turned my womb into one. This reaction was explicable, even logical, to myself and other people, and I used it as an acceptable shorthand.

I do not now believe, however, that my damned body was the real culprit.

It was myself, wherever that reality might be lodged and whatever form it might take. I think I never really wanted a baby because I was afraid of what might happen if I did have one. I was afraid of history, and tragedy.

This is our baby, we love him, he dies, it's my fault.

That was the reasoning and so every time my body conceived, my mind poisoned it. Out the potential big tragedy came in a wash of blood, only another small tragedy as yet. Not even named.

If you think that's crazy – believe me, so do I.

'I will be the judge of that,' Peter said mildly on the night we met, when I told him that I was mad. And he chose to bring in a verdict of sanity.

It was a strange mistake, for a clever and perceptive man who is usually so accurate in his judgements.

When it became obvious that we were not going to have

children, I lodged myself in Dunollie Mansions like a hermit crab in its shell. I loved the screen of summer leaves and filigree winter twigs across the windows. I loved the thick walls and floors, and the almost dreamlike sense of seclusion, and the way Derek soft-footedly took care of the building. I liked the other quiet, discreet couples and the safety of the solid doors. There was no shock or violence or mayhem here, nor could I ever imagine anything of the sort disturbing our calm routines. I became a recluse.

We still gave dinner parties, of course, and went out to dinners in return, and to the opera and weekends in the country and on holidays, but I became an emotional solitary. Peter and I continued to look after each other and no doubt loved each other, but the woman he had taken home from the photographer's party ceased to exist.

Obliterated by history.

Then came Lisa Kirk, with her red TARDIS and trendy furniture and the full heat of youth, smarting from Baz's rejection and wishing for the baby she thought should have been hers. She saw in Peter Stafford exactly what I had seen myself, all those years before.

As I say, it was therefore only a matter of time.

Until Christmas, I reckon, give or take a week or two. I never quite got to the bottom of how it began. When I put the question to Peter he answered, shamefacedly, 'We met for a drink, that's all. She wanted some business advice.'

'Where did you meet for a drink? How did it happen? Did she call you at the office and suggest this assignation?'

'Cary, does it matter? Why do you need to know?'

'Because I do,' I snapped. But he wouldn't tell me and in fact I didn't need to know. This is how things unravel, that's all. It's nothing unusual. I had even watched my mother go through it, when my father ran off with Lesley.

It was quite early in the new year, this year that has now

turned to October, and Peter and I were driving over to Fulham to have Sunday lunch with our friends Clive and Sally. It was one of those colourless London winter days when the sky and the river and even the buildings lack definition, and everything seems looming, as at the onset of seasickness. My handbag was at my feet, in the carpeted footwell of the current old car: an Alvis, silver-grey. Although Peter has now replaced it with a new BMW 5-series, no doubt at Lisa's instigation.

I looked down for the handbag, intending to blow my nose or swallow a headache pill or something, and I saw a fragment under the seat mounting. Peter's cars are always so impeccably looked after, it surprised me to see a piece of litter that might have been a sweet wrapper. I picked it up and looked down at it lying in the palm of my hand. Peter was occupied with the traffic at South Kensington.

What I had found was a little golden label, reading 'Bag Shot by Lisa Kirk'.

Like a business card, but more eloquent. I put it in my pocket and said nothing.

The signs had been there for some time and now I was able to read them.

I began a horrible regime of espionage. Whenever Peter was working late, or when he telephoned to say he had an unexpected meeting or a new client to see, I would slip up the well-swept shallow stairs to Lisa's door. I would ring the bell and then tap on the thick swimmy glass but – funnily enough – she was never at home either.

On the evenings when Peter did come home I would listen. I had never been able to hear Mrs Bobinski moving around, but then I had never tried to. Now I could suddenly hear the faint creak of floorboards, the vibrating bass of her music, the click of a door closing. Lisa at home.

'What's wrong?' Peter asked.

I know, but I'm not ready to let you know that I know. That's what's wrong.

I'm on the beach again, another day. The sea is very flat, aluminium-coloured under a high, hazy sky. There is no breath of wind. A sailing boat crosses the mouth of the bay, the masts bare and the engines drumming. A shadow falls across my book.

A tall man with a white shirt and loose trousers, and creased Moroccan slippers with squashed pointed toes. I can see a narrow crescent of suntanned foot, between the leather slipper and where the cuff of his trousers dips over the heel.

'Hello,' he says. 'I've got a copy of *The Times* here. Finished with it. Would you like it?'

Inglis man.

He holds out the folded paper and I am so surprised that I take it.

'Thank you.'

'Nice to know what's going on in the world,' he says. And then he moves on, diagonally across the sand to the margin of the silver water, where wet sand makes a khaki ribbon. I watch him walk along the water's edge, into the distance. The paper had bled a smudge of newsprint on to my palm and fingertips.

In the end it wasn't Peter I confronted. One evening when he was sitting in his armchair reading a report I left the flat and went upstairs to knock on Lisa's door.

She had the grace to look startled and apprehension dawned in her wide eyes.

'May I come in?'

She held the door wider and I marched inside. In the kitchen, with a yoghurt pot with a spoon stuck in it on the table – I felt that I was interrupting a child's tea – I turned on her.

'What are you doing with my husband?'

There are a dozen possible responses to a question like that. Innocence, affront, evasion, denial.

To her credit, Lisa only nodded quietly. After a moment's thought she said, 'Just what you imagine, I suppose.'

'What does this mean?'

She pursed her lips and mournfully widened her eyes even further, a risible expression that was her attempt at high seriousness.

'That we are in love with each other.'

I gaped at her for an instant, silenced by this mouthful of garbage. I remembered what she had said at the dinner weeks ago – *oh yes, once I knew you* – and how the airy assumption had infuriated me. But that was nothing compared with the ballooning rage I felt now.

What did this airhead know about love and what right did she have to claim Peter's?

With one arm I swept the yoghurt pot and its spoon and assorted bits of crockery off the table. With one foot I kicked the red door of the TARDIS so that it shuddered. If Peter had been in our kitchen below he would surely have heard it. When I could speak I yelled at her, 'Don't talk such *fucking* crap. Don't say another word.'

There was a mess of spilled yoghurt and broken crockery on the floor. But Lisa kept her eyes on me, and there was at last real shock and proper concern in her face.

I'll teach you about feelings, you china doll.

'You don't know anything. You'll never know anything about me or Peter. You are to leave him alone. To leave *us* alone. Do you understand?'

For extra emphasis I kicked the refrigerator again. There was a tiny dent in the lower corner of the door and my toes hurt.

'Cary ...'

Even in this absurd and undignified situation I could see how lovely she was with the light shining through her thin skin and the smooth flesh of her arms. Her thin fingers curled round the back of one of her uncomfortable chairs. Maybe she was contemplating how to lift it and bring it down on my head. Only she couldn't have reached high enough.

'Leave us alone,' I repeated, with the anger starting to ooze out of me. I felt like a crumpled paper bag.

'It's too late for that.'

There was the confidence again, bred out of youth and arrogance. I wasn't going to win. History decreed it.

What to do now?

'I don't care. It isn't too late,' I lied.

'God, look. I love him and he loves me.' Her words rang true now, suddenly, reality unleashed by my fury. Lisa Kirk wouldn't let go. This wasn't some monochrome Baz at issue; this was important to her.

But we weren't just two alley cats fighting over a fish head, either. There was a third person involved in this. It was Peter who would determine what happened, of course. Briefly I felt the warmth of his familiarity around me, a security blanket. All would be well, because he had always made it well.

'We'll see,' I said. I turned round and walked out of the kitchen, closed Lisa's front door behind me and ran back down the stairs to our flat.

Peter was still reading. He hadn't even noticed that I had gone.

I said nothing to him, not a word. I cooked supper and we ate together and watched the ten o'clock news. There was silence from upstairs. By being normal, I thought, maybe I could make everything normal. That shows how irrational I was.

There is a little covered souk at the centre of Branc.

I am lingering by one of the stalls, breathing in the scents of cumin and cinnamon. There are fat hessian sacks spilling out a dozen different spices and herbs, and heaps of glossy dates and dried figs. The stallholder is a fat man in a vast white shirt with a little striped waistcoat pinched around his shoulders. I am biting into the date he has passed to me to sample when a voice says, 'I've got another *Times*, but not with me. I can drop it into the hotel later. If you would like, of course.'

Inglis man, again.

I turn round and we look at each other. He is wearing a loose shirt, pale trousers and the leather slippers. He looks ordinary, unremarkable, but familiar. He fits in here in the souk – unlike me – but I find that I can imagine him equally at home on a cricket pitch in Hampshire or in a restaurant in London.

'Hello?' he prompts. I have been staring at him.

'I'm sorry. Thank you, that's kind.'

'Are you all right?'

The pretence seems more trouble than it's worth. I say very softly, on an expiring breath, 'No.'

'No. Would you like to come and drink some coffee with me?'

Whatever my intentions might have been I find that I am following him. We duck out briefly into the white sunlight and cross a square to some tables under canvas parasols.

And then we are sitting facing each other, with a tent of shade cutting us off from the heat and brightness. Little cups of Turkish coffee arrive, with glasses of cool water and a dish of almond kernels. I pick up a nut and bite it in half, examining the marks made by my teeth in the white flesh. Then I sip at the thick, sweet coffee and gaze across the square to a mosque and the needle points of the minarets. I realise with a shock that softens my spine that I am at ease in the man's company, am not talking or laughing or fending off. I am just sitting, enjoying the shade and the view and the faint grittiness of the coffee on my tongue.

'I have a boat,' the man says, before I even know his name.

And I have agreed to go for a sail in his boat, still before I even know his name.

It didn't take long for Peter to hear about my visit to Lisa. He came home early the next day, wearing an expression I had never seen before. A guarded look, edged with defiance.

'Is it true?' I asked him, once he had taken off his coat and put his briefcase down on the chair in the hallway.

'Yes.'

'I don't understand.' Although I did. 'Are you in love with her?'

He spread his hands, a gesture of expiring patience that brought the first dart of dislike out of me.

'No. Yes, I suppose so. I didn't go looking for it. These things just happen.'

Like getting hit by a bus, I suppose. You are just standing there, minding your own business, when adultery comes along and runs you over. Although, when I thought about it, having Lisa Kirk set her sights on you must be not unlike being ploughed over by a bus. The dislike intensified and it made me want to cry. The idea of disliking Peter was so outlandish.

After that there was a predictable series of ugly events and confrontations.

I wept, Peter retreated, Lisa widened her eyes. Instead of a calm backwater, Dunollie Mansions became a place full of gusts of misery and disbelief.

In the end, after weeks of grief and entreaty, Peter moved

out and into a flat in Baron's Court. Lisa drifted there with him and I stayed put. It was as if my husband and his new lover had climbed into the red TARDIS, pulled the door shut behind them and dematerialised. Some time later Selina had the idea that the two of us might go on a Turkish holiday together.

And now I am going on a boat trip. It is another unseasonably hot day, although the sky is hazed with a layer of thin cloud. The white sky slides into a pearl-grey sea with no line of separation. There is a small boat waiting at the jetty near the corner of the bay, as Inglis man told me there would be, and as I plod towards it I can see the man lying on the roof of the tiny cabin, straw hat tilted over his eyes and ankles crossed, apparently asleep. His hearing must be supernaturally good, however, because I am still a way off and treading quietly over the rocks when in one fluid movement he sits up and raises his arm in greeting.

He takes my hand and helps me down into the cockpit. There are cushions on the seats and the space is shaded by an awning, and I sit down with relief to be partly out of the brooding heat. Through the cabin door I can see a neat area with narrow bunks separated by a folding table.

'No wind,' the man says, hunching his shoulders.

'No.'

'I don't like moving under engine power, but I think we shall have to. Maybe we'll pick up a breeze outside the bay.'

I look down into the water, which is so clear that I can see the rocks ten feet beneath the surface as if they were lying under plate glass, and then up into the colourless sky.

'Maybe,' I agree. I don't mind whether we find a breeze or not, or whatever else may be going to happen. I'm happy to be here, rocked by the water and with the shipshape little wooden cockpit around me.

The man starts up the engine and a drift of blue smoke rises from the stern. He jumps on to the jetty and releases the bow rope, and as the prow swings outwards in a slow arc he unties the stern and leaps back to join me and the boat. A minute later we are heading out to sea. In companionable silence we watch the water, and my white hotel and its companions as they fall away behind us.

'I don't know your name,' I say.

He tilts his head sideways and looks at me. None of his features is distinctive, nor is the composite they make, yet the suggestion of familiarity comes back again. I know that I don't know him, but I feel easy in his company.

'Mine is Catherine Stafford. Cary.'

'Andreas,' he says. He makes a small adjustment to the tiller to bring us round parallel to the shore.

'There,' he says with satisfaction. And then, gesturing to the tiller, 'Do you mind, just for a moment?'

I slide across and take his place as he moves forward. He runs up a sail and at once the wind fills it. Water drums under the hull and a wake churns behind us and I tighten my grasp on the tiller. I lift my head to look at the masthead, and the wind and our quickening speed make me smile. When Andreas moves back again I start to move out of his place but he makes a sign to indicate that I should stay put.

'I can't sail.'

'You are sailing.'

And he is right, I am. Pleasure swells in me until I feel as taut as the white sail. We seem to skim over the water. I watch the coastline and the villages that run down into the bays like clusters of sugar cubes shaken in the fold of a napkin. The scenery is calm rather them beautiful, painted in shades of aquamarine and sepia. Andreas points out the places and tells me their names.

61

'Do you live here?' I ask.

'Some of the time.'

After a while we pass a massive outcrop of rock, where cormorants shuffle against the sky. Immediately behind the rock, hidden by it except from an oblique angle, there is a tongue of sand between two steep rock cliffs.

'That's where we are going.'

'It looks beautiful.'

He helps me to bring the boat round. In the shallows the water is brilliant turquoise. There are fish in synchronised shoals, flicking their shadows over the sand. Andreas lowers the sail and makes his boat fast to a small buoy.

'Welcome to my bay.'

I am hot, now that we are motionless again, and the water looks enticing. I pull off the shirt that covers my swimming costume and stand up too quickly so the boat rocks wildly. Andreas puts his hand out to steady me and I cling on to his bare forearm, laughing. My own hand looks chalky against his suntanned skin.

'Dive,' he says and I look over the side into the water. Deep enough. We link hands and I scramble up on to the seat feeling the rough canvas of the cushions under the balls of my feet. The boat is still rocking and we are both laughing now. He puts his hands on my shoulders to steady me while I rise on to my toes and arrow my arms in front of me. Andreas's touch is friendly, even brotherly, with no whisper of sex in it. He is protecting me and teasing at the same time. I feel a pang of loss with Peter at the centre of it, because he was my lover and I miss him so acutely.

'Dive,' Andreas repeats and to get away from the memory of Peter I launch myself from the boat. There is a smack and sizzle of water and I stretch, letting the momentum of the dive drive me down as far as the rippled sand. Then I am rising again and the cool water strips away the roughness of the last months and it is as if I am clean and smooth and in one piece again. When I break the surface in a dazzle of light, I notice that the sky's white haze has receded and the sun is shining. Andreas surfaces next to me and shakes a glitter of drops from his hair. We swim together to the beach and then sit in the shallows, sun-warmed, looking out to the little boat and the slice of open sea beyond the mouth of the bay.

'My favourite place,' he says lightly.

'I can see why.'

Later Andreas straps a knife to his ankle and takes a netting bag for a swim around the rocks while I lie in the sun. When he comes back the bag is full of black spiny globes.

'Lunch.'

We sit under the boat's awning.

There is coarse brown bread and a dish of tomatoes. Andreas cups the sea urchins one by one in his hand and twists the point of the knife into the underside. He piles them in front of me and I spoon the orange pulpy contents greedily into my mouth. The taste is pure sea and iodine.

When we have finished eating I lie on the cabin roof, letting the sun unpin me, and Andreas puts a tiny coffeepot on the blue flame of a gas cylinder. He brings me a little tin cupful and three figs, and I gnaw the fruit off ragged slices of skin while the juice runs down my chin.

'This is wonderful.'

'Good.'

'But I don't know anything about you.' I smile.

He takes the last fig from me and neatly quarters it with the knife. 'What do you want to know?'

I try to frame the questions – how old are you, where do you come from, what do you know and what are you doing here – but then the points of reference fade. There is nothing I need to ask because it is enough just to be here.

Andreas splits the flower-shape of fig segments apart, two for him and two for me. I look into his face and it is like looking into my own. As familiar as that.

'Have you eaten enough?'

I nod.

'Come ashore.'

There is shade under the east-facing cliff. We lie on the sand, facing each other, heads propped on our hands.

'What are you going to do next?' he asks quietly. It is as if he already knows about Peter. It is a relief not to have to fill in what has already happened, but to make an attempt at sketching out the future instead.

'I won't go back to London. I'd like to live somewhere different, where all those rocks of history don't weigh me down any more.'

'You could do that.'

'I could do anything' I start to say it with an ironic shrug, but looking into Andreas's face the words come out with me believing them. 'I'll start living, instead of hiding. You know, something happened to me a long time ago – no, not happened, I *did* something and it changed everything that came afterwards, for me and everyone around me. I'd like to be the person I might have been, if … if that thing had never happened.'

His hand uncurls and he touches my mouth.

'Shh. You can be, if that's what you really want,' he says.

And what he says is right. The certainty is soothing and I stretch myself out in the sand, suddenly drowsy.

'I could sleep,' I murmur.

Andreas yawns. 'And me, too.'

We lie down side by side and I fall asleep with Andreas's heartbeat and the ripple of water in my head.

That was how the day was. There was nothing complicated or buried or even unspoken about it; we were just easy in one another's company as if we were old friends.

When I wake up the sky has clouded again with the morning's thin white cover. There is only a hollow in the sand beside me and I sit up, panicky and still fogged with daytime sleep. Then I see Andreas in the cockpit of the boat and he lifts his hand to beckon me. The water feels chill as I wade in and unwillingly strike out. He helps me over the side and I wrap myself in my shirt.

'The weather is changing,' he says. Under the colourless sky the land looks bleak and the water is cloudy. It's airlessly hot now, but a breath of fear makes me shiver.

'What's happening?' I shake my head, trying to clear the sleep out of it.

Andreas is busy with the rope that has anchored us to the buoy. He hauls in the dripping length of it.

'I'll take you home.'

'Home,' I think and the notion was nothing to do with the white-skinned hotel. It's somewhere else, somewhere I can't yet locate. The sky has grown steadily darker and a few raindrops pock the water, but I hardly notice. Outside the confines of the bay there is just enough wind to stiffen the sail. We sit quietly and the coastline slides backwards until the beach hotels come into view.

We reach the jetty and he brings the boat alongside, passing a double length of rope through an iron ring to make us fast.

'Thank you,' I say uncertainly. The questions I dismissed earlier sound again. *Who? Why?*

Andreas says, 'We will see each other again, but it won't be another day like today.'

Why? Again, but I don't ask the question aloud. I already know that there will be no answer, not now, no answer that would qualify as such. Maybe he is about to go away. Maybe there are other considerations that I don't yet understand.

'I had a very happy day, today.'

Already in my mind it is set aside, marked out with a memory. With the rhythm of Andreas's company I have stopped thinking about Peter. There has been a whole chain of hours during which I have been completely happy and unmarked.

On the jetty, looking out at the brown hummocks of the Greek islands and the backdrop of pewter sky, Andreas briefly puts his arms round me and holds me close.

'So did I,' he says.

Then he kisses my forehead and lets me go.

I stand watching the boat slip away, but he has put his straw hat on and there is no glimpse of his face.

I am in my hotel room again. A handful of days separate me from the hours I spent with Andreas, but the effect of our strange encounter has stayed with me. I have been content with my own company, not needing to block myself out with reading or barbiturate-heavy sleep. My memories of Peter and our life together have been tender and untainted by bitterness. I am awake and anticipatory, and there is no weight on my back. I have walked on the beach and through the streets of Branc, looking at the people who live here and making up stories for myself about their lives. People have looked at me in return, nodding and smiling – casual greetings, just the way that ordinary people acknowledge each other. And I have not minded or shied away from the scrutiny. I feel that I have the freedom of myself.

Maybe this is normal, maybe this is the happiness of normality.

Maybe I have never known it since before my eighth birthday.

I can't sleep.

The clock at my bedside tells me that it is a little after one a.m. The close, thundery weather has lasted for three days now, since I went sailing with Andreas. A storm would clear the air, but it never comes, and the nights are long and airless. I find that I don't mind the absence of sleep, now, whereas only last week I would have obliterated myself with sleeping pills.

I slide out of bed and put on a pair of loose trousers, a thin shirt. I step noiselessly out of my room and walk down the hotel corridor, past the numbered and nameless doors, across the deserted lobby where the night porter is dozing in a chair behind the reception desk. Outside in the garden there is the faintest breath of wind and I pursue it down the steps on to the beach. The sand grates cool and pleasant under my bare feet. The sea is black, the sky starless. I walk for a couple of minutes, to the water's edge and a step beyond, soaking my feet and ankles and the hems of my trouser legs. Then I pace along to the jetty where Andreas moored the boat. I walk to the end and sit down. I hook my fingers in the iron ring and dangle my legs over the edge.

There is stillness and silence except for the restless water.

I look back at the darkened town. There are few holiday-makers left, the bars and clubs are mostly closed for the season. It is as if everyone in the world is asleep.

I sit and wait.

FOUR

'It's too hot,' Theo complained.

His grandmother held him on her lap and stroked his hair, murmuring a stream of Greek baby talk. It wasn't particularly hot now that it was dark, but the thundery air was oppressive. Olivia moved between the sink and the table, stepping around the chair where Meroula sat. She knew that her mother-in-law was watching her over the child's head and she tried to shake off both the awareness and the irritation that went with it. She didn't want Meroula sitting here in her kitchen. The older woman judged the way that Olivia ran her household and cared for her children, and always found the methods deficient, pursing her mouth so the creases ran out from it like slanting chisel marks. Olivia had no choice in the matter, however. Meroula took it as a Greek mother's right to place herself at the centre of her son's household and Xan tacitly concurred.

'When I was a little girl, Granny used to put Max and me to bed every night at seven o'clock,' Olivia said, although no one was listening.

They shared a room, when they were very small, just as Georgi and Theo did now. Olivia would lie under the blankets

68

and make up stories about runaway princesses and jungles and lost treasure. The stories had more exotic ingredients than narrative drive, she remembered. She had been very good at making up the cast list but rarely got beyond it into any action. Even so, Max would lie with his thumb in his mouth, watching her with enthralled eyes as she rambled on. She would get carried away with descriptions of the princess's golden hair and long pink dresses, and when she finally looked again to see how riveted he was, he would have fallen into sleep as suddenly as if he had dropped down a well. In the morning he would apparently still be lying in the same position, thumb in his mouth. Time to get up, Olivia would tell him, and he would open his eyes immediately, ready to scramble up and do what she told him in their games.

She could remember exactly how the house felt on those early evenings and mornings. It was quiet, as if nothing would ever change there, and yet there was an underlying sense that with just a single flick everything could alter frighteningly for ever.

'I'm too hot,' Theo repeated.

'He has a fever,' Meroula said to her.

'Let him get down and go and lie down in his own bed.'

'On his own, the poor child?'

Meroula wore a wide grey skirt with folds that allowed her to sit with her legs planted apart. She had thick lisle stockings, the colour of dried clay, and a dark cardigan with lapels and military buttons that stretched across her chest. She didn't always wear the same clothes, but she gave the impression that this was her unvarying uniform.

'I don't want to go to bed,' Georgi said from the other side of the table, without looking up from his drawing. 'I want to see Pappy when he comes in.'

'Of course he does,' Meroula said triumphantly.

Olivia was preparing squid for Xan's evening meal, slicing

69

off the heads and pulling out the entrails and the ink sac, and then dropping the torsos into a dish of oil and tomato juice. Squid stuffed with rice and onions was one of Xan's favourite dinners. The boys had already eaten their sausages and beans.

'Mother? You will stay and have some food with us?'

Meroula still lived in the house where her husband had died not long after Theo's birth. But in the winter, when there were no guests and tourists to keep her away, she spent plenty of time with her son and his family. She inclined her head now, her expression managing to convey that this would be a duty rather than a pleasure, but still a duty that she intended to perform.

'That's good,' Olivia said.

From the window over the sink she could see a corner of the square and the Taverna Irini. The owners had retreated to Rhodes for the winter; the windows of the bar were lined on the inside with newspaper, already yellowing, and the door was padlocked. The islanders preferred to use the place on the harbour.

The only light showing was in a blue wooden kiosk next to the taverna. Inside his square metre of shelter, stacked with cigarettes and chewing gum and lottery tickets, Manolis was dozing with his cheek on his folded arms on top of a pile of photo magazines. Manolis had a tiny head and a huge body, invariably encased in the same pair of greasy trousers that revealed a slice of woollen underclothing through the fly opening. Georgi said that his head wasn't big enough to hold a proper brain and it was true that Manolis was simple. But he was able to sell cigarettes and calculate the right change from a thousand-drachma note, and he kept the kiosk open all hours of the day and half of the night, summer and winter, because the only other place he had to go was a curtained alcove in his mother's tiny house right over the

70

harbour. Sometimes Manolis sat in the sun on a bench near his kiosk, but the approach of a customer sent him rolling back into the blue box. As Olivia watched now, his head bobbed up.

The customer was Xan. He pointed to something, pocketed what Manolis gave him, handed over money in exchange.

Olivia was smiling, her hands unfurling under the dirty sink water.

'Pappy's coming.'

Theo sprang out of Meroula's arms and Georgi threw his crayon aside.

'Pappy!'

Meroula sat upright and smoothed her grey skirt across her lap, as if she was about to see her lover. Olivia had noticed this often enough before and it both irritated and touched her. Xan was everything to his mother; there was no corner of her life that he did not irradiate.

Xan said when she tried to talk to him about it, 'It's the way it is, it's not unusual. But you are the one I am married to.'

She would put her hands on either side of his face and kiss him on the mouth.

'Don't you forget it.'

He came in, bulky and smelling of smoke and bar. His arms were held stiffly in front of him with the fists clenched so he marched like a robot. The boys ran at him and battered themselves against his legs.

'Left or right?' Xan demanded.

'Left,' Theo yelled and Georgi countered, 'Right.'

Theo amended his choice at once. 'Right!'

Ignoring their responses, Xan dropped a plastic bubble into each pair of cupped hands. Inside were a block of bright pink bubblegum and a plastic toy that demanded construction from four puzzle pieces. The boys stuck the gum into their mouths and dropped to their knees to put the toys together. Georgi's was a yellow car, Theo's a red man.

The first time she saw him, Olivia remembered, Xan had been handing out sweets to Bangkok street children with just the same robot movements. The children were milling around his knees, pushing and shouting for his attention, and his arms were outstretched above a thicket of grasping fingers. It was the end of the monsoon and the swollen, khaki-coloured river behind them carried a mat of floating weeds and branches. Olivia lifted her old Leica to frame the shot and Xan turned to look straight into the lens, through the tunnel of her eye and into her head. He emptied his bag of sweets into the waiting hands and came to her.

'It's a straight trade,' he said and took an Instamatic out of the pocket in his shirt. He held it horizontally and made as if to take the picture.

'If I were you,' Olivia pointed out, 'I'd frame it vertically.' He did as she suggested and clicked the shutter. They were standing in a sea of children now, all clamouring for more presents.

'Nice. Thanks. You know about photography, do you?'

'It's my job. I sell my photographs.'

'Is that so? You want to come for a beer?'

That was how she lived, in those days. She took flights, she drifted through foreign cities and rode buses up remote mountain passes. She took pictures in Soweto and Havana and Bogotá, and on Caribbean beaches and in the canyons of midtown Manhattan. Some of these she sold, to picture libraries and agencies and magazines. She owned little more than she could carry, and the tide of travellers and back-packers that flowed around the world was the current she swam in. She had drunk beer with hundreds of strangers and some of them had become friends. Some, even lovers.

'Yes, a quick one.'

When they were sitting under an awning beside the river Olivia began with the question that always followed the exchange of names. 'Where are you heading?'

Xan said, 'Home.'

The intense pleasure in the way he said it, the way he anticipated the prospect as if he was starving and about to be fed, filled her with a wash of melancholy. It wasn't homesickness – England and her parents' present house in the country, where she had never even lived, was hardly home any more. Yet she could feel the pull of home through Xan Georgiadis, the idea and significance and safety of a place rather than her own reality, like a thread passing straight through her innards. She felt a longing to be connected to a place again after so many years of wandering.

Over the rim of her glass she watched him, thinking how good-looking he was. There was an unfamiliar knocking in her chest. Don't get too excited, she tried to warn herself. But already it was too late for warnings. 'Where's that?'

'Greece.'

Xan had lived for five years in Melbourne. He had been working in his second cousin's building company, putting up cheap houses for immigrant communities on the city outskirts, and he was brawny from carrying and deeply suntanned, and an Australian twang overlaid his Greek pronunciations. But now, he said, his parents needed him at home. His father was getting old and his mother missed him.

'It's one of the islands, in the Dodecanese. You should just see it. It's paradise.'

Olivia had been to most of the world's paradise destinations, but she could easily believe that with Xan Georgiadis in it this one would outstrip them all.

'You are going up to bed right now. You can bring the toys with you,' Xan said.

The boys kissed Meroula and Olivia, and padded after their father. They always did as he told them.

'See, they are their father's children,' Meroula said with a broad smile of satisfaction. Olivia tucked the last of the stuffing into the last of the squid and slid the dish into the oven before her mother-in-law could tell her that Xan really preferred meat to fish. She could hear the thuds and scuffles of the boys romping with Xan overhead. Meroula nodded and smiled.

When he came back from settling the children they sat down to eat, with Xan at the head of the table and his wife and mother on either side of him. They had a dish of olives with bread and oil, and then the squid. Xan had been playing cards in the taverna and watching a football game on the television that hung over the bar, and he had come home hungry. Meroula ate a substantial plateful too, but with an expression of forbearance. She looked at Xan's plate every minute or two, to check that he had enough. The room was quiet except for the clink of cutlery. If Meroula had not been there, Xan and Olivia would have chatted and maybe even drunk some wine. These empty, out-of-season evenings when the children were asleep were among the best of their times on Halemni.

Olivia contented herself with looking around the room as she ate.

There were candles burning on one of the stone shelves and a row of books on another. There were logs stacked in a basket next to the stone hearth, but the fire was unlit – this luxury was reserved for the coldest evenings, or for the times when the island's power supply failed. Two comfortable old armchairs sat on either side of the fire, with cupboards for the boys' toys and games beside them. There was a bread oven at the side of the fireplace, but Olivia baked in the new gas oven that occupied the far end of the room together with all the cupboards and equipment for cooking for a dozen guests at a time. The big oak table filled the centre of the space, and windows on one side looked from the front of the house to the square and the sea in the distance. On the opposite side a row of doors opened on to the shaded terrace and the slope of hillside behind the village. In summer this was where life was lived.

Xan had built almost everything and laid the limestone flags of the floor. The doors of all the cupboards were painted with squares and diamonds and lozenges of brilliant colour, turquoise and saffron and tangerine and crimson – this was Christopher's work – and every spare piece of wall was covered with pictures by guests, the boys and Christopher, and with Olivia's photographs. There was no television, but there was a CD player and a radio. It had taken a long time to create it all on limited resources but it was a warm and comfortable place now, lit with the candles and low lamps.

'Have you had enough to eat, Mother? Xan?'

'Give him that last spoonful.'

Xan pushed over his plate.

'There's some fruit. We've got figs,' Olivia suggested.

Meroula shook her head. 'No fruit. Thank you.'

'I will make some coffee when I've finished,' Xan said with his mouth full.

'Let me do it for you,' Meroula responded.

Olivia let her. She was remembering what it had been like when she first came to Halemni. She had known Xan for only a few weeks, the time that it had taken for them to make their way slowly back to Europe and to know that they wanted to stay together. The last stage of the journey had been on a ferry out of Rhodes harbour. The hot, smoky bar and passenger lounge seemed to be full of weather-beaten men who knew Xan, and greeted him with full-on embraces and streams of questions. But after a brief talk with each of them during which he introduced Olivia as *my girl*, Xan preferred to stand the whole way, four hours of sailing, on the upper deck. Olivia leaned on the rail beside him, watching the curl of foam from the ship's bows and the cliffs and rocky uplands of the other islands, her hand tucked under his arm and the thought in her mind that she was giving up everything she had known in her life so far to follow Xan Georgiadis back home.

The idea created a hollow and pleasurable sense of the irrevocable in the pit of her stomach. The travelling was over. Whatever this place waiting over the horizon turned out be like, it was where she would stay because it was where Xan belonged.

'There it is.'

She followed the line of his pointing finger. A blue-grey smudge on the November horizon of the Aegean.

Forty minutes later the ferry made a complicated reverse manoeuvre in the bay of Halemni and brought the ship's stern up against a stone jetty. Olivia stood beside Xan in the ship's bowels as the massive steel door was lowered to reveal a widening rectangle of scenery. A rim of frosty blue sky. Rocky hillsides, brown and grey, and the whitewashed houses in a semicircle above the harbour. A narrow strip of shingle beach fringed with tamarisk trees and an expanse of pale-grey sea. It took a closer scrutiny for Olivia to notice the ruins of a castle on the highest rock cliff, and a more geometric composition of rock and stone clinging to the slopes beneath it. There were windows that looked like dark eyes.

'The castle of Agrosikia, built by the Knights of St John, and Arhea Chorio, the old village,' Xan said.

The steel door clanged into the horizontal against the jetty, and sailors and harbour men made the massive ropes fast. The little knot of people Xan and Olivia had been waiting with moved forward in a sudden surge and a couple of trucks nudged out of the hold.

'There they are,' Xan said. 'My parents.'

Olivia saw them. A stout woman with a square body and a square face under a wedge of iron-grey hair, and a much smaller, thin and colourless man with a cigarette cupped in his fingers. With all her belongings in one pack on her back, she followed Xan off the ship and into her life on Halemni.

When Xan introduced Olivia, Meroula's eyes travelled from her dusty boots to the top of her head. She was almost a foot shorter than Olivia, even when she drew herself up to her full height as she did now. The only son had come home at last, but instead of choosing to marry a Greek girl he had brought this outlandish creature with him. Nikos Georgiadis's friendly handshake hardly compensated for the chilliness of Meroula's greeting.

For the first weeks they lived with Meroula and Nikos, sleeping in the bedroom next to the parents' and eating every meal with them. Olivia learned quickly, putting Greek words and then sentences together, and always deferring to Meroula in everything. To her initial surprise even this didn't win Xan's mother's approval, but then she realised that nothing she did ever would win it because Meroula was her outright rival for Xan's love and attention. Xan himself ducked out of the conflict.

He spent his days fishing with his boyhood friends or working, when the weather allowed it, on the new buildings for summer tourists that were inching their way upwards on the margins of Megalo Chorio. To keep out of Meroula's way, Olivia spent her days exploring the island. In time she came to know every piece of it, from the sandy bays on the southern side to the wild rocks and remote inlets on the north and eastern flanks. It was ten miles from west to east and, at the narrowest point, a mile and a half from north to south. She walked and climbed, and sat on rocks and simply looked, and fell in love for the second time.

The weather changed with snapshot speed, from still clear days to wild storms followed by insistent rain, and then changed back again. The sea could take on every colour from almost black to pearl to turquoise, and the bare hillsides darkened with rain and then softened again under the afternoon sun.

Meroula said, 'You will have to marry, Alexander. You cannot go on living in my house like man and wife without the blessing of the church.'

Xan laughed. 'We will marry when we are ready, Mother. If you don't want Olivia and me to live together here I'll clear out and move in with Stefanos. Would you rather that?'

'You cannot live anywhere on Halemni but with your own mother and father.'

'Well, there is your answer.' Xan winked at Olivia, Meroula gave her a black look.

Christmas came and went. January brought the first of the wild flowers in sheltered places. Olivia discovered clumps of tiny white wild cyclamen and blue anemones, and found the furry rosettes of mandrakes with their central boss of flowers like flattened eggs in a bird's nest. She climbed between the wire-netting bushes and clumps of wild sage, up the steep goat path to the abandoned old village, and made herself at home in it. The stepping stones of the narrow streets were broken and tilted, with the spear-shaped leaves of arum and wild hyacinth pushing up between them.

The last few families had left in the Sixties, driven out by the lack of water and the hardness of life, retreating down to the coast to join the rest of their dwindling community. This was before the great money tide of tourism washed over the islands. The young men no longer wanted a back-breaking existence spent farming their family's hillside terraces with donkeys and their bare hands, and the young women refused to marry into such a life. The little stone houses were roofless, door and window holes gaping, home to the goats and a few snakes and lizards.

Olivia wandered through the ruins with her camera.

Each house had its own atmosphere. In some the bare earth smelled sour and the loose stones rattled underfoot. In others the bread oven beside the ruined hearth still felt almost warm and she could imagine the smell of baking on the air. The twisted trunk of an old rose bush leaned at an angle against one door, blue paint daubs marked family ownership on another. But the Halemni families would never come back to Arhea Chorio. The only inhabitants were ghosts. Sometimes Olivia could feel people, walking up the street to the ruined church to answer the silent bell.

'I can't live with your mother any longer,' Olivia said to Xan when spring had properly arrived and the hillsides were a picture of flowers.

'You don't have to.'

'What do you mean?'

'Vangelis is going to sell us his house. Bit by bit, as we raise the money. It's more expensive than buying it outright, but beggars can't be choosers. Let's go and look at it.'

They walked up to the potter's house. It was dirty and barely weatherproof, and full of the twisted remains of aborted pots, but Olivia and Xan knew immediately that they could make a home in it. They moved into one room, with plastic sheeting nailed across the window frame and fruit boxes for furniture. But the days were long and hot now, and they were happy to work all the hours that came.

'You can't live in that house together. You are not married. Do you know what people will think?'

Xan still laughed. 'I am not worried what one hundred and fifty people think on one small island. What if we were doing something wicked that the whole world might disapprove of? Which would make you more ashamed?'

'You should not make your mother ashamed at all.'

Xan laid the heavy flagstones in the kitchen, with the help of his friends Stefanos and Yannis. It was back-breaking work. At the end of one day he sat on the terrace with Olivia under a velvet midnight sky.

'Will you marry me?' he asked.

'What do you think?'

'I will take that as a yes.'

They were married in September, a Greek Orthodox ceremony in the church across the square from their house. Olivia spent the week beforehand staying in the house of Stefanos's married sister, and every night of that week Xan and his bachelor friends came and brought her presents, and took away the women's offerings of cakes and wine before embarking on a night of drinking.

'It's the Halemniot custom, always before a wedding,' Xan protested blearily in the mornings.

'What am I supposed to do meanwhile?'

'Work on your wedding clothes. Prepare the bed linen. You are marrying a Greek man.'

'God help me.'

'God has got nothing to do with it,' Xan said. He pulled her into the windowless storage room off Stefanos's sister's kitchen and rapidly made love to her against a sack of bread flour.

Olivia's parents and brother and three of her old friends from university came out for the wedding. Polly and Celia sat on the beach in holiday bikinis and Jack rubbed sun cream between their shoulder blades, and flipped through their magazines while they went swimming.

'I can't believe how lucky you are, coming to live in this heavenly place.' Polly sighed.

'And with Xan,' Jack added enviously.

Celia was the married one, with small children whom she

80

had left behind with her husband. She worried about them, and telephoned mornings and evenings from the public phone at the harbour.

'Won't you miss home?' she asked.

'Darling,' Jack protested. 'Olivia has hardly been home in ten years. Why should she start missing it now?'

'Well, you know what I mean. This is coming to live somewhere for good, starting a family. Putting down proper roots.'

'I can't think of anywhere else I'd rather be, root and branch,' Olivia said.

'I'll drink to that.' Polly smiled. They all raised their glasses to her in an affectionate toast.

Max liked Halemni as soon as he came ashore from the ferry. On her last day of being a single woman, Olivia took him for a walk up the hill behind the potter's house. She loved showing him the best view of the sea and the clear view of the Turkish coast from the rock ridge. They sat down on a stone outcrop with the sun hot on their shoulders and Olivia leaned comfortably back against her brother's knees. After working on Vangelis's house all through the long Greek summer Olivia was almost as brown as Xan.

'I'm so glad you came,' she told Max as he pulled at the ends of her salt-dried and sun-bleached mop of hair.

'You think I'd miss this? Look at this hair. Jack will despair of you,' he teased. 'I thought brides were supposed to spend days beforehand getting crimped and painted.'

'It's not like that on Halemni. Who would care?'

'I'm glad you're going to be married,' Max said. 'It will suit you.'

'I never thought I would be. It seemed so unlikely, ending up doing the same as Mum.'

Max laughed derisively. 'The same? I don't think so. And you aren't just marrying Xan, are you, and settling down to a mortgage and a routine? You are marrying this beautiful place and a life as unlike Mum's as it could possibly be.'

Olivia nodded. Her head felt as if it couldn't contain so much happiness.

'Exactly. I knew you would understand about the island. The others don't, not really. We always understood each other, didn't we?'

'Yes, we did.'

They had been a company of two, all through their childhood and teens. When she left university and set out with her rucksack and a camera it was Max whom Olivia felt guilty about leaving behind, not their parents. It wasn't many years before Max left England too, in her wake. He had recently come to rest in Sydney.

Now that the two of them were adults they sometimes talked about the uncomfortable marriage that their parents had endured. Its quality was monotony cut with menace, Olivia diagnosed, once she was old enough. Every table mat and duster and saucepan lid had its proper place in her mother's domestic order, there was a rigid programme of what was cleaned when and what was to be eaten on which day. Nothing was ever allowed to vary, but Maddie seemed always to be tensely waiting. When she was young Olivia never wanted to come too close to what the element of menace consisted of, although it shifted around the arguments that she and Max overheard when they were lying in bed, and her father's absences.

He came home, always, in the end, but there was an unspoken fear that some day he might not.

It had felt like the essence of freedom to Olivia to move out of their house and go as she pleased, and it was a freedom she had never dreamed of giving up, until now.

'Be happy,' Max ordered.

'I think I can promise that,' Olivia murmured, dreamily resting her head against her brother's knees.

'Where's Jack and the girls?' he asked after a while.

'Giving each other facials, I think.'

'Of course.'

They rolled on the brown turf, laughing as they had done when they were children.

For the wedding Olivia's mother wore a pink suit and her father a linen jacket and a spotted silk tie. Denis and Maddie looked tall and pale and formal, and quite bewildered among the fishermen and carpenters and goat men.

When she came out of the church in the wake of the priest in his black chimney hat, as Xan's wife, she stopped and kissed both her parents.

'That's my girl,' Denis said and she knew that he was pleased for her. Maddie had tears smudging her mascara and Olivia brushed them away with the tips of her fingers. Meroula was standing there too and Olivia gave her mother-in-law a kiss on each cheek. She wanted to say something about being a daughter rather than a son stealer, but she couldn't muster the Greek words.

Just as well, she thought afterwards. Meroula had no time for sentiment. She was as sentimental as a mousetrap.

The newlyweds gave a party on their terrace, under the newly planted vine. Everyone on the island who could get away from their summer work came, and the tavernas and restaurants operated for the night with a skeleton staff. Celia and Polly and Jack danced with the goat men, and her father got drunk and made a long speech interspersed with the classical Greek he remembered from school, to the bafflement of the entire company.

Xan and Olivia went to bed that night in their room still furnished with fruit boxes.

'Will your mother be happy now?' she asked.

She felt him smiling against her hair, his breath warming her scalp. 'No, of course not.'

'Why?'

'There must be sons.'

'Well, what are you waiting for?'

That was ten years ago. In that time they had built a business together, and they had had Georgi and Theo.

Meroula put down her empty coffee cup.

'I will walk back home with you, Mother,' Xan said, as he always did. Olivia kissed her and Meroula submitted to the embrace.

'Goodnight Olivia. I am grateful for the food.'

'And we are thankful for our family.'

It was a traditional island exchange after hospitality given and received. Sometimes Olivia had to grit her teeth around the utterance more than at others.

While Xan was out Olivia finished drying up the supper dishes and put them away in the cupboard. She blew out the candles and went outside to stand on the terrace. The wind was blowing from the wrong direction. Usually at this time of night she could hear the sea, but now she caught a sound from the opposite side, a goat bell from the herd that roamed the hill. She stood for a minute, listening. The goats should be in their shelter now, not restlessly moving. It must be the thunder in the air.

Upstairs the boys were asleep in their beds. Theo's arms and legs were flung out at angles and he held the red man firmly in one fist. Olivia kissed them both. In her own room she sat tiredly on the bed and peeled off her socks. It had been a long day.

Xan came in and closed the door.

When they were lying down together she asked, 'What time is it?'

'Half past eleven.'

'Did you hear the wind?'

'Yes. Are you sleepy?'
'I thought I was. But now I'm not.'
'That's good.'

It was an hour before they finally fell asleep, at half past midnight.

FIVE

In the darkness I am still clinging to my bed of rock.

I can see Peter's face and Lisa Kirk's smile, and Andreas, and my mother and a falling statue.

Again and again, over and over, the statue's stone arc cutting through a blue afternoon, and the terror that came after merges with the terror of this moment.

The jetty no longer exists. Even through a hanging pall of dust that thickens the darkness I can see that much. Everything has been transformed. The line of hotels along the beach front has been mashed into drunken, sloping relics. The brittle white façade of my hotel has fallen into creases with stark vertical pillars rising out of it. The corner that had once been my room is completely gone. The tall lights along the sea wall have been snapped like matchsticks and the sand in front is a greedy swirl of water.

I stagger to my feet like a drunken creature.

The jetty foundations are big, jagged boulders and I begin to scramble over them. All I can think is that I must get to the hotel. My belongings are all there, my clothes and my money and passport. Without these coverings and shreds of paper I am nothing, I am invisible.

Get to the hotel. Only a few yards away, but an interminable distance. Blocked by rubble and sea water. I must get to the hotel.

Somewhere ahead of me a woman starts wailing, a long, ululating sound of pure desolation.

Get to the hotel. People will need help.

I hear a booming noise behind me. I turn my head, a split second and out of the corner of my eye I glimpse a towering wall of water. The crest of it with an ugly lacing of foam is far higher than my head and it is racing at me, too fast to evade, even if there were anywhere to run to.

I fling up my arms to cover my head. The wave smashes into me, and my ears and eyes and lungs fill up with water. I fall and the force of the wave sweeps me away like a dead thing, arms and legs useless as I am churned in a soup of stones and sand.

The next thing I know I am lying head down, my torso twisted so I can't breathe or cough to expel the water from my lungs.

Move. But I am pinned by rocks and the notion flutters in my weary mind: stay still. Let go and then rest.

I gather a knot of strength from somewhere within myself and strike out against the rocks. Somehow I break free of the weight and the sky steadies overhead. I can see stars, pinpricks in the dark-blue span. I am lying among boulders in what was once the garden of my hotel, where the huge wave that followed the earthquake has disgorged me.

It is no longer a garden. Tables and broken beach beds and the snapped stalks of parasols lie in a reeking jumble with sand and mud and a wreckage of fencing and pedalos and torn-up trees. Among the debris, close to my face, is a woman's body. I can't see her head, but from the angle of her hips and her stillness I know that she is dead.

I lie with one side of my face in the mud, shivering with fear and cold, and the beginnings of comprehension.

The earthquake must have been massive and devastating. It has not just happened in my head or in the immediate envelope of space surrounding me. The line of hotels is destroyed, the whole of Branc must be in ruins.

Maybe I am the only person left alive.

I must move. Do something.

'*Move.*' I hear my own voice croaking out the word. And in obedience to the command I lever myself on to my hands and knees, and crawl to the woman's body. She is every bit as dead as she looks. I couldn't see her head when I first noticed her, because it isn't there.

I am not the only person left alive. There are shapes awkwardly moving in front of what remains of the hotel and I can hear shouting. Meshed with the shouts are thin, high screams for help. I struggle towards the figures and a shaft of light strikes across the mess in front of me. A man clambers past, dressed in fisherman's clothes and carrying a big torch, and I struggle in his wake, drawn like a moth to the beam of light. He half turns and shouts a stream of Turkish commands, waving towards the side of the hotel.

'I don't know. I don't understand,' I shout back. He takes no notice of me at all and another man scrambles past me to answer his instructions.

Belongings and passport. The thought comes back to me and fighting disorientation I veer towards what was once the door to what were once the stairs leading to my room.

Slabs of marble facing and chunks of torn concrete and twisted rods of metal make an impenetrable barrier. There is no entering the building because there is no entry left, and nothing recognisable remaining of this corner of the hotel. Everything has sheared away and toppled into a mess of rubble, and the acrid dust from the collapse hangs in the air like poison gas. I can't reach any of my possessions because they are buried under tons of masonry. If I had been asleep in my bed, I would be buried there with them. But instead I am outside in the darkness, unable to speak the language of the cries for help I can hear rising all around me. People are stumbling and shouting, and hauling at the wreckage.

I can't communicate with them. I don't know what to do. I am invisible.

I sit down in a heap against the spars of what was once the terrace bar. Only yesterday I was perching here on a tall stool, dipping my spoon into an ice cream that – after Andreas – I saw no reason not to allow myself: pistachio and almond ice cream, palest sea-green, speckled with nuts.

Now there is broken glass, a flag of half-buried awning.

The full scale of the devastation is becoming clear. I can read it in the anguished flailing of a man who is tearing handfuls of mud out of a bank of silt washed up against collapsing walls. He is shouting a name, over and over. It sounds like *Oma, Oma*.

There must be scenes like this all over Branc, and how far beyond that?

There are more people now and bobbing lights weaving across the ruined garden. The beams swing across a woman who is standing alone, screaming at the sky, her fists clenched above her head. They light up a man's face, caked with grey dirt and blotted with blood. In another place I see a knot of men with garden spades who have begun to dig at the mud bank. The man in fisherman's clothes is pointing and shouting directions but he is the only one who seems capable of organising any rescue attempt. And in the face of this devastation, rescue of any sort seems an impossibility.

Help. Sluggishly, my reactions impaired by shock, it dawns on me afresh that I should also try to help someone. Once I am on my feet I move clumsily towards the nearest light.

A woman in a torn and bloodied nightdress is crouching over the wreckage of the bar. I can see her hair hanging forward in a grey coil over her shoulder, and the filth caking her wrists and arms, because there is a girl of about twelve holding a tiny torch with the narrow beam shining on her. The woman is muttering and frenziedly hauling at a painted pole that once supported the bar canopy.

I shout at her, 'I'll help. Who is in there?' but she is too intent to hear me. The girl stands her ground, shivering and sobbing. When the pole comes loose the woman throws it aside without even noticing the weight. She kneels down and peers into the space and then doubles her efforts to haul away the rubble. Her hands are bleeding, but she is oblivious.

I can see a third hand, curled in the dirt.

The woman seizes it, her muttering becoming a moan. The child is shaking so much that the torch beam is jumping. There is a warning shout from further off and then a crack and rumble of a further collapse. I don't even look around to see. I crouch down by the woman instead and begin furiously digging with my hands, hauling away debris to expose an arm and shoulder dressed in a white waiter's jacket. The woman is pulling on the limp hand as if she could drag the buried weight out by it.

'Stop. Help me like this,' I order her. She doesn't hear or can't understand what I am saying so I labour on, moving the fallen spars as carefully as I can to spare the person beneath. It is a hard struggle, shifting the cumbersome pieces. I can see more of the waiter now. He is lying on his side with his back to us, part of his shoulders and head exposed by our efforts.

Tears are streaming down the woman's face. She looks up beyond me and shouts for help, her mouth pulled square with desperation. Two men run to her and join their efforts to hers. Within a few minutes enough of the man's body is freed to enable one of the rescuers to reach into the hole and work his arms under the shoulders.

I am standing to one side, my hands hanging loose.

I can't watch this, but I must.

The waiter's body is dragged out of its resting place and laid on the ground. His head lolls as they move him and the old woman runs to cradle it. The skin of the face is waxy, covered with mud and dirt. She rubs at it with a fold of her nightdress, whispering words of faith and encouragement, and as she smooths away the mess I recognise him. It is Jim. And I can also see that he is dead. It takes longer for the truth to dawn on his mother and sister because they fend the knowledge off with hugging the inert body and rubbing their cheeks against his.

One of the men mutters to the other and they move off to where another group of people is frantically digging and calling out. When I try to look away from Jim's mother I see that the same scene is repeated all along the beach front. Knots of rescuers have started to claw at the fallen buildings and disorientated survivors rush from one group to the next, crying out names.

Jim's mother is on her knees beside his body.

She can't any longer hope that he is alive. She gathers him up in her arms, holding him against her like a baby. And she wails, a raw note of desolation that cuts the noise around us and turns everything else to silence.

I can't bear to listen, but I can hear nothing else. The same deafening, despairing note has been in my head for ever.

Jim's mother becomes my mother. The debris of Branc is an English garden and the fallen hotel just a stone statue. The mother lifts up a child's body and cradles him, and her world and the rest of the world is torn to fragments.

The girl, Jim's sister, is standing a little to one side. The

91

torch lies at her feet, where she has just dropped it. She is white-faced and as mute as the statue and her eyes slide from her dead brother to her mother's living horror.

I see myself in her.

But this child is blameless. None of this, the wreckage, or the wailing or the flood of horror is her fault.

It is different for me and it always has been.

And now I am a woman in my forties left standing in the aftermath of an earthquake. A new world of grief plays itself out in front of me.

A hand touches my shoulder and I spin round.

Andreas is beside me. His face blots out everything else. As if I am a tiny child and he is my powerful father, a surge of relief washes through me, diluting the grief and easing my terror. I will be safe now.

'Look at this,' I say, pointing to the tableau. Jim's mother is kneeling almost at our feet.

Andreas takes hold of me. He is warm and solid, dry against my wet clothes. His arm circles my shoulders, protective and insulating. I feel myself being lifted to safety.

'I know. There's nothing we can do here. Come with me,' he says.

He does know, not only about what is left of Branc and here and now, but about the steps that led me here. It was this unworded familiarity that made our day in the boat so right and even here the rightness of it stays with me.

'We should help them.'

The girl has moved to her mother's side. Together the two women lower Jim's body to the ground and they sit on either side of him, holding his hands. They are both crying, but quietly now.

'What do you want to do for them?' Andreas gently asks.

There is nothing tangible, physical, of course. I have nothing, not even clothes, let alone light or digging implements or medical equipment. Maybe I can just tell them, I have been where you are now. You may not think it, but you can endure it. In a way, I think, looking at the young girl and remembering my six-year-old brother's dead body and my mother holding him; you can go on living, in a way.

But what could I tell them, in English, here and now? Even the thought is a presumption.

Andreas is waiting. I can feel the tension of it in his arm. 'I'm coming,' I say.

But still I hover. Under the mud and dirt, Jim looks as if he was tired and has simply fallen asleep. He must have been working one of his endless shifts and now I understand that he would have been the breadwinner for these two women. I bend down, close to the girl's thin shoulders, to express a mute goodbye. From the nearest knot of diggers there is a confusion of shouting and then terse commands leading to frantic activity. Someone else has been discovered, trapped, but this one is alive. There are many more people out now, pouring on to what is left of the beach strip with shovels and blankets and torches. A surge of them head for the new focus.

Slowly I stand up. Andreas takes my arm and leads me away.

We pick our way over rocks and through pools of filthy water. When we clamber by it I see that the woman's body has already been covered with a torn piece of curtain. Our progress is slow because of the debris that has been flung everywhere and the hampering darkness. But still I follow Andreas unquestioningly, holding on to the anchor of his hand. I have abandoned all thoughts of my belongings. They are buried and I have no need of them. Nobody has anything now.

I stumble beside Andreas, and as we near the end of the beach and my eyes become used to the darkness I can see beyond the major wreckage of modern buildings to the old town. Some of the whitewashed old houses are still standing, because they are low-built and constructed of stone. There are flickering lights in some of these and activity as survivors are hurried into shelter. The mosque looks mostly intact but I can't see the minarets.

There is now no sign even of the jetty foundations. The bay is a black gulf out of which huge waves rush to the shore and smash a chaotic jumble of splintered wood and hoardings and the remnants of jaunty parasols on to the ruined beach. The undertow makes a greedy noise as it sucks at the shingle.

Andreas leads me over bigger rocks, moving so fast that I am breathless. I am barefoot and the stones hurt me but I keep up with him because this is where the last thread of security resides. I can't imagine what I would do in this desolation if he were to disappear.

We reach the lee of the headland where the waves thunder into rocky inlets, but more naturally, as if all of this could almost be the aftermath of a winter storm. There is a boat riding crazily at anchor in one of the channels. It is sawing at the anchor chain and the dark outlines of the prow and tiny cabin pitch on the wave backs. It looks like one of the fishing boats that work up and down the coast.

As soon as I am aware of it it becomes evident that this is where Andreas is leading me. It is bigger than the boat in which we sailed to our secret bay, but not by a long way.

'Think of these people as friends,' Andreas tells me. He has to put his mouth close to my face and his breath is warm. I realise that I am shivering uncontrollably. Shock lends everything a dreamlike dimension and I don't question the boat or the friends, or what is about to happen. I let myself be steered, like a tired child.

Extraordinarily, there is a dinghy riding the vicious swell

between the boat and the rocks. A black snake coils through the air and becomes a rope that Andreas deftly catches. He steers me forwards until I am balanced on a rock while a wave roars up around my thighs and then swirls away again, and the dinghy pitches a yard away. The rope goes taut and I cling to it.

'Jump.'

I am past fear. Andreas's voice is clear and I do what he tells me. I launch myself forward and there is a second of space and then I fall hands outstretched in a wet space full of net and hard edges. There is one oarsman in the boat and he moves roughly past me as Andreas jumps and lands beside me. The man takes up his oars and bends double to pull us away from the rocks but we are almost submerged as another glassy hillside of water smashes over us. The ebbing wave propels us towards the bigger boat and we collide with the flat stern. More hands reach down for the rope and make us secure.

Moving in the wake of the boatman I swarm up a precarious ladder. As soon as Andreas has landed in the bottom of the fishing boat alongside me there is a thrumming roar from the engines and I feel the propellers start churning under my ear. I lie still, exactly where I fell, and the bows come round and head into the waves. The decks rise up to what feels like the vertical and I slide backwards, and then we pitch downwards into the wave trough and I roll inertly in the opposite direction. But I can tell that we are making headway I reach out and find a locker ring and hook my fingers into that. With this purchase to cling on to I stop slithering and lie as still as I can, salt water sluicing over me. Twin images are colliding in my head. Jim and the garden. England and Branc. My mother and his mother.

Someone bumps down next to me and puts an arm under my shoulder to haul me upright. It is Andreas. I sit with my head on his shoulder and let him support me. It is cold but he makes me warm, and after a moment I can look up and try to work out what is happening.

There are three men in oilskin dungarees and thick jerseys, one at the wheel and one beside him in the half-shelter of the open wheelhouse, intent on the instruments. The third is forward in the bows, watching the walls of water rearing up and vertiginously dropping away, and shouting instructions back to his crew mates. It is several numbed minutes before I realise that the language they are using isn't Turkish.

'Where are we? Where are we going?' I ask Andreas.

'To somewhere safe,' he tells me.

The tsunami wave struck the beach at Megalo Chorio at one twenty-six in the morning. It was generated by the shudders at the earthquake's epicentre on the sea floor off the Turkish coast and instead of just the surface, as with ordinary waves whipped up by the wind, the whole body of the water was moving. In the shallow Aegean the wave rapidly built up to a swell of forty feet and it swept westwards at a speed of more than a hundred miles an hour.

Halemni was partially shielded from the full force of it by a scatter of small uninhabited islands to the south-east, but the impact was still massive. The wall of water thundered over the crescent of beach, uprooting half the fringe of tamarisk trees. It smashed into the village houses, surging the length of the street and through the square at the end. The houses were stonebuilt and so resisted the major shock, but the wave tore into the rooms and swirled out again, carrying a scum of broken furniture, papers, branches and ruined possessions with it. The half-built shells of flimsy concrete tourist apartments on the village outskirts collapsed like the hotels in Branc.

The wave finally collided with the hill behind the village

and a backwash coursed through the houses and funnelled along the street in the opposite direction. Manolis's blue wooden kiosk was swept away and the old fig tree in the square was torn in half. The harbour wall withstood most of the impact but the bay became a heaving morass of flotsam that crashed over the harbour with every succeeding wave.

After five minutes of booming water an eerie stillness settled over the houses again, fractured with dripping and gurgling, and the creaking of broken structures. The people of Megalo Chorio slowly released their hold on whatever fixed point they had clung to to stop being swept away, then paddled through their flooded bedrooms to open the shutters and look out into the street.

There was no power because the island's generator station was flooded. One by one, points of candle flame wavered and steadied, and torch beams picked out the scum-laced khaki river where the cobbled road had once been. A dog howled somewhere and was answered by another.

Theo was screaming louder than the noise of the water. Georgi's cries were lower and more confused.

Dazed with sleep but with the shock of sudden adrenalin pounding in them, Xan and Olivia stumbled out of bed and covered the soaking pitch-dark distance from their bedroom to their sons' without stopping to light a candle or locate a torch. The familiar few steps had become an obstacle course of overturned furniture.

The screaming turned into hysterical crying as they plunged into the room.

'I can't see you,' Georgi shouted.

'I'm here. It's all right. It's a big wave, it's gone.'

'It's coming back,' the child sobbed.

Olivia found his shivering body and lifted him in her arms. 'No, it won't come back. You're safe.'

Theo's sobbing turned muffled as he clung to his father. His mattress was damp; thirteen feet above street level, the tide of water had just licked it. Xan held him, stroking his head with his free hand.

'I want my man,' he whimpered. 'My red man.'

'We need some light. Hold them both while I get the torches.'

Olivia and the boys crouched together on the raft of one of the beds. From beyond the window there was the noise of confused shouting. She hugged her children against her with their breathing interlacing in shocked gasps. They were alive and not hurt. Nothing else mattered, whatever might have happened downstairs, even if everything they owned was ruined. Gratitude hammered in her chest as she heard Xan running back to them. Torchlight sliced across the room and over their gaping faces.

'Here. Put these around you.'

Dry blankets were bundled around the shivering children. Xan had a fistful of candles and he put these on the windowsill and struck a match. In the wavering soft light they stared at the room. Water had been driven up the stairwell and slopped through the door, then drained away in the wake of the racing wave. It had pulled the rug with it, and the toys scattered on the floor, and the baskets of clothes and shoes that stood beside the door. These were toppled and the contents lay spread along the landing and down the stairs, black with sea water and mud, and limed with grey scum.

The children sucked in their breath and their mouths trembled at the sight.

'I want my red man, my red man,' Theo wailed.

'Shut up,' Georgi answered, looking up into his mother's face. Olivia's eyes met her husband's over the children's heads.

'I'm going to find Meroula,' Xan said. 'Stay here.'

He was already in the doorway.

'What's it like downstairs?' Olivia called after him.

'Stay there.'

He was right, she knew, to leave them and run to his mother, but she still felt a guilty lick of resentment. She made herself sit quietly and let the squirming warmth of her children seep into her. They were recovering themselves now, curiosity at the drama slowly overcoming the fear of night's unknown.

'Look at the mess,' Georgi said wonderingly.

'We'll clear it up. We're safe, that's all that matters.'

'I want my little man.'

'We'll look for him.'

Olivia stood up and stepped through the mess to the window. Already the room stank of salt and mud and sewage. Carefully setting the candles aside, she unlatched the shutters and leaned out into the square. The first thing she saw was the jagged pallor of the fig tree's exposed innards. The second was Yannis and his brother bending over a criss-cross heap of broken planking, splinters of familiar blue in the light of a lantern. Beyond the mess there was a big dark heap, at first like a pile of sacking. But even as she looked at it she saw that it was a mountainous human shape. It was Manolis. He must have been asleep in his kiosk when the tsunami hit, head on his folded arms on a heap of magazines and lottery tickets.

She turned quickly from the window and latched the shutters again in case the boys came to look too.

'Help me find him.'

Olivia ducked her head to the tangle of sheets and blankets. It was a relief to have something tiny to focus on.

Manolis was dead. She had seen the aftermath of enough disasters when she was taking photographs and enough death to recognise it at a glance. Fear of what lay outside the door jostled uneasily with the impulse to run out and do what she could to help their neighbours and friends. She didn't even fully understand what had happened but the first instinct was to stay here with the boys and protect them from whatever there was outside. She pushed the blankets aside, making an attempt to search for the plastic toy.

'I'm looking,' she said. 'Don't worry. Pappy will be back soon.'

The sea seems to grow a little calmer. The prow still rears up and then slides endlessly down into the wave troughs, but the waves no longer pour over the sides and wash over us and the pumps have stopped. The three men are in the wheelhouse together. Their orange oilskins make a luminous blur and I realise that the sky is lightening.

Andreas strokes the hair back from my face.

'It won't be much longer,' he says. This is a working boat and there is no shelter except the wheelhouse, let alone any blankets or dry clothing. There are no fish either, I notice now. The men must have been on the outward voyage when the earthquake struck.

'Why did they risk putting out to sea straight after the earthquake?' I ask Andreas. He glances at the three oilskin backs and then up at the sky. In the east, behind us, it is pearly grey with a faint barring of pink. The night is nearly over.

'Greek boatmen make night trips to and from the Turkish mainland for different reasons. They might not want to be caught in a remote Turkish bay, or to draw attention to themselves in Greece either.'

I understand. They are smugglers, hastily making for home in the wake of the disaster.

'Why have they brought us with them?'

'We needed the ride.' He is smiling as he uncoils his arm from around my shoulder and shifts his weight up on to his knees so that he can see over the side of the boat. 'Look,' he says.

I raise myself into a similar position. The light is strengthening all the time and the air has turned a dense milky colour. Over the flaking, salt-caked paintwork of the fishing boat's gunwale I can see a broad expanse of heaving water. The wrinkled surface is scarred with driftwood and chunks of wreckage, some of it darkened with mats of torn-up weed. In the distance there is an island.

I stare at it. It is a long, slate-grey mass with a jagged spine. In the pale pre-dawn it seems to float between the sky and the sea, tipping and tilting as the random waves slide beneath it.

'Is that where we are going?'

'Yes. It's called Halemni.'

'Why are we going there?'

Even as I ask the question I am aware that I won't get an answer that I can properly interpret. I think backwards, through the cold, and the shock of the earthquake and the images superimposed on it, beyond Branc and back to London, half intent on pinpointing the time when questions and their answers became disconnected. I can see the interior order of Dunollie Mansions, the tracery of winter twigs and the screen of summer leaves beyond the windows. I can see Peter sitting in his usual chair against a yellow wall.

'Why?' I repeat.

Andreas is watching the island, whatever its name was. We are drawing steadily closer to it. His profile melts against the grey mass of land and I lose my sense of knowing him. He is, I belatedly realise, a virtual stranger and I have come with him across the sea to a place I have never heard of. I glance sideways to the fishermen, trying to estimate whether I could call on them for help if I need to. There is a screech of static. One of them is shouting into a radio handset and the other is at the wheel, legs apart and back braced. The third moves forward past the cabin and steps up on to the prow again to the coils of rope that the heavy seas have displaced.

A shaft of yellow light slides past me. It is my imagination, but I could swear that I feel sudden warmth on my back that draws steam out of my sodden clothes. The sky lightens to bird's egg blue and the island steadies on the rocking sea. It is sepia and purple and lavender now, instead of granite grey. The sun has risen.

'Why?' Andreas echoes. 'Because it is safer here than in Branc and because there are people here who will look after you for me. Did you want to stay back there?' He tips his head in the direction of the ruined seaside.

'No.'

The thought of the people there, the hundreds of them like Jim, is so disturbing that I don't remember to ask why he should need anyone to look after me, if he is here himself. The moment of mistrust, whether it was an aberrance or whether it was an instant of clarity, is also past. Andreas is just Andreas again, with all my trust lodged in him.

I turn my back on Turkey and the rising sun because the horizontal light shines too brightly in my eyes. I study the island instead and the colours the sun coaxes out of the rocks. I can see little white houses now around a harbour and some ruins up on a cliff that look like a castle. The sea has grown eerily calm and the fishing boat glides towards the harbour, pulling the thread of its wake behind it.

It was better when the dawn came.

Olivia and the boys cuddled together under the covers of Georgi's bed and Olivia told them the story of Noah's ark. She had resorted to this because Theo's red plastic man was nowhere to be found.

'Will we need to build an ark?' Theo asked.

'No, we've got plenty of caiques in Megalo Chorio,' Georgi said kindly. 'We could go in Yannis's, with the sheep and goats two by two, all the way to Rhodes.'

Xan ran back to the house through the street's jumble of soaked furniture and belongings. Olivia sat upright when she heard the downstairs latch. A minute later he burst into the bedroom.

'Meroula is safe, she won't come up here until she has done what she can at her house.'

'Thank God,' Olivia said. 'I'm going down now to see what the worst is in ours.'

'Stay here for another few minutes.' The adult eyes met over the children's heads. 'I'll come back and let you know when.'

Xan went back into the square. A pair of tall fencing poles with wire lashed between them had been brought up and placed on the ground beside Manolis's shrouded body. Next Xan and Yannis and Yannis's brother Stavros and Christopher Cruickshank and two other men heaved the massive bulk on to the makeshift stretcher. They struggled to their feet under the weight and slowly shuffled to the blue-painted iron gates of the church. The priest stood waiting at the church door. His tall black hat was slightly askew on his head and the skirts of his long black coat were soaked and splashed with mud and wet sand.

The men carried the drowned man into the church and laid the stretcher down on the mosaic tiles in front of the altar. A small pool of water formed and a dark finger ran away from it, pointing to the slab of light that struck in through the open door. There would have been barely enough room to get the stretcher into Manolis's mother's tiny house and the priest had directed them to bring the body to the church instead. He nodded gravely to the men now and knelt down at Manolis's shoulder. They waited with their heads bent and hands folded while he prayed, and then filed out into the daylight. The priest came out and locked the door behind him, dropping the heavy key into his pocket.

'Look at this, will you?' Stavros sighed at the sight of the village square and the street leading out of it. Old women in soaking black skirts and younger ones in jeans and anoraks picked their way through soaking rubbish, retrieving a piece of flotsam here and there. Two or three of the older ones were wailing softly. The door of Manolis's mother's house stood open, and one of her neighbours was brushing filthy water out over the step with a coarse broom.

'You are still alive, my friend, at least,' one of the other men said.

Manolis, asleep with his huge body wedged in his wooden kiosk, was the island's only fatality. The other villagers had all been safe in their stone-built houses and although the tourist structures on the outskirts had collapsed, they had been empty. The damage was to property and to the villagers' sense of security in their houses so close to the water.

'I'm going home,' Xan said. Christopher followed him through the mud.

The fishing boat slides across the bay. The throb of the engines is amplified by an eerie post-dawn stillness.

When the fishermen have made fast against the massive bollards on the harbour wall, Andreas and I step ashore. The ground's solidity after the boat's pitching makes me stagger and he catches my arm before I fall over. When I look around again the three men are already hurrying away from us. They have their families and their homes to worry about.

At first glance, the village is a pretty place. A horseshoe of beach, white cube houses backed by a sweep of hillside.

High up on the hill, beneath the castle, there are more houses. But I now see that these are ruined, with black holes for windows and walls tipping down the steep slope, like a sinister mirror image of the new village. A second longer look reveals ruin at the lower level too, reflecting the upper desolation. The beach is a tangled mass of seaweed and broken planking, and the split trunks of trees at the fringe of it show jagged spikes of raw ochre and cream. The street is silted up with dark mud and a pathetic litter of tamarisk branches, torn shutters and sticks of furniture. People are trudging through it, their movements slow with shock.

The sun is fully up now, with the promise of a bright, warm day.

Andreas takes my hand and we walk along the harbour wall, past a taverna with the shutters dangling at injured angles. There is a stench of weed and dead fish and excrement.

The pictures and drawings that decorated the kitchen were mostly gone; those that remained were a grey pulp. The bright cupboard doors were plastered with muck, a foot of grey water lapped at Olivia's calves. The boys sat on the wet stairs, a sheet of polythene underneath them. Their excited curiosity had evaporated and they gazed at the devastation in round-eyed silence.

'It's only water,' Olivia said. 'We'll dry everything and clean it and the house will be as good as new.'

'Not my heaven picture, the one I drew for Christopher.' Theo pointed to the place where it had been pinned to the wall.

'No, not your picture. You can do another one, maybe.'

Xan churned through the water. He put his hands on either side of Olivia's mouth and rubbed the thin skin with his thumbs, then kissed her.

'It's all right,' he said.

She clung to him. 'I know. We're lucky.' A small lift of her chin in the direction of the church.

Christopher came with a yard broom. The water level was dropping and tidemarks of grey scum rimmed the walls.

'It's the same everywhere. Worse, lower down.'

Xan looked at his children's faces. Then he dropped on his knees in the water. They gave a joint gasp of surprise. He sat down with a bump and finally sank on his back until only his nose and chin jutted above the surface.

'Not often', he enunciated from the depths, 'that you can get a swim in your own kitchen.'

Georgi and Theo yelled with laughter.

There is a small, square-built woman struggling in the street in front of us. Her arms are piled with clothes and books.

Andreas has kept hold of my hand but now he detaches himself. I feel him at my shoulder and he seems to push me forwards. The woman has grey hair, unbrushed in a coarse mass and when she sees me she begins an instinctive movement to lift her hand to it. She remembers her load just in time and the pile totters, but does not fall. She has started towards me but stops short when she realises that I am a stranger. But her eyes are dragged back again and she is looking at me full on, and I realise that this feels like the first time I have been *seen*, except by Andreas, since the earthquake.

She says something in rapid Greek.

I stutter back, 'I don't understand. I'm English. I'm sorry, do you want me to help you?'

'English?'

'Yes.'

I glance down at myself. My arms are blue with cold. I am wet and dressed in the thin clothes I was wearing when

I left my hotel room to walk down to the beach. Was that only last night?

The woman looks up the street to a blue-painted house overlooking a square with a domed church. This must have been a lovely place before the water hit it.

'My son has an English wife.' Her accent is heavy but she speaks clearly enough.

'Yes?'

'I thought … you are tall. Like her.'

Her hands are shaking. The load is too much for her and I am afraid she is going to drop it in the mud.

'Let me take something.'

I slide my hands under the books and take their weight. I see now that they are old photograph albums. Of course, they are what most people would rescue first.

'Be careful.'

'I won't drop them.'

'You are cold.'

I am shivering, even though the sun is drawing steam off the soaking walls.

'You come with me to my son's house.'

The invitation has the promise of dry clothes and even a warm drink wrapped up in it and I seize on the idea. I look round for Andreas. He is standing motionless a little way behind me, watching and waiting. Maybe he hasn't heard our exchange. When I begin to follow the woman I tilt my head to indicate that he should follow us and I see his smile.

'Pappy lay down in the water,' Theo chanted. 'Dirty water, dirty water.'

Christopher and Xan were sweeping water over the step and the boys watched the small stream joining the larger one that trickled through the square and back towards the sea.

Olivia sorted through the mess on the lower shelves.

'Salvage this. Fling that. Salvage, fling,' she muttered as she worked.

'Mella's coming,' Georgi called. Olivia emptied the water out of her big saucepan and went to meet her mother-in-law as she splashed across the square. There was someone with her. A tall, angular woman with a stack of photograph albums held carefully away from her wet clothes.

There are people at the blue house. Two men, one big and dark and one smaller and sandy-haired, with brooms and sopping work clothes. And children. Two small boys. My eyes skip away from them.

A woman comes and stands in the doorway. She is bare-legged, with shorts rolled high above her knees. Long, stork's legs. She is as tall as the big dark man and looks just as strong. Her cropped hair is spiky with mud.

She is looking straight at me too, with her hands hanging curled at her sides.

I turn round, to Andreas, needing his introduction to these people. *There are people here who will look after you*, he said.

But he has gone.

The village street is full of strangers, carrying belongings, helping one another, beginning the work of clearing up, but there is no sign of Andreas. I can still feel his hand under my elbow, the pressure of his fingers motioning me forwards. His smile is fixed in my mind too, the features blurring and fading away until all that is left is the smile itself. Like a Cheshire cat.

I want his protection; why has he gone and left me all alone?

Slowly I turn back again. The tall woman is still waiting in the doorway.

SIX

Olivia gave the woman a cup of hot coffee. She put it carefully into her hands and only let go of it herself when she saw that the other had laced her bluish fingers securely around it. Olivia touched her shoulder lightly and then left her in peace to drink.

It had taken an interval of wading in the silted-up kitchen to find dry matches, to heat the water using the reserve gas canister, to clean out the coffee pot and empty sea water out of enough mugs for all of them. The new arrival sat on a stool at a corner of the table, with Meroula and the boys covertly glancing at her. Xan was busy with a shovel, clearing mud from the floor.

'Thank you,' the woman said, when her coffee was finished. She was still shivering.

'Georgi, go upstairs for me and get a thick jersey from the top of my cupboard, and a pair of dry jeans.' Olivia spoke Greek. Meroula looked from one woman to the other.

When Georgi came back with the clothes Olivia put her hand on the woman's shoulder again.

'Would you like to put these on instead of those wet things?' she asked gently, in English.

The only words the stranger had spoken since arriving at the door with Meroula and her photographs were I'm sorry and thank you. Meroula had muttered that she had found her standing alone in the street. She had seen that the photograph albums in Meroula's arms were too heavy and had immediately offered to carry them, even though she was obviously in difficulties herself. 'We are in this world to help each other, especially at times like this,' Meroula had said and crossed herself. 'And she is English,' she had added, although in a tone that suggested this was not an advantage.

'Yes, please,' the woman said now. She had a soft, neutral voice.

Olivia looked around, aware that there was nowhere clean or even dry to take her into.

'Come behind here,' she suggested and opened the door that led into the hallway. While the woman was concealed behind it Xan and Olivia raised their eyebrows at each other and the boys giggled behind their hands. Olivia put her finger sternly to her lips to warn them into silence.

A minute later the woman reappeared. Olivia's clothes fitted her well enough, although the other woman was thinner and the jeans made baggy folds round the waist and hips. She held up between one finger and thumb the clothes she had been wearing, then saw the heap of soaking rubbish that Xan was building out on the *avli* under the pergola. She walked quickly out to it and dropped her things on top. When she turned back into the room she was almost smiling.

'We could easily get them dry for you,' Olivia protested.

'No. Unless you mind me wearing yours?'

'Of course I don't.'

The woman's eyes moved to the mess of dark silt and Xan working to clear it.

110

'This isn't a good time for a stranger to turn up, is it?'

Olivia looked around too. She was thinking that she must telephone her parents, get a message to Max, let them know that they were all safe. As soon as the power came on again. Or there was Panagiotis, who owned the village store and a mobile phone – maybe he would let her make a short call.

'No.' Olivia smiled. 'Not really. But it's only a mess, it can be cleared up. We're lucky ...'

'Yes,' the woman said abruptly, as if there were images connected with the earthquake in her head that she didn't want to see again. 'I could help you. I'd like to help.'

'Are you on your own? Where have you come from?' Olivia asked.

There was a moment's hesitation. The woman looked out on to the terrace, as if she might see someone there. Then she answered. 'Yes, I am on my own now. I was on a boat.'

There were five pairs of eyes fixed on her. Even Xan was waiting, briefly leaning on his shovel. The silence extended itself but the woman kept her gaze directed outside and plainly was not going to offer any more than this minimal information.

'Have some more coffee while it's hot.' Olivia felt sympathy with her for whatever it was she had been through. If the stranger didn't want to talk about it now, or account for herself, that was up to her. We have been lucky ourselves and we have got enough resources, she reminded herself, to be able to help someone who needs it.

'I don't know yet what else we've got,' she apologised. The larder was a streaming mess, the bags of bread flour oozing grey glue.

'Let me help,' the visitor said again.

Theo had squirmed on to Meroula's lap, but now he jumped down. He paddled over to the woman and tilted his head to look up at her.

111

'What's your name?' he demanded. The boys were used to switching between English and Greek, and did so without even thinking about it.

There was another hesitation, this time a careful one.

'Kitty,' the woman said.

Xan shrugged, already bored with the nuances of this exchange.

'There's plenty to do. If you really want to help, start with the cupboards. When you've finished your coffee, of course.'

He pointed to the shelves. All the saucepans and dishes were full of black mud.

'Yes, all right. I'd be glad to.'

Olivia gave her some cloths and they started work. They were intent on what had to be done and after a while Kitty became just a part of the mopping and emptying and wiping machine. They were grateful for another pair of hands and for now they didn't ask any more questions. Xan had a transistor radio and they listened to news bulletins from Turkey, but then Theo grew tearful at the reports of children buried under wreckage and Olivia switched it off. Kitty worked harder, as if by her efforts she could obliterate more than mud stains.

It was October, but there was plenty of heat in the midday sun. The people of Megalo Chorio cleared mud and debris from around their houses, and helped each other to drag mattresses and sodden armchairs out into the kindly warmth. A thick, steamy mist rose from drying clothes, and the brackish smell of mud and water clung to everything. Nobody talked much, in the blue house or anywhere else, except to offer help and to direct operations. The atmosphere was sombre.

Christopher came up to help the Georgiadises. His own upstairs room had been only partly affected.

112

'This is Kitty,' Olivia told him. 'Kitty, this is Christopher Cruickshank.'

Kitty looked at him and stood still for a moment.

'Hello,' she said and then turned back to her task of wiping out the insides of saucepans.

By three o'clock all the wet clothes and furnishings were spread out to dry in the sun. Every window and door stood open to let the warm air circulate.

The mains water supply was off so they could do no more washing. Xan said the wells would probably all be contaminated with sea water so they must hoard what little there was left in their own reserve tank on the roof until the ferries came with emergency supplies of fresh water and food. Most of the mud and dirt had been shovelled up, and ruined food and soaking papers and broken crockery had been piled up ready to be put into rubbish bags. For now, there wasn't much more they could do.

Meroula sat down suddenly, her bowed legs revealing the rolled tops of mud-stained stockings. Her face sagged with exhaustion.

Kitty saw that she had had enough and bent down beside her.

'Have a rest now,' she said.

Meroula briefly patted her arm in acknowledgement. She had obviously taken to the newcomer.

'We've all got to have something to eat right now,' Olivia declared. 'Or we'll collapse.' The boys had eaten tinned fruit and biscuits, but none of the rest of them had had anything. Kitty hesitated.

'It's fine to stay, if you want to.' Olivia smiled at her. 'You've done a lot to help us. I can't promise anything gourmet, mind you.'

Kitty bent her head. Olivia noticed that she moved slowly and with a kind of conscious grace, but she had already assimilated and forgotten the fact of their similar height and colouring. They were different in many more ways than they were superficially alike.

'I'd like to, thank you. Just until I sort out where I'm going next.'

'Fine. That's good.'

Olivia went into the larder and took some tins of beans and tuna off the roughly cleaned shelves. Sometimes in winter the ferries were storm-bound for days on end and so the islanders were used to existing without fresh food. It was a problem to have no bread flour, and most of Halemni's home-grown fruit and vegetables were ruined, but meals of a kind were no immediate problem. Theo was tired and tearfully demanding his lost plastic toy.

Kitty went out into the hallway. After a moment she came back with something in her hand. She opened her fist to reveal it.

'Is this what you were looking for?' she asked Theo.

He gave a howl of delight and ran at her.

'My red man.'

Kitty stiffened as he butted against her legs. Then, as if she was half afraid to touch, she put her hand on his shoulder and just stroked his hair. Theo snatched the toy and whirled around the kitchen while she stood completely still, watching him, her hands outlining the space where he had briefly been.

Olivia watched Kitty watching her son.

'Where did you find it?' she asked.

'I saw it when I was changing. Caught in the corner of the stairs.'

'Theo, say thank you.'

'*Efharistó*,' the child said.

'Can we eat something?' Xan demanded.

Immediately Olivia went to the table. Meroula had washed seven plates and seven forks and knives in a minuscule quantity of fresh water and the food was spooned from the tins in carefully judged portions. There were tinned crackers to go with it. Each person took a plate and went outside, where the sun was still just about warm enough to make it easier to contemplate the wreckage of the garden than to sit inside the damp and reeking house. They all found a place to perch; the boys side by side on a low wall, Meroula on a wooden chair and Christopher on a flat stone near her feet. Xan sat on a rock and the two women together on a wooden bench that Xan had retrieved from a little way up the hill and set upright in its proper place once more.

Kitty rested her plate on her knees. Olivia noticed her eyeing the food as though she had never seen tuna and beans before, and was afraid that she was being disdainful. But then she dug her spoon into the heap and began eating. She finished her portion long before the rest of them.

'You were hungry,' Olivia said.

To her surprise, Kitty laughed. It was a deep-throated and attractive laugh that made Xan and Christopher and the two boys smile reflexively. It was as if they were sitting in a semicircle at the newcomer's feet.

'Yes. I really was. That was so good.'

'It was only tinned stuff.'

There was a sudden prickle in the air. Meroula was revived by food too and her grey head wagged as she looked from one woman to the other. Meroula never missed a thing.

At once Kitty's face set in wary lines. Her eyes skidded sideways, to the view of the bay past the side of the house. The water was almost flat.

'I just meant that it was nothing, nothing special.' Olivia murmured. She hadn't meant to sound defensive, but Kitty was disconcerting.

Christopher scrambled to his feet. 'Everyone finished?' He moved around the group and collected their plates.

'Where are they going?' Kitty asked and pointed to the hill.

A line of people was moving upwards. They were carrying baskets and bits of furniture, and their progress was slow but those out at the front had almost reached the ruined houses below the rocky ridge. The low sun made the blind window holes look blacker and intensified the purple shadows in the clefts that had been streets.

'They are going back,' Meroula said.

Olivia ran the palms of her hands over the boys' mattresses. They were dry enough for them to sleep on. She would spend the time between now and dusk making their room as habitable as she could, she decided. They were both tired enough to sleep properly tonight.

Tomorrow would be an easier day. They were lucky, she thought yet again. Not like the poor people in Branc. She looked across at Xan, in his filthy clothes, and thought how when they finally got to bed she could let her tired bones melt against his, and they would warm each other and be safe. Her tense shoulders loosened with pleasure at the idea and then she felt Kitty's watchful eyes on her.

'Back?' Kitty asked.

Meroula answered, 'It's the old village. We moved down from there, my husband and I, when the boy was four years. In nineteen sixty-one.'

The belfry next to the blue-domed church was a plain white tower with a single bell. The bell started suddenly tolling now, making them jump. A minute later another far-off bell answered it, the cracked note further flattened by distance and the moist air. The two children had been playing with the red man in a series of mud chutes but they both cocked their heads to listen. It was from the church up in the old village.

Georgi asked a question in Greek and his father answered it.

116

'Some of the older people are going back to their family houses,' Olivia explained. 'They think they will be safe higher up, if another wave comes.'

'There won't be another. It was a tsunami, from the earthquake.' Impatience intensified Xan's Australian accent, giving the end of his statement a mocking lift.

Christopher paused briefly in his collecting of plates.

'It's natural to be afraid of it happening again.'

'There's nothing up there. Just stones,' Olivia said to Kitty. 'The last two families abandoned it fifteen years ago.'

Meroula's head jerked. 'There is plenty there. My family home where I grew up. The bread oven, where my grandmother cooked for all of us, still beside the door. Four terraces where my father grew food for our family. My mother brought water every day on the back of a donkey.'

This was a long speech for Meroula to make in English for the benefit of the stranger. She stood up as she delivered it, her toes pointing outwards and her fists on her hips. She looked like a pugnacious house brick.

'I know. I meant there are only ruins of the houses now, no proper shelter for people.' Olivia forced herself to sound conciliatory.

'There is much more than nothing. You would not know. Families. My mother and father, in their graves up there.'

Olivia knew how easy it was to quarrel with her mother-in-law. She sighed. 'I'm sorry, Meroula. We're all tired. I didn't mean to be tactless.'

The bell close at hand was insistent, the other slowed to irregular clangs that tailed away into silence.

'I am going, for poor Evangelina.'

There were to be prayers for Manolis and the village women would support his mother. Olivia had seen a coffin being hastily carried through the church gate by the Halemni carpenter and his son, who made and supplied these things.

117

She guessed that Manolis's huge body had been laid out by Yannis's mother and would lie in the church until a grave could be dug. Tonight, when the boys were comfortable, she would have to tell them what had happened to him. They had both liked the poor mountainous man.

'Shall I come with you?' Olivia asked.

Meroula said stiffly, 'It is not necessary. But Alexander, you should come to church with your mother.'

Xan put down his tools with a bad grace that Meroula determinedly wouldn't see. Christopher went on tidying the remnants of the sketchy meal.

'If you stay in Halemni – tonight you must, because there is no ferry and we do not know for how many more days – there is a bed for you in my house,' Meroula said to Kitty.

'But I hope you'll stay here with us. We've got a room,' Olivia countered.

Hospitality was the backbone of the island. To be slow or deficient in providing it was a greater crime than laziness or incompetence. Olivia would have preferred to be alone with Xan and the children tonight, to wrap her arms round them in peace and let the shock of the day subside, but she also knew that she was going to make Kitty welcome. She had worked hard all day for a family of complete strangers and there was nothing tangible about her to arouse mistrust. Kitty was English, the cadence of her voice and her few words and even the way she looked, all spoke directly to Olivia. And she was bafflingly alone. The smell of loneliness hung around her, as strong as the reek of salt and mud in Megalo Chorio.

Olivia smiled warmly at her. 'It's my darkroom. I can make you a bed in there.'

Kitty's smile in return lightened her face. There were gaunt hollows and dark shadows under her eyes, but the smile made both men look at her.

'Thank you,' she said.

After Meroula and Xan had gone out of the front of the house and stepped through the littered square to the church gate, Olivia went upstairs. The boys continued their game of mud roads and Kitty and Christopher were left under the pergola to shovel the sad wreckage of broken crockery and spoiled paintings and family possessions into the rubbish sacks that Xan had given them.

Kitty glanced at him and began to say something, so that Christopher paused and politely waited, but she thought better of it.

'Sorry,' she said.

The sun was setting now. The beach and the white houses were briefly washed in silvery pink.

Kitty stopped work and straightened up to look at the view. 'This is a beautiful place.'

'It is.'

'What do you do here?'

While they worked he told her about the painting school and Xan's and Olivia's work in building it up over the years. 'Look at this mess. These were all pictures painted by guests, or by the children, and Olivia's photographs. It will make things much harder for them next season, an earthquake epicentre across the straits and a freak wave. It won't bring people rushing here for their painting holidays, will it?'

The little boys were still intent on their game of mud and soldiers, their heads bent to an imaginary world. The adults went back to shovelling the pulpy mess of a livelihood into refuse sacks.

'No. Not for a year or so,' Kitty said gravely.

The darkness came quickly. Without electricity there was nothing much more that could be done. Xan and Meroula came back from church and Olivia took the boys to the bathroom and performed the best cleaning operation on them that she could manage using one small bowl of water. Christopher slipped away to his room further down the street and on the way escorted Meroula back to her house. Xan stood out on the terrace and smoked, and Kitty left the empty kitchen and came out to sit on the low wall nearby. There were tiny yellow glimmers of candle and paraffin lights showing in the ruined houses up the hill, where the refugees from Megalo Chorio were settling themselves for the night.

'It's a long time since I've seen the place lit up like this,' Xan mused. 'It reminds me of when I was a kid and we moved down to the harbour. Some families were still living and farming up there. Carrying all their water on the backs of donkeys, and everything else that they couldn't grow themselves. This was an agricultural community then. Now it's all over. A bit of fishing and everything else is tourism. People come from a dozen different countries to lie on this beach, or sit up on the hill drawing pictures, or walk in their trainers up the track where my grandmother hauled water on a donkey. I'm not sure what'll happen to all of it now.'

'They will come back.'

'Do you think so? I hope you are right.' He threw away the stub of his cigarette and they both watched the red arc it made. 'Are you on holiday?'

'I was. I am, in a way.'

Xan shrugged. 'Stay here if it suits.'

They could see Olivia now, through the terrace doors. The light was yellow here too, from a combination of candles and gas lanterns, and her tall frame threw spidery shadows on the walls as she moved quickly to set dishes on the table.

'She's very strong, your wife. I've never met anyone like her,' the woman said quietly.

Before Xan could answer Olivia came out to them. She

was carrying an unlabelled bottle of thick green glass and three tin cups.

'I think this is what we need,' she said and poured from the bottle. It was local red wine, high in alcohol and with the raisin taste of hot weather in it.

'I wish you had had a better welcome to Halemni,' Xan said before he drank.

'I am sorry to see it at such a time.'

There was a Halemniot formality to the exchange that Meroula would have approved of.

In the dim light from the terrace doors Olivia looked from one face to the other and then drained her wine.

'Shall we have some food?'

The children came down in their pyjamas and sat at the table with them. The surface of it and the plates and cutlery were clean, but the stone floor was still curdled with mud and all the bright-painted cupboards were stained and beginning to split with the damp. The wood for the stove was too wet to burn, and the room was chilly in spite of the warmth of the candlelight. They ate quietly, another meal of tinned food from Olivia's store cupboard. The boys were pale and giddy with yawning. Theo's red plastic man lay beside his plate while he spooned up the food.

After they had finished Xan kissed the boys goodnight and put on his coat. It was merely damp now, following an afternoon steaming in the sunshine. He was going down to meet the other men at the kafeneion on the harbour wall. They would make salvage plans together.

'If you see Panagiotis, will you ask him if I can use his mobile? Just two minutes, to speak to my mother,' Olivia begged. She turned to Kitty. 'Do you need to call anyone? To let them know you're safe?'

Kitty shook her head.

Olivia took the children upstairs to bed. She told them

how Manolis had died and they lay under their blankets watching her with huge eyes. Kitty sat alone at the table with the lights in the old village just visible through one of the windows.

I have a bed, made up with blankets and clean sheets although my feet and legs are itchy with dried mud. There is a room around me and a roof overhead. The walls of the room are lined with shelves, the shelves stacked with art and photographic supplies that were mostly above the high-water mark. The old floorboards are damp but the smell of wet is already familiar enough not to be noticeable. I lie on my back, staring up into the darkness. I am weightless and disorientated with exhaustion.

I don't know where Andreas went, or why he brought me here. His face is already dissolving in my mind's eye. It is Peter I see when I close my eyes. His glasses flash opaque signals at me and then I take them off and touch my thumbs to the corners of his eyes.

The sense of loss is precise now. I can explore all the contours of it. Peter is in England, living with Lisa Kirk, and the shell of Dunollie Mansions has been cracked open. We will never be together again. I have seen an earthquake and Jim's mother kneeling in the wreckage, and now I am on a sea-smothered island, lying in a strange house, with the sounds of people on the margins of my awareness.

The husband, Xan, has come back from wherever he went. I can hear the creak of his feet coming upstairs and the murmur of voices.

The images of the day file past the Peter background: the little boys playing, with me wanting to look at them and eavesdrop on their Greek-English chatter. Usually I turn away from children, because of Marcus and because of my own undeveloped babies, but I want to edge nearer to these two.

122

The square-bodied mother, so strong and insistent, different from my mother in every way it is possible to be.

And Olivia. I want to watch Olivia and see what makes her move with such confidence. She has energy to make all the patterns in this house, the meals and the pinned-up drawings and the laughter that we haven't heard today because nothing is funny, now, although I know it has been and will be again. Everything stems from her. She is at the centre of this machine, she's the dynamo that keeps it running. She draws the love out of the family and refines it and radiates it again.

The sight and sound of her makes me understand what a shadow I have been, standing on the periphery, behind the leaf-screened windows of Dunollie Mansions.

And all that has itself faded into a shadow.

What is there left?

I close my eyes and will myself to sleep.

I wake up again very early. The window of this room has shutters, I now see, but they were left open last night and the grey light is unimpeded. As I lie on my side under the blankets the greyness turns faintly pink and then suddenly a narrow bar of gold slices the wall and a corner of floorboard. The sun has risen.

I push back the covers and sit up. Olivia's jeans and sweater lie folded on the end of the bed, where I put them when I undressed last night. A few seconds later I am sliding out on to the landing, where the other doors are firmly closed. Everyone else is still asleep.

The heavy front door creaks a little, but opens smoothly. There is no one in the cobbled square. The broken branches of a huge old tree have been roughly stacked with some torn blue-painted wood that reminds me of Jim's bar in Branc. The innards of the split tree trunk gleam raw ochre and orange. It is only twenty-four hours since I followed Meroula across here, balancing her photograph albums on my forearms. Olivia was standing in the doorway. It seems a much longer interval, as though I have lived through enough in that time to fill several weeks.

I walk down the slight incline of the village street, looking at the damage caused by the freak wave and at the work that has already been done to put it right. Torn shutters have been taken down, broken windows are roughly boarded up. The tidemark lines of mud and damp show high up on the whitewashed walls.

There is a bareness that only strikes at second glance. I realise that the day before yesterday these stone steps would have been crowded with blue-and green-painted cans planted with gaudy geraniums. There would have been messy lines of washing hanging from the windowsills and old wooden chairs put out beside the front doors. The wall of water has swept all this away.

It will take time for Megalo Chorio to regenerate itself, but it will happen. The first small features of the living landscape are already creeping back – the cats. An old tom the colour of coal dust slips out of an alleyway and prowls ahead of me, and an apricot-coloured one delicately tugs at some sacking covering a pile of rubbish. The sight of them in the deserted street gives me a beat of pleasure. I am wondering if by some sixth cat sense they smelled the wave sweeping towards Halemni and escaped up the hill in good time, way ahead of the villagers and their armloads of baskets and belongings.

I come out on to the harbour wall. The buildings facing the bay have taken the main force of the water and there is even more evident damage. A low white official-looking building has every window broken or boarded up, and through a door grille I can see an inner courtyard with a felled flagpole and a wreckage of tables and chairs piled like matchwood against the far wall.

The sound of a vehicle startles me and I press myself into the recess that gives on to the courtyard.

A second or two later a pick-up truck passes and skids out on to a jetty. The jetty is constructed from stone and has withstood the shock of the wave, although a mishmash of remains of what looks like fish boxes lie against the wall on the land side. The truck reverses sharply and comes to a halt with its tail to the bay. Two men climb out and leave the doors open. They walk along the jetty, deep in conversation, and even from the shelter of my doorway recess I can see that the younger is one of the fishermen from yesterday's boat.

I don't want him to see me. I want my anonymity to be absolute, for a reason I don't even understand yet. I watch for a second longer to make sure that the men are still absorbed in talk and then leave the doorway, keeping flat to the wall before turning the corner that places me out of their sight. A narrow alley lies between the white building and a closed-up bar or café. It runs for a few yards of blank wall and then peters out into a path leading uphill. The alley is choked with rubbish washed from the beach and the harbour, but I climb over it without too much effort. The hill on this side of the bay is steep and I am soon above the high-water mark. The path leads up on to the headland that encloses the eastern side of Halemni bay.

My pace slows as I mount above the village. It occurs to me as I walk with my fists balled up in the pockets of Olivia's jeans that if anyone is watching me from an upstairs window in the village they might well think at this distance that I am her.

The notion is comforting. My shoulders drop and my breathing steadies as I settle eagerly into this borrowed identity.

I am walking eastwards into a fiery orange sun that floats on a white sky streaked with cerise and lavender. The lurid colours are unearthly and I suppose that this must be the result of the dust and debris thrown up by the earthquake. Branc must lie somewhere ahead and to the right of me, if my bearings are correct, but the Turkish coast is invisible in layers of mist. The sea is the colour of diluted milk.

The path narrows but remains distinct enough and the rocks at intervals are daubed with blue-painted way markers. This must be a tourist walk, maybe leading to some secluded beach on the other side of the headland. I can imagine couples and families making their way over here on bright August mornings, loaded with beach towels and cold boxes. A sudden sliding noise above me makes me jump and I whirl around to see who is watching me. All there is is a pair of goats, affronted, on the crest of a rock outcrop. I stand still and they skitter down the rock and high-step across the hillside towards the skyline.

My route brings me to the summit of the headland and then dips down again. My guess was right; there is another much smaller bay down here with an eyelid of shingle beach backed by little trees and a steep wooded gorge leading upwards towards the old village. The wave has smashed through the trees and funnelled up the gorge, and the back-wash has dragged debris with it and left uprooted saplings and dead branches littered all over the shingle. It is hard to imagine the beach now with a serene patchwork of beach umbrellas and a fringe of swimmers in the turquoise water.

I turn my back and face towards the bigger bay. There is a flat-topped rock at the side of the path and I sit down, wrapping my arms round my knees and resting my chin. The immediate silence is intensified by the murmur of the sea on the rocks a hundred feet below.

I can see the entire village curved round the beach and the

harbour. It is tiny, much smaller than it seems from among the white cube houses. I can see the church with its sky-blue dome and the white belfry beside it, and the square, and Xan's and Olivia's pale-blue house. There are more people down on the harbour wall and out on the jetty. The mess is much less apparent from up here, apart from the flotsam and wreckage strewn on the beach itself. I can see how all this would look in ordinary times and I realise again how beautiful it is.

The sun is warming my back now. In an hour or so Olivia's sweater will feel uncomfortably thick. Scent begins to rise around me, coaxed out by the day's heat. It smells so clean up here after the reek left by the flood, sharp with citrus from the bushes and rich from the dewy ground. Absently I stretch out one hand and pick the nearest leaf, rolling it between my thumb and forefinger and then sniffing it. It is sage. It delivers an instant memory picture of the kitchen at Dunollie Mansions.

I am cooking, wrapping a loin of pork with a wreath of fresh sage leaves.

Peter comes in and stands behind me. His arms fasten round my waist and I lean back against him, closing my eyes for a long moment. The connection is perfect, like two halves of a balancing equation.

This recollection is so sharp and delivers such a kick of agony in its aftermath that I have to sit up and straighten my back to make space for it under my diaphragm. I find that I am thinking of Xan and Olivia, dwelling fiercely on them to deflect my own sense of loss.

And it is with these two images equipoised in my head, my own life and this other woman's, that an extraordinary thing happens.

Reality, present time, physical identity – suddenly all these dwindle and drop away. I am not sitting on a rock on a Greek headland. There is no blueness in the sky, salt in the air or blood in my veins, and these are only minor absences. There is no qualification either, none of the constraints of history or questions about the future. There *is* no past, no longer any memories of Peter or even Marcus and his death and my disablement. Olivia and the rest are gone and I am floating free, a speck of matter. Less than that. Pure essence.

It is more than intoxication. It is the first time that I have felt the swell of absolute vertiginous emptiness and of happiness that inhabits and exactly matches it. Everything equals precisely nothing and beyond or within this absolute zero there is ecstasy.

For a few seconds I know this with certainty.

From somewhere close at hand a low voice with a familiar timbre distinctly says, 'Now you know.'

Now you know.

I do know and the pleasure of knowledge suffuses me.

For a few more seconds I am thinking, if I try hard I can hold on to this instant. Maybe the voice was Andreas's. But as soon as the words *try* and *maybe* form themselves in my head I am already losing the vision.

I can feel the sun on my back again and the gritty texture of the rock. The scent of damp hillside floods back and colours come with it, and the sound of the waves. I turn my head and I can see a ship rounding the opposite headland. It is a bluntended ferry, drawing a wake of gulls and milky foam.

What was it, to feel nowhere, disembodied and at the same time enchanted?

As if I am waking up from sleep the fragments of memory and awareness drift to the surface and fit together into the old picture: Dunollie Mansions, Branc and Halemni.

Now you know.

As the vision, out-of-body experience or whatever it was rapidly fades, this is what I am left with.

What do I know?

Like the village in the path of the tsunami, it occurs to me that I have also been swept away. I have a nothingness that I can hold on to, an empty sheet like one of Olivia's from the sketch pads in the darkroom. The earthquake and the aftermath have wiped the world for me.

My mind is wildly racing now. Wait, wait. Let me think.

Everything I brought with me to Branc lies buried in the hotel room. Clothes, papers, money, belongings, passport. I was sitting on the beach with nothing but my thin nightclothes and even these have now been consigned to the rubbish sacks in Megalo Chorio. Andreas led me to the smugglers' boat, if indeed they were smugglers. I don't think Andreas will divulge anything about me to anyone, because everything about Andreas is mystery and secrecy. I hid from the fisherman this morning, and maybe I can hide from him and his partners until I leave Halemni.

Otherwise there is nothing to connect this person, perched on a rock overlooking the bay, with the woman in the Branc hotel. If I had been able to sleep, I would have died in the earthquake. In that rubble, amongst so much loss, who would ever know the difference? Who will know? I am gone and therefore I am effectively dead.

A faint echo of the euphoria of nothingness comes back to me.

I can be someone else. No longer Cary Stafford, ex-model, ex-wife. No longer Catherine whose little brother died when a statue toppled in an English garden. I can be a new person. I can begin again, without history.

I told Olivia that my name is Kitty. This is what my mother called me, no one else, ever. The pet name died with her. I doubt that my father or any of the Steps and Halves would remember it.

I was going to say something to Christopher Cruickshank

last night. Do you have a brother, a portrait painter? There is a family likeness. Just as if I were at some meaningless cocktail party, but something stopped me. Already there was the instinct for anonymity. I can be a new person.

Wait, again.

If I am dead, if it appears that I am dead, who will be affected?

Peter is with Lisa Kirk. He will mourn me, of course, but it will be a retrospective grieving, for a love that was already gone. My father and his new family, but after so many years it will be an arm's-length loss for them. A few good friends, who will console one another.

It isn't much to walk away from. There will be some sadness, I am not so withdrawn as to think otherwise, but I am certain that no one will be blighted or broken by my exit into another existence.

I sit and hug my knees close to my chest. My bones feel solid as the rock and my muscles ache with the memory of yesterday's physical exertions. I am entirely corporeal again. There is a leaf of sage still crumpled in the palm of my hand. When I open my fist a gust of wind catches the leaf and whirls it away.

I don't yet know how to work out the details of this plan. But I can collect myself here on Halemni for a few days, Olivia and her husband have both told me that I can stay. I can work out a new identity and invent a new history for myself.

The idea of it makes me laugh out loud, a crazy-sounding bark of mirth, but I don't any more believe that I am mad. I have a choice, I have already made it. The past and my ex-self can be erased and I can walk free.

The ferry has reversed and edged up to the blunt end of the harbour jetty. The fisherman's pick-up truck backs up to the open rear where a massive door has been lowered to form a ramp. As I watch, a little fork-lift truck trundles out of the ship's hold with packing cases stacked in its arms like Meroula's albums in mine. There is a crowd of people on the harbour, busy with the unloading. These must be emergency supplies for the island, sent maybe from Rhodes or Kos. It is too soon for a relief ship to be arriving from Piraeus. Big blue barrels are trundled out in the wake of the boxes and crates, these presumably containing fresh water.

Before I realise it, I have scrambled to my feet.

I should go back to the village and find a way to help, if I can keep out of the way of the three fishermen. The sound of the truck's engine revving reaches me a second after it shoots away from the ferry with its rear end piled with supplies. I watch while it buzzes along the harbour wall and turns the corner up into the village street.

With my hands stuck deep in the pockets of Olivia's jeans I begin to walk, and then run, back down the clifftop path towards Megalo Chorio. Big Village, I have worked out this is what the name means. And up on the cliff, under the Knights' ruined castle, is Old Village. Inhabited again, for now, with refugees from the wave.

SEVEN

Olivia led the way with Kitty walking behind her. They were winding uphill from Megalo Chorio to the old village. Both women were carrying heavy baskets filled with food for the refugees from the tsunami and the path was steep.

Olivia moved quickly and Kitty panted in her wake.

'I'm so unfit,' she groaned, as she stopped to catch her breath.

Olivia rested her basket and waited for her.

'Halemni's all walking, usually uphill.' She smiled. 'You'll soon get used to it.'

Just as she herself was getting used to having Kitty around, she thought.

Kitty wasn't difficult company – in fact, she was most noticeable for her determination to stay in the background. She sat in her room upstairs, watching the small comings and goings of Halemni through the window. Sometimes Olivia caught a glimpse of her pale face behind the glass and was pierced with a sense of how lonely she must feel. She did what she could to draw her into the circle. There was plenty of warmth to spare, she thought, in the potter's house.

'Come downstairs and sit with us,' she begged. But Kitty usually refused. Yet when she did join them she was easy to be with. She played with the boys, who had taken to her from the beginning. She did her share of the cooking and chores, and asked questions about Halemni that showed she was interested in the place and the people who lived there. Xan and Meroula opened up to her and proudly recounted the old stories that Olivia had heard a dozen times before.

As the days passed Olivia found herself drawing closer to Kitty. It was interesting to have another woman in the house, a woman who spoke English and knew what *Coronation Street* was and who could sing snatches of the same songs when they were washing up together. They could be friends, Olivia thought, and she was surprised to realise how much the prospect appealed to her. A real friend, an English ally, would be good to have. Even here on Halemni, where she believed she had everything, there was room for that.

If there was any uncertainty, it was because Kitty gave so very little away. Once the telephone connection was restored Olivia tried to persuade her to call someone – surely she must have relatives and friends – but Kitty politely insisted that there was no one she wanted to speak to. On another night Olivia gently tried to probe for information and Kitty told her the outline of her story. It was the bare bones, no more than that. Some of the things Kitty said, Olivia was certain, were untrue – even her name.

And yet, Olivia thought, we are all entitled to our own layers of being. If Kitty chose not to expose hers yet, for whatever reason, time would probably change that. Time was in abundant supply through a Halemni winter.

Olivia picked up her basket again. It was getting hot and she didn't want to make the climb to Arhea Chorio in the midday sun.

'Shall we get going?'

Kitty made a reluctant face, but it overlaid a smile. They began trudging upwards once more.

Most of the people who had retreated to the old village were old themselves, and couldn't fetch and carry food and water every day. The rest of the villagers had organised a relay service and Olivia contributed to this without even thinking about it. It was how Halemni worked. She had asked Kitty if she would like to come too, so that she would feel included, and Kitty had jumped at the offer.

'I'd love to see Arhea Chorio,' she said.

Our walk up to the old village takes us past the new grave-yard. At the far side of it there is a fresh mound of earth under a blanket of wilting flowers. It is not a bad place to be buried, I think, within this stone-walled compound on a hillside overlooking the sea.

Of course, I did not go to Manolis's funeral, three days ago now. But Xan and Olivia went with their children, and everyone else from Megalo Chorio, on a clear, cool afternoon with a wind blowing off the bay. There must have been close to a hundred people following the coffin up the track from the church. The six men who carried it walked very slowly, straining under the great weight.

After the burial people came back to the village square where there were tables under what remains of the old fig tree, and some food cooked by Olivia and two of the other women.

'Come down and eat something,' Olivia said, but I was happier to look on from the window of the darkroom that has now become my bedroom. I didn't then know anyone on Halemni except the Georgiadises and Christopher Cruickshank, and when the first emergency receded I began to attract inquisitive stares whenever I left the blue house.

The walls of Taverna Irini and the church were white

enough to reflect the afternoon sunlight, even though the high-water mark of mud still plasters them. There were cats under the tables and children chasing between the chairs, and mournful string music distorted by over-amplification booming out of a tape player.

The village must have closed in on itself in the wake of the tsunami. People stood or sat together in tight groups, talking in low voices. It was interesting to watch them, in a way that feels more involving than in any of the hours of staring into Kensington streets from the windows of Dunollie Mansions.

Family ties don't seem to be the primary connections here. However hard I tried I couldn't work out who was married to whom or which of the children, apart from Georgi and Theo, belonged to which parents. Age and gender were much more significant. The men all sat to one side, smoking and talking together. Xan was among them and I saw him pumping his fist against the palm of the other hand to emphasise his point. The women served out the food with busy efficiency. When everyone had been offered everything they sat down in their own huddle with the small children tumbling around them. I counted a dozen children altogether and two babies on – presumably – their grandmothers' laps.

The older women wore black clothes and headscarves, and they drew their chairs up to sit close to Manolis's mother. Meroula was there, and I could see her nodding as she listened and talked. The resemblance between her and Xan was clear in the way they both moved their hands and tilted their heads. The old men sat apart again, most of them silently watching with their hands spread on their knees or clasped on the head of a stick, or dozing until their heads fell forward to jerk them awake again. The long shadow cast by the church belfry moved across the cobbles, pointing admonishment at the sea.

I was intrigued by seeing all this and by trying to guess at the workings of the village. The tragedy of Manolis's death belonged to everyone in the square. I leaned my head forward and rested my forehead against the window, and my breath steamed the glass a little. I was remembering my isolation in Dunollie Mansions, with Peter and Lisa Kirk away in each other's arms.

One of the men replaced the tape, someone I recognised because Olivia had pointed him out as Xan's friend Yannis. Tremulous notes shivered across the square and the talking stopped. Two men stood up and waved to two more to join them. They wound their outstretched arms round each other's shoulders and began the dance.

They moved slowly and with extreme grace, dipping from the knees and hips, and pointing their toes from side to side. The music grew louder and the dancers undulated in their stately line, tending one way and then back in the opposite direction. They held their heads high and kept their eyes fixed on the same invisible distant point.

Manolis's mother was weeping. On either side of her a black-scarved old woman took her hand and tightly held it. Olivia was standing behind a row of chairs, watching, her hands resting on a chair back. Among the dark heads she stood out, tall and fairhaired like something out of Norse legend, but she also looked entirely and completely at home.

I felt the grip of benign envy then, for the way she was at ease with herself and for belonging in this enchanted place, and I feel it again now. She is walking up the track a dozen paces ahead of me, and her hips and thighs move with the easy strength of powerful muscles.

On the night of Manolis's funeral, the dancing went on late in the square. When darkness came the children were taken away one by one and the lanterns were lit. In the flickering yellow light the men performed their intricate and

136

mournful dance sequences. Bottles of brandy and raki were brought out, but the music never grew raucous. Yannis folded his arms on a table, rested his head, and apparently fell asleep.

I heard Olivia come in and the children going uncomplainingly to bed. Then she tapped on my door. I crossed from my place at the window and opened it.

'Come in.'

I stood to one side in the narrow space as she hesitated, then edged past me and sat down on the camp bed with her hands resting loosely in her lap.

'Are you comfortable enough in here?' she asked, looking at the shelves.

'Yes,' I answered. I was much more than comfortable, I was at home. It made me feel odd to realise that she hadn't understood this and that I had not considered the possibility that she might not.

'You were watching.' Her head inclined towards the unshuttered window.

'Yes. Did you mind?'

She was very warm and solid, and I could smell her hair and the vanilla scent of her skin. There were small brown freckles on her exposed forearm, a few shades darker than the remainder of her summer suntan.

Olivia shook her head. 'No. It was just that I kept on thinking about you up here on your own. I was worrying about it. It seemed inhospitable of us.'

'It was a funeral. I didn't have a part to play. You feel responsible for everything, don't you?'

It was one of the things that was so attractive and so vital about her. She took on and drew in and radiated outwards, and the patterns centred on her.

She laughed then, stretching out her arms and swallowing a yawn. 'Who else is going to?'

137

I liked that too, the confident acceptance that she was indeed at the heart of everything and that she could handle whatever was demanded of her. I thought that by getting close to her I could maybe absorb some of her confident physicality, become more material myself.

'What are you going to do, Kitty?'

It was fair that she should ask; I had been expecting it. Now, to my surprise, she kept her arm stretched out and took one of my hands. I let her draw me closer so that I ended up sitting down next to her on the bed. She kept hold of my hand all the time, massaging the skin on the back of it with her thumb in small circular movements as if to coax an answer out of me.

The idea I had had on the headland was still with me – more than an idea now. I began hesitantly, 'I would like to stay here.'

Olivia looked, said nothing. She was measuring me up, waiting, and I wanted to give her a coherent account of myself. It was hard, since my understanding of my own motives wasn't complete yet. We sat side by side with our hands linked and our thighs almost touching. In the stillness the house was noisy with creaks and snaps like little ricochets, the old wood drying out after the wave.

Go carefully, I warned myself.

'There is nothing I want to go anywhere else for. No one, that is.'

On the day when the phone was connected again Olivia chattered to her mother, a conversation full of reassurances. Later the same day the phone rang again and when she heard whoever it was on the other end she laughed with delight and her words got mixed because she was talking so fast.

After she hung up she said, 'That was my brother. He lives in Australia and I don't see him nearly often enough.'

I kept my face expressionless. You've got a brother, I thought. I envy you that, too.

She lifted the receiver then and held it out to me with a question in her eyes.

I know that my silence will be causing pain, at this minute, back in England. Peter and other people will mourn me and I should not cause them grief, deliberately, like this. But there is no other way to shake off the past. If I do this and hold steady, I will be free. 'No, thank you,' I said. 'There isn't anyone.'

I concentrated on what I should be saying to Olivia.

'I was married, like you, although I didn't have children. And then my husband left me for someone else and I … came away. Now that I *am* away I find that I don't want to go back and I don't know, yet, how to go forward. If I could stay on Halemni for a while I could maybe work out what is real and what is not. It's not a very original story, I'm afraid.'

'Did you love him?'

'Yes, I did. I think our marriage foundered because I was sad. Not because of him, but because of something much further back in the past. Long ago. Peter tried to make me happy in spite of that, but he couldn't do it and the failure told on him in the end. He was tired and so was I. Then someone came into our lives who was so full of energy and happiness and bright intentions, it was like a light being switched on in a twilit room. I don't blame him for wanting to be with her. Not really.'

Olivia put the corner of her thumb to her mouth and bit at it. The tips of her curled fingers were cracked and her nails were broken.

I could hear the unspoken questions and feel the resistance in her. What was this thing, back in the past? Why would she want another woman in her home, a mystery, bringing dark corners and doubtful motives into an ordered life? But it turned out that I was understimating her generosity.

'Why here?' she asked at length.

'It feels a happy place.' To me this was the obvious truth, even amidst the flood damage and on the day of a funeral.

'Yes,' Olivia cocked her head, as if to say that this was indeed so plain that it didn't need to be stated. 'I meant, why did you come here and where from?'

I didn't want to tell her what I had seen and heard in Branc. The images come constantly back into my head, especially Jim's mother and sister kneeling beside his body in the waiter's coat.

This grimness belongs inside me, not spilling out in Olivia's house.

I didn't want to tell her about the fishing boat either, if I can manage to keep that to myself, because that links me too directly to the earthquake and to Andreas. I can't explain Andreas's presence then or his absence now, but he is in me as much as the marrow in my bones and there is no accounting for him to anyone.

I realise that I can be cunning, when I need to be, and this in a way reassures me. I have dimensions, like everyone else.

'I was on a boat with some friends. We were caught in the high seas after the earthquake and they put in here, briefly, when it got light. I didn't want to get back on board because I was too afraid. I made them leave me here. I walked up from the harbour and I saw Xan's mother carrying things out of her house.'

I told Olivia this quickly, only stumbling a little in the improvisation.

She released my hand now and rested her chin on her clenched fists, considering what I had told her.

'Won't they worry about you, these friends of yours? Shouldn't you try to contact them?'

'I don't think I need to do that. They won't worry about me.'

Olivia turned her head to look me in the face now.

'What's your surname?'

A new life, a wiped slate, no history. A new name, therefore.

'Fisher.' The first name that popped into my head and not a very clever choice.

Her gaze didn't waver although her eyes narrowed. 'I see.'

There was a silence. I could either retract or blunder on regardless.

'I don't have any money or any possessions or ... anything much at all. As you know, as you can see.' From what I had already seen I believed that such things mattered on Halemni much less than anywhere else I had been in my life, nor did I imagine that anyone would ask to see my passport or birth certificate. 'I am sure I can do some work, find a place to live. Not be a parasite, if that's what worries you. It's what would worry me, if I were in your position.'

'So what do you do, Kitty Fisher?' Olivia's tone set the name in inverted commas. I must have looked disconcerted because she enlarged with deliberate precision.

'What skills do you have, that you hope to employ in Megalo Chorio?'

Ex-model wouldn't fit the bill, I realised, nor would ex-wife. The comedy of this mock interview struck me suddenly and I almost laughed. Olivia saw it and I am certain she nearly laughed too. A pair of lines like ironic brackets deepened at the corners of her mouth.

'Um. The usual practical things. Cleaning, childcare.' I can, I could look after children. 'And I can cook.'

'Of course, plenty of us here have lives that call for paid domestic help – nannies, cooks, housekeepers, that sort of thing. One really can't get the staff nowadays. You'll be a definite asset.'

'Please,' I murmured.

Then I waited while she thought about it. There was

141

nothing much else I could do or say. I could hear Xan moving around downstairs.

'Kitty, I'm not going to throw you out of this house, or say that we won't help you when you obviously need help. We haven't got much to give, but you have a bed here and you don't even eat as much as Theo does. And there's plenty of work to be done in Halemni right now, of the dirty manual variety. Stay here if you want to.'

Olivia Georgiadis didn't know how much she was offering me. Relief made me smile.

'Thank you. I'll do whatever work I can to earn my keep. I'm independent and I'm ... not afraid.'

She lifted one hand and let it drop, not wanting me to thank her too profusely. She got up and eyed me from the low doorway, standing with her head slightly bent under the lintel. I was still wearing the clothes she had given me to replace my own soaked things.

'I could find some other stuff for you to wear.'

I glanced down. Olivia was drawing me into the circle, even though her instinct might have told her not to. My admiration for her burned more fiercely, fanned by the envy that was becoming familiar.

'Thank you,' I said.

She turned to go and then swung back again.

'What do you want to tell people about who you are?'

I had been considering this.

'Um, perhaps we should just say that I am from England. I have had a difficult time lately and I want to have a rest. I lost my things in the sea, on the way here. Does that sound right?'

'It sounds okay.'

We were collaborators now. I smiled again, because I felt less lonely than I have done for months and I saw the way that made her look at me.

'Okay,' she said again, very quietly.

Now I am wearing a thick old pair of her trousers and a plaid flannel shirt because the weather is cooler, although the stiff climb to the old village at Olivia's brisk pace makes me sweaty and breathless.

'You look like my mummy,' Georgi said, when he came downstairs and saw me in these clothes.

'Do I? I'm very pleased about that.'

'You are like a lady in a film, but she is prettier.'

Xan made a sharp remark in Greek. He was lying on his side, repairing the piping under the sink in the kitchen. Running water was restored to Halemni and the renewed pressure had revealed cracks in the pipe seals. I was crouching beside him, passing tools and a tub of thick greasy substance on demand.

Georgi looked rebuked. 'She is,' he insisted, glancing from his father to me.

'It isn't polite to say so.' Xan's black shaggy head emerged from the cupboard. He dropped a wrench with a clatter and took the grease tub from me.

'I don't know about the film lady, but you're right, Georgi. Your mummy is prettier,' I told him.

He whipped round at once to his father. 'See?'

All three of us laughed.

Olivia came downstairs with Theo. The *demotikon*, the little school in Megalo Chorio that the two boys went to with the other Halemni children, had reopened and she was getting them ready to go.

'What's funny?' she asked.

'I said you are prettier than Kitty,' Georgi said.

'Really?' She looked from me to Xan and back again. She seemed displeased, more with the brief complicity between us than with the little compliment itself.

These are the things that I am remembering as I climb behind Olivia to Arhea Chorio. The baskets I am carrying are heavy enough to pull my arms out of their sockets, but I have plenty of thoughts to distract me.

The inquisitive stares have finished. Now I have begun to be awarded the occasional nod in the street, or even a murmured greeting of *kali mera* or *yia sou* as I pass by.

Olivia and I tell my story to whoever asks. I was travelling, recovering from some personal difficulties back in England. The earthquake caught me in a small boat, which had almost capsized in the high seas and from which my belongings had been swept away. I am a poor sailor and was terrified by the waves. The crew hurriedly put into Halemni to allow me ashore and then sailed off again.

I am grateful to Olivia for her brisk explanations whenever they are called for. I know she can't understand my desire for absence and anonymity – how could she? – but she is generous enough to allow me what I want.

I went down to Meroula's house the day before yesterday. It has been agreed between Xan and Olivia and me that I will help out by washing down her walls and fittings and repainting whatever needs to be repainted.

She stood among her water-damaged furniture with her hands on her square hips, square-jawed and solid-framed, watching my work. When she saw that I know how to use a mop and a scrubbing brush she relaxed and began talking, telling me about the old days on the island before the tourists came. Her English is good and her intelligence is obvious.

'Was the island a happier place then?' I asked.

She pursed her lips. 'Life was very hard. The young people today have no idea. They think everything is hamburgers and motor scooters.'

'Is that a bad thing? A hamburger is just a hamburger.'

'But old traditions are forgotten. There were songs and dances, and old stories, these were the things every child knew in his bones because his mother taught him. Now they are interested in American films and the clothes and games they see the tourist children have. My own son's children, they are just the same.'

'So the old days were better days?'

She wiped her hands on her apron and adjusted a green crochet mat underneath a glass bowl that stood on her dresser.

'No. I would have to say now.'

I reached down with my cloth to clean the furthest recess of a deep cupboard and laughed.

'That's progress.'

For some reason Meroula approves of me. If I had to guess why, it would be for no more complicated reason than that I am not Olivia, and therefore no rival for Xan's love and attention.

Xan himself seems indifferent to the presence of a stranger in his home. He is busy with repair work and his responsibilities on the island, and the company of the other men. Domestic affairs are Olivia's business and he leaves them to her. And the little boys, I catch myself watching them and eavesdropping on their games. I have never lived in proximity to children before. I wake up to the sound of their voices on the stairs and in my half-dreams they are mine.

We are almost at the first of the ruined houses. The path slants upwards in a last steep incline and then levels out. I can see steps made of blocks of stone, winding up into ruined alleys, uneven now because thistles and arum have pushed and sprouted between them. The sky is pearl-grey and the branches of trees knit against it. They are fig and olive and thorn, their leaves shrivelling in the wind. A little gust of wind funnels between the houses and drives a cloud of fallen leaves with it. I can smell woodsmoke and cooking – probably fish grilling over an open fire.

The other thing is that I can hear children. There is singing, a repetitive chant that might be a counting game, and further off noisy shouting and laughing, and the sound of a ball thudding against a wall. It sounds like a lot of children, more than I have seen down in Megalo Chorio.

The houses themselves are very sad. They are one-and two-storey stone buildings, with square low doorways and windows on either side of them, just like the houses down by the sea. But these are roofless, and the windows and doorways gape open, with rusty hinges and shards of wood swinging in the blank eyes. The little stone-walled enclosures in front are clogged with fallen stones and overgrown clumps of thorn and sage. In one or two of the abandoned gardens rose bushes have run wild and sent sprawling arms over the walls and in through the empty windows. I stop in one of the openings and stoop under the low door frame. There is a bare earth floor with a rusty pan lying among sprouting nettles and dock. The stones of the open hearth and chimney are still blackened with smoke, and to the side there is an arched opening. I put my hand inside the bread oven and I think that I can still feel the generous heat.

When I duck outside again I see that Olivia is standing waiting for me on a flight of broken steps that angle up and away from this alley under the branches of a ruined fig tree.

'It's a maze,' she says. 'The reoccupied houses are mostly higher up, near the old church.'

I climb more quickly, following her rapid steps. Her denim shirt is a blot of colour in the stone monochrome.

Close to the top of the hill we emerge from a narrow stone passage into a little square. The only building higher than us now is the ruined church, with its domed roof a sad concave reminder of one-time symmetry and the intricate pebble mosaic of the forecourt partly obliterated by fallen stones and dead leaves. But there are signs of life here. There are some chairs against a south-facing wall, rugs and cushions spread out to air on a heap of stones, a washing line flapping with singlets and shirts. Smoke is rising from a couple of chimneys. An old woman comes out of one of the doorways, pushing aside a blanket that has been hung over the space.

'*Kali mera*, Kyria Elena,' Olivia calls. She turns to me. She has tied a green ribbed scarf in her hair today, pulling her hair back and exposing the bones and lines of her face. She looks strong and concerned. 'There are about twenty people up here. They are all older and they are superstitious. They feel safer in the old houses, although it's so uncomfortable for them.'

I follow her across the square. Kyria Elena stands aside to let us into her house. It takes me a minute to get used to the dim light.

The single room is only a few feet square. There are sacks spread on the earth floor and a tarpaulin provides weatherproofing overhead. A low folding bed has been made up in one corner and there are two metal beach chairs with garish striped nylon backs and seats next to the hearth. There is a twiggy fire blazing, from which smoke occasionally billows into the room, making us all cough and rub our eyes. A few pieces of cutlery and crockery stand on a shelf, with a small box of food.

Olivia rapidly unpacks bread and fresh milk, and cheese and some tinned ham from the baskets. The ferries have brought in supplies and there is plenty of food down in Megalo Chorio now. The two women are talking rapidly in Greek. Kyria Elena takes one of Olivia's hands and rubs it between her two.

'*Ne, tie parakalo*,' Olivia says. Meaning yes, please. I am starting to pick out odd words from the unintelligible torrents

147

around me. Elena motions me forward too and indicates one of the chairs. There is a metal cooking pot hanging from a hook in the fire and she twists a cloth to lift it and pours water into a little tin jug. After a minute or two I am handed a miniature cup of thick, sweet Greek coffee. Olivia is sitting on the low bed, Elena and I on the chairs beside the fire. Shafts of light come through the tiny window apertures and veils of blue smoke drift within the bright parallelograms.

I can hear the children's voices again and smell fish cooking on a bed of wild herbs. Absently I stretch my legs and point my feet towards the fire. It is very tranquil here. I can understand why Elena and the others are drawn to the old village for the breath of safety. The spartan conditions seem minor, even irrelevant.

Olivia's voice speaking English startles me.

'Elena was born in this room, and three brothers.'

The old lady is nodding, beaming at me. Her fingers and knuckles are swollen knobs but she looks wiry and strong.

'She must remember a lot of things.'

Olivia's translation brings a flood of words.

We make visits to the other houses. The reclaimed ones are identifiable by the sacking or blankets nailed over the window and door apertures, and by the blue smoke rising from the chimney holes. Olivia leaves food at each house and talks to the old people inside. It should be a gloomy business, I suppose, this mercy mission, but somehow it is not. Arhea Chorio reoccupied has a sense of safety about it, even though the walls are falling down and the streets are choked with weeds and stones. I wander in Olivia's wake, looking up at the slits of sky visible between the houses, and at the shafts of sea and hillside revealed at the street corners.

The last house belongs to a very old man. Olivia explains that he is Xan's friend Yannis's grandfather, the oldest inhabitant of Halemni. Yannis's grandmother, his first wife, is buried in the old village graveyard at the back of the church on the hilltop. The old man, also called Yannis, insisted that his family bring him back to their house up here as soon as the water had receded from Megalo Chorio. Olivia greets him respectfully.

Yannis senior is deaf and querulous, and looks from Olivia to me with irritable confusion. I take the first opportunity to slip out of his pungent room and back into the fresh air. The church is close at hand and I wander across the courtyard, pushing dead leaves and rubbish aside with my feet to trace the pebble mosaic patterns. The wind is freshening, I feel the chill of it on my cheeks. On the other side of the collapsing walls there are tiers of dozens of terraces, the one-time cultivated land dropping away to the south in full sun. Once, this whole stepped hillside must have been a moving sea of grain.

The old graveyard is a rectangle of slope enclosed by crumbling walls. I walk between the graves, seeing how the stones have slipped and slid to leave gaping apertures. Even so, it is a comfortable place. There are clumps of wild thyme here with bees droning over the flower spikes, and tiny cobalt and sulphur-yellow butterflies settling in dots of colour. I sit down in an angle of wall and gaze out to sea, my thoughts suspended again.

I had a pair of red leather sandals with holes punched in the toes in a sunburst pattern. I remember ordinariness, the smell of soap and bath towels, and the unexpected – the first ice lolly I ever tasted with a sweet white kernel of ice cream hidden inside it.

Our father, Marcus's and mine, worked as an administrator in the big general hospital in the Midlands town near where we lived. He wasn't a medical man, as he used to put it, but several of my parents' friends were doctors. We lived in a house down a lane shaded with oak trees, not quite in the proper countryside but not in the town either. I used to climb the trees, swinging myself into the lower branches and daringly edging out over the ditch underneath, but Marcus wasn't allowed to because he was too young and too small. The difference in our heights seemed remarkable. I could look down on the top of his head and see the pallor of his scalp through the fair hair.

'She's tall for her age,' I remember my mother saying. I liked being big and being the older one. My father encouraged me but my mother used to warn me not to be too big for my boots.

'I don't wear any boots. Red sandals, look.'

I must have been a challenging child. I can remember a smile snapping my lips, confidence itself, and the dapple of sun on a green lawn.

A loud clang makes me jump and twist my head round. The church bell is rusty and hangs at an angle in the bell tower, and the wind or some other force must have drawn a single peal out of it. Now I remember that I have heard it pealing before, answering the tolling bell down in the village.

I stand up, stretching to ease the stiffness in my legs, and then stroll back around the church walls. There are terracotta shards of broken tile underfoot and I am just working out that they have slipped off the caved-in roof when I hear the children again. This time I catch sight of them. They are running away across the far side of the little square, and then they chase into an alleyway and are swallowed between high walls. I am blinking because the light is in my eyes but I am sure that there were as many as ten of them, or maybe even more.

Olivia is waiting by what is left of Kyrie Yannis's front garden. A dying fig tree dips at a crazy angle over the wall.

'Ready to go home?' She smiles at me and I hoist the empty baskets in response. We make our way back down the steps of the main street.

The steep path leading down the hill to Megalo Chorio already seems familiar. When it broadens out and the gradient eases I catch up and walk in step with Olivia. I am wearing a pair of her shoes, thick ones with laces and cracks in the leather across the toe creases, and I study our feet. Of course they look similar because Olivia's shoes are printed with the size and shape of hers. Mine slither a little inside the leather shells.

'How many children from down there moved back up to the old village?' I ask her.

She shrugs. 'None. Only the old people. Young families think the same as Xan and me.'

'There are children up there. Maybe ten of them.'

Now she looks at me. 'There are only twelve children on Halemni at the moment and two babies. Except for the babies they are all at school this morning, like Georgi and Theo. The older ones go to Rhodos Town, you know. They stay in school houses over there.'

I look back, briefly, over my shoulder.

'I thought I … heard them playing.'

'I don't think you can have done,' Olivia answers decisively.

Xan is working in the garden when we reach the blue house, clearing some of the broken and dead plants from Olivia's vegetable patch. He leans on his spade as we come out under the pergola.

'I'd like a cup of coffee,' he tells her and she turns back in through the terrace doors. I begin automatically to rake the decaying matter he has collected into more compact heaps – I am getting used to making myself useful wherever I can.

'What did you think of the old village?'

151

'Peaceful. Not as sad as I expected,' I answer him. We continue with our work, in companionable silence, until Olivia comes out again with little cups of thick coffee and a knob of bread. Xan hungrily picks it off the plate and tears off a chunk.

EIGHT

A month after the earthquake the people of Branc were connecting up their lives again. It looked a slow but determined process, Peter Stafford thought, as he abandoned the car he had driven from the airport at the side of the one passable road into town. He picked up the flowers from the passenger seat and set out to walk the last half-mile towards the sea.

He had flown out to Turkey once before, three days after the earthquake, against official advice, and had pressed onwards to the coast through the columns of rescue and aid workers. The beach and the seafront then lay under a metre of water, and the jumbles of masonry and twisted girders and concrete stuck up like weird geological formations. Cary's hotel, when he finally worked out which one it must be, was a honeycomb of square rooms at one end with the face ripped off to expose the innards, and at the other a shapeless heap of rubble. It was a partial collapse, an English-speaking engineer from one of the exhausted rescue teams told him.

Cary's room had been in the collapsed end. There was no chance that she could have survived within it. No one had been brought out alive in the last forty-eight hours.

153

Peter had turned round and flown home again, back to London and Lisa's ashamed and shaming warmth.

Now there were settlements of tents in the fields on either side of the road, miniature villages of canvas with washing strung from poles and communal cooking areas, and children playing in the scrubland. Peter walked slowly, and two or three scarved women with babies in their arms looked incuriously at him as he passed. He thought about how much they had had to bear and the speculation put his own loss into a flatter perspective. They were rebuilding here, as the trucks grinding past loaded with cement mixers and lifting apparatus and building materials clearly indicated. Reconstruction was possible, it was a matter of will and determination. But return was not. Cary was gone, she wouldn't come back. Even though he was wearing sunglasses and the November sun was covered with thin cloud, Peter put his hand up to shield his eyes.

The water level on the seafront had dropped a little. The concrete slabs and rusted girders of the ruined hotels were fully exposed now. The collapsed end of the one in which Cary had stayed had been almost completely removed, leaving the less damaged end looking raggedly and startlingly abbreviated. He glanced at it and then looked away.

Surprisingly, a kind of restaurant seemed to be operating at the corner of one of the streets leading back from the sea, on a raised platform that might once have been the ground floor of a big building. There were protective walls of canvas and a row of little stalls selling vegetables and grilled meat. Trestle tables and clusters of assorted chairs stood in an enclosure in the centre. People were sitting with their chairs drawn up, talking and eating and even laughing. Peter edged between them and approached a huge man who was turning the strips of meat on a griddle over the red coals in an old dustbin.

The man beamed at him and pointed to his cooking.

'Eat someting?'

Peter shook his head.

'No? Is good.' The chef was astoundingly cheerful, in his makeshift canvas kitchen.

'Mr Dulcik?' Peter asked.

The man tipped his head then, understanding. He looked at the flowers, put down the fork he had been using to flip meat and came out from behind his brazier. He dropped a weighty arm round Peter's shoulder and guided him back to the shelter's opening.

'There.' He pointed.

Down the ruined street, maybe a hundred yards away across canyons and banks of rubble, half a building was still standing. The walls were painted bright yellow and blue, as if in another world the place might have been a bar or a club. The side that the earthquake had ripped away and left exposed was shored up with planks and sheets of corrugated iron.

'Office,' the chef said, his face now puckered with sympathy.

Peter nodded his thanks and negotiated his way towards the blue and yellow building, feeling sharp stones through the soles of his shoes. A truck bumped in low gear along the road in the distance with a dusty car nosing behind it.

There was even a door in the intact wall, with official notices posted on the peeling paintwork. Peter knocked and then eased the door open. Inside there was an office with fax machines and telephones and computer screens, and a row of chairs. A woman with her hair tucked under a black scarf looked up from the nearest desk. Peter unfolded the letter and showed it to her.

'One minute.'

He took one of the chairs and waited. After a while the woman showed him into an inner office.

155

Mr Dulcik was wearing a blue short-sleeved shirt and drill trousers. He stood up when Peter came into the room and held out his hand. There was a neatly folded grey polythene bag on the desk in front of him.

'I am sorry, Mr Stafford. Please take a seat. As you know, we have not found your wife's body, but we have some of her belongings from the Hotel Flore. This is sometimes the way, you understand. Missing people in major earthquakes and then the small items of their possession are found. We cannot predict or explain. Some people we do not find, ever, although we know that they are there.'

His English was good, but full of 'ch' and 'gh' sounds, and rolled 'r's.

'I understand.'

Mr Dulcik picked up the package and passed it across the empty desk.

'Thank you.'

Inside was Cary's passport. It was dirty and swollen with damp, and the colour had bled from the covers to leave blots of dull red over the pages, but it was hers. Even in her passport photograph she had her head turned to the right angle, her eyes wide and her mouth artlessly shaped as if she was about to whisper something secret, important. He looked at it for a long moment, remembering her voice.

Her wallet was there too. The sight of it shocked him with its familiarity, although he would not have been able to describe it if he had been asked to do so five minutes earlier. Inside there were some Turkish lire and a hundred pounds in sterling. And the remains of a small, creased snapshot that was just recognisably of himself.

'These are Mrs Stafford's belongings?'

Also in the bag there were a few of her clothes. Neatly folded, by the salvage operators presumably.

'Yes.'

156

'I am sorry,' the man said again.

Peter stood up and they shook hands once more. Peter bundled the grey bag under his arm, his elbow pinning it against the aching cage of his ribs. In his other hand he still held the bunch of flowers.

He walked through the outer office. The woman there gave him a sheaf of official paperwork and he signed in the places she pointed to, noticing the pinpricked cushions of flesh surrounding her thumbnails. Out in the street again the light seemed too bright even with the protection of his dark lenses. He walked quickly, heading for the sea once more. He reached the water's edge and balanced on an outcrop of masonry, putting the package safely beside him. Everything seemed the same colour: mud-grey. The flowers were wrapped in paper, stripes of white and candy pink, looking gaudy in this monochrome environment.

He had wanted to bring lilies of the valley, Cary's favourite flower. But of course there had been none in the flower market he had been directed to this morning. The nearest thing – not a very close approximation, he thought now as he peeled off the cone of paper – was yellow and white freesias with a waxy sheen like plastic. He sniffed them automatically and then snapped the thin rubber band that held them in a bunch. Muddy water swirled close to his feet. He kept his back turned to the truncated hotel, unable to bear the thought of her buried beneath it.

He separated the stiff stems and held the first flower out over the water. When he dropped it a wavelet slapped the bloom against the stones, dirtying the petals, and then carried it away. He watched it submerge and surface again before he dropped the next, and the next. The last flower he held on to for a moment longer, then threw it out to join the rest. The petals rocked on the waves.

Peter bent down and picked up the grey polythene-wrapped

package of Cary's few belongings. He turned away from the sea and the trail of floating freesias, and picked his way over the rubble without a glance at the ruins of the hotel. He remembered as he walked that Cary hadn't cried at her mother's funeral.

'I hate funerals,' she had told him savagely. 'I don't want one.'

There couldn't be a funeral for Cary anyway, but he resolved that once he was back in England he would gather her friends together. There would be Selina and Marianne and the others from her modelling days, and Clive and Sally and the rest of their shared friends, even her negligent and selfish father. They could remember her with champagne and the music she liked, and the extraordinary pictures that the world's photographers had taken of her when she was at the height of her beauty.

Peter walked back to his hire car through the dirt and construction traffic with tears running down his face.

Cary had hardly ever cried about anything that mattered. She wept at sentimental films and soppy books, not real things. Tears were too shallow and passing to be a proper expression of the thick seam of melancholy that ran through her – her quick, yelping laugh with its edge of desperation came closer. The first time he saw her, over the bobbing heads at some bizarre party, she had been laughing with her head thrown back and the white curve of her throat recklessly offered up. In a room full of beautiful women she had looked outlandishly beautiful. It had been months before he had disinterred the reason for her sadness.

Once, at the beginning of their time together, he had woken up in the middle of the night. They had been in bed in Cary's apartment, a white-walled box containing more suitcases than chairs, more pills than food. She had been lying completely still, breathing evenly, but he knew that she was fully awake. He had put his hand, fingers splayed, in the sharp dip of her waist. Then he had moved it slowly over the swell of her ribs, tracing the ripples of bone like a pianist fingering the keys.

'Why can't you sleep?' he whispered.

Her answer had been the brief cough of laughter that was by then familiar. Her tragic merriment already excluded him.

'Can't you tell me?'

A rustle of bed linen indicated a shaken head. He felt her isolation and his ardour made him determined to melt it. He had pulled her close to him and then made love to her, fucked her, to try to force his way into her head. But although her body offered him everything, there seemed no entry beyond that.

'I love you,' he told her afterwards. The first time he had done so.

'I love you too.'

It was the truth, he was convinced of that much, but her kernel remained intact. Silenced, he lay with his hand over the curve of her ribs until a film of sweat slicked and glued their skin. In the end they fell asleep.

In the morning Cary was the same as she ever was. They didn't talk about the night. Even so, Peter was sure that sooner or later, maybe after they married or once they had children or when she finally felt truly secure with him, the sadness would break up. He convinced himself that there would be fewer withdrawals and longer intervals between them, until finally there would be none at all.

Instead, there had been Dunollie Mansions and Cary gazing out of the window into the long Kensington afternoons. She had retreated within their retreat.

He was almost back at the parked hire car. Dust blowing off the ruins had coated the bodywork. His mobile phone rang in his inside pocket and he fumbled for it.

'Are you all right?' Lisa's voice was concerned. He could feel her warmth reaching out to wrap around him.

'Yes. I'll be home tomorrow.' Whatever home meant, he thought. Disorientation made him feel momentarily giddy and sick. He swallowed, wondering if he might be going to vomit.

'What's happened?'

'I'll tell you about it when I get back. But she is dead.'

They had both already known this, but the official confirmation set a final seal on it.

'I'm sorry. I'm very sad,' Lisa said at last.

'Yes,' Peter agreed.

After the call he unlocked the car and sat in the driver's seat with the scent of warm plastic thick in his throat. With his hands braced on the wheel he thought of Cary's dislike of driving herself and the first time he had taken her home in the Jaguar. Her long legs were crooked in the carpeted footwell and the low roof grazed her head. She had talked too much and laughed constantly, and he had nothing in his head but how to soothe and silence her.

She was dead and she seemed more alive to him now than she had ever been.

The clothes were packed in two big cardboard cartons. They had arrived from Athens in one of the relief ferryloads and had been stacked on the harbour wall alongside the boxes of food and crates of water, and lavatory paper and cleaning materials. They had come from one of the international relief organisations. Most of the aid was going to Turkey, of course, but some pencil-stroke decision of distant bureaucracy meant that a small shipment of warm clothes had arrived at Halemni.

'Let's have a look,' Olivia demanded.

Yannis unfolded his knife and cut the seals on one box. Everyone on the harbour wall who had come to meet the latest ferry crowded closer to have a good look. There were the Georgiadises, including Meroula and a handful of her friends and Yannis, and Panagiotis the harbour master and his wife, and Kitty. The sea water slapping the harbour steps was clear, reflecting back the sky's grey pallor, and a fresh wind licked white caps on the waves in the bay. There was a cold-weather scent of rain and salt in the air, and the houses of Megalo Chorio looked drawn in for the winter.

Panagiotis stuck in his hand and lifted out the first garment. It was a stout pleated skirt that must have belonged to a good-hearted English countrywoman with a conscience, who had opened her wardrobe for the benefit of earthquake victims on the other side of a continent.

Panagiotis was a thickset, red-faced man with a neck like a bull's. He cherished his reputation as the island's joker just as fiercely as he defended his official role as overseer of all the harbour traffic. He glanced at his wife and then held the skirt up by its substantial waistband. He gave it a little shake so that the pleats swirled and then measured it up against himself. A twitch of the lips, a lift of the eyebrow and a shift of the hips combined to make a gesture so lewd and comical that everyone in the huddle burst into laughter. The men openly enjoyed the joke while the older women nipped in the corners of their mouths and half hid their amusement.

Kitty laughed too, saw Olivia looking at her, and laughed harder. It was funnier for them because Olivia recognised where the skirt must have come from and who would have worn it and she knew that Kitty did too. Awareness of their shared roots drew them together.

'Kitty should have first pick,' Olivia called out.

Panagiotis invitingly held the skirt out to her and everyone laughed again. It was Olivia who plunged her arms into the box next and began turning over the layers of fabric. She came up first with a pair of men's flannel trousers, long in the leg and usefully narrow in the hip. Kitty took them and measured them against herself, copying Panagiotis's suggestive wriggle. The laughter was louder still and Kitty smiled in pleased surprise. Watching her, it occurred to Olivia that she was unused to fun. Her expression was wary more often than relaxed. But now, suddenly, she did look almost happy. Olivia was glad to see it.

'They'll fit,' she encouraged. The next thing she brought out was a Breton fisherman's top, the thick navy and cream stripes faded with repeated washing. 'And this.'

'You make her look like a man,' Panagiotis shouted in Greek. Kitty understood the words from their innuendo and her eyebrows shot up in amused denial. There was sudden real warmth in the way that Meroula and the other women immediately closed around her, patting her arms and hips to reassure her that she could never look anything of the kind.

By the time the boxes were empty, Kitty had been fitted out with a basic if eccentric winter wardrobe of trousers and jumpers. There was even a pea-coat with the cuffs and collar edges worn to a shine but with plenty of warmth in the thick wool fabric.

'You have had nothing for too long,' Meroula said. 'All your things lost in the sea like that.'

'I've got everything I need,' Kitty assured her.

The procession made its way up from the harbour, following Panagiotis's pick-up truck and its load of supplies and relief clothing. Kitty's arms were full of her new acquisitions. Olivia fell into step beside her.

'That was a bit of luck, wasn't it?'

'Yeah. I need never go shopping again. No more credit card bills, no worrying about what's in style or out. And you don't have to go on letting me use your things,' she added.

'I don't mind that. You like it here, don't you?'

162

There had been a short succession of days in which life had taken on a kind of routine. Xan worked on the large-scale repairs in the potter's house, and at Meroula's and elsewhere in the village. Olivia did the fiddly small jobs, like reinventing the painted designs on the kitchen cupboards, and Kitty shuttled between them. She cooked some of the simple meals they all shared, and washed up and did the household chores. She looked after the boys, drew pictures with them and read them stories, and took them for walks on the hill behind the village. Down at Meroula's house she had already washed all the mud-stained walls and wood and furniture, and prepared them for repainting. And in the few hours of the day that were left she walked over the island, learning its contours.

'I love it here,' Kitty answered and the truth of it showed in her face.

Olivia considered. She liked Kitty and wanted Kitty to like her in return. Whether she was telling the truth about herself or not, Kitty whoever-she-might-be spoke the same language as she did and came from the same place. She answered a longing for a close friendship that Olivia hadn't even guessed at until now. But there was an uncertainty that tugged under the surface of her liking. It was partly because Kitty was so evasive, of course. There was also a wrinkle of jealousy, because of the way Kitty looked and the way that Christopher and even Xan responded to her. And Kitty was free to be and do whatever she wanted, instead of being pinioned by children and a husband, and a limited place. But these were small things, Olivia thought quickly. Kitty deserved liking and sympathy, not petty jealousy.

'Don't you miss home?' she asked.

There was a brief pause before Kitty said, 'No. I miss what was there and now isn't. I told you that. Do you?'

'Yes,' Olivia answered. The quickness and certainty of the

answer surprised her. Being with Kitty was uncovering feelings that even Xan didn't touch.

'The people there? Or England itself?'

She was being deflected, Olivia realised. They had reached this point in their conversations before and Kitty always turned the questions away from herself. She smiled. 'Both.'

Olivia let herself be headed off, for now. There would be time in Kitty's own time. In the end she would talk.

Olivia was thinking of woodlands and June mornings and frosty winter nights, with an exile's nostalgic and distorted longing. While she was travelling she had kept these memories alive in her mind, assuming that she would go home some day and rediscover them.

'Can't you visit?'

'No. There's no money. And Xan wouldn't think it was logical to be wanting a holiday or to go elsewhere when you already live in the most beautiful place in the world.'

'Tell me about your family. In England, I mean.'

'What do you want to know?'

They were coming up the village street. Meroula turned aside to her own house and Panagiotis's truck accelerated away from them. Christopher and Xan, Olivia now noticed, must have stayed down at the harbour taverna with Yannis. The two women walked side by side with their heads close together.

'The usual things,' Kitty pursued her. 'Who and what. You're such a focus. You're at the centre of a world with all these threads radiating from you.'

'Like a spider in her web?'

'No. I didn't mean that. I'm sorry. But then' – Kitty tilted her head over the pile of clothes – 'maybe this is a bit of a web. In a nice way. Look at me – what's something that exists all on its own? A hermit crab? Peter's gone. My brother and my mother are both dead, my father remarried a long time ago and has a complete family of his own. I am the opposite of you.'

This was a lot of confiding, for Kitty. Olivia was quick to offer information in return.

'My mother and father live in the country, in Dorset. They moved there from the Midlands, after my father retired. They have an old stone house with an acre of garden and they grow roses and keep a cat. It's a kind of tired truce. I don't believe they ever had an easy marriage. My mother lived under his thumb, she was always glancing sideways at him to see if he was approving or otherwise. I suppose otherwise was usually the case. He had affairs, the affairs made her miserable, he reacted against her unhappiness by having more affairs. Max and I always felt that home was an uncomfortable place, although if you'd asked us, when we were kids, we probably wouldn't have understood enough to say so. It meant that we both wanted to get away, as soon as we were old enough. We both developed a thing about freedom, about the world being our home. Not needing walls and rules and order and the tyranny of domestic unhappiness.'

Kitty nodded as if she recognised how this might be. Olivia continued, 'But we both found what we wanted in the end. I met Xan. Max has got Hattie, in Sydney. They have their two little girls, younger than Georgi and Theo. Max works in property, buying and developing. I think he makes money.'

'You're close to him.' It was a statement not a question.

They had reached the potter's house. Olivia pushed the door open, to make room for Kitty to walk in with her clothes.

'Yes. Max was always my friend and my ally, all the time we were kids. There's less than two years between us and we had a complete system for living, all our own. I was big and strong and confident and he was smaller, always my assistant in everything we did. Like an apprentice. As well as wanting to get away from the way our parents lived I think I needed to travel, both to make space for him and to learn to be single for myself.'

'It sounds as though it was an intense relationship.'

'It still is.'

Olivia had gone straight through to the kitchen. Kitty lingered behind her, out of sight in the dim hallway.

'Are you there?' Olivia called. 'Come on in, you don't have to wait to be asked. You live here.'

It was a second or two before Kitty did appear. She kept her head bent as she dropped her new clothes in a heap on the table. Olivia rustled through them. 'Go on then, let's have a look.'

She waited and then Kitty grinned. 'Shall I?'

She took off her plimsolls and peeled down the jeans belonging to Olivia that she had worn since arriving on Halemni. The flannel trousers proved to be a much better fit. They didn't even need a belt to keep them in place. The striped top came next. Kitty bundled her hair up on top of her head and posed for Olivia. 'What do you think?'

Olivia stared. 'My God,' she said slowly. 'I think you've done this before, haven't you?'

'I used to be a model. A long time ago. Not a notably successful one, but I did get work.' After she had blurted this out Kitty ducked her head and fiddled with the buttons of the trousers, as if it were a painful admission.

If we're going to be friends, Olivia decided, I should say what I think.

'Why do you put yourself down, Kitty?'

'What?'

'Like that. Why do you say, "I was no good. It was nothing." You do it all the time. "I'm Miss Nobody, from nowhere." I don't believe it. Looking at you, I think you were probably an amazing model. You're a chameleon. I'm a photographer, I understand these things. I also know there's

166

a whole lot of things about you that you're not telling. Like everything. Who are you, anyway?'

Kitty slowly turned her head. The kitchen went very still and the stillness seemed to bleed from the windows into the daylight outside. The two women stood with their eyes level, watching each other.

'It doesn't matter.'

Olivia put down the coat she had been holding out ready for Kitty to try on.

'It doesn't matter what you say, or it doesn't matter who you are?'

There was an edge of humour as well as a flat note of finality when Kitty answered, 'Both.'

Olivia laughed in spite of herself. 'Do you *know* how annoying your refusal to give away anything about yourself actually is?'

'Yes. Or I can guess.'

Olivia waited and when nothing more came she shrugged her shoulders.

'Well, I must say, you're very cool.'

'It isn't that. But I think you do know me anyway. Not the details maybe, but the essence. Don't you? I think we both feel it.'

'Perhaps. Or perhaps I haven't a clue what you're talking about.'

There was another eerie moment of stillness, but this time they could hear the wind scraping the trees on the hillside.

Olivia shivered.

'Winter's coming.'

She made a quick movement, deliberately breaking the tension that had gathered in the room. Picking up a fine paintbrush that was sticking up out of a jar on the table she beckoned Kitty with it. 'Come here.'

Kitty did as she was told. Olivia twirled the brush and then came close. With two strokes she painted a moustache on the other's face. Kitty didn't even flinch. She was used to being made and remade. Olivia stood back again to judge the effect.

'Aha. I knew you reminded me of something in that get-up. Twist your hair up again.'

'Like this?'

'Exactly. Mmm. A hat, that's what we need.' There was a baseball cap belonging to Georgi hanging on a wooden peg behind the door and Olivia seized it. She put it on Kitty's head sideways, with the peak behind one ear. They were both caught up in the game now.

'That's it. Now, take a look.' She steered Kitty to the mirror propped behind a jumble of salvaged household pieces on the shelf over the stove. 'What do you see?'

Kitty looked and laughed. 'A small-time conman?'

'No, *no*. Look harder. How about Jeanne Moreau in that film, *Jules et Jim*? You know it, you must have seen it.'

Their two faces were reflected back at them. Olivia's was bright with the success of her dressing-up game and the light from the terrace windows. Kitty's was shadowed and startled behind the painted moustache.

The kitchen door swung open.

'What are you doing?'

Xan had a blue plastic bag in one hand. Christopher came in behind him, then hesitated in the doorway. The two women broke apart as the men stared from one to the other.

'Trying on Kitty's new clothes. You must look. See?'

Olivia hoisted her Leica from its place on a high shelf, out of the boys' reach. She focused, framed the shot and the shutter clicked. The sound stirred a perfectly automatic response in Kitty. She made a Jeanne Moreau pout and then dissolved it into a bruised cinematic smile, while Olivia danced around her, firing off more shots.

'Too dark,' she wailed. 'Give me more light.'

Xan reached for the light switch on the wall. Bright electricity flooded the room. Kitty blinked in the dazzle and at once the photographic spell was broken. She took off Georgi's cap and shook her hair around her face, then rubbed at the moustache paint with her thumb. Olivia slowly lowered her camera.

'I think we interrupted something,' Xan said to Christopher.

'Just trying on clothes,' Kitty told them, dispelling the moment as she dropped Georgi's cap on the table.

The blue plastic bag contained fish, a silvery shoal of smelts and whitebait.

'*Psaria*,' Xan said. 'Fried fish for supper.'

Georgi and Theo came in from afternoon school and they helped Christopher to bring in logs and light the stove. Kitty made tomato salad, then dried the fish and shook them up in a paper bag full of flour. Olivia fried them in hot oil and chopped up wedges of lemon to go with them, and Xan turned off the light again and lit candles. It was dark outside now, with the sudden blackness of November evenings that made the meagre lights of Megalo Chorio look dim, and the tiny pinpricks showing from the old village an even feebler reflection of them. Inside the big room at the potter's house it was warm and welcoming.

The six of them ate their meal of fish and salad and bread. Afterwards the boys removed themselves to the far end of the table to draw pictures, and the adults drank wine and talked. Olivia stretched her legs and rested her feet in thick socks in her husband's lap. She laced her fingers, still fishy from the meal, in her ragged hair. Christopher watched her through the nimbus of candlelight, but he looked away if he thought that any of the others might notice. Kitty had pushed her chair back a little way from the table.

'I've got an idea,' Olivia announced.

Xan groaned. 'What is it this time?'

'Something simple. If Kitty is going to stay here we should give her one of the studios to live in. Make it winter warm, everything. Then she would have somewhere of her own to call home. Don't you agree?'

'Are you going to stay?' Xan asked her.

'If ... I may. For a little while.'

'Good.' He smiled.

Kitty looked at Olivia, but Olivia's eyes were fixed on her husband.

'That's settled, then,' she said, but thoughtfully, as if something had just dawned on her.

NINE

I have a room – nearly a home – of my own.

It is the end unit of Xan's and Olivia's row of holiday studios, converted from the potter's old outbuildings and cleaned up after the tsunami especially for me. I have a mud-free and freshly white-painted room with a tiled floor – clammy with cold at this time of year – and an alcove with a pine-framed double bed. Olivia has given me the best studio. This is the only one that has its own outside space; two armchairs face doors that open on to a miniature terrace. There is a sort of kitchen against one wall, with a sink and electric rings and a cupboard with some basic cooking utensils, but no oven. Beside the kitchen there is a drop-leaf table with two upright chairs. And leading off the main room there is a tiny mosaic-tiled bathroom with a shower corner, even hot water when the sun shines long enough into the face of the solar panels angled on the roof of the studios.

I particularly like the way the walls of the room are decorated with pictures, some framed but most of them just roughly pinned to the plaster. Olivia and I chose them from the folders kept in her darkroom, my old bedroom. They are all the work of summer guests. Some of them are very good, especially a set of charcoal drawings of the old village with gaunt trees spiking a stormy sky. I can sit in one of my two armchairs looking at the holiday painters' work, then change the angle so I look out at the real scenery. Across a corner of the square I can see a narrow sliver of the beach and the sea beyond it. On windless days the water looks like a sheet of wrinkled metal.

I have a job, as well.

This is a piece of pure good fortune. Halemni seems to be like this – what you need is somehow delivered, maybe not in the form you might expect or would necessarily wish for, but still an answer is supplied.

Panagiotis the harbour master's wife is much younger than he is. Olivia told me that his first wife died of cancer and he married again less than a year ago. The first marriage was childless, but now this second wife is pregnant. She is a dark-haired, doe-eyed creature of maybe twenty-five, with a sweet submissive smile.

The larger and slightly less chaotic of the two shops in Megalo Chorio is owned by Panagiotis and his brother, and Helen, the new wife, has been running it for them. But Panagiotis is very protective and he has recently decided that the work will be too much for her in future.

He told me about the shop and his concerns one afternoon when I met him on the headland. I had been for a walk to clear my head of the thick fog of paint fumes – I had been redecorating in the airless spaces of Meroula's house and then drinking coffee and listening to her stories of the old days – and Panagiotis had obviously been off to attend to one of his multitude of subsidiary businesses. If somewhere as tiny as Halemni can support a Mr Big, Panagiotis is the candidate.

After an exchange of polite greetings in Greek, which is still about as much conversation as I can manage, although

I am beginning to understand much more, he remarked in English that he was looking for someone to help him.

I nodded encouragingly.

It would be just a few hours a day, Panagiotis said. There would be lifting and carrying work, to stock shelves and manage the storeroom. I could be a pair of hands for Helen. The language should be no problem, because he or his wife would tell me exactly what needed doing. I would be paid in cash, on the basis of hours worked. And he winked at me. 'This will be a nice job for you. I think you stay in Halemni for a few weeks, for a quiet time, Olivia tells me.'

It wasn't difficult to work out what he was really saying. He wanted a willing worker, without ambitions, or the complicated ties of Halemniot family loyalty. I would be unlikely to overstay my welcome, or make awkward demands on my employers, and best of all I spoke so little Greek I wouldn't understand any of his business dealings and I couldn't eavesdrop or gossip about anything I might see or hear while I was in the shop. I would be exactly that, a pair of useful but unthreatening hands.

I smiled down at him. Panagiotis was engaging, and it would be a great relief to have some cash of my own. I couldn't even participate in the island's barter system because I had nothing to bring. The freedom of possessing nothing had been exhilarating for my first days on the island and at the same time Olivia and Xan had looked after me as if I were their third child, but now I was beginning to feel embarrassed and indebted.

'How much do you pay?'

He gave me a cunning glance. 'One thousand five hundred per hour.'

It is a long time since I have earned anything at all of my own; I have been Peter's wife. But the contrast between my long-ago modelling rates and Panagiotis's offer made me smile briefly.

'Three.'

He winced and turned down the corners of his mouth. 'I have a wife, a child coming. Seventeen hundred, although this is more than I can afford.'

'Two thousand five hundred.'

'Ah, you make this very difficult for me. Shall we say two thousand?'

I pretended to consider my position. 'Okay. When shall I start?'

'Tomorrow. Ten o'clock.' Panagiotis held out his meaty hand and I shook it.

No one, except the island fishermen, gets up early in winter. There is no point.

'Okay.'

And so this is my job. I love the shop. The only windows are at the front, and these are smeared with salt and dust. The walls are lined with steel shelving and piled up with dry goods of all kinds to make a messy, colourful cavern. If there is a storage system I haven't worked it out yet because clouded polythene bags of cheap sunglasses for the summer visitors sit alongside tins of tuna, with torch batteries and dusty tubes of sun cream next to them. There are more tins with fading labels stacked up everywhere; beans and sardines and coffee and tomatoes and condensed milk and big square green and gold ones containing litres of olive oil. These are the basic supplies that everyone in Halemni relies on when the weather holds up the ferries.

There are vacuum packs of olives and ham and vine leaves and halva too, all stored in their cardboard cartons, and piled packets of biscuits and crackers and cereals. Down one long wall on the floor beneath the lowest shelf there are hessian sacks with big open mouths. These contain broken pasta and bulgur wheat and barley, plain and wholemeal

174

bread flour and rice. Metal scoops lie half buried in the mealy contents. There are smaller sacks of dried bayleaves and peppercorns, and on another shelf near to Helen's ultra-modern cash till – the only shiny new item in the shop – there are barrels of olives, anchovies and feta cheese preserved in brine. Against the other long wall there is a big chest freezer, the resting place of dubious joints of meat that lie like logs of wood, and anonymous packets of fish. The walls of the chest are thickened and swollen like a fat-furred heart with layers of frost crystals; I suggested to Helen that I could do a defrosting job but she only looked alarmed and insisted that I would have to consult Panagiotis.

Helen's main area of interest in the shop is the tiny drapery and haberdashery section. There are needles and thread, and children's ankle socks, combs and tampons and tissues and women's stockings. She likes to arrange and rearrange her stocks, and when this task is complete for the day and we are not overrun with customers (this has never happened yet although I suppose it might, if everyone in Megalo Chorio were to choose to come in at the same time), she sits down next to the cash register and watches a tiny black-and-white television set balanced on a high stool. She knits at the same time – matinée jackets and bonnets in white or lemon acrylic. I watch her, covertly, and the swell of her stomach. The baby is due in eight weeks' time.

Sometimes she looks up and catches my eye, and gives me her sweet smile. I make a little pot of Greek coffee, using the electric ring in the washroom cubicle behind Helen's chair, and put the cup into her hand. She always looks a little startled and thanks me more than once, as if the attention makes her feel uncomfortable.

The rest of the time I keep myself busy. Panagiotis doesn't have much fresh produce, just a tray or two of tomatoes, bunches of flat parsley, lemons, and bruised imported apples that no one ever buys, but he likes these to be displayed outside on wooden racks that stand at right angles to the shop door. It is my job to put the things out in the morning and to bring them in again when we close up for the night. He also has netting bags of faded beach balls, flip-flops and plastic beach toys, and even now, in winter when there is not a single visitor on the island, he insists that these are also taken out every morning and hung up on the arms of the shop awning. Maybe, with a real shopkeeper's optimism, he believes that each arriving ferry could bring a crowd of tourists who will spot his inviting display from the harbour wall and hurry to stock up on beach goods without being tempted by the rival shop, owned by a cousin of Yannis's, who does not bother with such things.

Inside the shop I dust the shelves and pile the dry goods in tidier sequences, making decorative buttresses of canned tomatoes or cereal packets. I like doing this, making trivial domestic order, and I am good at it. Much better, at least, than I am as a painter and decorator. The miniaturisation of routines reminds me of Dunollie Mansions, a little, but this is more satisfying because I have no sense of being a disappointment here. No one knows who I am, or expects anything from me that I can't deliver, and accordingly nothing matters very much. Therefore I am free to take pleasure in the smallest things: the picture on a tin of tomatoes, the baby-fingernail shells on the beach, the church bell dinning the village's old women in to prayer.

I restock the shelf goods when necessary from the supplies housed in the dark storeroom that opens off the back of the shop, saving Helen from having to do any lifting or carrying. I sweep up spilled flour or wheat and I mop the floors regularly, keeping an eye out for mice or other vermin, as Panagiotis discreetly instructed me. I also serve customers – most of the goods are clearly priced, and when in doubt

I can refer to Helen who lays down her needles and placidly checks for me. I can operate the till and give accurate change. The people who come in are beginning to take my presence for granted and will exchange a few words with me or Helen almost indiscriminately.

The shop smells deliciously of vinegar and spices and local honey, and the constant handling of food makes me hungry. I have never had an appetite like this before, but now I am ravenous after working and from my walks up the stony spine of the island or over the coast headlands. At night, when I don't eat an evening meal with Xan and Olivia, I take pasta or tinned fish or beans back to my studio, and I make sloppy platefuls of food and greedily consume everything.

I am happy. The discovery shocks me at first and then I learn to savour it.

Every day I put on the striped top that came in the aid shipment and the flannel trousers that are now beginning to feel slightly tight round the waist. I remember that the outfit when I first put it on reminded Olivia of the film *Jules et Jim* and think of the coincidence of my talking about the same film to poor Jim the waiter in Branc. Then I remember Branc itself and the night of the earthquake.

The memory still makes me shake, even though I am in the spicy warmth of the shop or sitting close to the wood-burning stove in Olivia's kitchen. I have seen graphic pictures of the aftermath in the local papers and on the news on Helen's television. The thought of the suffering endured there by Jim's mother, and a thousand other mothers, skewers me and my weird happiness trips over the reality and falters away into sadness.

It takes a long walk or a day's work to restore it again, but it always does come back. I am beginning to trust in it.

Sometimes I think about Peter. But the thoughts are

detached and his voice is fading in my head. I imagine him in London with Lisa and the way that his sorrow for me will be tempered by present comforts. He has what he wanted and to my surprise so do I. I am breaking free of the past, just as I hoped.

As if to demonstrate my freedom my hair is growing out of its high-maintenance London cut and colour, turning shaggy and sticking out at odd angles, and developing a thickening dark strip at the roots. My city manicure was destroyed on the night in Branc. Now I keep my nails clipped brutally short and my hands are rough with cleaning and washing up. I chop at the stubble on my legs and under my arms with a man's disposable razor, and I haven't worn any make-up since leaving the Turkish hotel because I don't have any. I don't pluck my eyebrows or use body lotion, or any cosmetics at all except the cheapest moisturiser, soap and deodorant from Panagiotis's shop. In this, I am getting more like Olivia every day.

We are alike in other ways too.

Exploration of her shelves shows me that we enjoy the same books and music, we laugh at the idiosyncrasies of our village neighbours and at Christopher Cruickshank's wry asides, we like cooking and all-weather walks, and evenings by the warmth of the stove. But we are dissimilar in much more profound ways.

Olivia has the luxury of loving and being loved, and the self-confidence that allows her to take and to give. Olivia believes in herself. I find myself envying her with a greedy and passionate longing. I wish I lived her life.

I wish I could *be* her.

I am closing up the shop for the night. Helen has already gone home, walking slowly up the main street towards Panagiotis's house with her knitting bag held close against her side. Usually Panagiotis arrives to drive her in the pick-up but tonight he has gone with his brother, who works as a fisherman, to sell or deliver some of the day's catch to Halemniots who live in remote corners of the island. I haven't met the brother yet, because he lives on an inlet further down the coast where he moors his fishing boat.

'You like him,' Panagiotis teases me. 'He nice-looking, good working man.'

There is a great shortage of marriageable women on Halemni. Most of the girls prefer to move away to Rhodes or one of the bigger islands as soon as they are old enough to leave home. The traditional way of life is hard.

'I'll have to see,' I joke in return.

I have taken down the netting bags of beach balls and flipflops, and dragged the wooden outside shelving under cover. The locking up is an unnecessary precaution because there is no one on Halemni who would take anything, but I am preparing to go through the motions when the door opens and pings the little bell that announces a customer. I come out of the storeroom with the keys in my hand and see Christopher Cruickshank. He is standing at the shelf where we keep the bottles of wine and spirits – dusty square-shouldered bottles of brandy, slim and lethal little bottles of raki and ouzo, a few of Demestica and an unlabelled almost black-looking rank of the local red.

'I'll have a couple,' he says, holding up two bottles of these.

I take the money and he puts them one in each of his two coat pockets. He is still standing around in the darkened street when I have finished locking up. It is a cold evening with rain spitting out of the blackness.

'Come and have a drink?' he asks me, as we turn away from the shop together.

I have never been inside his apartment and I look around

it with interest. It is the upper floor of one of the houses in the main street. The stairs are wooden and very rickety. Downstairs, he tells me, are summer rental rooms that are too cold and dark to be comfortably occupied in winter. His quarters are not exactly warm, either, although I am learning to be less sensitive to the cold. Xan brought out of storage and plugged in a pair of electric radiators for me, the old-fashioned ribbed kind that remind me of school classrooms, and these heat my studio well enough in all but the coldest weather. I keep my pea-coat on and wear woollen gloves if I have to. Christopher has just one radiator and I can see our breath clouding in the air. I pull my coat closer around me.

There are dozens of pictures here too, covering the walls. Most of them are watercolours, recognisably his own work. I wander along, looking at them. The floor space is cluttered with books and papers and painting materials, the bed is heaped with clothes. In a second room that opens off this one, presumably the kitchen, I can hear Christopher rattling glasses.

It occurs to me that he has had a few drinks already. Probably he has been in the kafeneion with Yannis. He comes back at a stumble.

'This do?'

He gives me a tumbler full of dark-red wine. I try to warm it a little with my hands before venturing a gulp. Luckily, even though the temperature is close to *frappé*, the wine itself still tastes of heat. I take another gulp.

'Sit down.'

There is a table, two upright chairs. We sit, facing each other. Christopher takes out his leather tobacco pouch and makes a roll-up with exaggerated care and concentration. He is not quite drunk. All the time he is frowning and adjusting threads of tobacco I am staring covertly at him.

He *must* be Dan Cruickshank's brother. The resemblance is suddenly striking.

I remember the evening of our dinner party. The night Peter and Lisa met for the first time, and Dan gossiping about painting the portrait of one of the royals. For a minute with the taste of wine on my tongue I am back there, in the candlelit dining room at Dunollie Mansions. The words are almost out of my mouth – *are you related to Dan Cruickshank?* – before I manage to stop myself.

The two worlds run dangerously close, threaten to collide and merge. I remember the time on the headland. The hit of euphoria that came with realising that I can be free, with all the shackles of history gone.

Now you know.

I don't, not properly, but I do know that I should keep *now* separate from *then*. Not only should, but must.

The certainty is reassuring and relief makes me smile. Dunollie Mansions fades away.

Christopher touches a match to his roll-up. He inhales and blows out smoke, then squints at me through the cloud.

'God. You looked like her just then. When you smile like that. I never noticed.'

'Like … ?'

'Olivia,' he says. He rests his cigarette in the lid of a jar that serves as an ashtray, takes a long gulp of wine. I was right. He's slightly drunk. I am also making other connections.

Looking around the room, I can see that among the books and CDs and the heaps of clothes there is no sign of a suitcase or a rucksack or any indication of packing being done. Christopher is making no move to return to England even though I remember that he was supposed to leave a few days after the tsunami.

He gets up from his chair, banging against it so that it almost falls over and I reach out to steady it.

'Bugger.'

He was en route to the CD player. Now he picks one from the scatter and snaps it into the machine. Sheryl Crow, I think. When he has safely regained his chair we sit for a while listening to the music. It's comfortable here. Although my fingers and toes are still cold the wine goes a way towards warming me. Christopher finishes his cigarette. He's older than Dan and much less handsome, but he has a puckish smile and there is a restlessness about him that makes him interesting.

Are you staying on? For the winter?' I ask. I can sense that there is a conversation waiting to start and this is only to prompt him.

He looks around the room with a touch of exasperation.

'I don't know.'

'Do you want to leave?'

'No. But there's no real reason to stay.'

I wait, turning my glass in circles on the table. He considers, a touch blearily, and then decides that he will confide in me.

'No reason at all, except that I want to ... be close to her.'

This is the conclusion I had already reached. I nod, thinking that life on Halemni is not quite as simple or idyllic as it seems.

'I was ready to go at the end of the painting season. It's my third year here, I'm used to not seeing her for months at a time. But the earthquake turned it all upside down. Opened buried seams and exposed them. I'm afraid that if I go something terrible will happen and she won't be here when I come back again.'

'Yes.'

'So I want to stay here and watch over her. You can call that ridiculous since she has Xan to protect her, and her boys and everything else that she wants, and she certainly doesn't need some failed painter wistfully hovering on the margins of her life, but knowing it's absurd doesn't change the way I feel about her. It exaggerates it, if anything. Ridiculous, eh?'

'Does she know?'

He glances at me again through the veil of smoke, tilting his head to one side as if measuring the proportions of my face before setting out to draw me. This makes me self-conscious and I look quickly away.

'Don't women always know these things?'

'Yes, I suppose so.' I know, for example, that he has only opened up to me now because I looked like her, fleetingly and through the bottom of a glass. (I am aware that there is a slight resemblance because of our height and the Englishness of our features, but it is really only superficial.) So a degree of female intuitiveness might therefore be assumed, if you are talking vague generalisations of this kind.

'Have you ever told her about it?'

He laughs, refills our glasses and sets about the papers and tobacco again. 'Jesus, no. What could I say? "Darling Olivia, I love you more than breath itself, I want to hold you and keep you safe for ever, or at least to live in the same square mile as you so I can see you every day? I can't offer you anything like what you've got already, by the way. Or anything much at all, in fact." It's not terribly enticing, is it?'

I laugh too. I like Christopher and the way he talks, and his self-deprecating Englishness in this Greek redoubt. The wine is making my head swim, but I'm still cold. I nudge my chair closer to the radiator and curve my hand over the cream-painted fins. At first I feel nothing, then the hot metal burns my fingers. I snatch them away again.

'You're cold.'

'Um, yes.'

He stands up, not quite managing the vertical, and lopes to the bed. He pushes to one side the assorted T-shirts and holey jumpers, and picks up an afghan blanket crocheted in multicoloured wool.

'Come and sit here.'

He shoves cushions against the wall and when I sit on the edge of the bed he wraps the blanket round my shoulders. He adds a further layer of his own arm and we settle back against the pillows. He smells of tobacco and soap, which reminds me faintly of my father and the complicated time of my childhood.

'That better?'

It is, surprisingly. My head rests on his shoulder. This is my first exchange of physical warmth – I think back, through the grainy days – since Andreas and I clung together on the fishing boat. Touch is soothing, like a dressing placed on a burn.

When he turns his head to resume our talk I can feel the warmth of his breath on my neck.

'I love her, that's all. It's simple, irreversible and insoluble.'

'So do I,' I shrug. 'If there's any comfort in that.'

He doesn't think I'm a lesbian, I can tell. He nods and we meditate separately on Olivia's vitality and her enviable place at the centre of this Halemni web, and our own peripheral and shadowy natures by comparison.

'Not a lot,' Christopher says at length. 'This is nice, though, isn't it?'

Even though he's drunk he isn't going to try to kiss me, I know that much, and I am relieved. To cuddle each other and thoughtfully drink our wine is enough for both of us.

'I'm warm now.' It's true, I am.

'Good. Any time.' His words are slurring now and when the music finishes and the only other sound is the creak of a loose shutter, I can hear that he has fallen asleep. For a while I half lie curled up against him, looking at the room and his pictures and possessions. The strong rhythm of his breathing is comforting and the catch in his throat that hasn't yet grown into a snore.

I don't move until there are warning pins and needles in my side and down my arm, then I slide away from him and silently stand up. I unwind the afghan from my shoulders and tuck it around him, and before I leave I make sure that his cigarette is out and that there are no fragments smouldering in the ashtray or among the strewn papers. Then I let myself out into the night.

It is pitch-black and windy. But I know the way back to the potter's house studio now, every step, and I walk comfortably. The wind smells of cats and wet dirt and cold brine.

My other day job, when I am not at Panagiotis's shop, is still helping Meroula. This I do, of course, in order to repay Xan and Olivia something for their generosity to me, but I also enjoy doing it. Xan's mother is a perfectionist and whatever I do in her airless little house has to be to the highest standard, but in spite of this – or perhaps even because of it, for I have perfectionist tendencies too – I enjoy her company. She watches me while I scrape away ruined Anaglypta wallpaper or sand down woodwork ready for repainting and points out if I have missed a crack. I go back at once and carefully attend to it.

The mud and debris from the wave have long been cleared and Meroula sees the present situation as an opportunity to improve her decor. The only gloss paint currently available on Halemni, from some depot of Panagiotis's, is a pale stone colour with a shine on it like glass and Meroula loves it. I have applied it to doors and skirtings, three coats. Wallpaper, however, will have to wait until she makes a ferry trip to Rhodes Town to choose something suitable.

While I am working we talk. Or rather, Meroula smooths her grey cardigan front and crosses her ankles in the grey lisle stockings and talks to me.

I know about her husband and their happy life – although times were hard, work was hard, I must understand, they were still a good match. Her face softens and she pats the sides of her hairdo as she recalls it. Meroula almost got away from Halemni and the hard life. She went away to study in Rhodes Town and learned English, and she tells me that she could have had a good job, maybe as a secretary or a receptionist in a hotel. But then she fell in love with Nikos and – she smiles – after that there was nothing to be done.

'How did you meet?'

This innocent question makes her slap her knees and shake with laughter.

'On Halemni you do not meet people. All your life you know them. But then a young man and a young woman look at each other and suddenly, *ppffff*, they are seeing a quite different person.'

'How old were you when you noticed a different Nikos?'

'Eighteen years. Married one year after that.'

'That's very young.'

Meroula shrugs. 'What is to wait for?'

And then they were blessed with Xan. Xan is her sun. He can do no wrong, nothing that she can do for him is too much.

I listen to all of this with fascination, and Meroula loves to have an audience.

When I have completed whatever the day's task happens to be, Meroula offers refreshments and I accept. To refuse her offer of hospitality would be unthinkable. At the beginning, since I am English, she did her best to make tea for me but now I have convinced her that I prefer coffee. In fact, it's true that I have developed a taste for the thick, very sweet

186

Greek coffee favoured by Meroula herself. She brings it on a tray with a lace-edged traycloth, in tiny gilded cups with a glass of water set alongside. There is also invariably either a plate of little sweet biscuits out of a tin lined with corrugated crimson paper, or else an arrangement of the sticky honey and almond sweet pastries that Meroula makes herself from a family recipe. I eat, eagerly, while she watches and nods her approval.

Once, seeing me glancing at them in their place on her shelf, she brought down her photograph albums, the same ones that I carried up to safety at Olivia's on the morning Andreas and I arrived here. They have thick grey card pages interleaved with flimsy waxed sheets, and there are black-and-white photographs fixed with geometrical precision and captioned in Greek that I frustratingly could not decipher.

There is a picture of Meroula and Nikos on their wedding day. He has a full moustache and a solemn stare. He is dressed in a high-collared wool jacket with a full white shirt beneath, and Meroula is wearing a wide gathered skirt with an apron, and a laced bodice over a fine lawn full-sleeved blouse. She looks very pretty.

She pointed to herself. 'This, our island dress. You do not see much, today.'

'That's a shame.'

Most of the pictures are of Xan, as a baby and a small child. He was plump and pale, and dressed in what looks like far too many complicated layers of clothes. Meroula noticed that I looked closely. I saw her glance pityingly at my ringless fingers.

'No children yourself.' This was a statement of the obvious. If I had children of course I would be with them, not painting doors.

'No.'

'Not married?'

'I was. Divorced now.'

I suppose this was the easiest shorthand. I wondered what Peter would do – was doing – and told myself that of course he must by now assume my death. The photographs blurred in front of my eyes and my mouth felt clogged and rancid with the sweet pastries.

I was too aware of Meroula's measuring scrutiny. 'Kitty? Something is wrong with you?'

'No. Nothing, really. How old is he here?'

'Ah, five years.'

I fixed my attention on the albums again. The photographs that interested me most were those that show the old village as it was, before the families left and moved down to the coast. There are very few of them and they are faded to sepia so they look as if they belong to a much earlier date than the early Fifties.

The houses are the same, but the crumbling skeletons are fleshed with doors that close, windows with painted shutters. The gardens are tended and there are vines trained over frames of wood and wire, roses tumbling over a low wall and children shading their eyes against the sun to stare at the unfamiliar sight of a camera. An old woman walks up the steep cobbles with a load of hay trussed up in a sack on her back, and a donkey with heavy panniers is led through a narrow alleyway by a bent old man.

'My father,' Meroula said. 'He brought water up every day. His donkey, he loved as much as his wife and children.'

I started to smile, then realised that she was simply being candid.

'People here now, young people, they don't understand. The old ways, before the tourists came. My son's wife does not understand. They want everything to be easy.'

It becomes more and more evident that there are difficulties between Olivia and Meroula, and it is easy enough to work out why. Olivia looks after Xan and all his domestic needs with a submissive attentiveness that seems at odds with her confidence in herself and his love for her. But even so, this isn't enough to please Meroula. Olivia doesn't prepare his food properly. He has to make his own coffee. She is a negligent mother, by Meroula's standards, although to me she seems to offer the boys plenty of love and enough discipline. And Meroula is jealous of her, because it is Olivia who lives with Xan. As I guessed almost at the beginning, it is partly because I'm not Olivia that Meroula is disposed to like me.

'You've made a friend,' Olivia said to me once, crimping her face in a comic expression that still showed her concern.

'It's because I'm not her daughter-in-law.'

Olivia laughed. 'Greek men never leave their mothers and they are never unfaithful to them.'

A question trembled in the air between us but I didn't ask it, not yet.

I closed Meroula's album, making sure the waxed paper didn't lie in a crease between the boards.

'I think Olivia does very well. Much better than I ever could.' I had to defend her; I couldn't listen to Meroula's criticism and not do so.

Meroula pursed her mouth. 'She is good, I know that. But Greek boy should have a Greek wife, Kitty. You are not Greek either. You do not understand these things.'

That's it, I suppose. Meroula likes me and if Olivia were in my place she would like her too. But Xan's wife, that's completely different. Whoever Xan married, I suspect, Meroula would be opposed to her.

Even Olivia's idyll has its flaws, then. I feel a ripple of sympathy texturing my envy.

Today I have put Meroula's books and albums and carefully washed china ornaments back on the painted shelves, arranging everything according to her directions. My hands and lips feel hot and cracked from the dusty work and I tell myself that I must get some cream for them. There is a scuffling out on the step – now the freshest and whitest-washed on the street – and Georgi and Theo scramble in from school. On most days they come to visit their grandmother on the way home.

'Mella, I'm hungry.'

'Look, I made a model. It's a castle.'

Meroula already has fruit juice and biscuits put out for them, and another pot of coffee prepared for us. We sit cosily in the kitchen, with rain rapping at the windows. The children are used to seeing me here and they push between Meroula and me to get up close to the table.

At seven Georgi is wiry with a thick thatch of hair, but five-year-old Theo is still plump and babyish. I put my arm round him while he drinks his juice and he lets me do it. He even presses closer and I can smell his skin and see the light through his eyelashes.

'Show me your castle,' I ask.

He squares it up on the table, his lopsided structure of painted cartons and sticky tape. Without thinking I scoop him on to my knee so we can both see better and he wriggles to make himself more comfortable. Without any warning my heart contracts and then bangs in my chest. He is warm and solid, and I am longing to bury my face between the wings of his shoulder blades. I want to slide my fingers through the silky strands of his hair and feel the bones of his skull.

'See, this is where the people go in.'

I content myself with folding an arm round his shoulder. It feels complete to sit with a child on your lap. This is what my own children would have felt like, the babies I couldn't hold on to. Holding Theo in their place matches a need and creates a greater one. Now it is as if it is all I can do not to

190

seize both the boys and find some way of subverting them away from Xan and Olivia and making them mine altogether.

I am afraid of this feeling – it creeps up on me sometimes at the potter's house, and so I try to keep a certain distance from Theo and Georgi. Down here at Meroula's their parents are further off and my longing seems as if it could almost be gratified, for an hour at least.

'The animals live in here.' Theo points to an enclosure made from a strip of glued card.

'What animals do they have?'

'Goats and sheep. Some donkeys,' he says, enjoying the fact that I don't know.

Meroula is watching me. I feel guilty at once, but what I see in her square, heavy face is compassion. She heaves herself to her feet and comes round the table, then pats me on the shoulder.

'Eat some this *ghlika*,' she says, passing me the little tray of sweetmeats. To offer food is her way of showing concern. Georgi tries to take one too but Meroula slaps his hand away. The boys aren't allowed these adult confections, they have chocolate wafer biscuits instead. The sweetness in my mouth is comforting.

'Look at my writing book,' Georgi insists. He doesn't like Theo getting all the attention. He opens a red exercise book ruled off in squares and shows me the lists of words.

'I can't read a single word,' I laugh. It's true: I have picked up a bit of the spoken language, but beyond puzzling out some of the labels in the shop I haven't tackled the written one yet.

'And you are grown up.' Georgi is scornfully delighted.

'You could show me the letters, to start with.'

'I know letters,' Theo shouts.

They are fighting for a place on my lap now. Georgi

191

flattens the pages of his book with a clenched fist and smudges the pencilled words.

'*Alfa, vita, ghama,*' they chorus. Georgi carefully writes the letters, his tongue sticking out between his teeth.

'Like Kyria Tsatsas,' Theo tells me. 'Our teacher.'

'Now you do it.'

I take the pencil and copy the letters, filling a square with each one. Faint images of classical inscriptions float in my head and I regret that I know so little about Greek culture. I'll read, I promise myself. There's time for that.

'Quite good,' Georgi judges. He is writing out the rest of the alphabet as Theo chants, '*Omicron, pi, ro, sigma.*'

When it is complete all the way down to *omega* and I have copied every one of the letters, Georgi gives me the page. 'Now you have to learn it.'

'I will,' I promise.

It has stopped raining now, but the light is fading. Olivia will be expecting her children home.

We say goodbye to Meroula and I walk up the village street with them. It is deserted except for the slinking cats. The boys take my hands and swing on either side of me, pleased with their writing lesson, and then I hear a car coming up from the harbour wall and slowing down behind us. My arms are pinioned by the boys and I am in any case thinking about them and nothing else, so the car has already slowed and then drawn level with us before I look round.

'*Yia sou, Olivia,*' a loud voice calls. It is Panagiotis in his pickup truck. I am wearing my dark coat with the collar turned up, and with Georgi and Theo pulling at my hands it is a reasonable mistake to have made in the dusk. But I can see his briefly startled expression before he grins, showing his teeth. 'So sorry! Kitty I mean, of course.'

'*Kali spera, Panagiotis.*'

'I have someone with me.' He beams. The passenger door

on the other side opens and a man half climbs out, to look at me over the roof of the cab. Before Panagiotis can introduce him I am staring up and down the street, pointlessly wondering where I can hide. It is one of the fishermen, or smugglers. The oldest one, who stood braced in the little wheelhouse and steered the boat through the huge seas.

'This is my brother, Michaelis,' Panagiotis announces with only the faintest suggestion of a leer.

I stand dumbly, waiting for the clap of recognition and the explanations that will have to follow it. Amazingly, there is nothing. Michaelis doesn't betray even by the faintest flicker that he has ever seen me before. His night-time fishing activities must be kept even from his brother.

Either that, or Andreas and I were invisible.

'*Kali spera*,' we murmur politely to each other.

'Maybe we meet again,' Michaelis says. Then he reverses his slither back into the passenger seat and the pick-up grinds on up the street.

Olivia opens the door of the potter's house. A bright shaft of light strikes past her and there is a warm scent of fish and tomatoes. The boys peel away from me and dash into the house.

'Thanks for bringing them home.'

'I was at Meroula's.' I am about to turn away towards the studios, but Olivia is still standing in the doorway. She seems to be waiting, holding the door open in just the same way as the first time I saw her. My hands are hot and itchy.

'Do you have a little bit of hand cream I could use?'

The door opens wider. 'Sure. Xan isn't back yet. Come in.'

TEN

They went upstairs to the bathroom and Olivia took a basket of cosmetics out of a cupboard.

'Here,' she said, passing a tube to Kitty. Kitty smoothed a worm of hand cream into her cracked fingers while Olivia stared into the mirror propped behind the basin. It was just big enough to reflect their two faces. Olivia's expression changed. She shook her head slowly, disbelievingly, as she took in the contrast.

'God. Just look,' she breathed. She teased a strand of her cropped hair between her fingers. Just look at me, compared with you.'

Kitty put the hand cream aside. Their eyes met in the glass. 'What?'

'How old are you?' Olivia asked and Kitty told her.

'Same as me.'

Olivia was still staring. She saw that her face was lined with laughing and frowning, clefts bracketing her nose and chin, and corrugating her forehead, and her skin was patched with brown blotches from too much sun. This was the longest time she had spent looking in the mirror for months, even years, and she hated what it revealed.

There was no women's hairdresser on Halemni in winter-time. Meroula and the other women of her generation assisted each other with rollers and perming lotion, and the younger ones mostly grew their hair long or went to Rhodes. Defiantly Olivia had the island barber trim hers at the same time as the boys' and Xan's. Now she saw that the cut left her ears unflatteringly exposed. Her lips were chapped and her eyebrows were thick and grew in all directions. And there were coarse hairs sprouting from her chin that she had never noticed before.

Whereas Kitty ...

There were all kinds of different and complicated shades of sun in her silky hair. Her face was as smooth as if she never smiled or scowled and her skin was the colour of warm double cream.

Olivia put her hands up to cover her face, but she was still staring horror-struck through the chinks in her fingers.

'This island,' she whispered. 'It's either paradise or prison, I'm not sure which. Can anywhere you can't escape from really count as paradise?'

Kitty took hold of her wrists and gently lowered her hands again. 'Halemni seems to me as close to paradise as you could ever get.'

There was no doubt that Kitty meant what she said. There was an intensity in her voice that made Olivia want to back away, laugh off her moment of panic and vanity, and talk about something else. Of course Halemni wasn't a prison. What was she thinking?

But she was still recovering from the shock of their joint appearance. She kept her eyes averted from the glass.

'I used to think so. But I never leave the place. There isn't the money, or any reason to go elsewhere. I used to know the world out there; now I'd be almost afraid to venture into it. I'm set in island ways. I need Xan, I couldn't leave the boys.' The corners of her mouth tightened. 'I look ... old. My horizons have shrunk. It's too late to do anything but what I'm doing now. So this *is* a kind of prison, isn't it?'

'What else do you want?' Kitty asked.

Olivia thought about England and her parents. She would like to go back home once in a while, yes, but Denis and Maddie came out to Halemni every spring. Polly and Jack and the others loved to come to lie on the beach, whenever and as often as they could. And in any case England wasn't *home* – this, here, was home, nowhere else.

She would love to spend more time with Max because she missed him every day, but going to Australia was out of the question.

It would be pleasant to be out of Meroula's critical sight, just for a little while.

And I hate myself, Olivia decided, for even wishing for more than I already have. It's because of Kitty. It's Kitty being here that makes me dissatisfied with my life.

Her eyes slid reluctantly back to the mirrored reflections.

Kitty had put her fingertips to Olivia's jaw and was thoughtfully turning her head this way and that. She fluffed the other woman's hair, trying it with and without a parting. Olivia let her do it, although usually she hated what she thought of as being messed about with. Kitty had once been a model so this – hair and make-up, and having your face stared at – was what she was used to. No wonder she managed to look the way she did, even dressed in earthquake aid clothes on Halemni in November.

'There must be something,' Kitty prompted.

Olivia's instinct was to fend her off. She shrugged deliberately.

'I don't *know* what I want. I haven't a fucking clue.'

They started to laugh, loud laughter that startled them

both. They looked like friends playing about in front of the bathroom mirror and the silvery surface hid their separate depths.

Olivia dismissed the issue. 'I'm too busy to think about it.'

'Tell you what. I could do you a make-over,' Kitty offered. She pursed her lips and rummaged in the basket of cosmetics. 'You know, before and after.'

'Are you mad? Have you been drinking?'

'Yeah. Coffee, with your mother-in-law.'

Whatever she had been doing, Kitty's mouth was softer and her eyes sleepier than she had seen them. The relaxed look suited her.

'Wanton. Wild woman.'

Kitty unpeeled a lipstick and stretched her lips to show Olivia what she wanted. She began busily painting. Downstairs they heard the front door slam.

'Pappy's home,' the boys were yelling from their bedroom.

Olivia sighed and hooked her head from beneath Kitty's hands.

'Some other time.'

'It's a deal.'

Xan was big and dark in the hallway. He kissed Olivia and then stood back.

'What's this?'

'Lipstick. You won't remember it.'

In the kitchen the telephone began to ring. It wasn't a common sound in winter, when the business was fallow.

Olivia went to answer it.

'*Max?*' she said.

She listened intently, holding her hand up to silence the boys. She kept nodding her head, smiling at first and then looking more serious.

'Of course you can. Just you? Yes, yes, of course I do. Whenever you like, I'd love you to, Max. You know that ...'

The boys pulled at her legs, demanding to be allowed to speak.

Kitty mouthed goodnight to Xan and went out to her studio. It was so cold inside the room that her breath clouded in front of her face. Determinedly she clicked the 'on' switch of her radiators, then pulled her coat closer around her. She stood by the window, looking across the angle of hillside towards the black gulf of the bay.

Xan's breath smelt of raki when Olivia kissed him. He had had a couple of glasses but she had shaken her head when he held up the bottle. She rubbed her mouth against his lips, letting the stubble on his cheeks scrape at hers. They had eaten and she had cleared away supper and the boys were in bed, and now they were sitting in front of the fire together.

'Who was there?' In the bar earlier, she meant.

He shrugged one shoulder. 'Stavros, Yannis. Michaelis and Panagiotis.'

No surprises. This was the winter pattern. The men drank and played cards or backgammon, and went fishing when the mood took them. The women did what they always did. A thumbprint of dissatisfaction coldly pressed the nape of Olivia's neck, then lifted again. She cuddled closer to Xan.

'Let's go to bed.'

He yawned and drew his arm tighter round her. 'Sounds like a good idea.'

Afterwards they lay in the dark.

'Why do you think Max wants to come for *Christmas*? Leaving Hattie and the girls behind. It doesn't sound good, does it?'

Xan sighed. 'No idea. I'm sure you'll find out.' His voice was thickening and she knew that he wanted nothing more than to go to sleep.

She nudged his bulk with her hip. Her brother telephoned

out of the blue, asking if he could come on his own to Halemni for the holiday, and she wanted to talk about this and try to work out what might be wrong in Sydney. But Xan wasn't interested in discussing the dynamics of other people's relationships, let alone last thing at night. Olivia's need to connect with him grew suddenly sharper. Loneliness began to crystallise at the margin of her consciouness.

'What do you think about Kitty?' She put the name delicately in quotation marks, not for the first time, but Xan was deaf to this too.

'Think? Um. I think she's entitled to do what she wants. Now she's got a job, she can pay her way. My mother obviously likes her. It's none of our business why she chooses to hang around here, is it?'

This was either commendably generous or lazily incurious – Olivia couldn't quite decide which.

'She sees quite a lot of Christopher.'

'It would be surprising,' Xan said patiently, 'if Christopher wasn't interested. There isn't a lot of choice around here, is there? Unless he gets into mother's age group.'

It was true, there were plenty of widows on Halemni.

Olivia was used to what she chose to think of as the Christopher problem – so used to it that the idea of its finding a solution made her oddly uncomfortable. Christopher's devotion gave her a kind of insurance. It couldn't be transferred to Kitty.

Kitty … The name made a faint but disconcerting echo in her head.

'I don't understand why she's here.'

There was a silence and then Xan rolled over and presented his back to her.

'I don't understand why you won't let me go to sleep.'

Olivia lay and stared up at nothing. Her thoughts scraped and rustled like mice in straw, darting from Kitty to

Christopher to Meroula, from Max to Theo and Georgi. Xan was already asleep and the effort of lying still next to his inert bulk wound Olivia's limbs into coiled springs of tension. All season, she thought, she looked forward to peace and privacy without guests to take care of. And then, almost as soon as they were gone, she felt restless.

She was frowning now. Dissatisfaction on this scale was a new sensation. Olivia knew that she had always been good at accepting what came and what couldn't be changed. She was happy. Happy was normal, wasn't it?

In one fluid movement she pushed back her half of the covers and swung her legs out of bed. Theo hadn't walked in his sleep lately, the last time had been before the wave. But she would check on him now. Xan grunted something unintelligible from under the surface of sleep as she slid out of the door.

The boys' room was completely dark but as soon as she was into it she knew that all was well. She could smell the warm scent of them both and her sharpened ears picked up the sighs of their breathing even before her hands connected with the sleeping shapes. Georgi was curled in a tight ball, Theo lay spread out like a starfish. She sat on the end of Theo's bed and listened to their sleep.

This was where satisfaction lay, and happiness. If her children were well then all else was well and boredom or frustration or anxiety were only waves on the surface of a body of still water. Love for her children was solid and unquestionable inside her.

The silence of the house was soothing and it became pleasant to be the one who was awake, at the heart of it. In her mind she roamed through the rooms, checking the order of everything and in this thoughtful quiet, at the farthest limit of perception, she could just hear the sea. She leaned back against the wall to listen and her eyelids drooped.

'Mummy?'

It was Georgi's whisper.

'I'm here.'

'Is the wave coming again?'

'No. Nothing like that. Go back to sleep.'

He sighed and turned over, taking her presence for granted and her reassurance as absolute. In a minute he was asleep again.

Olivia went back to her own bed, where Xan lay in the centre of the mattress. She slid under the covers to warm herself against him.

Xan went with Meroula to Rhodes Town on the ferry. Meroula's widowed sister lived there and they would stay a night with her, buy wallpaper and some photographic materials for Olivia and toys for the boys' Christmas presents, and come back the next day.

Olivia called in to Panagiotis's shop and found Kitty sealing a big bag of bread flour for Stefania, Yannis's long-suffering wife.

'Come and have supper,' she said to Kitty, when the three of them had finished exchanging greetings. There were so few people on Halemni that they met constantly, but the polite standards were still maintained.

'I'd like that,' Kitty said.

When she had locked up the shop for the night she walked the familiar route to the potter's house but instead of crossing to the row of studios she went straight to the front door. On Xan's and Olivia's bookshelf she had recently found a tattered, backless book called *Portrait of a Greek Mountain Village* and this she had been reading in the evenings while she huddled in her coat beside the blessed radiator, or ate big, comforting platefuls of food, but the prospect of talk and a glass of wine was still much more inviting than learning some more about Greek manners and customs.

She held up a brown-paper bag when Olivia opened the door. Eggs came from the misanthropic chicken farmer who lived down a rough track near the island's eastern tip and were brought down to the shop by Panagiotis in the truck.

'Eggs. Today's.'

Olivia took them from her with proper gratitude.

'Lovely. Come in.'

It was a cold night, with rain driving in on a rising wind. The kitchen was lit with a big wood fire and candles, and Kitty looked around with a wide smile of appreciation.

Theo climbed on Kitty's lap at once while Georgi made her read a list of Greek words: '*Meli, psomi, kafe, tsai.*'

Georgi fiercely corrected her pronunciation and Olivia looked up from slicing bread to see the three bright faces pressed close together over the exercise book. She straightened up with the point of the bread knife digging into the board.

'Food's ready,' she said loudly.

The two women drank a glass of wine while they ate, then another.

'Have you seen Christopher?' Olivia asked.

Seeing meant not just encountering on crossing the street or over a tin of olive oil in the shop, because that happened all the time in the claustrophobia of Megalo Chorio. It meant a meeting out of the general eye and talk that might not necessarily be appropriate for relaying across the village.

'No,' Kitty said truthfully. Rather the opposite, he had seemed to keep out of her way.

After the boys had gone to bed and, at their insistence, Kitty had been upstairs to say goodnight, she came down with the basket of Olivia's cosmetics from the bathroom.

'I could finish your make-over,' she coaxed.

Olivia hesitated. Then she tipped the last half-glass from the bottle of wine and shrugged. What am I dodging away from? she wondered. Is it Kitty herself? 'I'll open another one. Live dangerously. Sure, let's do it.'

She pulled her chair round so that her face was to the light, slid down and tilted her head back.

Kitty took her face between her hands and gazed intently into it. Then, with the delicacy of a surgeon selecting a scalpel, she took a pair of tweezers out of the basket's jumble and set to work on Olivia's eyebrows.

'Ouch. That hurts.'

'You have to suffer to be beautiful.'

'Is that so?'

'I'm going to trim your hair too. Can I use these scissors?' She snipped at Olivia's crop, thinning rough tufts into sleeker spikes.

'How did you learn all this? Did you have one of those mothers?'

'Mother-and-daughter visits to the salon, you mean? "Darling, always use a good cuticle cream, exfoliate twice a week, and I promise you'll grow up to look exactly like me"? No, I didn't. I just spent years on the receiving end of all this. I'm glad to be getting my revenge.'

Olivia laughed. It was enjoyable, this women-together game, even if the other player was Kitty who was as solid as smoke. She didn't, she realised, have nearly enough female company in this stronghold of men. It was good that Kitty was here.

I don't remember much about her before Marcus died. She was just my mother. She didn't have a job, although some of my friends' mothers did. Clare Colley's was a doctor, even, and Jessica Parks's worked in a bank. Mine baked cakes and wore high heels to go out with my father, and looked after us and the house. Then everything changed and the way that she changed was the most frightening of all. I remember the crying. It was nothing human. It was more like a cat, or an animal caught in a trap, a long, high wailing that I would hear behind closed doors. I would sneak along a hallway or silently tread down the stairs to press my ear against a crack or a keyhole. I had to hear it. I knew that this was what I had done, all this grief was because of me.

Later my mother would come out from wherever she had tried to lock herself away and her face would be like a mask with dark holes in it, her mouth all pulled awry. I would run to her and she would pick me up and I could feel in my arms and legs that she was making herself do it, trying to hold me close against her when every fibre of her wanted to push me away for not being Marcus.

I stopped running to her in the end and the crying stopped too, or at least the kind that you could hear did. She was just very quiet and thin – I remember the tops of her arms, you could see that there were two bones joining her shoulder to her elbow.

We didn't talk about clothes or lipstick, no. Nothing like that, because when I was old enough to take an interest in such things it was already far too late.

Olivia's face under my hands. I feel that I could easily remodel it, as if it's made of potter's clay instead of bone and muscle. She has a square jaw and a wide forehead, I'll need to shape and slim the contours. The skin is lined and damaged by the sun. Halemni extracts dues for its summer generosity.

I am enjoying – *loving* – the sense of power, the idea that I can make something of her other than her strong self.

With a sponge and cotton wool Kitty began to apply foundation. She worked for a long time, building up layers of highlight and shadow, then covering the whole with a thin mask of colour. She turned Olivia's face into a smooth, featureless oval.

Olivia fidgeted. She was tired of sitting still. 'Haven't you finished yet?'

'Hardly begun. You need patience in this game.'

'Give me my drink, at least.'

'Finish it before I do your lips.'

There was quite a range of make-up, in cracked and dusty tubes. Kitty worked with the mascara and shadow and lipstick, painting a new face over the one she had blotted out.

'I'm bored. My neck aches,' Olivia complained.

Kitty stood back to consider the effect.

'All right. You can look now.' She passed her the mirror.

Olivia stared.

Her hair lay flatter, leaving her face bare for scrutiny. The lines in it had been filled in to leave her cheeks stiff, with the threat of cracking in them if she ever smiled again. Her forehead looked like marble, her mouth was a wide and shiny scarlet gash.

It was more them just cosmetics, more as if Kitty's expertise had wiped away experience and emotion, denied them entirely, except for the eyes. The eyes were huge dark hollows, ringed with shadows, as if Kitty had punched holes in her face. They seemed to contain all the feelings that were absent from the face mask, and all these feelings were pain.

'My God.'

Even speaking felt strange, with the tightness and unaccustomed heaviness of her skin and the slicked gloss on her lips. The thick black eyelashes drooped, temporarily veiling the wells of grief.

'I look *nothing like* myself.'

'No.'

'I look sad. No. Like a death's head.'

'You look amazing.'

It was only a face, Olivia thought, still staring into the

mirror. It was nothing to do with identity. Time and truth and history still remained and could never be painted out. Yet it was bizarre to be made to appear so different, just with some tubes of coloured cream. Kitty's alchemy was disturbing. She could come from nowhere and bring nothing with her, and yet seemed able to exert influences beyond what was reasonable. Olivia wondered if her uneasiness, if the dissatisfaction that had crept over her, *was* all to do with Kitty. Or was it in herself and Kitty had only tapped it?

Olivia turned away from the idea. It was too fanciful.

They were just two women who were slightly bored with wintertime on a small island, lonely for female company and playing with a bag of make-up. Like children, testing boundaries, trying out the face that their mother presented to the world.

Olivia remembered the way her mother always put on lipstick and foundation in the mornings, and a slick of mascara that made her lashes look spiky and stiff. In the Sixties she was already middle-aged, but she gamely shortened her skirts to reveal plump knees and the effect was awkward combined with her tidily set hair and boxy handbags. Olivia was still wearing preteen pinafore dresses and ankle socks, but the sight of her mother caught on the edge of tectonic plates of shifting style made her fidget with embarrassment. She had tried out those cosmetics herself, of course, wobbling eyeliner across smooth eyelids and blanching her mouth with pale lipstick, but the effect had been funny, not transfiguring in the least.

Max had crept in once and caught her. He didn't often find the opportunity to make fun of his older and stronger sister, and he took full advantage of this one. They had circled each other, taunting and then jabbing at each other with balled fists. Their mother had run in and pulled them apart, Olivia remembered, and grabbed the little zipper bag of make-up out of her hands.

She had been sent to her room to wait for her father to come home.

Much of life, it seemed, for all three of them, consisted of waiting for him to come home.

'Hello?' Kitty teased her. 'Have I lost you?'

Olivia found her balance again. It *was* only a face. A magazine make-over, a stylist's trick for the lens. 'Let's take a picture.' She smiled. The slap was already cracking as her cheeks moved.

She picked up her camera from the shelf, checked the light and the focus, and handed it to Kitty. She tried to pose with Kitty's automatic, lens-drawing hauteur while Kitty prowled around her in a parody of the intrusive photographer. The shutter clicked three times.

Olivia took the camera and put it back in its place. The fire had burned low and she took an armful of logs from the basket and kicked up a shower of sparks as she stirred the embers into life. Kitty drained her wine and refilled the two glasses.

'Did I tell you,' Olivia said, 'that my brother is coming to stay for Christmas?'

She didn't know why she said this now. Maybe because he had just been in her head, but also to fill the awkward little moment that followed the make-up and the photography when they hadn't known what to say to each other or where this game might lead.

'That's nice,' Kitty said softly. 'Well. Is it?'

'Oh yes, it's better than nice, I want to see him more than anyone else in the world. But he's coming without Hattie, that's his wife, or their children and I'm worried that ...'

There was someone at the front door. The door of the potter's house had a heavy old iron knocker, rusty from the salt air, and the sound was one muffled rap. Someone trying to make himself heard without creating too much noise. Olivia went to answer it and came back with Christopher. He was wearing a coat with the collar turned up and a scarf wrapped round his throat. His sandy hair fell forward, neatly bisecting his face, but when he saw the two of them in the light he straightened up and raked the hair away. His eyes slid from Olivia to Kitty.

'I'm sorry, I didn't know you were here, Kitty. I just thought …' He gestured, revealing that he was holding a bottle. '… I'd come by and see if Olivia felt like a drink.'

'Kitty did my face. What do you think?'

Olivia knew that the spell was broken. The mask had cracked and now it was no more than a clumsy theatrical overstatement. She might have been about to play in some outlandish piece of amateur dramatics.

'Are you auditioning for a job as a geisha?' Christopher asked. But he was still glancing from one to the other. The juxtaposition was clearly more disturbing than he wanted to indicate.

'Don't be rude about my handiwork,' Kitty laughed. She had been running her fingers through her hair as she worked and now it stood up on end. She screwed caps on tubes and replaced pots in the basket. 'I'll put this back, Olivia, and be on my way.'

'Stay,' Olivia said quickly, turning to Christopher. 'She should stay, shouldn't she?'

He came to see her sometimes, the occasional nights when Xan was away. It wasn't a secret, it would be hard to keep a secret of that kind in Megalo Chorio. It was just an understanding between them. He would sit and watch her while she cooked or mended clothes and they would talk about pictures or photography, the sort of conversation that didn't much interest Xan. She had had in her mind when she invited Kitty on the spur of the moment to supper that Christopher might well materialise. And without properly articulating the thought she had imagined it would be useful to see his reaction to the two of them, and maybe to gauge his loyalty.

Did he love her because there was no one else and would that change now that Kitty was here?

And if it did, would she herself resent it or would she be relieved to have the Christopher problem solved?

Then, in the weird involvement of the face-painting, she had forgotten all about him.

'Yes, stay,' Christopher said to Kitty. Demonstrating his familiarity with the room and its routines, he found three clean glasses and poured brandy from the bottle he had brought with him. This was a routine too.

'*Stin iya sas,*' he said, making the Greek toast as he lifted his glass to them both.

Olivia fed a CD into the player. It was local music, plangent with strings. Kitty and Christopher had taken the two armchairs close to the fire and she gestured to them to stay where they were. She sat down on the floor with her back against Christopher's knees and he rested his hand on the top of her head. At the same time he drew Kitty's foot on to his lap and held it, and they sat linked, listening to the music and watching the fire.

Rain was driving against the shutters. The village was dark and the lights in Arhea Chorio had gone out hours ago. Waves scoured the shingle crescent of beach and broke against the harbour wall, and wind whipped the remaining tamarisk trees. Inside, the minutes drifted in soft folds with ambivalence interleaved in them.

Christopher didn't look at either woman but Olivia could feel his vacillating susceptibility to both of them. There was her new embellished but denatured face, and there was the different Kitty who smiled more and who had the spark of happiness in her eyes. Instead of one woman who talked to him about Diane Arbus or Frank Auerbach while she dutifully performed her tasks, there were now two lounging against him, and those women changed their faces to become four and those four reflected others, like mirrors, into an erotic infinity.

Nobody moved or spoke. The fire provided safer pictures and they looked into the heart of it instead of at each other. The sound that broke in on them was a scream.

Olivia leapt to her feet.

'Theo,' she said.

She ran up the stairs and into their bedroom. Theo was sitting upright in his bed and she scooped him up from the tangle of covers and held him. He buried his hot face against her neck and she rocked him and stroked his head and murmured motherly automatic words: 'It's all right, I'm here, you're safe.' He had been having one of his nightmares. He was only frightened, not ill or hurt. The screams slowly subsided into sobs.

Georgi had woken too and Olivia stooped awkwardly in the darkness to reassure him.

'Theo had a bad dream, that's all. Go back to sleep.'

At the sound of her voice and the touch of her hand he settled back under the covers.

Then, with Theo held on her hip as she used to carry him when he was a baby, she made her way downstairs. She would sit by the fire and soothe him out of his terrors so Georgi would not be disturbed any more. Kitty and Christopher were still sitting in their places but Kitty had withdrawn her foot.

Theo lifted his flushed face from his mother's neck and blinked in the sudden light. Then he craned his head round to look at Olivia. There was a second's silence while he sucked breath into his lungs and then he loosed a scream straight into her face. His body went rigid and he twisted violently in her grip. Kitty and Christopher jumped up and Theo stored over Olivia's shoulder at Kitty. At once he stretched his arms imploringly to her and kicked wildly to get out of Olivia's grasp.

His mother couldn't hold him. Kitty reached and wrapped

her arms round him to stop him falling. She rubbed her cheek against his head and smoothed his heaving back and tried to whisper the right words.

Olivia was left standing with her hands empty and outstretched. Her mouth tried to shape dismay at the child's recoil from her and then her fingers flew up to cover it. Understanding dawned as she felt the forgotten mask.

'It's my face, it's the bloody paint,' Olivia cried.

She ran across the kitchen to the sink and cupped her hands under a plume of cold water. With Theo still wordlessly screaming and Kitty trying to calm him, she splashed her eyes and cheeks, and then scrubbed at them with a towel. The first result was a grotesque circle of black round her eyes draining down to her cheeks and a mouth that looked like a stab wound. Kitty glanced and shook her head, and turned Theo's back so that he couldn't see. He clung to her as if he wanted to climb inside her body.

'Let me,' Christopher said. He took the towel out of Olivia's hands and scrubbed at her skin. She pressed her lips and eyelids closed and let him.

'That's better,' he told her at last. Her skin burned from the rubbing and the towel's rough texture.

'Look at me now, Theo. It was a game, it was silly. Look. Just face-painting.'

Reluctantly he lifted his face from Kitty's shoulder. He was shuddering and gasping with fear and shock but he saw that she was his mother again. He stretched out one hand to her and she gently met it with her own. At once his grip tightened on her.

'I'm sorry,' she whispered. 'Mummy was silly.'

He reached towards her, whimpering, and she lifted him out of Kitty's grasp. Now Kitty stood with her arms hanging at her sides. Olivia sat down in the armchair and closed herself around the child.

'I want Pappy,' he sniffled.

'He's gone to town with Mella, you remember? He might bring surprises for you and Georgi.'

It was plain that there was no one else in the room for her now but Theo. Kitty and Christopher stood in silence for a moment, then edged towards the door. Olivia nodded as they murmured goodnight and smiled briefly at them over Theo's head. His thumb had found its way into his mouth.

It was cold outside, but the rain had stopped.

'What was all that about?' Christopher asked. He shoved his hank of hair aside as he spoke, as if to leave his own face unequivocally exposed.

'Just making faces,' Kitty answered. She was looking away from him, peering into the dark.

'It scared Theo. I thought it was pretty disconcerting myself.'

'Why? It wasn't meant to.'

'You both looked different. Quite unlike yourselves. More like each other. I didn't know which one of you was real.'

Kitty said, 'Faces don't mean anything. You can change them. It's what you are this minute that matters, that's what's real. And what you want to be.'

Christopher shivered and stuck his hands in his coat pockets. 'It's too cold out here for deep talk. Do you want to come and have another drink?'

She shook her head. 'Thanks. Not now.' She came a step closer, bent her head a little and kissed him on the cheek. 'Some other time. Goodnight.'

'Goodnight,' he said, watching her walk away.

I can't forget his childish scent. The heat and weight of his body clinging to me and the wet of tears and snot soaking my neck. For a single minute I knew exactly what it feels like to be a mother. I could feel the urgency and the fierceness and the animal determination that no harm should come to him. And there was a pain like a birth pang afterwards when Olivia took him out of my arms.

If I could have *been* her then, when she sat down with him by the fire, I would gladly have leapt into her being.

Standing here in my cold white room, I imagine what my mother must have felt. I have tried this a hundred, probably a thousand times before, but tonight I understand that I have never even come close to knowing it for sure.

ELEVEN

Meroula told me that if the weather is fine for the feast of Aghios Pandelios, the island's patron saint, a peaceful and prosperous year is certain to follow.

Today is the feast day and it is perfect – as soon as I open the shutters of my room I can see that the early morning sky is an unbroken bowl of porcelain-blue. This is what happens on Halemni when the rain stops and the wind blows itself out. The clouds break up and drift away to settle on the horizon in pink and silver turrets, while the sky shimmers with the illusion of heat and the sea reflects it in a sheet of intense cobalt rippled with navy-blue. Under the brilliant sun the shadows in the clefts of hillside deepen to purple and slate-blue, and the exposed slopes reveal a hundred different tones of sand and sepia. There is just enough warmth in the sunlight to draw the scent of sage and thyme into the air. In this Aegean landscape of water and rock and shrub, where lush greenery plays no part, it is hard to believe that it is not midsummer. In fact, we are already into December and I have lived on Halemni for two months.

This is an important day. Not only will there be the feast,

the biggest celebration in the island's calendar, but Olivia's brother Max is due to arrive on the ferry from Athens.

Olivia has been counting the hours – she told me so, but she also said that she is anxious to find out why Max is coming here without his family.

'I hate the idea of him having problems, maybe being unhappy. I love him and he lives so far away. If I could see him every day or even every week I'd have a better idea and I could do more to help.'

I listen carefully, containing my feelings. Of all the things I envy Olivia for, the existence of her brother and her closeness to him is almost the first.

'And he must feel the same about you,' I say.

'Yes. Yes, I know he does.'

I want to meet Max, but I feel my jealousy of Olivia like a rock under the surface of deceptively calm water. I shall have to navigate my way around it. And I am also apprehensive that the arrival of another person will unbalance the calm pattern of life here. I have been happy for these past weeks and I am afraid of change.

As soon as they see by my opened shutters that I am awake, there is a pattering of hands on the door of the studio. Theo and Georgi have taken to running across from the potter's house to see me each morning before they set off for school.

I open the door to them and they tumble in. Even in the few weeks that I have lived on Halemni I have noticed a change in them. At the beginning they seemed barely distinguishable, except by size. They were little children from whom I needed to turn away because in looking at them I risked memories of Marcus and longings for my own barely formed babies. But now this is changing.

Georgi seems to grow taller every day. He is becoming more thoughtful, more observant as the consequences of what he does and says become apparent to him. Two or three times I have noticed him hesitating as he works something out, with his bottom lip drawn between his teeth. His movements are more controlled and his voice has grown quieter.

Theo is still a baby. His spread-out hands look like starfish and there are dimples over the knuckles. His legs are plump, not skinny and elongated like Georgi's. He cries easily, whenever he is thwarted or disappointed, but the tears dry quickly. He smiles and chatters, and is eager to be cuddled. I love the feel of him in my arms, but I value Georgi's more measured approval. And the younger still follows the older's lead. Georgi has decided that I am a good thing, so Theo's allegiance is given almost automatically.

'Max is coming today,' Georgi reminds me.

'That's right. On the big ferry, isn't it?'

'Because it's Tuesday, yes.'

The big ferry calls on its round trip only once a week, an eighteen-hour outward journey from Piraeus, and in wintertime only if the weather permits. Like everyone else on Halemni I chart the weeks by the ferry timetables – although unlike everyone else I never board one, even to visit Halemni's closest island neighbours. I feel superstitious about it. If I leave this place it might not be so easy to get back again.

'He'll be coming to the feast too, I expect,' Georgi says and I nod.

'I wouldn't want to miss it if I was him.'

There is going to be a service in the half-ruined church of Saint Pandelios up in the old village, as there is every year, Xan tells me. Usually the party that follows takes place down at the coast but this year the partial reoccupation of the old houses has triggered the idea of holding the celebration in the Arhea Chorio square up the hill, where it always used to happen. Xan and Panagiotis and the other village men all agreed that this would be appropriate, to celebrate in the old way after the wave's devastation. The eye of still, warm weather that has opened in the face of winter is taken as a sign of divine approval.

But Theo has already lost interest in this discussion. 'Where is he today?' he clamours.

'That's for me to know and for you to find out.'

Two or three weeks ago I was dusting shelves in the shop and among Helen's haberdashery stocks I found a little bag of tiny soft toys. One of them was a grey felt mouse with ears lined with scraps of pink felt, black bead eyes and whiskers of stiff nylon thread. I held it up by the tail, laughing, and she pretended to flinch from it with her hands crossed over her mouth.

It happened that it was pay day. Later, when she handed me the brown envelope of folded thousand-drachma notes I felt a soft bulge inside it. It was the mouse. My shriek of pretend horror and our laughter afterwards brought Panagiotis running to see what was going on.

This new possession was instantly noticeable in my bare room. The boys seized it on the first morning and named it Squeak.

'Because he doesn't,' Georgi explained seriously.

On the second morning they demanded to know where the mouse had gone.

'He's hiding,' I told them. In fact, he was in the pocket of the flannel trousers, which were now so tight across my hips that he made an obvious bulge. It was Theo who spotted it first.

Hunt the mouse is now our regular game. Every night I find a new place – not an easy task in this small and sparsely furnished space – and when the morning comes they run around the room shouting Squeak, Squeak, until they find it. Today the door on to the little terrace stands open to the sun and I have balanced the mouse on the outer catch of the shutter. They aren't used to looking outside and they look under my saucepan and in my cup and in the toe of my shoe, all places I have already used, while I tell them no, freezing, getting warmer, and finally hot, hot, scalding. Today it is Georgi who finds the mouse. Their score is about even, luckily for me.

'It's time for school now,' I tell them.

'Only half a day, half a day.'

It's true. For the Saint's day, the school and the shops and even the men's kafeneion will all close at midday. Everyone on the island will go to the church up the hill, including me. I have stopped worrying that one of the three fishermen might recognise me and ask questions that I can't answer. I am Kitty now, and Kitty only began to exist when I set foot on Halemni. The old Cary, even the ghost of her who came across in the boat with Andreas, has simply been wiped away.

I hold the door open for the boys. Olivia is coming across from the house.

'I found him today,' Georgi calls to her.

Olivia has dark smudges under her eyes, as if she sleeps badly, and she looks to me as if she has lost a little weight. But her new haircut suits her, and so do the arched brows that I shaped for her. And I notice that she is wearing a slick of mascara. Maybe this is what gives her eyes the heavy look.

'Time for school,' she repeats.

'Shall I?'

I am going down to open up the shop – eight thirty is plenty early enough to be there in sleepy winter – and I could easily walk the little distance beyond to leave the boys at the school door.

'No, thank you,' Olivia says. 'I'll go down with them myself. I need to see Dimitria about the *melijanes*, aubergines, for tonight.'

218

I make the offer most mornings. At first she regularly accepted but nowadays she always refuses.

At one o'clock I am home again. The shop has been busy all morning with women coming in for last-minute needs for the feast. Helen can do little more these days than sit and knit with the tiny lemon or white garment balanced on top of her bulge. In the last two weeks her bulk seems almost to have doubled.

I make myself coffee and a plate of tinned tuna and beans, and carry the food out on to my little terrace. I sit on the stone flags with my back to the wall and the sun on my face, eating and enjoying the distant view of the beach and the sea. Contentment rests inside me like a warm pebble. I don't have to review the past any longer, or revise myself within the context of it. I can bask empty-minded in the sun, live from day to day, play hunt the mouse with the children. It seems, now, that it is no major achievement to be as happy as Olivia is. Set free from history, in this beautiful place, it is only natural.

I can hear a truck, probably Panagiotis's, passing down the street. There is a rustle in the air, not so much the sound of people moving as the buzz of expectation. The ferry is due and it is a holiday. There will be a crowd out on the harbour wall waiting to meet it.

Almost against my will, I find that I am drawn towards the harbour too. I leave my terrace and walk slowly down the hill. Most of the flood damage has been restored now, although some of the houses that lie empty through the winter are only temporarily boarded up. The washing lines are back and the occasional chair beside a whitened step, and the cats pursue their shadowy business beneath them. There are no geraniums or marigolds in painted tin cans yet, though. These will have to wait for the spring.

Just as I expected, there are several knots of people waiting on the harbour. The kafeneion is closed but a group of men is lounging outside under the metal framework of the summer awning. I can see Xan smoking a cigarette and talking, and Yannis's bear-like frame. I scan the groups for Olivia and then I notice her standing a little apart, facing the sea. She rocks on the balls of her feet, backwards and forwards, watching for the ship that will bring Max.

Theo and Georgi are here too, of course. They run around the vehicles that are waiting to load and unload provisions from the ferry. I stay in the background, keeping to the shadow of the port buildings, thinking like one of the skinny smoke-coloured cats that I will only watch and not intrude.

The ferry is late, but this is not exactly unusual. The schedules are wonderfully elastic. Olivia walks a short distance along the jetty, then back again, but she never takes her eyes off the point where the ship will round the headland. Xan is absorbed in his conversation with the men and the boys begin to be bored with the wait. They climb up the wheel arches of one of the trucks and are shooed off again, then clamber up on to a lowered tailgate and jump off it, clamber and jump. When this palls they are drawn to a pile of pallets and fish crates behind the line of cars. As I watch, Georgi stacks two crates one on top of the other and Theo hauls one more towards the structure. Two other children, Michaelis's son and daughter, I think, run to join in the game.

The corner of my eye catches some movement out beyond the rocks to the west. As soon as I have seen it I register that it is the ship's funnel. A second later the prow comes into view and the ship glides into Halemni bay. I am always surprised by the size of these ferries, their massive blue-and-white superstructure towering over the flat sea and spreading a fan of white water in their wake. A flock of gulls dips behind, and I can hear their cries over the thrum of engines and trucks reversing, and voices calling instructions.

Once the ferry is inside the bay it has to perform a complicated reversing manoeuvre so that it approaches the last few
yards to the mooring stern first. It looks too big, out of scale
compared with the tiny harbour and the people waiting. As
always, I watch in admiration as the massive hull swings in
a circle and the engines go into reverse thrust to bring it up
exactly in line with the massive, chain-scarred bollards on
the quay. The stern door is already open by a chink and
lowering to form a bridge between ship and harbour wall.

Olivia is dancing up and down, waving her arms in an
exuberant double arc. Peering up and shading my eyes against
the southerly sun, I can just see a man on the stern deck,
leaning over the rail to wave back at her. Then he turns and
hurries away, presumably to descend to the stern door. Xan
has thrown aside his cigarette butt and is strolling towards
the quay edge. As I watch, a rope coils through the air from
the ship's side and is expertly caught. There is a roar of
engines and a powerful smell of diesel fuel. Everyone is
moving towards the ferry door as it opens like a trap.

Something makes me turn aside.

I see a rickety structure of pallets and wooden crates,
perhaps six feet high, half hidden by one of the trucks. They
have been piled up to make a set of crazy steps and at the
top there is an upturned box like a lookout post. Wooden
corners stick out at threatening angles. A child is clambering
up the steps and the weight of him makes the tower sway.
Two more children, one of them Georgi, are crammed into
the box itself.

Standing in the lee of the tower, with his thumb in his
mouth and all unawares because his attention is on the ferry
as it docks, is Theo. The vessel's stern door is open to make
a bridge.

There is a warning cry in my ears.

I am already running, the cry trailing thinly out of my mouth.

My eyes are locked on Theo but elsewhere, inside my skull, there are other pictures. They show up in a split-second flash, lurid as lightning. I can see Jim, in his pool bar, and Manolis's splintered kiosk in the wave-wrecked square. I can also see an English garden heavy with the scent of grass and roses, and mild sunshine in my eyes.

Then there is a tumbling arc of sky and branches, and the strange sight of my feet whirling above me in red sunburst sandals.

I can hear a cry of warning, my mother's voice with a raw note I have never heard in it before, already too late.

Georgi and the other children are shouting, eager-to-be-scared shouts with cadences of exciting fear in them. They know their tower is tottering but they have childhood's certainty of immortality. Theo's thumb slowly drops from his mouth.

I plunge at him, snatch him up and whirl him out of the jagged shadow. The children whoop in Greek. Theo's head jerks up and smashes into my jaw, pain stabs my tongue, but I have got him safe. The crates make a wild last see-saw and then topple sideways. There is a crash and three children plunge in a jumble of planks and limbs. Theo is in my arms but I am frozen with fear for the other three. My tongue hurts as if it has been stabbed.

Rather than hearing or seeing anyone, I feel a movement of the air beside us.

'What's all this, mate?'

A man has come up behind me. Theo ducks again, rubbing his head where it cracked into my chin and I twist my face instinctively to avoid another blow. I can sense too, rather than see, that three children have crawled or rolled out from under the fallen crates. They are all laughing and shouting with the thrill of their escapade. I am suddenly gasping with relief while my eyes simultaneously water from the agony in my mouth.

'Don't you know your Uncle Max?'

I look now. There is a man with the afternoon sun throwing his shadow towards me. Xan and Olivia are on either side of him and I blink, squeezing out more tears of pain, because for a confusing second I think he is Andreas. My mouth opens and a small river of blood gushes down my chin.

'Holy shit,' the man says.

Olivia gives a little scream at the sight of me.

'Uncle Max, Uncle Max.' Georgi is dancing around the man's legs. Xan takes Theo away from me and Olivia and the man seize one of my arms apiece. He is not Andreas, of course.

'What happened?' he asks.

Olivia dabs at my chin with a handkerchief and I weakly shake my head.

'Bih my hongue.'

'Let's have a look.' He peers at the carnage in my mouth. 'Holy shit,' he murmurs again. 'I think you'll live, but it's going to be a close call.'

I feel faint and sick. Not from the bitten tongue, but from the shock of seeing the tower fall. There is a circle of people around us now. Stumbling a little, I push my way through and find another fish crate. I sit down and let my head hang, but that sets off another shrill of pain and a further rush of blood. Olivia's brother and Xan and Olivia pass children and handkerchiefs and advice from one to the other.

'Kitty,' Theo wails.

'Horry,' I say to them all, for ruining the welcome party.

'Don't talk now.' Max gives me a folded white handkerchief, blamelessly clean. 'Put this over the bite and press. Tongues bleed a lot and hurt like hell, but it isn't nearly as

223

bad as you think. I didn't mean to scare you, I was just trying to be funny. I'm not always such a fool.'

I try to say 'It's not that', but I can't manage it because I have a mouth full of handkerchief and blood. Georgi and Theo have been reassured that I am not badly hurt in spite of all the gore and the crowd of onlookers breaks up as the unloading and reloading of the ferry goods catches their attention.

Olivia squats down beside me and rubs my hands.

'Thanks for grabbing Theo. Did you think they were going to fall on top of him?'

The truth is so much more than that, I can't keep the look of it out of my eyes even though I try to. She stares into mine for an instant and through her hands I feel a jolt of dismay that's followed by a little galvanising current of fear.

I don't want her to be afraid of me.

I'm not afraid of myself any more, because I have walked away from history and its tentacles. I am here on this sunny quayside with the waves splashing the harbour wall and Theo's round eyes watching me, and there is the tug of potential happiness in my chest.

No. It is not potential, that would be to diminish it. It *is*.

Olivia and I are still looking at each other. I can feel the others, two men and two little boys, way out on the periphery.

I nod my head and then expand the gesture into a shrug.

'Mmhm. Hupid. Hen I bih myself.' A smile is just about within my capacity.

Olivia stands up, relieved, and briefly draws my head against her hip, as affectionately as if I were one of her boys.

'Poor you. It must really hurt. Let's go on home, if you are all right. Max?'

He has two canvas holdalls. He hoists one on his shoulder, like a sailor, and picks up the other. Xan carries Theo on his back, and Georgi comes between Olivia and me, taking both our hands. With my free hand I hold the handkerchief in place so it doesn't chafe the wound in my tongue and we make our way up the street in procession.

'Great to be back. That was quite a welcome,' Max calls over his unweighted shoulder. He has a wide smile and the ends of his sentences finish with an antipodean up-note. Olivia and I let Georgi swing between us, and he chants 'one, two, *threeee*'.

The old church is lit with dozens of candles and the yolk of light partly conceals the fact that the shell of the building is cracked and broken. The whole population of Halemni is gathered inside the stone walls. I can even see the reclusive egg man. The old people have chairs, rickety wooden ones or the folding beach kind, others have made benches from weathered planks and a couple of stones. Helen has a chair, of course. I can't imagine how she managed the walk up here. The rest of us sit on the ruined mosaic floor or stand, waiting.

There is no talking, or even whispering. Even the children are silent.

I stand right at the back, behind the Georgiadises and Max. At this end the roof is almost entirely gone except for a couple of beams bisecting the sky. It is nearly six o'clock and the light has faded.

The cracked bell peals six times and on the sixth peal there is the sound of slow steps on the stones. I turn my head and watch as two boys pace by with a rectangular shape swathed in fabric borne between them. Behind them comes the Halemni priest in his black robes. He swings a brass censer and thick clouds of incense drift past our heads. Behind him come two more priests, visitors for the occasion from nearby islands. When they reach the semicircular stone apse end under the still intact dome, the boys lift the draped object on to a rough stone altar and stand back. The priest hands one of them his censer and lifts away the covering.

I can easily see over the heads in front of me. The icon is of the Saint himself. He has a long, flat face with oval heavy-lidded eyes that stare impassively out at the people. Behind his head are the four branches of a cross, the dull gold paint catching the candlelight.

There is a sonorous blessing, for which we all kneel, row upon row of us, and the incense drifts again over our bent heads. Then the three priests begin a plainchant under Saint Pandelios's gaze. The music makes fingers seem to walk down my spine.

When the singing finally stops there is more movement at the back of the church and the sound of footsteps again. Four of the island's young men, hardly more than boys, come forward. Each of them is carrying a wicker basket in his arms and different smells compete now with the thick waft of incense. There is a glossy heap of the new season's olives, a silver glitter of fish topped with a spiny crown of sea urchins, a mound of lemons and some loaves of bread. The baskets are laid on the stone table in front of the Saint and the priest lifts each one in turn, holding it up to the icon and then to the people.

After the fourth basket has been presented, the priest draws himself up and spreads his arms wide. A little old man sitting to the side of the church lifts a kind of violin – but this is an odd, old instrument with only three strings, balanced on his thigh instead of tucked under his chin – and draws out a chord. There are tiny bells on his bow, and their sweet tinkle is a signal. The priest's arms swing up in a great lifting gesture and we surge to our feet. There is a collective drawing-in of breath that seems to fill even my unprepared lungs, and then a great shout of singing. The flames of the candles flicker with the gust of air from so many opened mouths.

To my surprise, what emerges is a rollicking song with a

shouted chorus that is taken up with clapping, and tapping of hand drums and the chiming notes of a mandolin as further accompaniment. I don't know the words, of course. And even if I did I wouldn't be able to sing because my tongue is too swollen and painful to do anything but be allowed to lie in the trough of my mouth and try to recover itself. But I do clap and stamp like everyone else. It is a warm night for December, but even so it is chilly to be standing still for a long time in the clammy stone shell of the old church. The rhythm brings the blood back into my fingers and toes.

We are celebrating the year's fruits, from the earth and the sea. Each verse belongs to one of the baskets and the olives, the fish, the fruit and the bread are held up again in turn as the singing and stamping grows louder.

The harvest song ends with a loud chord and a shout of exultation. A forest of arms waves in front of me, blurring the candles and making it look as if two hundred hands are reaching out to touch Saint Pandelios. The four youths pick up their baskets once more and process back through the church, followed by the priests, and then we all crowd outside in their wake, with the music and the pealing of the old, cracked bell to accompany us. The Saint is left to continue his watch over the empty church.

It is fully dark now although there is the suggestion of white light just misting the sky, maybe from the invisible moon or the sea's reflection. I follow on behind Olivia and the others in a tide of bobbing heads. Xan and Max have a child apiece on their shoulders. Someone bumps against me and I look down to see Meroula.

'Is good, eh?'

I can't do much more than nod and smile, but that seems enough.

'Even this year, with the wave and poor Manolis, we have

227

many things to give thanks for. Halemni is good place.'

Indeed, I think. Better than good. There was immaculate logic in Andreas's bringing me here, although it is a weird variety that follows no rules I have ever heard of or even imagined.

We are in the old square now. Village industry has cleared the drifts of dead leaves and piled the fallen stones to one side. In the middle of the cobbled space a huge bonfire of logs has been lit and allowed to burn down to a crimson core that sends out intense and welcome heat. Over the fire a kid is roasting on a spit. Fat drips from the haunches and makes the fire leap with yellow and blue flags. There are other animals already cooked, I know, enough to feed us all and plenty more, but this one is the symbol, like the baskets of olives and the rest that are now placed in the middle of a long, laden table against the south wall. We have all done our share of carrying food up to the old square this evening.

'Feast time,' a familiar voice says at my shoulder and I look round to see Christopher Cruickshank. 'I've never been here at Saint's day before. I'm glad not to miss it for once.'

Since the night of Olivia's face-painting, talk of Christopher's possible departure date for England has stopped altogether. It seems accepted now in this unusual season that he is here to stay.

'How's the tongue?'

There are two deep gouges in the tip, on one side so deep that a slice of tissue is almost severed. Max examined the damage back at the potter's house and declared that it would heal without a stitch. This is just as well, since the only emergency stitching on Halemni is done by Anna Efemia, the island's nurse-midwife. There was a doctor but he married a girl from the next island and now lives there with her during the winter. He visits Halemni twice a week for surgeries, but otherwise he is almost half an hour's fast boat ride away.

'You a Conor?' I asked Max, not very graciously because I was in so much pain.

'Nah. Engineer. Did a course in bush first aid, though.'

'Oh goo.'

I nod in answer to Christopher's question. Talking is just too much this evening. So is eating. The only nourishment I am going to be able to manage for the next day or so is liquids, taken via a straw. Olivia has found a pack of fluorescent pink ones at the back of a cupboard and I have a couple ranged in the top pocket of my pea-coat, like biros in the school swot's jacket. Christopher smiles at me and puts his arm briefly round my shoulder. I see that Olivia has turned to look at us.

Two or three of the old people who evacuated themselves from Megalo Chorio have descended to sea level again, but most of them are still here. There are candles burning in the windows of Kyria Elena's house, and Yannis senior's, and the doors stand hospitably open. Chairs are set out at the doorsteps.

Meroula is on my other side again.

'It looks like the old days,' she murmurs. The lines of her heavy face are softened with nostalgia. Even the iron-grey ridges of her hair look looser. 'When I was married first, this was the way we had our Saint's Day. Always, year after year, until too many people had left and gone down the hill. Maybe, you know, this means some of the old ways will come back.'

Max pushes back through the crowd around the table and finds us. He is holding up two cups and gives a little bow.

'Here you are, ladies. A drink for you.'

Meroula accepts hers and thanks him, *efharistó*. I take mine with considerable eagerness. I want a drink very badly. I dip the straw into it and suck. I have been expecting wine,

229

but this is fiery raki. The spirit stings my tongue so viciously that I cough and raki dribbles down my chin, but an equivalent amount somehow goes down my throat. The alcohol warms the pit of my stomach.

There is a wonderful smell of roasting meat and oil and herbs. I am almost drooling with hunger, and now that I am used to letting myself eat whatever I want I can hardly bear the thought of not being able to satisfy my appetite. I take another suck of raki instead and wander at random through the crowd with the cup and straw held close against my chest. The movement of the crowd towards the tables of food has separated me from Max and Meroula. There seem to be many more people pressed together here in the square, eating and drinking and laughing, than the total of Halemni's sparse population. My face is familiar to many of them now, after my weeks of work in the shop, and there are murmured greetings, *Kali spera, yia sou, Kyria Kitty* ...

The raki goes down well, once you get used to it. And it warms the parts of you that aren't exposed to the fire. I finish the cup, greedily slurping up the last drops through my pink straw.

I am hungry for more than food and drink.

I want to submerge myself in all this. I want to be more and more part of Halemni, swallowed up and bound in here with my heart muscle. The fact that I am in pain, that I am now mute as well as an interloper, somehow intensifies the longing. If I could press myself against the stones, if I could pull all these people close and meld myself with them, then I would do it.

The next person I see is Olivia, towering over a row of Meroula's friends. She becomes the focus of my desire to obliterate myself. I glide closer to her, hold out my arms, and our shoulders and cheeks connect in a lopsided embrace. The crowd surges and briefly locks us together and the scent and shape of her is intensely familiar. I grope for the source of this familiarity but I am already tipsy from the alcohol sluicing in my empty stomach. I am dizzy, too, with the smell of lemons and baking bread, roasting kid and sweet olives. But Olivia detaches herself when the crowd shifts and I can't even interpret her expression. There are only the firelight and candles and torches to see by.

'You need some soup or something,' she says, as if I am Georgi or Theo. 'We should have thought to bring it.'

'Thih ih okay.' I show her the paper cup.

'Painkiller,' she says and I can't see a smile.

I want to say, *I don't need any*, but my mouth is too sore.

There is a great quantity of food, but it quickly disappears. The bread and the glistening new olives all vanish, and the sea urchins are cracked open and their tangy, iodine interiors scooped out. The sight of them makes my mouth water and I think of Andreas, and work my way round the loop of questions about him that is already too familiar to offer any hope of an answer. Panagiotis has fried the other fish in a pan over the red-hot fire, and the lemons are sliced and squeezed over the crisp result. I manage to capture a single lemon for myself, and I sniff the thick rind and then scrape it with my thumbnail to release the oily citrus scent. My mouth is still watering and I feel so hungry that I am almost floating.

After the eating comes the music. The players group themselves in the corner and begin with the slow, mournful love songs and sailors' laments that all the Halemniots seem to love. Old men and women and children listen, swaying a little to the rhythm and joining in the choruses. The fire has burned low but Xan and two other men drag more wood across the cobbles and stoke it up once more. As the flames crackle and leap upwards, the music livens up. Two violas and a flute have joined the *lyra* and the mandolin, and there is a whole line of drums and tambourines. A circle of people

231

at random, men and women and children, link hands around the fire and dance, and at once another circle forms around them and moves in the opposite direction.

At first I linger on the margin, watching. But then someone snatches my hand and draws me into the chain. I look sideways and see Christopher again. He links his fingers in mine and squeezes, and we are moving with the dance. The circle moves clockwise, counterclockwise, clockwise again. We're going faster now as the music begins to race. The fire flickers between the legs and arms of the two sets of dancers and the alternating glow and shadow is hypnotic. I see suddenly that there is yet another ring of dancers enclosing ours, this one all children. There must be twenty or thirty or maybe even more of them, from Theo's age to early teens, with the red burnish of firelight on their faces. I knew I was right, I think. There are more children than Olivia counted up. The crowd beyond the circles seems to have swelled too: I have the impression of hundreds of faces all looking inwards.

My tongue and jaw pain sharply from the jolting dance but I can't stop or pull away. Christopher is holding on to me too tightly. On my other side, I now see, is Yannis, capering like a drunken bear.

Then, across the chains of dancers and the fireglow and on the other side of the square beyond the silent onlookers, I catch sight of something.

Max is standing in the lit-up doorway of Kyria Elena's house. His head is turned a little to one side so that I see his profile. He looks like Olivia, of course.

But he is younger and his face is set in meditative lines that makes me suddenly want to look closer, to put my hands to his cheeks and turn his head so that his eyes meet mine. A jolt passes through me, like electricity flowing into my fingertips and escaping through the soles of my feet.

Of course, I think. So that is it.

The words ring in my head. Not as clearly as those on the headland – *Now you know* – because the music tries to drown them out. But still, I hear.

Max is familiar also in some way that I can't identify. Maybe because of Olivia. Or maybe it is the other way round, I seem to recognise Olivia because it is really Max I know so well, at some level much deeper than where we have both been until now and whether our physical paths have crossed or not ...

So that is it.

I'm breathless from dancing and the pain in my mouth is almost unbearable. I wonder if I'm drunk although I can only remember downing the one paper cup of raki. I try to pull my fingers away from Christopher and Yannis, and I see them both grinning and shaking their heads at me, looking like Hallowe'en lanterns in the lurid red light.

My legs are going to buckle underneath me unless we can stop soon.

With a crash and a long-drawn chord, the music does finish. The circles judder and slow down, and then snap apart like broken bead necklaces. I pull my hands back to my sides and walk slowly through the knots of people. There aren't as many as there seemed to be from the thick of the dance. It's colder now, and there are shawls and coats and hats appearing as everyone gets ready to leave. Aghios Pandelion's festival is over for another year.

Max has moved away from Kyria Elena's doorway. He is standing in the shadows to one side of it, waiting. And then, when I reach him, we stand looking at each other, our eyes level, our hands almost touching. I want to talk, but I can't say a word.

Instead he reaches up and just touches my lip, at the point where my gashed tongue lies inside the barricade of teeth.

'Poor mouth,' he whispers.

I do raise my hands and put the palms flat to his cheek-bones, and hold his face so that he can't look away. I know, at my back, that Xan and Christopher Cruickshank and Olivia are all eyes. The minute seems to last many minutes and then I pull my hands back again.

'I can't kiss you now,' Max says, as though we have been discussing this. And in a sense we have, without knowing it, ever since he stepped off the ferry and I opened my mouth and a river of blood ran out of it. 'But I will.'

It is strange to be mute when there is so much to say.

A child runs full tilt into my legs. 'Kitty, Kitty! I was dancing.'

'Nh,' I tell Theo, intending to convey *Yes, I saw you with all the other children*, although I hadn't seen him, in fact. He must have been there, somewhere, in the midst of them.

'Come on, Theo and Georgi. It's time to go home now.' Olivia's voice is chipped with ice.

I turn round and I see that the square is busy with people scooping litter into rubbish bags, piling dishes and trays ready for the trek back to Megalo Chorio. Helen and Panagiotis move slowly past, his arm so tight and protective around her that he is almost carrying her. She gives me her shy smile.

I move to the trestle tables and gather a random armful of dishes and food boxes to make a load. Max takes up a black plastic bin liner filled with debris and we bump into each other as we back away, linked by amusement at this mundane business as well as our amazement at what has just happened. We follow the procession of islanders out of the square. I can see Olivia's fair head and Xan's dark one ahead of us. The boys must be with them.

Even the strange whitish glow has now faded out of the sky and the darkness is intense. The stone steps through the ruined houses are steep and uneven, and the dozens of feet walking downhill make a steady clatter. I can't see where I am going except by watching the head of the woman in front. I recognise her now as Anna Efemia, the island's nurse. There is a surge of movement from behind, someone coming down the steps too fast, and the surge passes on down the line like a ripple on a lake. With my arms full I almost stumble, but manage to steady myself and just about keep my balance. I walk on more slowly, peering ahead to work out where to put my feet.

As we make our way down the zigzag bends the groups find their own pace and the column stretches and thins out. It is like being in some devotional frieze, with worshippers bringing offerings for the deity. I find myself walking alone now, although I know that Max is somewhere close behind me. A freshening wind off the sea touches my face with cold air and I catch the smell of rain. The good weather eye must be closing again.

We are on the last steep rocky section before the track broadens and runs gently downhill to the slope at the back of the potter's house. I am looking at the sprawl of the village and the lights showing in a few of the windows when there is a sudden sharp cry from below me and a sliding rush over the stones followed by the sound of breaking crockery. Someone has fallen.

A minute or two later I round the next bend and see a mound of smashed plates, a group of people gathered round and Olivia sitting in the middle of them. Anna Efemia the nurse is already kneeling alongside. I put my own load down at the side of the path and ease my way into the group. Someone has produced a torch and shines it on her. Olivia looks up at me and as the nurse leans over it I can see a nasty jagged cut on the soft inner skin of her bare arm, running from the crook halfway down to the wrist. Black seams of blood trickle down to her elbow. The palm of her hand is badly grazed.

'We haven't had such a good day, you and I, have we?'

235

she says, trying to hide the curl of pain in her voice. 'This is what you get for rolling your sleeves up.'

'Mummy fell down,' Theo tells me.

Anna Efemia speaks briskly in Greek. A wad of kitchen paper is produced from someone's basket and the nurse presses it over the cut while Xan holds Olivia's other hand.

I sense rather than see Max at my shoulder and his sister scanning the ring of faces for his.

'Quite a day,' he says softly. 'Are you all right?'

'I'm okay.' Olivia seems to lose patience with the business of being attended to. She stretches and flexes her fingers and then winces. 'It's only a graze. Thanks, Anna. Let's go on home. God, look at the plates.'

Xan and Max help her to her feet, with a flood of Greek warnings and instructions from Anna Efemia. They retrieve their own loads and leave the shards of broken crockery where they lie, and the boys bob anxiously in their wake as they move slowly on down the hill.

Christopher Cruickshank now walks beside me. His hair falls forward on this side to hide his face, although there isn't enough light for me to be able to see his expression anyway. There are questions spiking the air but I deliberately block them, with my shoulder and my silence.

I just want to get back to my bare little studio room, to think.

I can see Olivia's gash too vividly in my mind's eye. My own arm stings and throbs as if the damage is mine.

And my tongue feels like one huge wound.

TWELVE

Olivia and I are washing up. Max and Xan have gone down to the bar together and the boys are asleep. It's dark outside and when I look out of the window all I can see is the room reflected back at me.

Olivia hands me a dripping plate and I dry it with smooth circular strokes. We haven't been talking as we work but now she abruptly breaks the silence.

'You like him, don't you?'

'Yes.' We both know who we are talking about and we both know that a warning is being sounded.

For a week, ever since the feast, Olivia has been watching Max and me. We have never been alone together – Olivia has almost always been there and, if not, we have been with Xan and the boys and Christopher, or with Yannis and Stefania or Panagiotis. (I understand that this is an unusual winter, after the wave. Olivia says people have a greater need to be together and so they sit in each other's houses smoking and drinking and making music or telling stories.) Yet I have had the feeling that Max and I are only waiting for our private opportunity. Biding our time. Olivia knows this too and I can feel the tide of her jealousy pulling against us.

Max belongs to her and every time I speak to him, or even look in his direction, I sense her possessiveness. She doesn't want to share her brother's love and attention with anyone. Least of all me.

'We had a long talk,' she says now. 'He and Hattie are going to be all right, he told me. He hasn't left her or anything like that. He's going to go back as soon as he's had this opportunity to take stock.'

'That's good,' I lie.

'I thought I should tell you, you know, just in case you were thinking anything different.'

This is candid, at least. My neck and fingers stiffen defensively. Olivia is still talking. 'I know it must be lonely for you, living here and seeing me with Xan, and Yannis and Stefania. Panagiotis and Helen. I think you know where Christopher's interests lie, as well ...'

I put down another dried plate. I can see our twin reflections in the black glass, our heads turned aside, the lights of the warm room behind us making us two dark masses.

'I understand,' I say quietly.

At the same moment I make the decision that tomorrow morning I will ask Max if he would like to come for a walk with me.

We could go up to the Knights' castle. The highest point of the hill overlooking the bay of Halemni is a sheer cliff with the ruins of the castle perched like a broken tiara on top of the rock face. The old village lies beneath and a little to the left, surrounded by the steps of abandoned terraces.

Max was right. Tongues do heal quickly.

I test the tip of mine against the roof of my mouth and feel numbness in place of pain. The new scar tissue gives it an awkward thickness that blurs the edges of my words, and also takes away the flavour of my food. I still eat, though.

238

Quantity, the sleepy taut pleasure that a full stomach gives, more than compensates for the loss of the sweetest and fullest tastes. All the extra fuel inside me makes me feel strong, while the walking I do has made me fitter than I have ever been in my life. I think I could easily walk all day. Even now, although we have been scrambling for half an hour up this slope of broken rock, I am hardly out of breath.

I want to laugh or sing because I have never felt so alive. It is like losing a layer of skin, or being able to see in an extra dimension. The greys and purples of the rocks and sea and the sepia folds of the earth shimmer with extra intensity, and the smell of salt and wet vegetation is even sharper than usual.

We are alone together now.

When I asked him, Max hesitated. With my new clear sight I could see longing and circumspection pulling in different directions like tiny electrical pulses under his skin. I want to touch the skin, feel the living warmth of it. But I waited calmly for his answer.

'Yes, let's do that,' he said at last.

I can look down from here on to the sunken roof of the old church. The only movement that catches my eye is the goats hopping over fallen stones and the smoke drifting from chimneys around the square.

'Can you climb this?' Max asks me. He is still unsure about coming all this way up here with me and is focusing his anxiety on my physical capabilities.

I look up at the rock, measuring the difficulty.

'Yes, easily.' With my thick tongue it comes out as 'yeth'. 'I want to see the castle.'

'Coming down will be harder, remember.'

'I can do it.'

'I'll go first, then. Put your hands and feet where I put mine.'

The limestone is rough and pitted, hollowed by the weather to make hand and footholds, and it is steep but easy enough to climb. There are minute, fascinating gardens of sedum and lichens growing in the crevices. I follow on Max's heels without thinking about the drop beneath me. When he hauls himself over a low parapet of stone I do likewise, and jump down beside him into the shelter of the castle. We lean against the wall and look around us.

The ancient enclosure is a small area of coarse grass and rock, heaped with rough-hewn stone blocks that have fallen inwards during the castle's five-hundred-year decline into ruin. The landward side is marked by no more than a ragged outline of blocks but I can see that the slope is more gradual here and that there is even the suggestion of a path leading down to the island plain. This would have been the original access to the fortress, but a long and tedious way round for us. We have made the direct assault on the stronghold, the way that invaders come.

Max has turned aside and is resting his arms on the waist-high parapet as he stares out to sea. It is a grey, windy day and my unkempt hair whips into my eyes. Two birds that I guess might be buzzards circle high above the castle.

'Do you know who built it?' he asks.

'The Crusaders. The Knights of St John. They came from Rhodes in the early fourteenth century, occupied and fortified most of the Dodecanese.'

I have been reading the books. I can see the Crusaders with their little ships in the bay, black-faced men storming up here and building their rock fortress. The air smells of smoke and something thick like blood. It makes me cough and turn away to stare out to sea, like Max.

'Is that so?'

He isn't really interested in the history – he is too absorbed in the conflict of here and now. Our arms are almost touching and I feel the small hairs on mine stand up like tiny antennae.

240

'Look,' I point. The ferry is rounding the headland into the bay. It is exactly a week since Max arrived on Halemni, a week since I almost severed my tongue and fell in love for the second time in my life.

'I'm glad we climbed all the way up here,' he says. 'I never bothered, the other times I visited.'

Nobody ever comes to the castle; even Olivia has only been once, with Xan, when she was first on the island. There is, after all, nothing here except a few stones, and history.

Now that Max and I are in this isolated place together, we are about to cross a boundary. I feel easy with this, but all my senses are painfully charged.

While we watch the ferry way below making its complicated reverse manoeuvre on the purl-knit water, Max takes my hand and intertwines our fingers. I find that I have forgotten how to breathe properly and a sweaty glue makes my palm feel like the suction cup tipping the arrow from a child's toy bow-and-arrow set. Marcus had one, I remember: yellow wooden arrows, dark-red rubber cups. You licked the cup before firing the arrow, to make it stick to its target.

'I don't know. I just don't know,' Max is saying under his breath. I can feel the movements of conflict in him now, the flickers of electricity under his skin. My thumb traces circles in the vee of flesh between his thumb and forefinger.

I understand the indecision. In the week that has gone by we have talked, even though Olivia or Xan or one of the others has always been with us. He has told me about Hattie and the two daughters called Ellie and Lucy, aged seven and three. There is the house on the water in the Sydney suburb and a good job and plenty of friends and enough money.

'And?' I prompted him, when he came to this point.

Max said quietly that he loved his wife and his kids, of course he did. He met Hattie when he was travelling the world in his older sister's wake, as restless and adventurous

241

as Olivia but without her single-mindedness. He had married early and settled down, and now Hattie and he were circling around each other, too often looking for each other's faults instead of the good points.

'We just agreed that we should stop arguing and take a break. I arranged some leave and came over here to see Olivia. We've always been close.'

Yes. They fit together, sibling halves, Olivia the dominating older sister who had softened with age, Max the smaller brother who had grown up to meet her. But that matching seems imperfect compared with ours, his and mine. I now think that I know Olivia better and more deeply than our short relationship justifies simply because of the way she reflects her brother.

I look at him while he seems intent on the ferry's arrival. He has his sister's colouring – and so, to an extent, mine too – and her long upper lip and some of her bone structure. But he is made on a finer scale than Olivia, with a narrower face and jaw. He is a little shorter than me, but he has powerful shoulders and hands.

'And me?' I ask in my new measured way.

The hand holding mine suddenly twists me round to face him. He shifts his hips so that I am pinned against the castle wall with my back to the sea. I can see the light through his eyelashes, and the glitter of shaven hair high on his cheekbone.

He is more familiar than my own hand and at the same time more exotic than the outermost point of the world.

He is thinking and choosing his words carefully: 'This is probably a wrong thing to do, Kitty. But I can't help it. I don't know how not to do it.'

I choose my words too. 'Nor do I. I'm not in the same position as you, I don't have responsibilities or loyalties to anyone else in this world. But I believe even if I did, even if

242

I risked everything else I hold dear, I wouldn't turn my back on this. On you. I couldn't and I wouldn't want to.'

He puts his thumbs to the corners of my mouth and lowers my jaw so that he can look at my tongue. I know that it is misshapen at the tip and puckered with scar tissue and I want to hide it.

'I don't want to hurt you, if I do kiss you.'

I shake my head, finding that there are tears in my eyes.

'You couldn't hurt me.'

When our mouths meet I remember Peter, the first time he kissed me, the only man I have kissed between then and now.

Then I think of nothing, except this.

After the kiss finishes he puts his hands against my cheeks. He is looking hard at me, our eyes not quite level, the wind still whipping my hair across my mouth. He hooks a finger round the strand and tucks it behind my ear, and the gentleness of this, the intimacy of the touch after being so long on my own, is like a second kiss. I am smiling at him and I know there is light in my face.

'Who are you, Kitty?'

'You know who I am.'

I mean this on two levels, the more important and deeper one being that he *knows* me, the way I know him, without the need for questions and history. I am a different person from the old Cary Stafford, mired in guilt.

I am Kitty Fisher now. Free.

'Do I?'

Our mouths are still almost touching and our noses, his arms have slid around my back to pull my hips and the rest of my body in a long line against his. I hear the blast of the ferry hooter and I briefly imagine the bustle of loading and unloading down on the quayside: netting bags of potatoes; wooden crates of oranges and lemons; brown sacks of cauliflowers.

'I'll tell you whatever you want to know,' I whisper to him.

'There will be time.' I can feel the pull of small muscles round his mouth. He is smiling with his face against mine. He has come to a decision, reckless or not.

There will indeed be time, but not now. For all of this week, ever since the night of Saint Pandelion's feast, I have been like a teenage girl. Looking for him round corners and then looking away when he appears. Forgetting how to breathe, forgetting where I am, thinking of nothing but *this*.

Max feels the same, I know because I know him. He winds his arms round me, pulling me closer.

'Siren,' he says. Briefly, I think of Lisa Kirk and her seduction of my husband. She was the siren, with all her youth and cruel confidence. Am I the same, for Hattie, even though I am neither young nor confident? Yes. No. Maybe. And now, in any case, it's too late. We are already entwined in each other and it would take another earthquake to shake us apart.

There is a slot of dry grass here, hammock-shaped between a double line of fallen stones.

It's a fierce coupling, with the heat between us and the wind cold even within the sheltered circle of the castle rock. I hold him close against me and my damaged tongue needles me with little irrelevant stabs of pain all the time our mouths are glued together.

Afterwards he holds me and pulls my clothes tighter around me.

'You're cold. You feel like ice.'

'I'm not. I'm warm all the way through. I'm happier than I can ever remember being.' And this is the truth.

Max laughs at that. He rubs my hair and my hands, and kisses the planes of my face. When he touches me, when he made love to me, I realise that there are new folds and creases around my body. There are expanses of smooth flesh that slide over and soften my bones and offer themselves up to be kneaded and tasted. When we first knew each other Peter made me feel voluptuous, even though in reality I was brittle and stretched, but this is different. Now I know that I *am*, this new luscious fatness is all my own. I have made it. It is part of the liberation, the re-creation.

'And you?' I ask.

He sighs. He is rueful and I admire him all the more because he wants to be loyal. 'Kitty. I've been with Hattie for twelve years and I've never been unfaithful to her. Never even come close. And then I decide to come over here because we've been quarrelling a bit too much, paying too much attention to work and money, and not enough to each other. I thought it would mark a space, and that when I got back we would be able to do better. So I come to visit my sister and her family. That's a normal and ordinary thing to do, isn't it?

'And then I see you standing on the quayside with Olivia's child in your arms and I think, *who's that*? You open your mouth and a river of blood pours out of it. I think you're going to die and the first thing that flashes into my mind is you can't die yet. I've only just seen you and I want to take hold of you and I can't let you get away from me like this. My heart is *hammering*.

'But all the same, I'm seeming to take charge and making you show me the damage and saying dumb-Aussie stuff like you're going to live.'

The recollection makes me smile, and his face loses some of the fierce lines that trying to say things truthfully have dug into it.

'And then there's the Saint's party. All that candle-light and incense and ripe fruit and shadows dancing. It was holy and pagan at the same time, and like nothing at home, nothing else anywhere or any time in my life, and with you right at the centre of it. You were *there*, even though you were a total stranger. And I watch you coming across that old ruined square towards me, threading your way through the crowd like you're pulled on a wire. And I know what's going to happen as though I've already seen it. *I can't kiss you now*, I say. *But I'm going to.*

'Why did I say that, when I hardly knew you?

'And then I have this week of trying to be with you and not to be with you at the same time. Thinking about Hattie and the girls, and then not thinking about them.'

He looks away over my shoulder. 'So we come up here and we end up lying down in the ruins together. Who did you say? The Crusaders?'

'Yes. The Knights of St John.'

Pirates and plunderers, as well as Christian emissaries.

Max shakes his head wonderingly. 'Do you wonder that I ask who you are? When this happens between us, with no … introduction, or explanation?'

'Passion doesn't follow social rules,' I mumble.

I can see Lisa Kirk again at my dinner party and feel the subtle change in air pressure that announced the beginning of the end of my marriage. Only now, like a blade of light passing through the plates of my skull, the realisation comes: *I'm glad.* Otherwise, how could I be here, with Max? And no longer Cary, but Kitty.

'I know that. At least, I know the theory. I have never experienced it before.'

'Good,' I tell him. 'I don't want to think of you with anyone but me.'

Max props himself on one elbow. I am stiff with lying on the cold ground and I ease myself away from beneath him and sit up, resting my shoulders against the castle wall.

Because the ground slopes away on all sides, all I can see is a tumble of clouds and the circling buzzards.

'You don't have to think of it, for now. Now is now. But what will happen in a month or a year ... I can't say.'

I accept this offering, with its limitations. Even my improved vision isn't quite sharp enough to read the future. *Now you know*.

Except that I don't. Only partly, only with a glimpse of what freedom means.

It is suddenly too cold to stay in one place. We kiss each other again, pressing our chilled faces together, then I scramble to my feet, pulling on his hands to make him stand up too. The sea and the island plain come into view. The ferry has long gone and the harbour is deserted. It's time to do the climb back down to Megalo Chorio because the winter dark will soon descend.

'I understand,' I tell him.

We walk back along the wall to the point where we scrambled over and into the castle. Max leads the way and I peer over, watching what he does. The drop looks much steeper and further from up here, although it is probably not much more than twenty feet.

Max reaches the cliff foot easily and stands with his face turned up to me.

'Slowly,' he calls.

I climb up the inner wall and kneel on the parapet. The wind is much keener and the stones seem to rock under my knees. My palms go wet again and I feel the sick loom of vertigo. I turn my back on the drop and reach down carefully with one toe, feeling for purchase. My fingers dig in to the top of the wall and for a moment I think I am stuck here, unable to go down or up.

'Move your hands lower.' The voice is steady and very close at hand, and briefly I think it is Andreas. My rescuer, again. Tremblingly I drop one hand and then the other, fitting the clawed fingers into stone lips in the wall. I find that I can move my feet, down a blessed few inches and then a few more. I am on the cliff face now, with its tiny gardens of lichen.

'Keep going. You're nearly down.' It is Max calling out, of course. I concentrate, hands down, balance, then feet down. Two more moves and his hands catch my waist. I am gasping with the exertion and the ebb of fear. 'You are safe now. And look.'

Spread out below us is the ruined village with a tiny cluster of lights at the heart of it like a diamond ring in a magpie's nest, and much further below lies Megalo Chorio itself. There is the sparse string of lights along the seafront, shimmering a little because they are strung on cables that swing on the wind. The houses behind give up a powdery glow. It will soon be dark.

A smile peels my lips back, and a wash of warmth swims up my chest and into my throat.

I didn't fall.

I love this exquisite island and the quiet rhythms of living here. I love the smell of the shop and the plain delicious food that I can eat without counting, and playing hunt the mouse with the two children. Now there is Max and a sense of completion that is more than love.

I measure and weigh the value and the effect of all this, and I hold the realisation inside me – *this* is happiness. The opposite of it, hollow instead of solid, base metal instead of gold, is what I have felt ever since Marcus died. Always, until Andreas brought me to Halemni. My guiding star, whoever he was.

At the top end of the village I can just pick out the lights of the potter's house.

'What about Olivia?' I ask Max.

'Olivia?' He doesn't want to answer the question. But she is a part of this equation, maybe even the x itself. Because of the way she makes a bridge between Max and me. His sister, my opposite reflection.

'Will you – we – tell her about what's happening?' I want her to know and in some way to be included, but I also fear it. Why? Because I am jealous of her?

I was jealous of Olivia's life, I think. But I am not any longer.

Max has taken my hand and is guiding me down the steep slope. Thorny bushes catch at my ankles.

'I don't think we'll have to tell anyone anything. My guess is they'll know everything that's happened just from looking at us.'

He is right, of course. I look forwards, down the hill, to the village lights and let gravity do its work so that we are skipping the bushes and then running and leaping with loose stones and earth ratding behind us.

Olivia turned the dough on the board and kneaded it into a snout, then turned it again and kneaded and turned. The cool elastic feel of it between her fingers didn't give her as much pleasure as it usually did.

It was almost dark outside but she went across to the terrace doors and looked out. The hillside was a dark line against the paler sky with the castle standing up like a black paper cutout. There was nothing to see, no one moving. Of course there wasn't, this was Halemni in midwinter.

'It's nearly time for the boys to come home,' she said.

Xan was sitting in one of the armchairs next to the hearth, although the fire wasn't lit because they were saving firewood for Christmas. They were both wearing extra jumpers to compensate and Olivia had to keep pushing the sleeves of hers back to stop the cuffs catching in the bread dough.

There was a bandage round her forearm covering the cut from where she had fallen on the way down from Saint Pandelion's feast and the sleeve kept snagging on that as well. The wound was a short, deep gash that wasn't healing cleanly. Olivia thought that maybe she would ask Anna Efemia to dress it for her.

Xan's eyes were closed and he was listening to music through headphones, and he gave no sign that he had heard her speak.

Once, even until recently, she would have wanted to listen too just in order to be sharing it with him but now she was glad of the interval of peace and silence. She didn't even particularly want to know what piece it was that so absorbed him. She finished kneading the dough and put it in a bowl with a cloth covering it. Then she sliced some aubergines for dinner and salted them, and left them in a grooved dish to drain.

Either Xan or she would have to go down to Meroula's to pick up the boys. They could easily come the short distance up to the potter's house by themselves, but Meroula often either didn't remember or didn't care to send them home promptly. She wouldn't just phone, either. The telephone was for business or emergencies and all other messages in Megalo Chorio were delivered in person, assisted more often than not by a cup of *metrio*.

Olivia thought of England. If she lived in London, or in a market town or a prosperous village with laburnum trees in the garden and ducks on a pond, she would probably be part of a mothers' casual network linked by phone and short car journeys, and taken-for-granted shared ground. There was none of that on Halemni and perhaps this was why she had drawn close to Kitty. Kitty wasn't a mother, and she was often strange and opaque, but she was still familiar. She knew England, and English ways and the rhythms that had marked

Olivia's childhood, because they had been her rhythms too. Or at least, from the few details that Kitty had actually told her they sounded exactly the same.

It was odd that as a young woman Olivia had tried to escape the bounds of all this and yet now found herself wistfully thinking of the life she might have been living. She felt lonely, it was true, lonely for woman talk and intimacy, and Kitty's company had lifted that. Yet now that Max was here, seeing the two of them together made her jealous.

Perhaps this was the pattern of getting older, Olivia thought, and a smile without much humour in it twitched her mouth. You started wishing for what you might have had, and what you did have seemed less simple and graspable than it once had done. She was tired and it seemed that the inviting paths that once multiplied around her were petering out into arid dead ends.

In that case she was getting older too quickly.

She twitched the cloth away from the bowl to check on her dough. The cut on her arm throbbed a little.

She warned herself that she must stop thinking these things. Nothing had really changed. It was an odd winter, Kitty's being here disturbed the balance, she was worried about Max and Hattie. She didn't want to speculate about what might be happening between Max and Kitty, although it was impossible to stop her mind continuously working around it. The images swam in her mind like fish in murky water.

'Xan?'

He opened his eyes and removed the headphones.

'Xan, someone's got to go and get the boys from Meroula's.'

Instead of answering he wound his arm round her thigh and tried to pull her towards him.

'Don't.'

His arm dropped at once. 'Why are you so irritable these days?'

251

They heard the clink of the front-door latch and the boys running into the hallway. There was another voice following them. Christopher's.

Olivia stepped back. 'I'm not. I don't mean to be,' she said.

The kitchen door banged open and Georgi and Theo came in. Christopher's head craned round the door, sandy hair hanging forward.

'I took Meroula some fish from Panagiotis. She was just sending these two home.'

Olivia nodded. This was ordinary, it was how Halemni worked this winter. People dropped things off, stayed longer to talk, accompanied someone to the next house to continue the conversation. A tiny fingernail of claustrophobia scratched at her. It would be a welcome relief to have just an interval of anonymity or an element of choice in who came and went.

'Thanks, Christo.'

Xan hoisted himself out of the armchair at last. He wrestled briefly and air-punched with his sons.

'Something to drink, Christopher?'

The painter glanced quickly at Olivia, then raked his hair back from his face.

'A quick glass.'

Theo had gone straight to the terrace door, from where he could see Kitty's studio. There were no lights showing.

'Where's Kitty?' Georgi demanded.

'She went for a walk with Max.'

'Oh, I wanted her to play a *game* with me.'

Both boys looked disconsolate. Olivia put aside her knife and chopping board. Supper could easily wait a while. 'I'll play with you. What would you like? Backgammon?'

'You're no good at it,' Georgi said. It was true, she was not.

'Monopoly, then?' She made her voice persuasive to cover up dismay and irritation. Why was it that her children wanted to play with Kitty, not with her?

'Okay.'

The boys sat down at the end of the table and Olivia fetched the board and pieces. Christopher came with his glass of red wine and took the chair next to Olivia, and Xan yawned, then lounged across too. He lit some candles and leaned over Georgi's shoulder for a minute, then let his sons persuade him to join in. They had done this before, the five of them, and Olivia fought against the feeling that this time was different, that too much of the easiness had gone out of it. She heard herself chattering in a bright voice as the dice rattled and she moved her small silver shoe around the board. The boys took it in turns to have the racing car. This time it was Theo's. He rested his chin on the table to bring the car to eye level and made little engine noises in his throat while he waited for his throw of the dice. He nudged the car forwards with his fingertip and Georgi immediately complained that he was cheating.

'No, he's only playing,' Olivia said.

Xan poured wine for himself and Christopher.

'Don't I get any?' Olivia asked sharply.

'You don't usually want it.' Xan shrugged.

'Usually,' she echoed.

Everything was still usual. But it had once been comfortable and now it was not, as if a cold draught had crept into the room or there were invisible hairs prickling inside her clothes. The distortion made her feel giddy and nauseated, and she took a long, defiant gulp of wine when Xan poured it for her. Christopher turned to glance at her, she felt his movement through her shoulder, but she kept her eyes on the Monopoly board.

It was completely dark outside before they heard Kitty and Max at the door. Kitty was laughing, full-throated laughter that filled the hallway.

Olivia half stood up, then dropped back into her seat again. Georgi put down the dice shaker and Theo lifted his eyes from the racing car.

The door opened and they came in.

Each of the three adults saw it at once. Kitty's and Max's hands were almost touching, but crucially not quite. From the light in their faces and the electricity around them, they might as well have been glued together. There was a beat of silence.

Georgi broke it by pushing back from the table and launching himself at Kitty.

'Come and play,' he implored.

Xan lounged up from his chair and reached for two more glasses.

'Have a drink,' he said drily.

They were still standing there, the two of them. Olivia clenched her fists in her lap.

It was not possible, not *tenable*, that this stranger should come into her life and take it over. Kitty's influence seemed to creep everywhere, to her children and Christopher, and now even to Max, although Max was hers. All the fife that she could remember he had been there, her assistant and her supporter.

Kitty couldn't have him, not as a lover, she couldn't. That connection would be closer than her own; why should Kitty Fisher be allowed it?

Olivia's eyes travelled to Xan, her big, easygoing and lazy husband. He would be next. Kitty would subvert him next, if she hadn't already done so. *Why are you so irritable these days*, he wanted to know. These days meant since Kitty had come, didn't it? Yet even that possibility seemed not fearsome compared with the truth that she had taken Max. Here they were with identical delight and disbelief in their faces.

Hot anger and jealousy erupted in Olivia and ran down her arms into her fingers. She balled her fists under the shelter of the table.

'Come and play,' Theo was dragging at Kitty's hand.

'Well ...'

In a cold voice quite unlike her own Olivia said, 'This is a family game.'

The words fell into silence. Kitty stepped back, reaching for the door latch.

'I understand. Of course. Another time, Theo. Goodnight everyone.'

The door closed behind her.

Christopher stood up.

'I think that rules me out, too.'

'You're family,' Olivia blurted, 'of course you are.'

'Just the same, I think I'll head for home. Thanks for the drink.'

Olivia pushed the board to one side. Her mouth burned but the rest of her felt cold. She got up and went to the dish of aubergines, thinking that she would carry on with cooking supper and try to make things ordinary again.

But Xan came behind her and pulled her round to face him.

'Don't do that ever again under my roof,' he said in soft Greek that Max couldn't understand.

Olivia knew that she had broken the rules of hospitality, the worst crime for a Greek wife next to infidelity. Defiance licked up inside her.

'Don't tell me what to do.'

Just to say it made her remember what the world had felt like before Xan. She put down the dish of aubergines. 'You can cook your own supper, Xan, and your children's. I'm going out. I want to talk to my brother.'

Xan's mouth fell open in amazement. Max had hardly moved from beside the door. He had been listening to all this, but he had said nothing. Now Olivia hooked her coat off the peg and pulled it over her shoulders. 'Come on, Max. We're going to the pub.'

'Mummy,' Theo began to wail, but she cut him short.

'Pappy will cook you something nice.' Although Xan never made anything except coffee. He had transferred his domestic dependency straight from Meroula to his wife. 'Uncle Max and I will see you later.'

A moment later Olivia and Max were out in the square. Olivia took her brother's arm and they began walking downhill. She wanted to apologise and rub out her angry words.

'I'm sorry, I'm jealous of Kitty,' she said.

'I understand,' Max answered simply. That was how it always had been. They did understand each other, without rancour or difficulty. 'I knew you were going to be. But you did make a scene, Ovvy.'

Ovvy and Max was what they had called each other as tiny children, being unable to get their tongues around the proper names.

'I'm sorry.'

'It was like the old you.'

'Stroppy bitch?'

Max laughed. 'I'll say this for Xan, my darling. He did tame you.'

'With happiness,' Olivia agreed.

The taverna on the harbour wall stood out of the dark like a beacon with a line of electric bulbs slung between the struts of the summer blinds. The windows facing the sea were steamed up so that they couldn't look inside and check the occupants.

'Come on,' Olivia said and pushed in through the door. A dozen faces looked up at her.

It wasn't that women were barred, or even unwelcome. They were simply not expected, not in winter when the men gathered after fishing. Or instead of fishing. Olivia knew every one of them, of course – Panagiotis and his brother,

Yannis and his father, and all the others. There was a second's silent stare before they nodded greetings and returned to their cards or backgammon boards.

The bar in the corner was zinc-topped, smeared with spills and cluttered with bottles. There was an old coffee maker, a glass cabinet of uninviting pastries, ranks of cups and glasses. The barman, a Panagiotis cousin, heaved himself up from the nearest table where an involving hand of cards drew everyone's attention. He jerked his chin at the newcomers and Olivia ordered a glass of wine, Max a beer.

With their sticky glasses in hand they withdrew to a table near the window. Coarse net curtains and pallid, leggy geranium plants masked the lower half of the glass, and condensation beaded and dripped on the upper. They drew out their chairs and sat down across a puddled expanse of brown laminate. The two old fruit machines next to them were unmanned and silent, but a television mounted on a high bracket in the corner relayed Italian football.

Olivia opened her mouth to speak but the words were drowned by a yell of triumph and roared oaths from the two factions of card players.

When they could hear each other again Max put his hand over his sister's.

'You were saying?'

'Just that I really am sorry.'

'Is that for being rude to Kitty, or for being jealous of her?'

Another yell was accompanied by thumping on the tables. The backgammon players ambled over to see what was going on and Yannis poured himself another tumbler of raki.

Olivia sandwiched Max's hand between hers. 'I wish I hadn't been rude. Xan's angry with me.'

He nodded. 'But there was a flash of you that was the pure old Ovvy. From before you came here.'

They looked around the bar.

'*Do* you think Xan tamed me?'

'With happiness,' he reminded her.

Olivia drank some of her wine. It was good and gutsy, the best local stuff. The men knew what they liked.

'So. What happened?' she asked.

'When?'

'You know when.'

The backgammon players had drifted back to their places, except for a couple who stood in front of the television to watch a penalty.

Max pinched the bridge of his nose between two fingers. He looked tired.

'Okay. We both know what happened.'

Olivia recoiled. 'I can't think about it.'

'Then don't. Think about something else. Maybe you're not the only one who's jealous. You belong to this place now, to this island and Xan, instead of to me like you always did.'

Their eyes met, warily.

'Do you remember the games we used to play?' Olivia asked.

There was one called Grown-Ups. One of them played the wife and the other the husband – a smaller, more biddable and reliable husband than their closest role model. There was a good deal of going to the shops and to the library, and eating meals off dolls' plates. It was a safe world they made together, in which wives didn't wait for their husbands to come home or cry while they were doing it, and where nobody argued or raised a voice. They must have been five or six and seven or eight, Olivia thought. Round about the age of Theo and Georgi now.

Max said, 'Yes, I remember.'

They played weddings too, with dressing-up-box draperies for the bride and a pair of stiletto-heeled shoes of their mother's. The bridegroom outfit consisted of a bus conductor's peaked cap. They changed the roles around perfectly equably.

'It's one of the reasons why I came over here,' Max said. 'Hattie and I were arguing too much. I didn't want our girls to have to listen to the domestic bloody battles that we did.'

Olivia remembered lying in bed, on a summer evening when the drawn curtains barely dimmed the broad daylight outside. The room was full of the day's breathless heat. She felt as if her knees and elbows were locked and her stomach was skewered to the mattress. Her father's voice was loud with bruised edges, and her mother's thin, sharp and tearful. The content, she supposed, once she was old enough to interpret the memory, was the usual tennis match of accusation and denial. Other women, failures of satisfaction at home while appearances were kept up outside.

At the time she had had no inkling of any of this. She had forced herself out of bed and padded downstairs.

'Go away. Go back to bed.' Her father's face was mottled and livid.

Her mother crumpled herself into an angle of the sofa, and she didn't extend her arms or her reassurance either.

'Yes, go on now. Mummy and Daddy are ...'

'Incompatible.'

His muttered word still sounded loud. She didn't know what it meant at the time and she had retreated to her room.

One of the reasons she had loved Xan so readily was because he offered a different way of living. No suburban routine, no commuting to an office, no little English means of mutual torture. This was what she had escaped from.

And yet, and yet ...

Only this afternoon she had longed for Volvos and laburnum trees. And were she and Xan as happy on their island as she had always needed to believe? Briefly she closed her eyes and tried to set her mind straight.

'We had a happy childhood,' Max cut in, setting the untruth in quotes in the way Olivia did when she gave Kitty her full name.

And yet it hadn't been unhappy. They had had one another for company. There had been Christmas presents and summer holidays and weekend outings. A cousin on their father's side had a big country house with formal gardens that featured terraces and a tennis court, and they had often gone there to play. Those summer afternoons seemed like long, shimmering tunnels of green shade.

Their parents had stayed married and remained so to this day. After their children left home they moved from the outer suburbs to a house in the proper country. Olivia thought of the way that her father had shrunk once he no longer had his job or his mistresses. The air just leaked out of him. The loud voice had become a wheeze, and the bravado mutated into querulousness. His wife was a kernel of anger inside a shell of indifference. Everything he did irritated her, from the way he folded his newspaper to biting too noisily into his breakfast toast. They were locked into their house of annoyance, however. Death would be the only way of turning the key.

'Oh, God,' Olivia said. Her head felt thick as if she might be getting the flu and her arm still ached. The bar was full of smoke, everyone must be chain smoking. 'What's the matter with me?'

Max didn't try to wisecrack or to second-guess her. He nodded to the Panagiotis relative for two more drinks and simply waited.

'I know that Xan and the kids and Halemni might seem to mean more to me than you,' she said carefully. 'I love them and this place. You know I do, the same as you with Hattie and the girls. But you are in a different part of me,

260

and that will never alter and never could.'

After two more smeared glasses had been set in front of them she asked, 'Are you going to fall in love with Kitty?'

Because she feared Kitty's intrusion in a way that she had never feared her sister-in-law's.

There was another outburst of shouting. This time it was a dispute. Yannis tossed his cards on to the table and stormed away. He marched up to the fruit machine and fed a short stack of coins into the slot while the argument raged behind him. Olivia and Max crouched in his shadow.

'I'm trying to tell the truth,' Max said after a while. 'I don't think it's a matter of going to. I think it has happened already. I have never known anyone like her. Except you, maybe.'

The fruit machine grudgingly coughed up a couple of coins in response to Yannis's tugs on the handle. He fed them back again, muttering.

'I see,' Olivia said bleakly.

'I wish I did,' Max rejoined. They sat and looked at each other, with the bar noises washing around them.

'And what are you going to do?'

They had often talked like this, asking questions about each other's plans and decisions, and the connection had held secure through long-distance phone calls and months and occasionally years of physical separation. They were on the edge of a different, much less comfortable alignment now and they were both wary of it.

Max put his hands flat on the table as if to show that he would hide nothing.

'I will stay here for a while longer. Spend Christmas with you, as planned, if I may.'

This was an English Christmas, the kind Olivia liked to make for her children. The Greek calendar Christmas fell in early January and was not made much of on Halemni. Saint

Pandelion's feast was the bigger festival.

Olivia waited, with her wineglass empty again, but Max didn't seem to have anything more to add. Yannis's pile of coins was all gone and he turned away from the machine and shuffled back to the card table. He was reabsorbed into the game as if nothing had happened.

I can oppose Kitty and lose Max anyway, Olivia thought desperately. There was every possibility that this would be the outcome. Or I can try to live through this and maybe it will burn out and Max will go back to Hattie, where he belongs. It has only been a week. It's only *today* that they began. It just seems much longer.

And also, even though she was jealous and suspicious and resentful of her, she didn't want to sever herself from Kitty either. Kitty was under her skin. Olivia took a breath and found that her chest hurt. She nodded her acceptance of what she couldn't change in any case.

'One more?' Max asked.

'Definitely.' Olivia put her hand in the pocket of her jeans and drew out a handful of change. Maybe she'd win the fruit machine jackpot.

It was late when the two of them made their erratic way back up the street. They were last to leave the bar, except for Yannis, who was asleep with his head on his folded arms.

'Do you remember,' Olivia mumbled, 'the bus conductor's cap?'

'And the high-heeled shoes. One of my fondest. I wonder what became of them?'

'Might come in handy, you mean?'

'You never know.'

They stumbled in through the front door. On the kitchen table the boys had both left drawings for her, crayoned at the bottom with their names and rows of kisses. It was such a rare event for her to be out at night, to miss their bedtime.

She rubbed her mouth with the back of her hand. Alcoholically induced tears stung her eyes.

'I must go to bed,' she whispered.

Max put his arms round her. 'I'm still here,' he said.

'So you are.'

Olivia tried to move soundlessly, but she kept bumping into the bedroom furniture. Xan sighed. 'It's all right. I'm awake.'

She slid under the covers, cold-skinned from undressing in the chilly room, and he wound his arms round her.

'I'm sorry,' she mumbled.

'How much have you had to drink?'

'A lot.'

'I love you,' Xan said, with his mouth to her ear. His hand slid over her breast and across her belly.

'That's good. I'm tired now.'

She fell asleep almost at once, her mouth gaping a little against the thick mat of his chest hair.

With his hands still on her body, Xan thought that his wife felt different. She was thinner, he could feel the knobs and shafts of bone beneath the skin. There was an acrid scent to her too, unfamiliar, as if she was running a slight fever. This was what it must feel like to be in bed with Kitty, he thought. For a second or two he dwelt luxuriously on the idea, then he pushed it away.

THIRTEEN

The time we spend together is precious: already I have the sense that there is going to be too little of it. It isn't like it was with Peter, when our lives seemed to stretch ahead for ever. This time every minute has to be made to count and I know that there is a lot to fit in.

One evening, when we are sitting in my little studio room, I say abruptly to Max: 'This is what happened. I want you to know about it.'

It was a midsummer afternoon when I was seven years old and my brother Marcus was five, and we were playing together in a beautiful garden. There were big trees that cast dense green shadow depths and floated translucent islands of sunlight between them. There were stone steps with the treads worn into hollows that held the gritty residue of evaporated puddles, and there was the scent of lavender and the throaty conversation of wood pigeons.

Or maybe my memory has added these embellishments, overlaying the time *before* with the necessarily sweet details of a world that was on the point of detonation. Just because the time *after* was so devoid of incidental beauty.

There were statues in the garden as well as trees and flower borders, and these statues had fascinated me for most of my life. Every time we visited the family who owned the house I asked to be taken outside to look at the stone animals. They were the massive heads of strange beasts, mounted on pillars of ribbed stone. I remember a horse with a curled mane, the curls seeming so real that I would try to twist the petrified hair round my fingers. There was a lion with its mouth open in a roar, a unicorn, a strange dog with a forked tongue and my favourite, a gryphon. I didn't even know that was what it was called, I just liked its cruel face with the curved beak and unblinking eyes, and the powerful feline shoulders that fascinatingly didn't belong with the bird's head. One of my earliest memories is of being held up to stroke the feathered neck.

Or maybe this is another trick of the mind.

On this summer's day I knew that I had grown much taller since our last visit to the house.

'You are a big girl,' the adult cousins told me.

'Marcus has shot up too,' they added.

I stood up on the balls of my feet, conscious of my size and strength, and of being able to see and reach much further than my little brother could. Once the two of us had been admired and praised, however, the attention shifted away. The adults were sitting talking in a room with velvet-covered furniture and doors that stood open on to a terrace. I wanted to run out into the garden to play.

'Take Marcus with you,' my father said.

'Don't climb on the statues,' my mother warned me.

I know this one isn't a trick of memory. I know the words were actually spoken lightly, even absentmindedly. I can still hear them, but the faint vibration of concern is amplified with hindsight into a thundering roar.

The sun was warm on my head when I escaped outside.

I blinked in the sudden brilliance. Marcus was trotting beside me and we went straight to the gryphon.

I'm going to ride him, he's my bird horse.

Can I play? What can I be?

You can be my groom.

I scrambled up the pillar, scraping the leather of my new sandals against the ribs of stone. I gained the top and held on tight, hooking my knees round the gryphon's shoulders.

The creature was my magic steed. We would fly, or gallop on massive paws, through the shade depths and across the sunshine islands. We would take off into the summer air and discover new worlds together.

My imagination lent me body weight. I rocked on my stone charger and this set the gryphon rocking too. The pillar shivered and threatened to break free of its base, and I felt the answering tremors and rocked harder, caught up in the imaginary flight. And at the foot of the pillar Marcus faithfully stood, holding an imaginary bridle.

Memory doesn't distinguish for me whether the scream came before or at the very instant when the pillar started to topple.

I heard it and I felt the movement and froze, my hands clasping the bird's beak and trying to hold it upright. But we were already falling through an arc of blue air. My feet were above my head and the trees spun between my legs and the sky. I was thrown clear and my face hit the grass. There was a mushy thud behind me, the terrible sound of a heavy weight striking something soft and unresisting.

I remember the scream and the way it went on and on, a high note of pure terror that cut the soporific afternoon. It burned itself into my head and stayed there and will stay there, for ever.

I sat up, thinking my mother's scream was for me. I was unhurt but I was trying to decide whether or not to cry. Then the rush of people came, not to me but to Marcus. He was lying motionless under the pillar. His head was hidden beneath it but I could see his pale bare legs, and his feet askew wearing the same sandals as mine, only smaller. My father and two other men were battling to lift the weight off his small body. My mother just stood there with her knuckles pressed into her mouth. And all the time the scream went on in my head.

When they hoisted the pillar, with the strength that desperation generates, Marcus didn't wriggle and get up. He just went on lying there. I could see that there was blood on his head and his clothes. There was a confusion of voices and movement now, and someone running back to the house. But the three of us stayed still, Marcus and my mother and me.

That long moment of immobility was when everything changed. History began, the past that you can't rub out and which marks you for ever. All my life, from that day, I have lived with the knowledge that I was responsible for my brother's death.

Those few minutes of play in a summer garden sent my mother off into a spiral of grief from which she never recovered.

The loss of their child drove a wedge between my parents and my father in the end left this family to start another, the Steps and Halves, with Lesley.

And I, I became the person I am. The woman who married Peter Stafford, who longed for a baby and doubted her ability to care for one, whose womb in any case would not hold on to a child. Dunollie Mansions was my shelter, my whittling down of a life to a point that excluded almost everything except breathing. And then there was Lisa Kirk.

All of this brought me to Branc and the earthquake. Those images of devastation and Jim's body in the wreck of a hotel bar resonate so piercingly with that other image of a crushed body.

And after that came Andreas and a chain of events that

delivered me here to Halemni, to Olivia and Xan and Max and the moment on the headland.

Now you know, that was what I heard.

I didn't, I don't know whatever it is, but I did see the chance of an escape from history.

Kitty Fisher in the present, without a past.

On this island with its rocks and thorn bushes and five hundred years of ruins, I am not the woman who caused her brother's death. I am a version of her, a close relative or a recreation with the tragedy wiped away, but I am not her.

Look.

I am unkempt, unpainted, dressed in bag lady clothes. I am fat and I am free. I have chosen to be happy. I can feel the smile as if it belongs on my face now, although the creases that it gouges in my cheeks are still unfamiliar.

Max holds my hands and rubs them.

'Kitty, I am glad you told me. It helps me to understand the look in your eyes, that first time I saw you. I can't think what it must have been like for you, growing up in the shadow of that. Even though it was an accident.'

He says the same things as Peter, the same as the very few other people I have ever told about Marcus and me.

'It was hard, yes.'

I am glad to admit it although the words convey nothing of the reality.

But there is an anomaly here. If I wanted so much to be a clean blank page, why have I just written this story on it for Max, of all people?

'Did you tell Olivia about it?' he asks me.

Olivia? I think. And I'm briefly surprised to remember that I haven't.

'No. But I will do, some time.'

Maybe my ability to talk just shows my new-found

268

strength. I have told Max my story straight, in a way that I have never done before. In the past it has only come out of me in little dismembered pieces, most of them prised out by Peter. And now I have said it, offered it, I may find that I can move away from the darkness.

History isn't other people. It is yourself.

I have chosen to start afresh.

We have been sitting at the little table, with empty plates and dishes between us. We have eaten and drunk well tonight, Max and I. The lights in the potter's house were turned off hours ago, Megalo Chorio is in total darkness. It feels as though the two of us are alone in the world together.

We stand up now and move the two steps to the bed. The studio is cold, as always, and we don't try to take off our clothes. Instead we crawl under the covers and into each other's arms. Rough wool and flannel scrape against our cheeks and fingers meet the resistance of awkward buttons.

I thought sex with Peter was good, but this is a different matter. It's more urgent than I have ever known, but it is also natural and unhurried, and it has a logic and a rhythm that is completely new to me. It needs no words or explanations, but we talk all the same. The words pour out of our mouths and straight into the other's head, almost without the formality of language, more like the murmur of the sea. This meeting and matching is new to both of us. There is nothing to discover, because we seem to know it all already, and yet there is everything.

Afterwards we fall asleep in a tangle of trouser legs and underclothes, and sleep, and sleep.

The Christmas tree at the potter's house always stood in the hallway. It was not a real one – there were no trees for cutting on Halemni, of course, and certainly no ranks of them drawn up on the pavements outside greengrocers' shops, the way Olivia remembered from her childhood.

It was a family routine. Every year she and Max would go with their mother to Mr Weekes's shop in the high street to pick out the tree. There was always a debate about which one. Max invariably wanted the tallest, which was not always the most perfectly shaped. Sometimes the biggest trees had a nasty bald spike at the top, which even the tinsel star would not conceal. The best tree might be a foot shorter, but it would be a beautiful shape with a thick skirt of lower branches tapering to a neat point. Olivia always got the one she wanted in the end, because she argued more forcefully than Max. Mr Weekes tied a label with their name on it to one of the branches and their father would call later in the car to collect it. Not usually the same day, because he didn't come home from work in time, but the following weekend. It was an agony of waiting before he carried the thrilling scent and trail of early shed needles into the house. Their mother would come behind him with the vacuum cleaner, complaining about the mess.

Olivia's tree had been sent out from London by Celia, when Georgi was a baby. It was made of thick, dark-green glossy synthetic material and it looked quite convincing. But there was no sharp, resiny scent, of course, and she missed that. It had become the Georgiadis tradition to decorate it on Christmas Eve, although Xan didn't take much interest. He had no patience with all this northern European pagan forest nonsense, as he called it. Christmas to him meant either Halemni's religious festival, or the blistering beach barbecues of his years in Australia. But he let Olivia put up her tree and watched his sons arrange the carved wood nativity scene that went underneath it.

He did fix the lights every year. They were an old-fashioned set that Olivia's parents had passed on to her, and they were temperamental in association with Halemni's variable electricity supply. But Olivia loved them. They were candles of yellowed plastic with dribbles of plastic wax down the sides, and the bulbs were teardrops of clear glass. There had been a box of spare bulbs when the lights first arrived from England, but they had all been used up. When the next bulb failed there would be nothing to replace it with, but for now the whole set worked. Xan laid the string out on the floor and for once they lit up as soon as he plugged them in.

The boys breathed in sharply at the golden light spilling along the hallway and then hooted with pleasure. They were overexcited and noisy, running up and down the stairs and tripping over rugs as they chased each other.

The candles were fixed to the tree's synthetic branches with fiddly metal crocodile clips. Olivia nipped the little lights to the tips of the branches while the boys strung up the other decorations. They were simple, mostly plain wooden shapes or painted stars and animals made by the children and Christopher.

When they had finished, Olivia stood back and looked at it through half-closed eyes. It was beautiful. It could, almost, have been the tree of her childhood. Only the scent was missing.

'When can we hang our stockings up?' Georgi asked. He had asked the same question every five minutes for the whole day.

'At bedtime, I told you.'

She had made a red felt stocking for each of them. Their presents were simple, a wooden construction kit and tools for Georgi and a toy digger for Theo, and some crayons and paints and books and sweets. They didn't have many toys and their greedy anticipation about what they were going to get on Christmas morning was almost uncontainable. She still had the wrapping to do, once the boys were finally asleep.

Olivia went and found Xan who had retreated to read at

the kitchen table.

'Come and look. It's done.'

He put his book down and followed her. The stone-flagged floor made the hall seem arctic, whereas the kitchen was merely chilly. Olivia stood close to him, trying to forget her headache, and he put his arm round her shoulders.

'Pretty,' he said.

She wanted something else from him, something more than this. It was a feeling she had quite often nowadays.

'Are we going to eat soon?' Xan asked.

She slid away out from the crook of his arm. 'Yes. As soon as Meroula gets here.'

Xan swung Theo off his feet and let him dangle by his hands.

'Christmas is coming,' Theo yelled. He kicked out and his feet just missed the tree branches.

'Be careful, you'll kick it over,' Olivia snapped.

All three turned to stare at her. They looked absurdly alike, with the same circumflex black eyebrows. A gap seemed to have opened up between her and the three of them, and she didn't know how to step back across it or even what the distance might be. Xan lowered Theo gently to the floor.

'You're different, hair makes you different. And your face,' the child said to her.

'No, it doesn't. It doesn't one bit.'

She put out her arms and took him from Xan. He wrapped his legs round her waist and rocked himself while she buried her face against his hair. She breathed in his baby smell of hay and skin, and felt protective tears prickle in her eyes.

Georgi didn't want to be left out. He put his arms round her hips and hugged.

'You're always just the same,' he assured her, butting his head against her belly.

Theo felt incredibly heavy but she couldn't bear to put

him down. The warmth of her sons, their resilience and their vulnerability and the depth of her love for them made her cry, and she couldn't conceal the tears. She sniffed as they ran down her cheeks.

'Hey,' Xan said, smiling uncertainly at her.

They heard steps coming to the door and then Meroula's knock. As her mother-in-law let herself into the hallway Olivia let Theo squirm to the floor and hastily wiped her eyes. She kissed Meroula, noticing the defensive bulk inside the dour clothes, the strict curl of her iron hair, the guarded look in her eyes.

'Come in, Mother,' she said.

Meroula was a mother, of course. She felt the same way about Xan as Olivia did about her sons, and this should unite the two of them more than their age or their different cultures divided them.

It was Christmas, Olivia told herself. She would put aside her tiredness and forget her headache and pull her family together. Greek or English truly didn't matter, nor did jealousy over Xan or unspoken disputes about how the boys should be brought up. The family itself was what mattered.

Meroula flicked her a surprised glance in return.

'Look at this,' she said, about the tree.

'Christmas is coming, the goose is getting fat,' the children chanted. Olivia had taught them carols and Christmas rhymes. There were no geese on Halemni, however. The misanthropic egg man reared a few turkeys and Olivia bought a fat one from him every year.

'It looks very fine,' Meroula continued, pursing her lips.

'Come in and get warm. Let me give you a glass,' Olivia said. This would be a family evening. They would sit down to eat as soon as Max came in; he had gone down to the taverna for an hour or so with Yannis. Christopher tactfully claimed to be busy tonight and Kitty was down in the shop.

The two women had seen little of each other in the few days since Kitty and Max came down from the castle together. But they would tomorrow. Both Christopher and Kitty were coming to spend Christmas Day at the potter's house.

Meroula sat down in the comfortable armchair and took the glass of wine Olivia poured for her. 'Just one mouthful,' she insisted, as she always did. Olivia began to lay the table and Xan moved his book to one side.

The slam of the front door and an even more piercing cold draught signalled that Max was back. They heard his shout of surprise.

'The tree. He likes the tree,' Georgi said.

He came in, cold and bringing with him a waft of cigarette smoke and close air from the bar. He looked to Olivia just the way he had done when he was a little boy, late for supper and full of excitement and secrets. Surely he must have been with Kitty, not with Yannis and the others at all. Love and jealousy made a queasy knot under her diaphragm.

What is the *matter* with me? Olivia thought.

'Ovvy, those must be our old fairylights from home. Just the sight of them takes me straight back to Pelham Road.'

The ordinary house where they had lived a semi-suburban childhood. The Christmas tree there occupied one corner of the front room, next to the television cabinet. Usually they ate at a table in the kitchen, brown Formica-topped with fold-down leaves, but for Christmas and birthdays and anniversaries they used the dining room. It always smelled polished and unused, and Olivia had a sudden memory of spaces between spurts of conversation and the clink of cutlery failing to fill the silence.

Max made his way around the room. He had only been out of the house for a couple of hours, but he understood the importance of Halemniot greetings. He kissed Meroula, managing to inject a flirtatious note so that she put up her hand afterwards to pat her hair. He kissed Olivia too and exchanged mock punches with the boys and grinningly clasped hands with Xan. The two men liked each other; sometimes they seemed to belong to the club of men as much or more than they belonged to any family. Everyone sat down at the big table and Olivia brought the food. Conversation pattered around her, in English for Max's sake. Xan and Max teased the boys about whether they had been good enough to deserve any.

Olivia pushed her food around her plate.

Where was Kitty right now? She didn't have her own children, or a family around her. Jealousy was ugly.

In spite of her determination to create unity the room split and quartered and wildly subdivided into factions that she had recognised but never properly considered before. Mothers and not-mothers. Greek and English. Children and adults, men and women, brothers and lovers, married and alone. Herself and Kitty. Kitty and herself.

She was trying to work out why it was that Kitty affected her so much. She was a stranger here, she had materialised out of nowhere and had brought nothing with her. Yet she seemed to have slid a thin blade of threat into the heart of everything Olivia most valued. She's too close. Our separate selves seem to collide, Olivia thought. It's almost as though she is me, or wants to be me, as though we are fighting to occupy the same space.

I'm feverish, she told herself. I must be running a fever.

Everything had become so complicated. Tension intensified her headache into a jagged split that ran over her skull and throbbed above one eye. She put her knife and fork down.

'Where's Kitty?'

Max turned to her. He was still laughing at something Xan had said about Panagiotis.

'With Helen, I think.'

Not sitting alone in her cold studio, at least.

Everything would be all right. She would make it all right again. She would finish the boys' presents and get the food ready for tomorrow.

For the first time in her life Olivia felt daunted by what she had to do.

Meroula had eaten a large plateful. She looked across at Olivia's untouched portion.

'You must eat food, my girl. You will end looking like Kitty.'

The boys giggled, Xan's black eyebrows arched.

'I don't think so.' Olivia deliberately lifted a forkful of minced meat and placed it in her mouth. She chewed hard on the gristly pellets and found a way to swallow. The food tasted like dirty rubber.

Helen and I have set the shop straight. At least, Helen has directed me from her seat beside the shiny till.

She is huge, like a fruit about to split open. The baby is due in two weeks, and in a few days' time Helen and Panagiotis will take the ferry to Rhodes to wait for the birth. This is what most of the young women on Halemni do, since the doctor moved off the island. Only a very few nowadays opt to have the baby delivered at home by a midwife, although this was always the way in the old days. Meroula gave birth to Xan in the old stone house up in Arhea Chorio, attended by the village midwife and two neighbours. She told me the story, with relish: 'We had no need of doctor. Many hours labour, but a fine boy at the end of it.'

Olivia had the doctor for her boys, because he was here in those days, but Meroula implies that this was an indulgence.

I will not be left in sole charge of the shop, of course. A Panagiotis cousin from the other side of the island – and therefore safely oblivious to the finest points of Megalo Chorio power play – will move in to oversee matters for the family. But Helen wants everything to be in perfect order before she leaves and so we have spent hours after the shop closes minutely rearranging shelves, moving stock in the back room, dusting every jar. I love all this. I love the making of order as much as Helen does and we work well together even though we can barely exchange a word in each other's language.

It is very quiet, behind the shop windows, with rain on the glass and the hum of the big deep freeze. The smell of herbs and cheese is stronger at night, mixed with the hemp scent of the hessian sacks of flour and rice.

Helen looks tired tonight. There are dark circles under her dark eyes. It must be difficult to sleep with a stomach swollen like hers.

I lift the little coffee pot to ask whether she would like a last cup before we lock up, but she shakes her head. I put my hand on her shoulder.

'You should go home and have a good rest. There isn't anything else to do here. It's all perfect. And I will look after everything for you, you know that.'

She understands the gist, even if not the actual words, and she gives me her sweet smile. Then suddenly she lifts my hand off her shoulder and places it on her belly. Under my fingers, distinctly, I feel the restless kicking of a tiny heel. The baby is there, beneath the thin sheets of skin and muscle, her presence is as vivid as if there is a third person in the room. Amazed tenderness floods through me as I stare down into Helen's face.

She nods wearily and then her smile fades into a wince as she shifts her position.

'Time to go home,' I tell her again. We hear Panagiotis hooting in his truck outside.

After Helen has gone with her husband I check the freezers

and the window shutters, and switch off the lights. I lock the shop door behind me and turn towards the sea. It is a still, perfect night and the sky is a sweep of stars. I can hear waves breaking and the sound draws me along the street, past the darkened houses and the broken remnants of trees to the beach. I stand at the edge of the water, staring out to sea, as calm and unexpectant as the island itself.

It doesn't feel like Christmas Eve. But then, I think, I am no expert in these things. We didn't celebrate Christmas much, when I was a child. We remembered instead the six Christmases that were all that Marcus had been given and I felt that I had no right to enjoy the ones that followed.

A bigger wave breaks and I run backwards, too late because black water has briefly swirled into my shoes. I laugh at my carelessness and make my wet-footed way back up the beach and along the main street. There is a light still on downstairs in the potter's house, but I slip quietly past and into the silence of my studio. I will sleep, tonight, as sweetly and soundly as I do every night.

Xan was asleep, too, in his chair next to the hearth, with his book askew on his chest. Olivia placed a square of butter-soaked muslin over the breast of the turkey. It would do better than tinfoil when the time came to roast it. The stuffing was done, a hybrid of English sage and onion and Greek rice and olives, and she had filled the breast cavity with it and stitched the skin in place with coarse black thread. Her fingernails were rimmed with onion and chopped herbs, and she yawned as she went to the sink and ran water to wash them. Her arm still throbbed, she noticed, as she let the water run over her wrists. She was exhausted now, but maybe she should dress it again before she finally went to bed. There had been no time, this week, to show the cut to Anna Efemia.

Olivia held the safety pin from the bandage between her

278

lips as she quickly unwound the old dressing. She inspected the exposed cut with a critical eye.

It was healing, at last. The raised margins of the long, jagged scrape were shiny and purplish but the wound itself seemed to be drying out. The scab had turned crusty and it puckered the tight skin around it. She dabbed some disinfectant on to a cloth and patted it over the whole area, then quickly rebandaged the arm.

Xan sighed and stretched his legs, retrieving his book from where it had dropped.

'What time is it?'

'Nearly one.'

'Happy Christmas.' He grinned.

Olivia glanced around the room, reviewing what still needed to be done. Most of it could wait until the morning. There were just two small piles of presents to be taken out of hiding and the red felt stockings to be retrieved from the ends of the beds and filled up. Xan went upstairs to fetch them.

They sat side by side at the table and stuffed one stocking apiece. Last year, Olivia remembered, they had drunk a lot of wine and the complications of fitting hard-edged packages into floppy felt had made them giggle. This year they did it quickly, not saying much. Then they carried the knobbly results upstairs and laid them at the ends of the beds. The room smelled of innocence.

In their own bedroom Xan locked his arms round her and tried to steer her backwards to the bed. Olivia felt her knees buckle and she folded sideways on to the blanket. In her head she struggled for the memory of desire and comedy but they were gone as if they had never existed. All she wanted to do was sleep. To be nothing, and nowhere.

'I'm so tired,' she whispered.

FOURTEEN

At daybreak on Christmas morning the flat sea turned from pewter grey to milk white. Then the sun rose out of a low layer of cloud on the Turkish horizon and pointed a thick stripe of silver-gilt across the water to Halemni.

Olivia saw it because her children were awake. They ran into her bedroom with the red felt stockings in their arms. They tore into their presents and left a bright litter of paper across the landing and bedroom floors. Xan watched with sleepy indulgence from under the bedclothes; the door of Olivia's darkroom, where Max was sleeping, stayed firmly closed. The shutters of Kitty's studio room were closed too.

'No, of course you can't,' Olivia whispered when the boys said they wanted to run across and show her what they had got. 'Wait until it's morning.'

'It *is* morning'

'No, it isn't. Not yet.'

It wasn't so on Halemni but in other places, across half the world, this same scene was being played out. She imagined how it would be in England, down a hundred thousand suburban avenues and country lanes and city streets. She could see the grey curtains of a wet northern dawn, and empty town centres, and parish churches decorated with evergreens. Forlornly, just for a minute, she let herself connect to the pictures.

I can't be homesick, she told herself. Not for England, when I am here on this island with my family and with everything I ever wanted or cared about all mine for the taking.

'Come on, get into bed. Let's cuddle and get warm again.'

'I'm not cold. I want to play.'

But she scooped up her children and pulled them under the covers with her. Theo dragged in his red and yellow digger and the hard angles of it dug into her as she tried to put her arms round him. The two of them squirmed in the warm hollow between their parents' bodies and then gradually settled into stillness. Outside, the light grew stronger.

Olivia thought of the turkey and how long it would take to roast. Georgi's foot pressed against her shin and she noticed how big and broad it had grown. It was exactly the same shape as Xan's, even down to the toenails. He must be needing new shoes.

Theo had his thumb in his mouth, he was busily sucking at it like a baby. Max had sucked his thumb for years and she, the big sister, had mocked him for it.

Xan lay on his side, untroubled and asleep again.

Lying awake made her feel lonely, even with her children's smooth backs curved against her belly. How many more Christmases would they share like this? What if some tragedy came, as unexpected as and more devastating than the wave, and tried to sweep everything away? How would she keep them all safe?

The uneasy thoughts speeded up until they reeled into a blur in her head. Something hollow and slippery lodged in her chest and swelled until it pushed the air out of her lungs and made her gasp for breath. The skin at the nape of her neck prickled. Olivia twisted her head on the pillow and stared at the wall, as if she could look through it and across the terrace to the studio where Kitty was sleeping.

What she was feeling, she understood, was fear. She had never been afraid before, or only of things that were explicably threatening like violence, or poisonous snakes, but a great suffocating draught of it rolled over her now. She couldn't breathe and her skin crawled, and a lurid light flashed in the buried place behind her eyes.

Olivia forced herself to lie still. She concentrated on taking one breath at a time and waited for the panic to subside.

I lie on my side and watch Max. He has been sleeping deeply but now he's rising to the surface like a fish under water. His eyes move behind the curve of the lids and I feel jealous of the dream landscape, whatever it is, that I can't share with him. The bed in my studio is narrow but I press closer still and he moves obligingly to make room for me, his arm settling over my shoulder to hold me tight against him.

He feels so solid, when I slide my hand over the slab of his hips and up to the ribcage, more like some smooth warm piece of heavy wood or stone than just bone and muscle. Even though he is asleep he murmurs something and smiles, and I feel him stirring against me. From the colour of the light skewering the studio's shutters I can tell it is morning. We have to wake up early when Max sleeps with me, so that he can slip back into the potter's house without making anyone aware of where he has been. Xan and Olivia must know about this on some level, of course, but it is easier not to make our arrangements too obvious, especially for the boys' sake.

On this Christmas morning we have overslept but I allow myself two more minutes just to float in the satisfaction of warmth and scent. While I study the thickness of his eyelashes

282

and the tiny colourless margin that separates the tanned skin of his chin from the silky texture of lower lip, my breathing automatically synchronises with his. It would be easy to drift into sleep again. Instead, I force my eyes open.

'Wake up. Happy Christmas.'

Immediately he stirs and stretches, then looks at me. One of the things – one of many – that I love about him is the way that he wakes up happy. Before consciousness takes hold, before he remembers whatever it is that the day offers, his first and natural state is happiness. It is only afterwards when memory seeps back into the clear pool and he remembers where he is – cheating with me in my bed, instead of lying next to Hattie where he belongs, or at least sleeping virtuously alone – that guilt clouds the water. Then he deliberately accommodates again and allows himself the pleasure of me, and the prospect of another Halemni day. I can read all this in his eyes before he has spoken a word. This is how well we seem to understand each other.

Max's arms tighten round me as if he wants to hold me down. I like this, although I am hardly insubstantial enough any longer for there to be any risk of the wind carrying me away. He grins lazily with his mouth against mine.

'Hello. Happy Christmas.'

'Mmmm.'

'What time is it?'

I don't have a watch, of course, but I can tell from the light and by a clock inside my head. Max is already peering at his watch, a big rubber underwater and outdoor-activities affair with multiple dials and bezels.

'Half past seven.'

'Later. Twenty to eight,' he contradicts me, smiling, and peels the covers off our naked bodies. The icy air of the studio makes us both shudder. 'Come on, better get up.'

But it's already too late. Even as I sit up with my arms

wrapped round myself in an attempt to save some body heat, there is a thundering at the door.

'Kitty, Kitty, wake up, look what we've got.'

Max and I look at each other in pantomime dismay. He is wriggling into his jeans and layers of sweaters as I roll off the bed and claw for a random garment or two.

'Help.'

I pull on the clothes and rake the bedclothes together as Max opens the door and the shutters. Pale sunshine pours into the room, making us both blink.

'Beat you to it,' Max says easily to the children. They rush to me, too intent to ask questions, bumping against my legs, holding up their presents.

'I made a truck, like Panagiotis,' Georgi says. He shows us both a structure of wooden struts fastened together with bright coloured bolts. Theo is already on the floor, driving a red and yellow plastic digger between the table legs. Max kneels down beside him while I examine the design of Georgi's truck. We are so busy, the four of us, that we don't realise Olivia has followed her children. The first thing I see is her feet, in her boots but with the laces trailing, then I sit back on my heels to take in the rest of her.

She is leaning against the door frame, arms folded, watching us. Her face is flushed and the spiky haircut I gave her on the make-over night stands out around her head like a thorn-bush.

'Merry Christmas,' she says flatly.

'And you,' I answer.

Max stands up, goes to her and gives her a kiss.

'I made some breakfast,' she says to me. 'Would you like to come across and have some with us?'

'I'll come later,' I say, lifting my hand to indicate my mess of clothes. 'But thank you.'

I want to leave them the space to have a family breakfast

together. I also want to retrieve the boys' presents from the place where I have hidden them and slip them under the tree in the potter's house.

'Squeak!' Theo and Georgi are shouting now. Georgi has already begun methodically hunting the mouse, in my shoes and under the cups and all the favourite places. Theo goes straight to the bed and starts sliding his hands under the pillows and between the sheets. I tell him quickly, 'Cold.'

Olivia misses none of this. I feel caught out and defiance rises in me to meet her jealousy. Our eyes meet, with Max out on the periphery, and we consider each other.

It isn't a warm appraisal. This is our business, Max's and mine, I am thinking. You can't be the queen of everything, even though you imagine it's your right to be.

'Come on, guys,' Max says quietly to the children. 'Let's go and get some breakfast.'

'Squeak, Squeak,' Theo calls. He has found the mouse, down the spine of a fat book of Greek history I borrowed from Christopher that is lying open and face down on the table. The spine makes a good tunnel and the mouse's tail hangs out, but it is a hiding place I have used before and they are both disappointed. I should have found somewhere special for Christmas Day.

'I'm coming,' Georgi says. He is glad to dismiss the mouse hunt, since he is not the finder. Theo drops Squeak without a second thought and picks up his new digger. Olivia leads the way back to her house with her head up and her shoulders set, and the three of them follow behind her. Max glances back briefly. His face is straight but his eyebrows make funny peaks of concerned acknowledgement. I do smile back, defiantly.

It is a beautiful morning. The sky is clear and there isn't even a whisper of wind. I make a little pot of coffee and take the cup outside. Sitting with my back against the wall,

I idly watch an island tomcat stalking through the scrub a little way up the hill. He moves stealthily, stomach to the ground, and then when the shrew or mouse is in range he pounces. He looks like a streak of grey smoke. Just on the margins of audibility there is a tiny shrill bat-squeak.

I rest my head against the wall and close my eyes, sighing.

This time and place are too perfect to mar with disputes, even with Olivia. No, with Olivia of all people. I know she is jealous about her brother and she wants to protect this idyllic realm of hers from me, because I might change the balance here just by the way I relate to Xan or to Christopher or her boys. I believe I understand her, even though that understanding now seems only to point the way to Max. But I am not going to recede and efface myself, as I ended up doing in Dunollie Mansions. I am Kitty now, not Cary any longer. I want to taste and touch, and turn my face up to the sun, just as I am doing at this minute. The unexpected midwinter warmth of it touches my cheeks and floats yellow discs under my eyelids.

I am surprised by my own determination.

And I let myself dream, inside the iron support of it.

Perhaps Max and I can escape, run away somewhere together. Maybe we can find our own island and construct our own idyll. Like Olivia's, but our own.

Maybe.

Meanwhile, today, I stretch my legs against the stone blocks that make the terrace. My trousers are tight and straining across the thighs and at the zipper, and I don't care. I'm hungry and I am going to eat.

After my breakfast I wash my hair and carefully choose my clothes from the very limited range of possibilities. I wonder about tying a cotton scarf round my neck, then decide not to. Dispassionately I study my face in the little mirror in the shower room. There is a definite rounding of flesh under my original chin, my eyebrows have grown wings, my hair dips and straggles around my neckline. And when I smile at recognising how little all this matters I see that there are laughter lines round my mouth. *Laughter lines*.

Finally I take the presents I have made for Georgi and Theo out of their hiding place and walk through the slice of morning sunlight to the potter's house. It is already almost midday.

There are candlelights glowing on the tree in the dim hallway, so that it looks almost like Christmas at home. I hesitate for a minute, after Xan has opened the door, to look at it. Waves of memory wash over me. Christmases that my mother and I spent alone together and before that, just a sense of contrast rather than a memory, the safe feel of the years before Marcus died. I know it's the same for everyone. Christmas trees are just one of those switches that turn on the past for all of us.

In the kitchen the doors to the terrace are standing open and sunshine is pouring in. There is a big fire burning, but the bright light douses it and makes the heat unnecessary. There is a strong smell of roasting turkey and tangerine peel mixed with the outdoor Halemni scent of aromatic herbs. Olivia is at the stove but she turns when I come in. She is wearing a little knitted top in pale violet that I have never seen before, with a scoop at the neckline that shows the brittle span of her collarbone. Her eyes are glittering and there is a spot of red high on each cheek.

'You look very pretty,' I say and it is the truth. 'The top suits you.'

'Max gave it to me.'

I am aware of the two men at the doorway on to the terrace. The children are out there playing. Olivia and I look at each other and away again. A truce, then, for today, in this subtle struggle between us.

There are presents to exchange. For the boys, from a kit I found on a shelf in Helen's shop, I have sewn a family of grey and pink felt mice with extravagant whiskers and tiny bead eyes. They are immensely pleased with these. For Xan and Olivia, also from Helen's shop, I have bought two decks of playing cards because I know that theirs are dog-eared and greasy.

There are presents for me, too. Chocolates, from Rhodes, in a shiny box with gold and brown pleated paper cups. Olivia and Xan both know how much I love and crave sweet things. But I like Georgi's and Theo's gift even better. They have made a collection of beach jewels – white and green and amber chunks of bottle glass, rubbed smooth by the sea – and filled a glass pickling jar with them.

I haven't even tried to find a present for Max. We are, I calculate, enough of an offering for each other. But he has something for me and when Olivia has turned back to the stove he casually passes it across. It is a bouquet, but a Halemni version. He has collected dried twigs and teazles and wands of grass and wiry puffs of spiny burnet, and tied them into a posy with a length of red ribbon. The effect is spectacularly, sculpturally beautiful.

There are chairs out on the *avli* under the bare vine branches but we hardly have time to sit down before Christopher arrives. He too has presents for everyone – he has drawn a cartoon of each of us and framed them properly with glass and stained wood. He is a talented artist and they are very good. Theo's spiral of curly hair is exaggerated into a frothy billow that almost submerges him. Xan's eyebrows are great caterpillars clamped to his forehead, and Max is dressed in shorts with a tinny in his hand and a grin like a shark's. When I see mine, I think Christopher must have handed me Olivia's by mistake. I am towering above a tiny table and chair, feet apart and hands on my hips, a smile

288

consuming half my face. The size of me and the confidence I radiate remind me of my first sight of Olivia, in the doorway of this house, as I came soaked and shivering out of the sea.

Olivia is looking down at her picture.

'Let me see, Mummy,' Georgi asks and she holds it up. Christopher has drawn her as an elongated creature with endless legs and a bird's body. She is more fragile and her face more delicate than the real thing, but then I look again and I think, no, he's caught her exactly as she is today.

'You flatter me, Christopher,' Olivia says and goes back to her cooking. He follows her with his eyes and then collects himself. Xan has already turned away to pile logs on to the fire.

'And there's one more thing,' Christopher says. From a scruffy paper bag he produces three lemons, two big bottles of Schweppes tonic water and a half-litre of Gordon's gin. 'Tadah!'

'Gin and tonic,' Max breathes in awe. 'Let me be the master of ceremonies.'

We all take our drinks out under the pergola. I look up briefly before I try mine and see the twigs and a few dead leaves sharp against the sky. It is so still that we can hear tiny waves breaking down on the beach.

The taste of gin makes me think of London and the yellow walls of our drawing room at Dunollie Mansions. Last year our old friends Clive and Sally Marr came to Christmas dinner. I wonder what Peter and Lisa Kirk are doing at this minute, but I don't feel any stab of sorrow. I lift my glass instead and drink a wordless toast to them and to myself. I am not going back and what is there to mourn?

Meroula is the next arrival. In honour of the day she has swapped her navy-blue armour-plated cardigan for an almost coquettish pale-blue one. There is another round of presents to be exchanged. I love the inventive frugality of the hand-knitted scarves and crochet mats.

Max goes inside and puts on a CD of carols. To a background of the Coventry carol and 'The Holly and the Ivy' it is decided that it's warm enough to eat outdoors, and the men carry the table out into the sunshine. Two large gins make me lazy-headed and thick-fingered, but I lay the table with the crackers that Xan managed to find in Rhodes Town piled in the centre. Christopher and Max are dealing with vegetables and Xan is uncorking bottles of red wine and ranging them on the dresser. Olivia has come outside and is standing at the edge of the terrace, leaning against one of the pergola supports and looking out to sea. Even though her back is turned, I can suddenly read the weariness in her. I am about to go and ask what else I can do to help, but Christopher beats me to it. He tilts the Gordon's bottle to freshen her glass and carries over a chair so that she can sit down.

The turkey and roast potatoes and dishes of vegetables have all been demolished. The pudding was doused in Greek brandy and it blazed beautifully, and Olivia took photographs of us wearing the paper hats from the crackers. The gin is finished, and several bottles of wine as well. We have done the riddles and Max and Xan have played Racing Demon with Georgi and Theo, and Meroula has fallen asleep in the chair in front of the fire, not without remarking first that it's too warm for such a blaze. Christopher and I are washing up, making a companionable rhythm of passing dripping plates from sink to draining board. Olivia is outside again, sitting in the chair that Christopher carried out for her. Two or three times during the meal I caught her with her eyes fixed on someone's face, frowning a little, as if she was trying to weigh them up. I have never known her so quiet, although everyone else made enough noise to compensate.

Xan suddenly throws down his hand of cards. 'Come on. Let's all go for a walk.'

The sun is low, but there is still warmth in the air. Christopher whisks a cloth over the last pan and the boys jump up from the card game and run out to Olivia. I can see them pulling at her hands.

Meroula wakes up and adjusts her cardigan. 'I will stay here and watch the fire,' she says.

There is a move towards the door. Olivia stands up unsteadily, holding on to the back of her chair. I hadn't noticed it, but she must have drunk as much as the rest of us. I feel a bit unsteady too, but pleasantly so.

'I'm *coming*,' Olivia says. She puts another jersey on over her violet top and pulls on her boots, puffing a little with the effort.

The street is deserted except for basking cats. We move off in a bubble of noise and laughter. Xan and Max each have a boy on their shoulders and Christopher and Olivia and I walk just behind, heading for the silver slice of sea beyond the houses. The beach is a curved ribbon of polished shingle, and after the fumes of food and wine the clean salt air races through my head like another intoxicant. I want to sing and run.

'Race you,' I call to the boys. They slide down from the men's shoulders and a second later we are all running, scrambling and gasping with laughter, along the edge of the beach where expiring waves slap against our shoes. Max is beside me and he reaches for my hand and swings it as we run in the boy's wake. All through the Christmas meal I have just been one of the family around the table and this has given me pleasure, but this demonstration of plain affection makes my heart jump into my throat. I glance back, automatically, over my shoulder to see what Olivia is doing.

She is running with her arms tucked into her sides. Her eyes are fixed on the shingle and the red spots on her cheeks have spread to a flush. There is a look of blind concentration on her face that troubles me with its familiarity until I realise why. The expression is *mine*. I have caught it on my own face often enough and it says: I am going to hold on, I am going to do what is expected of me. To stop will be to disintegrate.

We are all panting and, except for Olivia, laughing with exhilaration when we reach the end of the beach. Running has made everyone hot. There is a peeling off of constricting winter clothes.

'I think we should go in for a Christmas swim,' Max says. 'Like in Oz.'

I can't tell if this triggers off a thought of his wife and daughters, on a beach in Sydney without him.

Xan isn't going to be told what to do on his home territory. He is already pulling off his boots and jeans and the children are leaping around him in encouragement.

'Last one in,' he shouts.

'Xan ...' I hear Olivia say.

'It's only a swim,' he retorts. 'It's Christmas. Be happy.'

The sea is so clear that you can see the grain of every pebble, all down the sloping shelf into deep water. Close to the surface a shoal of tiny fish is rocked by the miniature waves.

Olivia looks to Christopher to support her veto, but even he is taking off his clothes. I hesitate for a moment, then I strip down to my second-hand vest and the cotton knickers I buy from Helen's haberdashery stock. There is a whoop and a huge splash as Max and Xan simultaneously hit the water. Drops of spray catch the light and shimmer like diamonds. The two boys dance in the shallows, a pair of skinny brown eels, and then plunge in too. The beach silence is split with shrieks as the cold hits them.

Christopher slides past me, a pale pillar, and dips into the waves. He comes up at once, swimming strongly. With his pointed features and his hair slicked flat back from his forehead he looks like a clever water rat. Then Olivia wades in, straight-shouldered and with her arm angled to pull back her hair. She must have decided that she will not be left out. When the water reaches mid-thigh she tips herself forward and silently submerges. I am the last one in.

'Kitty, cowardy,' Georgi shouts at me.

The pebbles bite the soles of my feet and I screw up my toes as I edge deeper. Waves lap over my knees and I am giggling with anticipation and then filling my lungs with air before taking the plunge.

The cold hits me like a car smash. I gasp and yelp and strike out in a shower of silver spray. Cold water slides over my skin and salt stings my eyes and lips. But it feels wonderful. I dive under the surface, down and down, pulling with my arms until shingle scrapes my thighs and I have to head upwards again with my lungs burning for air. The brown arms of the headland are a long way off and I am thinking of Andreas.

Where is he? I feel his nearness now, as if he is watching us. I have never spoken about him to anyone on the island, nor ever tried to ask if anyone knows him. *Now you know.* I still don't know, not fully, but I understand that he isn't a part of this place. I wouldn't want to be met with a shrug or stare of incomprehension if I mentioned his name. His otherness is my secret, even from Max.

I am heading out to sea, pulling with long smooth strokes. I don't feel the cold for now, only the perfect exhilaration of air and water and salt. The sleepiness of heavy food and drink is washed clean away.

When I stop swimming at last and pause to tread water I am a long way from the others who are chasing and splashing each other in the shallows. I curve my arm over my head to show them that I am all right and let myself float. The sky is an unbroken shell of pearl. With water filling my ears and salt shrivelling my tongue, and the cold beginning to gnaw at my flesh again, I know that I have never felt so happy or so free.

I roll over like a porpoise, ready to swim for the beach. But before I strike out I look towards Megalo Chorio, sinking into the purplish dusk now, although the old village and the heights above are still touched by the sun. On the road at the back of the beach, behind the ruined tamarisk trees, there is an old man with a donkey. He is standing watching all the cavorting in the water. Then I notice there are children on the flat land behind him, running in and out between the remains of the ugly summer blocks. I stretch my arms in a lazy vee ahead of me and start to swim.

Everyone else is hopping on the beach as I wade out of the water. They are rubbing gooseflesh with scratchy sweaters and trying to pull socks on over wet white feet. Theo's lips have turned blue, but we are all exhilarated.

'Christmas swim,' Xan says in triumph. 'We'll have to make it a tradition.'

'Give me Bondi,' Max protests.

'Brandy, a large brandy', Christopher wails, 'for a drowning man.'

Olivia sees to the boys, rubbing them down with a T-shirt apiece. Only when they are dressed again does she start putting on her own clothes.

My thick woollen vest is dragging and heavy with water. I strip it off and drop it at my feet and for a few seconds, until I have regained the first sweater, I am naked to the waist. The two little boys are oblivious but I feel the three men all looking at me. At once, immediately, I wish I had stayed covered up.

We begin the walk back into the village. The old man has gone and so have the children. Olivia is behind again and I notice that she is convulsively shivering. I retrace two steps and put my arm round her, meaning to try to rub some warmth into her. But she pushes me away, rough with anger.

'Don't,' is all she says.

Outside the potter's house we separate. I want to go back to my quiet room and I assume that the Georgiadises will want a peaceful evening. But Xan smiles and winks at me. 'Come back in a while. There's going to be a party.'

Olivia has already gone inside with Christopher. Max sketches a kiss to me and follows them.

'A party?' I repeat stupidly.

'You haven't seen a proper Halemni party yet.'

'All right. No, I mean of course, thank you. And it was a wonderful day.'

'Swimming at Christmas, eh?' Xan is plainly tickled by this.

I laugh with him. 'The donkey man must have thought we were crazy.'

'Donkey?'

'On the beach road. While we were in the water.'

Xan shakes his head. 'No. Not on Halemni, not any more. All we have is Panagiotis and his trucks.'

I am going to contradict him and then I change my mind. I don't mention the children, either.

The kitchen was still littered with playing cards and the debris of crackers and half-empty glasses and cups. Olivia moved robotically, tidying up and trying to ignore her headache. All she wanted to do was lie down and sleep, and then to wake up again free of the dread that she was being edged out of her own life.

It was Kitty's fault, all of it. She didn't want Kitty here, basking in Max's desire, taking off her clothes in front of them all, laughing with Xan and Christopher, playing with her children. She couldn't bear to hear Georgi and Theo even one more time begging to be allowed to go and see Kitty.

She would have to tell her to go. It would be simple, but final.

Leave us alone. Go back to wherever you came from.

'Look at all these empty bottles.' It was Meroula, muttering in Greek with her mouth down-turned in disapproval.

'There were a lot of us,' Olivia tried to smile and not to point out that Meroula had had her glass refilled more than once. 'And it is Christmas.'

'Christmas,' Meroula sniffed, managing to make it sound like some pagan depravity.

Christopher had gone home and Kitty had made herself scarce for once. Max was moving round the margin of the room, looking hangdog, just as she remembered from their childhood when he had done something she didn't like and wanted to ingratiate himself with her again. She ignored him and concentrated on putting the kitchen to rights. Xan was doing something outside, making some busy arrangements and directing the boys to help him. She couldn't quite work out what it might be.

'Where do these go?' Max asked, indicating clean saucepans stacked beside the draining board.

'The cupboard to the right of the sink,' she said. She moved to show him and as she did so she saw through the terrace doors exactly what was occupying Xan out in the crisp twilight. He was lighting the big barbecue in its special pit, just as he did on the guests' last evening every two weeks all through the summer. Georgi and Theo were carrying logs in their arms, from the special store that they never touched themselves even in the coldest winter. She frowned in confusion for a moment. The big barbecue, tonight?

'What are you doing?'

Xan paused. His white smile flashed in the failing light. 'What does it look like?'

'Why?'

'Ah, I've asked some of our friends to come. It's a surprise.'

Olivia's knees sagged. 'It certainly is. Who?'

'I thought it would be nice, eh? A Greek party to finish off the day.'

Xan felt outnumbered, that was what it was. He wanted to demonstrate that he was still the Greek father in his household.

'Who?' Olivia insisted.

He shrugged. 'Ah, who do you expect? Yannis, Stefania, Michaelis and Nikos, Evgenia …'

'No,' she interrupted.

'I will grill meat, a few sausages, not much. Maybe you can open a few cans, some beans, perhaps chop a few tomatoes. Perhaps we can have some music and dance a little.'

'Xan, I said no.' The idea was hateful. Her headache felt like an ice pick jabbing into her skull and ever since the swim in the sea she had been shivering. Her jaw and shoulders felt rigid with suppressed juddering. She couldn't think of anything but lying down and letting darkness fold around her.

'No?' he repeated, as if he had never heard the word before.

'I'm tired, I want to go to bed early. I don't want the house full of noise and people.' Her voice rose with the swelling of a sob in it. Max put the saucepans down and came towards her but she held up her hand to keep him off. There were too many people. What had happened to everything that had once seemed so simple?

'I have asked everyone to come, now. I thought you would like the surprise.'

'I … would have liked it, any other night. But I'm too tired now and I don't feel very well.' This was the first time she had said even to herself that she might be ill. The admission didn't bring any relief. 'Tell them all it will have to be some other night. Please, Xan.'

Xan's face lost its genial lines. She knew this stubborn expression. He didn't even hear what she was saying.

297

'You want me – expect me – to tell our friends that they can't come to our house?'

This was a serious rebuke. Hospitality was everything. Olivia took two steps to rest her hands on the back of a chair. Without this support she thought she might fall over. Georgi and Theo were still moving logs and Meroula was fussing at the sink. She was listening to every word, of course.

'Not tonight,' Olivia whispered.

'I will make a few bits for you and your friends,' Meroula called to Xan in Greek. For Olivia, she switched to distancing English. 'You should go and have a small sleep, maybe. You will feel better.'

She couldn't suppress the shivering any longer. Her whole body was racked with it. It was flu, that's what it was. She was coming down with flu.

If Xan wanted to invite every soul on Halemni to the house tonight, he would just have to look after them himself. She didn't have the strength to argue with him or his mother.

An hour or so, she thought. If I lie down for a while now I can get up again later and show my face, at least.

'Thank you, Mother,' she said. 'If the boys ...'

'You can leave them to me,' Meroula said with grim pleasure.

It was an effort to climb the stairs. The risers swam up to meet her and the treads seemed to drop away beneath her feet. She walked unsteadily to her bed and crawled under the covers. Her face burned but she thought she would never get warm again. What had she been doing, swimming in the sea?

There was a soft knock on the door and Max came in with a cup of tea. He put it on the chair beside the bed.

'Thanks,' she managed to say. The thought of the cup filmed with tannin and greasy milk brought her close to vomiting.

'Xan did honestly think you'd be pleased with the idea.'

Why was her brother trying to tell her what her husband thought? Why did everyone try to edge her into the corner of her own fucking picture? Anger briefly gripped her and ebbed away again, leaving her mute and exhausted.

'Well. Have a kip. See you later.'

Almost at once, it seemed, she was pitched helter-skelter into dreams. Kitty was towering in the middle of them, bare-breasted, wet-haired, directing the movements of tiny unrecognisable people who swarmed around her.

When Olivia woke up again she was disorientated. Her mouth was tight and dry, and her face swollen. She struggled to remember what day it was and why she was alone in the bed at the wrong time, with something else out of place in the house that she couldn't at first identify. After a confused minute she realised that it was unaccustomed noise.

She sat up at once and swung her legs over the side of the bed. They seemed not to perform quite in the way she wanted them to but she straightened them out anyway and stood up. They almost gave way under her weight, but she caught hold of the bedpost in time. Her wayward knees hit the chair at the bedside and the cup of cold tea tipped over, sending a brown stream splashing over her ankles. She mopped it absently with a discarded sock and made her way to the door.

The noise downstairs was louder with the door open. It was voices and laughing and music.

The kitchen had been cleared for dancing. The table was pushed against the wall, with a barrel of home-made wine set on it, and the chairs had been shoved out into the hall. There seemed to be a huge crowd of people when Olivia slipped in between them. She was only half aware that her clothes were twisted from sleeping in them and her hair stood up on one side in a pillow crest, but no one noticed in any case. They were exuberantly dancing *ballos*, the island dances. There was even a band. Michaelis was playing the local pipes, accompanied by Nikos on a fiddle. The third musician was Christopher Cruickshank who had a set of bongo drums gripped between his knees and was beating out the rhythm with his eyes blissfully closed and his face slicked with sweat.

Xan was in the thick of it all, dancing with Kitty.

But as soon as he saw Olivia he gave a whoop of happy welcome and dived to catch her hand.

'Dance with me.'

His arms drew her into the rhythm. She let him do what he wanted, cupping the nape of her neck, nudging her hips into the music. Kitty had been commandeered now by Max. Her hair flew up and down in thick hanks and Max brushed it away from her mouth. They were trying to look as if the dance had just flung them together but there was enough electricity between them to illuminate the room without any need for candles.

Xan was an energetic dancer. Olivia tried to follow the steps. The music boomed in her head, faster and faster, and the press of bodies bumped around her. She felt that she was going to spin off the floor, out of Xan's reach, on some fatal trajectory of her own. She couldn't stop or even slow down, not with the music so loud and insistent. But at the moment when she was about to reel away it did slow and then stop, so that the piper could take a long draught of his wine and mop his face with a yellow handkerchief.

The scene lost none of its hallucinatory quality. But she could see now that there were no more than twenty people here. Meroula and Manolis's mother were watching from the corner, with Theo asleep between them. Georgi had been shyly dancing at the edge of the room, his hand held by Anna Efemia. He wriggled between the laughing groups and came to his mother.

'Why didn't you have supper with us when everyone was here?'

'I was asleep.'

'*I* didn't go to sleep.'

'You have got more energy than me.'

'I think so,' he said, nodding seriously.

'Good party, eh?' Xan crowed. Now that she was here he had forgiven her for her deficient hospitality.

Kitty was clapping her hands for more music and Yannis cupped his hands to his mouth, shouting for an encore. Olivia sidled to the table, her mouth and throat burning with thirst. She found a glass and took a gulp of wine. There was a long-drawn-out quivering fiddle note that held the room under a spell of expectation, then the music leapt up and they were all dancing again. The floor seemed to buckle and surge under Olivia's stumbling feet but she accepted it as what would be.

I never much liked dancing, but this is much more than a mere dance. The fiery rhythms and the intricate moves get under your skin and burn your bones. It isn't just the wine that does it either, although there is a river of it washing through me by now. It's the closeness of the room and the faces in the candlelight, and Max and the music itself. Olivia is dancing with Xan, faltering instead of swinging her hips, but he takes her hands and steers her. She closes her eyes and sways as if she is giddy, or drunk.

While I am noticing this I see something else too. Meroula's friend got up and went to the door, and now she is bringing a new arrival into the room. It is Panagiotis and he is looking around, elbowing between the dancers, searching for someone. Anna Efemia the island nurse is still at the far side of the room with Georgi swinging from her hands and as soon as Panagiotis sees her he makes straight for her.

Anna listens to whatever it is he is saying. Panagiotis tugs at her arm and she nods and asks a question, putting her mouth close to his ear to make herself heard. Panagiotis shouts something in response, and Anna frees herself from Georgi's grasp and begins to follow him. I am watching with a thought of Helen forming in my mind when there is a thump followed by a crash of furniture and some confused exclamations. The music falls apart for a couple of bars and then stops.

At first all I can see is people crowding around and stooping over something. Into the silence left by the music I can hear Xan calling out in Greek with a sharp note of anxiety in his voice.

Then I see Olivia lying in a heap on the floor. Stefania is kneeling beside her and Xan is trying to clear a space around them, and I make a move forward and check myself at the same instant. Georgi is scrambling between people, trying to reach his mother.

Panagiotis has already propelled Anna Efemia as far as the door, but she stops when she hears the noise of Olivia falling over. She rushes back across the room and the others make way for her. When they stand back I can see Olivia's closed eyes and her legs and arms crooked from the way she fell. She looks huge and helpless and terrifyingly inert. There are surges of movement around her but Xan holds everyone back except Anna Efemia who kneels down as Stefania makes room. Out of the corner of my eye I can just see Panagiotis making little frenzied waves in the open doorway. Theo has woken up and is kicking and crying while Meroula restrains him.

Olivia has fainted. Anna Efemia checks her vital signs unhurriedly, and even as she does it Olivia's eyes open and she rolls her head.

Xan kneels over her, holding her hand and murmuring to

her. The shock in the room subsides a little and the spectators start turning to each other and talking in low voices. I can hear Christopher saying to Max that of course she wasn't feeling well, and Stefania soothing Georgi. Anna Efemia helps Olivia into a sitting position with Xan supporting her. A glass of water is passed across from the sink and she sips at it. Her lips are pale and the red spots still show on her cheekbones.

Panagiotis is wringing his hands now. He darts forward and back again, and then catches sight of me.

'You come,' he says, jerking his head to the door.

'What?'

I can just pick enough Greek words and meaning out of the rejoinder. Helen's baby is on the way, early, with no doctor on the island so Anna Efemia must come at once. And Helen has been asking for me, too. Helen's mother is dead and her married sisters no longer live on the island.

'For me?'

Panagiotis's eyes roll in affirmation and he pulls at my sleeve. When I hesitate, out of surprise rather than unwillingness, he clenches his fists and punches his temples. Anna Efemia looks up from attending to Olivia and says something brisk to him. The gist of it must be that she will come as soon as she can.

Now I take Panagiotis's arm.

'I'm coming,' I tell him. 'Whatever I can do.'

Max nods across the heads that separate us. Panagiotis steers me out of the room.

It's cold outside and pebbles clink like metal under our feet as we hurry down the hill.

FIFTEEN

I have never been inside Panagiotis's house before. The floors are mottled marble and covered with slippery little rugs, and the furniture is very tall and shiny brown. Every horizontal surface is covered with mats or doilies, and packed-together china ornaments and framed pictures and bewildering trinkets. It is very clean and there is a chemical scent of potpourri and air freshener.

He hurries me down a hallway lit by a bright bulb under a green lacy shade and opens the door of a ground-floor room. Helen is lying on her back on a double bed with a high headboard and piles of crochet-covered cushions. I can smell her fear as soon as I sit down on the edge of the bed. I smile as confidently as I can, and take hold of her hand and ask her how she is feeling.

There is another woman with her, whom I recognise as the wife of a Panagiotis cousin. She stares at me in surprise and no wonder, since she was expecting the nurse and the strange oversized English shop assistant has turned up in her place. But Helen does her sweet smile back at me and I'm touched to see that she looks relieved that I have arrived. The fine dark hairs on her top lip are shiny with sweat and there are dark rings in the armpits of her cotton wrap. A thick hairy blanket lies over the huge mound of her stomach.

'You're fine,' I tell her, with no particular basis for doing so. I know nothing about childbirth, obviously, except for what I have seen in films and medical soaps.

'Anna Efemia will be here in a minute. Olivia wasn't very well and she stayed to ...'

My stream of information that Helen can't understand in any case is cut short. Her eyes widen to the point where I can see a margin of white all round the dark-brown irises and then squeeze shut. Her teeth clench and her arms begin to thrash although she keeps a tight hold of my hand. Her nails dig into my flesh so fiercely that I am wincing myself. Then her mouth opens and she gives a long howl that lasts a full ten seconds before tailing away into a gasping groan. Panagiotis makes a terrified echo somewhere between a squeak and a wail.

'One pain,' the cousin's wife says grimly.

No kidding, I am tempted to reply, but I find a towel on the bedside chest instead and mop Helen's face and neck with it. 'It's okay,' I tell her. 'It's a contraction.' From my anecdotal knowledge of obstetric procedure I am dimly aware that we should time the minutes between contractions. I even glance at my wrist, but I still don't have a watch. On the bedside table there is an enamel alarm clock with flowers and butterflies painted on the face, so I note that it is seven minutes past the hour without bothering to wonder which hour.

The contraction has fully subsided and Helen opens her wet eyes. She looks past me to Panagiotis and indicates that she wants to say something to him. He bends forward and she whispers in his ear. Whatever it is makes him even more anxious and his eyes flicker from me to the cousin's wife.

'*Parakalo*,' Helen begs him.

There is a muttered consultation between Panagiotis and the woman, while I sit beside Helen and concentrate on rubbing her hands and trying to exude calm. The next thing I hear is the two of them leaving the room. As soon as the door closes behind them Helen gives a long sigh of relief and fixes her eyes imploringly on mine. It dawns on me that I am to be her designated birthing partner. My response is surprise, squeamish dismay and a sense of being greatly honoured, in approximately equal parts.

I swallow hard. 'I'm here,' I assure her. 'If you are sure that's really what you want.'

At thirteen minutes past the hour there is another contraction. The screaming seems to be even louder this time and to go on longer, and she kicks her legs and tries feebly to roll over. While I am mopping her face afterwards I remember that I have read somewhere – probably during one of my own short-lived pregnancies – that a woman in labour should be able to move around if she wants to, to find the best position for herself. The one other thing I can remember – from a slightly earlier era, no doubt – is the importance of lots of hot water and newspapers. Maybe I should set Panagiotis to filling saucepans.

'Try sitting up.' I put my arm under Helen's shoulders and help her to struggle upright against the pillows. She breathes more easily and pushes the heavy blanket off her stomach, so I take it away altogether. Her plump bare legs are smooth and very white, veined with blue above the parted knees. I don't have to work too hard to convince myself that I shouldn't try to investigate any further. What could I do about whatever I might discover?

The next contraction comes much more quickly, after only four minutes or so. Helen screeches in Greek, words that I've never heard but can more or less fill in. Where the *fuck*, I think, is Anna Efemia?

After this one has subsided Helen is even more restless, shifting her bulk around on the bed like an upturned beetle and trying to find a way of getting comfortable while pinned on her back.

'Do you want to try moving around?'

It's hopeless. I seem to have forgotten every word of Greek. Helen's arm hooks around my neck and I almost tip over on top of her.

'Come on. You can lean on me.'

We seem to have the same idea despite the language problem, so I shift her buttocks to the edge of the bed and then I half lift and half drag her to her feet. She is gasping and sweating, but I calculate that to work on this at least diverts her full attention from the upcoming contraction. Like a pair of pantomime drunks we lurch a few steps from the bed to the door, from the door to the foot of the bed. Then she grasps the footboard and grunts and hunches her shoulders. She is sinking into a squat with my arm under hers for support, and yelling a string of imprecations. I put my free hand on her belly and try to rub it, but her head swings up and she snarls at me. 'Okay,' I mutter. 'No massage.'

But she is riding this contraction better than the others, I am thinking, when she gives a hiccup of surprise. Fluid splashes all over our feet and gushes across the floor. She isn't peeing, I realise. The waters have broken. Oh *God*. I am going to have to deliver this baby on my own if someone doesn't get here quickly. She is moving again, groaning and shouting, and I drop the hairy blanket one-handed over the puddle of amniotic fluid and shuffle with her. By the time the next one comes she is kneeling on all fours, panting and howling and I am shouting nonsense about keeping calm and willing the terrified Panagiotis and his relative to come back through the door right now and save me from emergency midwifery.

'Ahahahaha,' Helen grunts.

'Hold on now,' I order her.

Then, blessedly, the door does open and Anna Efemia materialises with Panagiotis and the cousin's wife gaping over her shoulder. She shuts the door in their faces, puts down a white metal case and marches to Helen. There seems to be almost no interval between contractions now but somehow the nurse has come in on one. She shakes Helen briskly by the shoulder and gives her an instruction. Get into bed at once, appears to be the gist of it. Helen nods with exhausted meekness and the nurse clicks her fingers in my direction. Together we ease her to her feet again and propel her to the bed, me at the head end and the nurse at the other. I get the impression that this is the only birthing position that Anna Efemia is prepared to countenance. Helen is flat on her back once more with her knees spread apart by the time the next contraction comes. This time she is purple-faced and straining, and the blood vessels stand out on her neck like thick string. I try to edge backwards to indicate that my role is over, but her hand clamps round my wrist.

Anna Efemia has opened her case and snapped on a pair of thin rubber gloves and a paper face mask. She conducts a survey while I mop Helen's face and murmur encouragement. It can't be long, I think.

Between us we spread out a thin plastic sheet and some paper towelling. Helen is allowed to prop herself up on her elbows, with me and the pillows for extra support. Her mouth stretches in a wide grimace. Anna Efemia counts and gives instructions – thank God – and Helen obediently strains and pants and strains again, while I rub her shoulders and look south and then quickly look away again. Is this what it's always like? How does anyone ever get born?

Push. Good girl, another push. Now rest, breathe. I can suddenly understand Greek again. In fact, I could probably understand this in Mandarin or Swahili. Helen embarks on another yell but Anna Efemia tells her to stop that and concentrate on pushing, and to my surprise she does as she is told. The flowery clock gives a small click and I glance across and see the minute hand move past the twelve. It isn't Christmas Day any longer. This doesn't amaze me. The day already seems to have stretched out to week-long proportions.

But the finale of the performance, when it arrives, seems almost easy compared with the run-up. Helen's mouth opens in a perfect circle of surprise. Between her raised knees I see Anna Efemia gentling a round, shiny, wet, black-and-crimson head. There is a pause while we all wait, silent and with the breath ragged in our lungs, and then the nurse orders another push and Helen screws up her face in a last effort of will. A pair of red hunched shoulders, a twist of purple-red umbilical cord and two sets of miniature folded limbs are delivered into Anna Efemia's hands.

The baby lies between her mother's legs on the sodden and bloodstained paper towel and Anna Efemia bends over the tiny creature and clears her airways, then lifts her up and a tiny bleating cry emerges. Helen cries too, tears streaming down her face, and reaches out for her. Very gently, the nurse places the baby on her mother's breast and Helen cups her hand around the wet head.

'A girl,' Anna Efemia confirms.

I kiss the top of Helen's sweaty head and gaze down at the baby. Her face is squashed and streaked with blood and some waxy white stuff, and her eyes blink open. They are tiny slits of bottomless blackness.

'She is so beautiful.'

I am trembling like a jelly. I have never seen anything so amazing. There is a new person here who was not before: creation's conjuring trick.

Anna Efemia takes over again. The baby has to be wiped and wrapped up, and I know there are other messy tasks to be completed. She looks at me briefly.

'Tell Panagiotis, please.'

Yes, of course. This isn't our baby, Helen's and mine, although by now I feel as though it is.

'Well done,' I tell her mildly as I move into retreat and she flashes me a smile of pure elation with all the shyness rinsed out of it.

I don't want to leave the room. It feels like the centre of the earth, but I don't have a place here. At the door I remember that the birth is not the only thing that has happened in the world today.

'Is Olivia all right?'

Anna Efemia nods curtly. 'I believe so.'

I find Panagiotis and the cousin's wife in the kitchen, sitting at a table with two cups of coffee and a brimming ashtray. Panagiotis seems to have worked his way through a full pack of cigarettes in the last hour. Their heads swivel and they start up from their seats.

'Congratulations. You have a beautiful daughter.' I deliver this classic line with great pleasure, and Panagiotis jumps up and wrings my hands with as much gratitude as if I am responsible.

'Thank you, thank God,' he stutters.

'I can go in?' he asks when we have all shaken each other's hands.

'Wait just a few minutes,' I suggest, thinking of what Anna Efemia is currently doing.

The cousin's wife offers me a cup of coffee with polite hospitable gestures, but I decline. I want to be on my own now.

Once I am outside, I know I don't want to shut myself away in my studio. I am so excited, so astonished by what I have just seen that even the black dome of the sky seems too confining. I drift between the village houses, up little cobbled alleys that lead nowhere except to scrubby wasteland, moving easily in the darkness like one of the island cats.

I am thinking about physical links and the way one body emerges from another – pushed out, with all the blood and yelling, to start up a fresh life. Witnessing it for real made me comprehend it in a way I never have before, even when I was briefly carrying my own children. Helen's mother gave birth to her and Helen to her daughter tonight, and this crimson scrap of humanity will have a baby some day and so on, making a chain of mothers and daughters all down the generations before us and on far beyond our limited range of vision or understanding.

This is hardly startling in itself, I know, even though the perspective is new to me. What is surprising is how utterly soothing it is to contemplate this unending chain. It puts the drama of individuality into a smooth unbroken sequence. The implacably repetitive process of birth itself, birth after birth, rolls on and washes over me and Olivia and Max, and all the rest of us just like the sea over shingle. I am comforted to feel so diminished.

I walk up through the village square and leave the church and the potter's house and the taverna behind me. I have come this way so many times that I can follow the path across the hillside without thinking about it. The pumping and zinging of adrenalin in my arteries gradually slows down and my mind clears and expands in its aftermath.

I am sorting my store of memories, re-examining them through the lens of tonight's events. It's like looking down through the crystal water where we swam this afternoon, down to the gardens of the seabed.

My mother gave birth to me but the chain – this tiny strand of it – stops here with me. I would have wanted a daughter, if I had been given the choice. But I am childless.

I don't often think of my mother and now I wonder why this is. Having watched Helen cupping her baby's head tonight I know she must have touched me as a newborn in the same way. The idea sends a wash of reverse tenderness through me as though she were the child and I the mother. I wish she were still alive, to begin the conversations we never had even though I sat beside her bed all the time she was dying.

Even then, when she knew that she didn't have long to live, we didn't talk much. We were too careful with each other.

I can remember the exact colour of the trim on her bedjacket, catch the waft of her Arpège perfume, see the pleats of her Burberry skirts and the clasp of her old but good leather handbag. But I can hardly see *her*.

I knew the dimensions of her grief and I am ashamed to acknowledge to myself that I resented it. I can't say this for sure but my father probably resented it too, and the way it filled the recesses of our too-quiet house. In the end he gave up and went off to exuberant Lesley and her brood of children, and started all over again. That I would quite like to have gone too only increased my determination – my obligation – to be careful with my mother. I tiptoed around her, almost afraid to speak in case it stirred a painful memory. And such careful attention helped me to contain my guilt, too.

I am so *tired* of guilt.

It has strangled me for so long, I think I died at the same time as my brother.

If he had lived, I would have been someone quite different.

The path leads past the graveyard and the place where Olivia fell on the night of the feast, and zigzags upwards across bare turf and rock towards Arhea Chorio. The Knights' castle on the highest point is just a denser black against the black

312

sky and the thought of Max wings through my head.

I don't want to climb any higher tonight – not even as far as the old village. I sit down on a rock instead, wrapping my arms round my knees because of the cold. It is so plain and beautiful here, and what I have just witnessed seems to anchor me even more firmly to the stone of Halemni. This birth does belong to me, I think, if I want it to. It is the antithesis to so much death.

I am so glad to be here. I am so grateful for the freedom I have found and for the new person it has allowed me to be. I am not going to give it up. Andreas brought me here, why and how I still don't know, but it is where I am meant to be.

Determination takes hold. I am without ties, without responsibilities or relatives or old history. I don't even have a passport, or a single possession from the old life. And none of this matters, because I am *here*. My tongue slides behind the double ridge of my teeth, testing for the edges of pain. The tongue tip still feels thickened and sore although the bite itself is healing to a pale sickle mark.

I am going to stay where I am and be happy, whatever it takes. I don't have a child, a daughter, and in this I am a tiny blind end. But the chain still goes on regardless and magnificent, and I can flourish for myself.

The thought of all this makes me feel drunk: light in the head and giggly and unsure of my limbs. I *can* flourish, plainly, because I *am* doing.

There are no lights down in Megalo Chorio. Everyone is asleep, even Anna Efemia and Helen and Panagiotis and the baby. I am not quite sure how long I have been out here, wandering in the dark. A long time, perhaps. Olivia is asleep, and Max and Xan and the boys.

Olivia has no daughter, so she isn't perfectly knitted into the seamless chain either. I must ask her if she would have liked one, or if boys in the image of their father are enough.

I saw that she had fainted, just as Panagiotis was imploring me to come to Helen. Anna Efemia said she was all right, so I haven't thought about her again until now. The point under the tip of my tongue where the teeth stabbed right through it chafes against the lower incisor as I continue the exploration of my mouth. Olivia doesn't want me to stay here. I can feel the swell of her hostility everywhere: in the potter's house, when I play with the boys, when Max slips away to be with me.

If it comes to a straight contest for possession of the kingdom of Halemni, I wonder who will win. I was weak, but now I am strong. And as I gain strength she seems to fade.

It is an absurd thought, of course.

The wind doesn't even seem cold any longer. The first steel-grey shimmer of light is just visible to the east and the island lies so still that I can almost feel the earth rolling on towards the sunlight.

The kitchen looked as it never did. There were dirty glasses on the floor and on the shelves, and spilled food and dribbled candlewax on the table. Theo and Georgi came downstairs in the early morning, in their pyjamas, and gazed in fascinated distaste. After Olivia fainted she was revived by Anna Efemia and Stefania, and then helped up to bed by Xan and Meroula. All the people who had been at the party drifted home and the house went quiet. Xan came afterwards and made sure they were in their own beds, and told them to go to sleep and that their mother would be fine in the morning.

But something was still wrong, this mess made it obvious.

Theo was about to turn and run to look for Olivia but Georgi stopped him.

'We can eat what we want for breakfast.'

'Anything?' Theo asked.

'Yes, of course.'

They both sensed that this morning was odd enough to allow them freedom. Georgi led the way into the larder and they looked along the rows of tins and jars. Georgi took down a jar of chocolate spread and Theo selected a tin of tomato soup. This seemed a modest choice to both of them and they found a packet of biscuits and then the sweets that Olivia kept for treats and rewards. They took the food back into the kitchen and cleared a space among the dirty crockery on the table. Georgi found the tin-opener and managed to puncture the lid of the tin so Theo could pour cold soup into a cup. They began to eat.

It was enjoyable to start with, dipping biscuits into the chocolate jar and alternating mouthfuls of soup with sweets, but in the end the breakfast didn't deliver as much pleasure as they expected because the room was cold and smelled bad, and the silence of the house was uncomfortable.

After a few minutes Theo let his spoon drop.

'I want Mum.'

'You're a baby. They're still asleep, actually.'

'Kitty will be up, I expect.'

They slid off their chairs without discussing it any further. It was grey outside with a sullen mist lying over the sea, but they didn't stop to take note of the weather. Georgi was already banging on the studio door. There was no answer, so he tried the handle and the door opened. Kitty's bed was flat and smooth. There was no one in the bare room or in the bathroom cubicle. They stared at each other, their mouths rimmed with chocolate and orangey crusts of soup.

'I don't like this,' Theo said.

They were turning to leave when a long shadow in the open doorway made them both jump.

'Hello,' Kitty said. Then she laughed. 'What have you been

315

eating?'

'Breakfast.'

'Where have you been?' Georgi asked. He stood with the table between Kitty and himself but she came anyway and crouched down and put her arms round him.

She put her face against his hair and breathed in hard.

'You smell of biscuits.'

'Where have you *been*?'

'You'll never guess what's happened. Helen's baby was born in the night. It's a little girl.'

'Can we see her?'

'Yes, I'm sure you can.'

There were no demands for hunt the mouse this morning, no more questions about the baby either. The boys edged closer together.

'Mum and Pappy are still asleep, and Max.'

'I'll come and make you a proper breakfast.'

In the kitchen of the potter's house Kitty gazed around.

'Just look at this. It's time for some clearing up. But I'll make you breakfast first, shall I?'

'I don't want anything,' Theo muttered. 'I am full up.'

But they sat down at the table anyway and watched as Kitty screwed the lid back on the chocolate jar and collected up the shiny sweet papers. And they accepted yoghurt and honey, and the toast she made when it was put in front of them.

Olivia lay in bed, listening. She could smell toast and coffee, and there was the sound of running water and the rattle of plates. It was disturbing to hear the sounds of her own activity – these were her tasks, no one else would do them – and yet to be disconnected from them. She wanted very badly to get up, but her arms and legs felt so heavy that it was too much of an effort to move. Xan was lying beside her, the underside of his face squashed against the pillow. His lips were parted and he was breathing with a tiny catch of a snore. Olivia listened again, through the kitchen noises and her husband's sleep sounds. She was sure that Max was still asleep too, on the low bed in her darkroom.

It was Kitty downstairs, working in her kitchen.

'My kitchen,' Olivia spoke the words aloud. A cold finger of fear ran from the base of her spine all the way up to her hairline.

Xan opened his eyes. They were bloodshot.

'Uh. My head. How do you feel?'

'AH right.'

Somehow, she managed to sit up. She pushed her hair off her face, then she put her feet to the floor and shuffled upright. Someone had taken off her jeans but she was still wearing the soft little knitted top that Max had given her, the colour of violets. She remembered that she had passed out last night in the middle of the dancing. They had put her to bed, leaving the sweater on for warmth. She felt gritty and sticky, with sweat under her arms and in the creases of her groin. But she found the jeans on her chair and put them on.

'I'll go,' Xan mumbled without moving.

'No,' Olivia said.

The boys were sitting side by side at the bare kitchen table. It had been freshly wiped. They had cups and bowls laid out in front of them, just as she always did it herself. They looked up at her with round, troubled eyes.

'Mum?'

'It's okay.'

Last night the rugs had been rolled back for dancing and now Kitty was sweeping the bare stone flags. She paused, leaning with two hands on the broomstick.

'Would you like some coffee? How do you feel?'

Olivia put her hands up to her face, checking that the

contours of it were still familiar.

'No coffee. I want to talk.'

Kitty looked surprised in her calm work of setting the kitchen to rights and attending to the children. 'Yes?'

'We could go across ...' she nodded to the terrace doors, not wanting to say *your room* '... to the studio.'

'Do you feel all right?'

The boys were looking from Kitty to their mother and back again. Theo's spoon hung halfway to his mouth, trailing yoghurt and honey.

'Stay here and finish your breakfast,' Olivia ordered them, ignoring the question. In fact, she felt barely real. 'Or go upstairs to Pappy.'

She led the way out into the chilly morning and across to the room where Kitty had been living. She noticed the books on the table, the few clothes neatly hanging on pegs. Christopher's cartoon was propped beside the bed, Kitty standing four-square, smiling broadly. This was a *home*, insidiously establishing itself alongside her own and Xan's. The dried bouquet that Max had made for her had the place of honour closest to the pillow. Olivia didn't even want to look at the bed itself.

'Would you like to sit down?' Kitty asked gently. 'Helen had a little girl, just after midnight. I've never seen a baby born. It was a miracle.'

'I want you to go,' Olivia said, brutally cutting into this benign monologue. Even in her own ears her voice sounded cracked.

Kitty took a step backwards. 'What?'

'Don't you understand? You can't stay here any longer. It's time you went back to wherever you came from.'

Kitty said nothing. She half turned to look through the door towards the sea under its bed of mist.

The silence stretched out with no end point. Olivia thought

318

that they might just stand here for ever with the unpricked balloon of their hostility swelling between them. She couldn't even now have defined what gave the balloon its queasy tautness. They were alike, they had many things in common – at least as many as there were differences. They might easily have become friends, as the early signs had indicated. But they had not done so. Her skin crawled with feverish repugnance.

Kitty had attended the birth of Helen's baby. She had poured milk for her own children. She came between Christopher, Max, even Xan, confusing what had once been simple. It was an *intrusion*. It was Kitty's presence here that made Halemni a place of pitfalls, where it had once been safe.

Since the tsunami, that was it. The water had come and gone, washing Kitty up on their beach like a piece of flotsam. Now they needed another tide, a cleansing one.

Kitty sighed, in the end, and turned back into the room. 'Why?' she asked.

Olivia thought, I could say that I am jealous of you. That's true enough. That I don't want you in my house, taking my place. Trying to do so. These things were reasonable, weren't they?

'You don't belong here,' was what she did say.

Kitty considered this. 'How do you know?'

'It's my place.' There is not room for both of us.

They were face to face now. Their eyes locked, on a level because their heights matched. They didn't quite circle each other, but the possibility was there. Olivia folded her arms in defence, feeling the soft pile of the violet sweater under her palms.

'Yours,' Kitty said thoughtfully. She didn't need to add anything like, *so being yours means it can't be mine*? This was understood. We do understand each other, Olivia thought, although we don't attract. Like poles repel.

'And if I am happy here?' Kitty asked, in the mild tone she had used all along. 'If I want to make it mine too?'

'You can't. It's my place,' Olivia reiterated. I was here first, as a child might chant, as Georgi and Theo often taunted each other.

Kitty went to the small sink and took a glass down off the shelf. She filled it with water and with a folded tea towel dried the base because the water had slopped over the rim. Then she came and put it on the table within Olivia's reach. Olivia ignored it, even though her throat was parched and fingers of heat combed through her hair. She wouldn't accept even this much of a gesture that demonstrated possession, establishment.

'I'm going to sit down, anyway,' Kitty said. 'You can do what you want.' She pulled out one of the two chairs that were drawn up to the table and settled herself. After a moment Olivia sat too. She didn't want Kitty on a different level either, not now when she thought she had her pinned. She was suddenly sure that she was thinking with great clarity and acting with total effect. All she had to do was say go and Kitty would be gone.

'Is it because of Max?'

Olivia smiled. She could probably afford to be generous now, but she wouldn't be.

'You don't know about Max.'

'What does that mean? I think I do.'

'After a couple of weeks?'

'A couple of hours was enough.'

Olivia laughed.

Kitty reached out for the bunch of dried flowers. She laid it on the table between them, touching the tips of her fingers to the teazle spikes and minutely outlining the geometric thorns of the burnet. A leaf of dried sage dropped away and she pressed it between her thumb and forefinger, delicately scenting the dried-blood smell.

'He always knows how to charm,' Olivia told her. 'He always did.'

Kitty lifted her head at this. She seemed to be listening hard, as if she could hear beyond what was audible, a change of pressure in the room.

'I have seen him do it often enough. In his teens and twenties. How many times? Hundreds. When we were both travelling I used to hear about it. He'd write to me, telling me about the latest Ingrid or Lisa. Because women have always loved Max. My mother was his first conquest – he was the favourite boy, the son.

'And I was the only one who eluded him. His sister. Don't you think that's interesting? He always followed me because I was bigger and stronger, and I did everything first and he adored that.' She knew that she was babbling, boasting like a child, but the words came before she could censor them.

'Yes,' Kitty smiled. 'I'm sure he did.'

Looking at her, seeing how she had filled out and grown strong in her weeks on Halemni, Olivia felt the familiar swoop of fear again. She wanted to manhandle her away from here. She stared at Kitty's hands, lying loosely on either side of the bouquet. They were rough, with short nails and torn cuticles, just like her own. There was something buried, something fetid here that she couldn't understand, but her subconscious scented it and recoiled. Olivia's fists clenched in her lap. She was sweating.

Kitty said softly, 'I had a brother. He died when he was Theo's age. A statue I was climbing toppled over and killed him instantly. Did Max tell you that?'

Another moment of silence, Kitty listening again.

'No.'

Max hadn't told her. He must have thought of it as a

confidence, between himself and Kitty, but even so the fine blade of jealousy slid a millimetre deeper into Olivia's core. And at the same time she thought that this was the first real thing she had ever learned about Kitty Fisher – the inverted commas still interposed themselves – and her history. About her background, marriage, the divorced parents, the English childhood not so dissimilar from her own, she had learned or had mostly filled in for herself, but the death of her brother was the first and only defining truth.

'You must have felt that it was your fault,' Olivia said. She was too hampered to edit her words.

'The facts indicate that it *was* my fault.'

Kitty's hands still rested on the table. As Olivia watched her the light changed, yellow ousting opalescent grey like a loaded paintbrush washing over canvas. The sun was breaking through the winter sea mist. It would be another unseasonably warm and sunny day. Kitty tipped back her head and sighed with satisfaction at the stillness, the promise of heat. The contrast between her bleak admission and this voluptuous pleasure stabbed Olivia again. Kitty was calm and happy, and she seemed to have achieved this by insinuating herself, eroding the Halemni ground, making equivocal what had always been sure. She had arrived as the half-drowned fledgling and she had become the oversized cuckoo. Olivia felt sick and overheated.

'You can't stay here. The season will start, I need the room for guests.'

'It's December the twenty-sixth.'

Olivia half leaned, half fell across the table. She cupped her own hot hands over Kitty's and for an instant the contact sent a shock up her arms. She pushed the woman's hands off the table.

'I want you to leave on the next ferry.'

Kitty's eyes glittered. 'That is not very hospitable.'

'I want you to leave. Hospitality wears out.'

If she expects me to look away first, Olivia thought, she is going to be disappointed.

In the end it was Kitty who ducked her head.

'You take it for granted, don't you? Who you are?'

Olivia got to her feet, her mouth taut with triumph. She didn't want to hear any more of this, or trade any more history.

'No,' she retorted.

'I think you do. You take happiness for granted. Did you realise that?'

'None of this is anything to do with you,' Olivia shouted. The loudness of her voice shocked them both.

She left Kitty in the studio and walked back across to the potter's house.

Xan was up, unshaven and chaotically dressed.

'Are we going to have something to eat?' he asked her.

'If you make it,' she told him.

Max was in the kitchen too. She didn't spare either of them more than a glance. The boys were desultorily playing with their Christmas toys in front of the ashcovered hearth and she noticed that Theo looked ominously pale. He didn't have a strong stomach and if he overate he was liable to be sick. Leave them to it. Olivia had the sense that she was walking an inch or so outside herself as she swept straight through the kitchen and on up the stairs. Leave them all to it, make Kitty clear out, then somehow start up again.

She went into the bathroom and opened the box where they kept their stock of medicines. When she looked at herself in the mirror, as she swallowed painkillers for her headache, she saw how peculiar she was looking. Flushed cheeks, overbright eyes, mouth tight and twisted.

I have got flu, she told herself. I should go to bed for a couple of days.

The thought of the hot, crumpled bed just vacated by Xan

didn't entice her. Instead she splashed her face with cold water, gasping with the shock of it on her burning skin. Then she went into her darkroom. Max's bed was made, with a blanket smoothed and folded at the corners. His clothes were folded too, in a tidy stack. He had always been neat, even as a little boy. She had been the splashy, reckless, improvisational one.

The darkroom was where Olivia withdrew, in ordinary times, when she needed a sanctuary. Although, it came to her now as she closed the door behind her, she hadn't spent more than a few hours in here in total in all the years since Xan had light-proofed it for her. To look back at *before*, from this perspective, was like peering down from a high window at a view that was quite out of reach. She reached from the real window for the outer catch and closed the shutters, then drew the inner blind to blot out the last finger of sunlight. Then, in the pitch blackness, she slid her hand along the wall and clicked on the low red lamp. She felt safe in the dim glow. Her eyes accommodated quickly and stopped burning.

She hunted along the shelves where she stored her photographic materials. Some of the chemicals came from Rhodes, others had to be ordered from Athens, but there was plenty here for what she intended to do. She wasn't skilled but she did do her own processing, usually, because it gave her satisfaction as well as being quicker and cheaper than sending the films away. It was a relief to concentrate on something mechanical now. Her capsules of exposed 35mm film stood waiting on the wider shelf that doubled as desk and bench. She listened to herself breathing in almost total darkness as she worked with the developing and fixing solutions.

Fifteen minutes later she hung up the first strip of celluloid to dry. There were half a dozen family pictures. At first glance it looked as if there might be a good shot of Georgi, perched on a rock and looking like a bird with his head turned into the wind and feathers of hair fluffed out behind him. There was another of Meroula sitting out on the *avli* – a snatched picture that caught her with her knees parted and the lines of her face loosened. And there were some pictures of Kitty. She was wearing the striped Breton top that had come in the aid shipment and a cap with her hair bundled up underneath it. Olivia had used a paintbrush to sketch in a moustache. In the negative it was a pale flourish in a shadow of face.

Dressing up, they had told Xan and Christopher when they came in and found them. They had been remembering Jeanne Moreau in *Jules et Jim* and this had seemed to strike a chord with Kitty. But in fact they were trying out roles. Model and photographer were the obvious, familiar ones and at the same time they had been auditioning for friends or confidantes.

Olivia looked at her watch again. They had not become friends.

She developed and fixed a second reel of film. She felt more than half out of her body now, as if she was watching someone else developing pictures. Maybe it was the pain-killers, she thought. She would finish the developing and then go to bed after all.

She was just taking the second length of film off the reel when she heard Xan calling her. Without looking at it she hung it to dry beside the first and went to find out what he wanted.

Theo had been sick. He was sitting in the chair beside the remains of yesterday's fire while Xan lugubriously sloshed about with cloths and disinfectant. Georgi looked smug. Max was nowhere to be seen.

'Where were you?' Xan asked.

'In the darkroom.'

She sat down and lifted Theo on to her lap. She felt his

forehead. It was cool to the touch.

'What did you eat?'

Theo told her, with a touch of pride, nuzzling against her as he did so. The smell of him made her gag.

'I'm not surprised you were sick, then.'

She would have liked to put him down immediately and go back to her solitude in the darkroom. The intensity of her children's need for her – and her husband's – seemed to suck the marrow right out of her bones. But she waited with Theo on her lap until it seemed unlikely that he was going to be sick again, then she bathed him and found clean clothes for him to wear. By the time all this was done his colour had come back.

When they came downstairs Xan was playing cards with Georgi.

'You heard about the baby?'

'Kitty told me.'

'I thought I might call in and see Panagiotis. Have a glass, just to wish them well.'

Olivia met his eyes. 'I am printing some pictures. You can take the boys with you, or you will have to stay here.'

He called after her, when he had recovered himself, but she ignored him.

In the darkroom the negatives were dry. She took them down and scissored them into shorter strips before slipping the strips into sleeves. Then she held them up to the light to examine them more closely.

The second set of pictures shocked her.

There was a whole series, a dozen of them.

They were pictures of Kitty again.

Only it was Kitty who had *taken* the pictures. She couldn't have been behind the lens and caught in its eye at the same time.

Olivia filled two baths with developing fluid and fixer, and a third with clean water. Her hands were shaking, which made her clumsy with uncapping and pouring.

A few minutes later she hung over the developing tray and watched the positives swim out of blankness. There were two sheets of contacts, twenty-four prints on each. Wash and fix again, then wait for them to dry.

They were still tacky when she put them down in front of the window. That was too bad. She snapped up the blind and pushed the shutters open to let the sun pour in.

Olivia didn't need her little magnifying glass to study them. Tiny as they were, the pictures burned straight into her head.

Kitty with her hair pushed under a cap, a moustache cheekily painted over her mouth.

And then Kitty with her eyes heavily made up, her lips pouting with layers of colour, her hair snipped and flattened. But not Kitty. They had changed roles that time, Olivia remembered. She was the model that night, because she had submitted to having her face painted. A make-over, Kitty called it. Kitty had played photographer, prowling round her objective with the invading camera. They were good shots, she obviously had a talent for it.

Olivia bent her head over the sheets again.

Jesus, we look identical.

I look so like her, I thought it *was* her when I saw the negatives.

She painted me up like that to make me her. It was an act of possession.

Christopher had come in, that was what happened, and he had been startled to see them. And then Theo woke up with a bad dream. She remembered his scream so vividly that it seemed to belong to now and she half started to the door, thinking he might be ill again. But that was then: she remembered how she had carried him downstairs and he had looked at her face in the light and started screaming again.

Kitty had lifted Theo out of her arms while Christopher

helped her to clean the muck off her face. Dear, calm Christopher. Kitty had taken hold of Theo as if she needed, intended, to keep him.

Olivia was shaking with fear and confusion. She wanted to run downstairs to the studio, to drag Kitty out of there and to pile up her possessions and set fire to them to purge her out of the potter's house for ever.

You told her to go. The next ferry. She *is* leaving, because she can't stay here.

Making herself breathe evenly, Olivia studied the contacts again. She marked two shots, one of Kitty in the Breton jersey and one of herself as Kitty, as Kitty had made her. This one caught her with her head a little dipped and her eyes turned away out of the frame, a withdrawn look that was characteristic of her when she first came to Halemni.

She closed the shutters and the blind, and turned on the crimson darkroom light again. She took two more sheets of photographic paper and warmed them between her hands, imagining that by making the pictures, teasing them out of their photographic reticence, she could somehow coax a ghost into visibility and therefore exorcise it.

And then she watched the faces as they lay in the developing tray, the curve of an eyelid taking shape from nowhere and the glint of light finally sharpening to a minute star in one wide eye. Olivia concentrated until the prints were dark enough to satisfy her and then she swished them out of their bath and washed and fixed them. She hung the pictures side by side to dry.

Two five-by-seven black-and-white portrait prints, interestingly composed, sharply focused, adequately printed. Two tall women, strikingly alike.

The effort of concentration had exhausted her. She couldn't, now, think why she had taken so much trouble to do this. They were only photographs, Kitty posing in jumble clothes, herself unrecognisable under inches of make-up to answer some whim of Kitty's and because she herself had felt old and unattractive.

She felt ill now.

She opened the shutters once again and switched off the light.

With one hand sliding along the wall for support she made her way from the darkroom to her bedroom. The house was quiet. She pulled off her dirty clothes and dropped them on the floor. Then she lay down in the crumpled bed and closed her eyes.

SIXTEEN

'How is she?' I ask.

We are out walking again – there seems to be nothing much else we can do. The potter's house has closed itself around Olivia and even my studio doesn't feel as much like home as it did before Christmas. So Max and I have taken the one metalled road out of the village and followed it up to the island's ridge back. From here we can look down on the island's other main settlement which is no more than a cluster of houses in a dip of land. Light glints off something moving as we stand and watch – maybe the wing mirror of a motor scooter or a window being opened. Neither of us looks towards Arhea Chorio or the Knights' castle.

'Not very well. Xan says she needs the doctor.'

It is the morning of the third day after Christmas. I will have to turn back, soon, and go down to take over from a cousin in the shop.

'He is coming, isn't he? Tomorrow?' It would be his regular surgery visit and Panagiotis told me he would come to see Helen and the baby afterwards. They are both doing fine; this is only a matter of routine.

Max nods his head. 'Yes.' He is facing away from me,

eastwards towards the brown crenellations of Turkey. The wind catches the word and blows it away from us so I step straight in front of him, forcing him to look at me.

'It is flu, isn't it?'

He half nods. His evasiveness, not just about Olivia but in everything contained in the six inches of empty space between us, makes me feel colder than the wind.

'Max?'

'What is it?'

'I want to ask you the same question.'

Here we are, stuck on the rocky fin of the island; I feel that everything new I have found and fallen in love with here is blowing around us in ragged wisps. My fingers encircle his wrists and dig into them. I can gauge the amount of effort that it is taking for him to stay still.

He sighs. 'Listen. Olivia is sick, therefore I am worried about her. There's something wrong that I can't identify. I don't know why it is, it's not just that she's ill. She's unhappy in a way I've never seen before. I just came for a few days' holiday over here, to see my sister and to try to set things straight in my mind. And now there is this with Olivia, and you. I have to think about Hattie and the girls as well, don't I?'

I made it on to the list, at least. I want to tighten my grip but I force myself to let go.

'Olivia will be better in a day or so. The doctor will give her antibiotics or something. Xan ought to do more to help her. I don't know anything about Hattie or Ellie and Lucy, how could I? But I do know about you and me.'

He looks confused and rueful, both elements of a complicated expression I often saw Peter wear, at the end.

'Kitty. I have to go back to Oz soon.'

Protestations form. But I don't give voice to them.

'Is that what you want?'

'It's what I have to *do*.'

'I suppose so,' I say.

It's his turn to wheel me around now, making his back a shelter for us both against the wind.

'Kitty,' he cajoles. 'You know what I feel.' He is looking at me with Olivia's eyes.

We seem to tip one way, towards destruction, and then to slide back the other, to the promise of happiness, and then to teeter on the knife edge between them. If he goes, I believe there is nothing. If he stays, we will have all this. As much as Olivia has herself.

'Do I?'

He kisses me for an answer, but absently. Over his shoulder I watch the buff folds of sunlit turf and the dark-grey fingers of stark shadow that comb between them. The sea is flat blue in the bay, lined with dark-blue cat's-paw ripples stirred up by the wind. The shallows are a startling pale turquoise.

I can't leave this. Neither Halemni nor the person I am here.

'Do I know?' I repeat. The rawness in my voice makes him step back. 'What do you feel?'

'I care about you. I have … loved these days with you.'

Now I am wiping wind-blown strands of hair away from my mouth, trying to rub away the taste that makes my lips sour.

'Is that what it meant to you? A Christmas fuck?'

He winces. 'No. Of course not.' A look of dumbness, helplessness, comes over him and I want to shake him to make him understand. Then I think cruelly, he is only a man. This must be how Olivia sometimes feels about Xan. My complicity with her swells and then abruptly withers as I remember that we are now, somehow, adversaries. I suddenly very much want to see her.

'Do you want to walk a bit further?' I ask Max.

'No, not really.'

'I've got to go to the shop, anyway.'

We turn round together and he takes my hand. His thumb strokes mine and this innocent touch makes my desire for him flare up all over again. I drag our joined hands up to my mouth and kiss his fingers, and pull his face close to mine. He stares into my eyes and then, gradually but inevitably, he succumbs. His hands slide under my layers of clothes, cold on heated skin.

In a moment we are kneeling on the lumpy turf, our mouths feeding on each other.

There is an outcrop of rock to shelter us.

It is like the first time, up in the castle ruins. Except that afterwards Max doesn't hold me or stroke my flesh. He moves away an inch and sits up, gnawing on a stalk of grass and looking down to the sea.

There is something else, too. When I say his name he flashes a look at me and I can tell that he is starting to be afraid of me.

Why is he afraid, of me of all people? Words start to spill out of me. I am trying to talk his fear away.

'I don't want you to go back to Sydney. I don't want you to be with Hattie, I can't bear the idea. Okay, you'll have to go for a while, to tell her what has happened. But you will come back. And then we can be together. We can live here. All right, no, not here, I understand why not here because of Olivia. But we can find somewhere like this. Maybe, maybe we could even have a child. It's late, but not unheard of ...'

'No,' Max says quietly.

With the soft contradiction I understand everything; we have come on this walk so that he can let me know just this. I was and am desirable. Maybe he even loves me. But there is no future time. And he is afraid that I will make difficulties about it. Make demands that he cannot meet.

Now do I know?

Disbelief and then anguish rise and start to spiral inside me. I don't cry. Tears are a long way off. Instead, I kneel upright, because I want to keep the unravelling to a minimum. If I move too much I will spill, oozing into the dry earth and vanishing.

'Don't look like that,' Max whispers.

I seem to remember that Peter used the same words, once, before he left with Lisa Kirk.

How am I supposed to look?

I have forgotten. This isn't me, this is someone entirely else. Where am I?

There is a shudder of anger vibrating in me now, as violent as the earthquake. For a voluptuous moment I think of giving way to it. It would break me apart. My top lip lifts to show my teeth and I hear my own little whimper of near-submission as my eyes threaten to close. There *is* a red tide behind them, yes. I look again into Max's frightened face.

I don't give way, not yet.

Instead, I pull my clothes together, doing up the buttons that he undid, fastening my belt. Then I climb slowly to my feet, stiff as an old woman.

'I understand,' I manage to say.

'I don't have the right to expect ...'

'Olivia told me. That you are – what's the word? – a bit of a player. With women. Is that right?'

He hesitates, long enough for me to think that I love him and want him, and I still feel that I know him better than anyone and that it is unbearable for us not to be part of one another. It is a bereavement.

'I have tried not to be,' Max answers humbly. 'Since I married Hattie. But ... once I saw you. Down on the quay there, your mouth pouring blood. Once ... that was it. I'm sorry. I'm sorry for me too, because it hurts.'

334

'Yes,' I say. And after another minute I ask, 'What's the time?'

He tells me and I am already late for the shop.

We start walking down the hill, into the familiar view. I am thinking, I want to be happy here. Can you choose happiness, after all?

The question is incongruous, I know, with the surge of anger boxed inside me.

We part on the bend in the road nearest to the potter's house. Max heads towards it and I call after him, 'Tell Olivia I'm asking after her. Tell her I'd like to come and see her, if she feels well enough.' Then I walk on down the street to Panagiotis's shop. Yannis crosses in front of me and lifts his arm in a wave. Down on the harbour wall, in a little group of men, I can see Christopher Cruickshank lounging in wait for the big ferry.

The shop smells as always, of sacking and cheese and dried anchovy. The Panagiotis cousin looks at her watch as I come in and I murmur in Greek that I am very sorry. There are gaps on some of the front shelves. I take note of what is missing and move through into the storeroom. I am just *English woman, in shop*. The reduction, the near-anonymity, is briefly comforting.

Max found Xan in the kitchen, laying spoons and plates on the table. There was a saucepan on the cooker and the boys were expectantly waiting for their midday meal.

'How is she?' he asked.

'She came down for an hour. But she felt bad so she went back up to bed again. I think she's asleep now.'

'Kitty was asking after her.'

Xan looked at him and Max gave a small, eloquent shrug. They were silently drawn together by the challenge, the sheer size of their tall women. Max went to the fridge and found himself a beer.

Xan spooned food from the saucepan on to plates.

'Pappy, what's this?' Georgi sighed.

'Beans and tomato. Very good.'

They tasted it, one spoonful into each mouth.

'I don't think it is.'

'You are wrong and so am I. In fact, it is *excellent*.'

'When is Mum going to get better?'

'In a day or so, I should think.'

Theo looked miserable. 'I wish it was today.'

'So do I,' Xan told him.

Olivia lay on her side, looking at the light beyond the angle made by the shutters. The room itself was dim because too much brightness hurt her eyes, yet she was afraid of lying in the dark. Daylight or the suggestion of it was reality; darkness made it too easy to slide into the dreams.

The dreams were terrible. They made her fight to sit up, clawing to pull the sheets from around her throat, drenching her in sweat, crowding the room with grotesque faces. Over and over again, she lost her children. Theo slid under the surface of clear water, stretching his hand imploringly up to her while she struggled to catch it. Georgi wandered between the gnarled trunks of trees in a forest, straying further away from her even though she called him and tried to run after him. In the end his small figure vanished into the green light. A knot of people on the beach stood watching as the tsunami swept towards them, and then she was in bed again and suffocating, and Xan was in the room and wouldn't help her. She struck out with her arms and knocked a cup off the chair beside the bed. It didn't break but the crash on bare floorboards jerked her into full consciousness again.

There was the light beyond the shutters. She was lying in a coil of sweat-soaked bedclothes.

Someone knocked on the bedroom door. It wouldn't be

Xan, of course, nor would either of the children bother to knock. She shrank under the covers. She knew she was weak; weak was vulnerable ...

'Olivia? Are you awake?'

Christopher, only Christopher, thank God.

'Yes.'

He edged around the door. 'Hello. I brought you a drink.'

'Thank you.'

Her mouth was parched and even to speak a couple of words made her cracked lips split.

'How do you feel?'

She took the cup from him, trying to shrug and smile, but she could read the shocked concern in his face.

'Not so good.'

'You should see the doctor. The ferry's in. We could take you now.'

'Is it?' She couldn't imagine not knowing exactly when the ferry was due, yet she had lost track of the days.

Christopher touched her damp shoulder. 'Drink that for me.' He went downstairs again. Max was washing up, Xan seemed to be straightening some of the disorder in the room.

'I think we should get her on the ferry now. Take her across to Rhodos Town,' Christopher said.

It was a four-hour sea journey, but there was a hospital at the other end.

'Pappy?' Georgi's head jerked up.

'Okay. There's no need for that. The doctor will be here tomorrow.'

'I think she should go now.'

'Wait a minute. No, it's too complicated.'

Xan was perplexed. It was always Olivia who made decisions like this; he didn't know what to do when she was the one who needed to have them made for her.

Christopher turned to Max who was wiping out a

saucepan. He looked dulled, as though he didn't even hear the conversation clearly.

'Max?'

'Uh, I guess – you know, against a long ferry ride, having the doctor come here would be better.'

The three men stood in an awkward triangle with the boys staring at them.

'Will Mum be okay?' Theo whispered.

'Of course she will,' Xan said. He gave Christopher a look intended to silence him.

Christopher hesitated, unsure of whether to push harder. He cared more about Olivia than anyone else in the world, she was the only person he loved, but she was Xan's wife, not his. He gave way.

'I think it would be a good idea to get her temperature down, then. Sponge her with cool water. Ask Meroula or Kitty to do it, maybe.'

Xan said that he would go and see Meroula about it.

'I'll walk with you,' Christopher said.

Outside, Xan scratched at his scalp with the fingers of both hands. 'Jesus. I don't know what's going on. Everything feels wrong in this place. Olivia's never been ill, all the time I've known her.'

Xan was not particularly adept at putting his feelings into words but Christopher knew what he meant because he felt the same. There was a shiver of threat in the air, the tiny vibrations of it touching everyone in the potter's house. He was reminded of the hot, heavy days before the earthquake and the wave.

'Let's make sure she gets better quickly, then,' he said at Meroula's door.

Xan grasped his arm. 'Thanks.'

Christopher went on to his own house. Xan would be less grateful if he knew how Christopher felt about his wife. How much he wanted his wife. But this wasn't exactly new. And

338

it was typical of Xan, Christopher reflected, that he never noticed how things were. When Kitty arrived, Christopher made himself believe just for a handful of days that she might be his Olivia. But Kitty was surface, illusion, even physical mimicry on the make-over night. She had none of Olivia's wholeness and depth. Even when Kitty first came, when the troubling, precious essence of Olivia had seemed briefly mirrored, doubled in its effect, Xan had seen nothing. He loved his wife, that was all. It was an enviable simplicity.

Meroula came upstairs with a plastic washing-up bowl that she filled with cool water. Olivia still lay under a film of sweat, restlessly moving her arms and legs. She let Meroula help her over on to a towel spread out on Xan's side of the bed, but she resisted when her mother-in-law wanted to peel off the soaked T-shirt she had been sleeping in. There was a brief, almost comical tussle as Olivia held on to the hem and Meroula tried to pull it up and over her head.

'No,' Olivia protested. 'No, no. I want to keep my clothes. I need my clothes on.'

Meroula did the best she could by sponging her arms and legs and her face and throat. Olivia tried to push her away at first, but the cool drops felt delicious on her burning skin. She let her body go limp and Meroula swept the sponge up over her knees to her thighs, and from her wrists to the insides of her elbows. It was wonderful to lie still and watch Meroula's grey head bobbing, and the intentness of her face as she worked. Her expression was severe but there was a thin seam of affection in it. Olivia had seen it occasionally when she looked at Georgi and Theo, but never for her.

She thought with weak gratitude that it was like having her own mother to look after her. She was in the bath at home, on a midsummer evening before her father came in. There were wood pigeons in the trees in the garden. Her mother sponged her face and neck as she lay back under the water. She always squeezed the sponge out over her hair, that was the game.

'My hair,' Olivia said.

'You don't want to lie there with wet hair,' Meroula answered.

Olivia knew that she understood the Greek words because of course it made sense, not to have wet hair in bed. But she couldn't understand where they had come from. She opened her eyes wide and stared at Meroula.

'What are you doing here?' she asked in sudden terror. There were shutters at the window, not bathroom curtains.

There was a long, mournful wail from outside. It was the ferry hooting as it slid away across the bay.

'You have a fever. I am cooling you,' Meroula answered.

When she was dry and quiet, Meroula persuaded her to put on a fresh T-shirt. Olivia sat up and turned her back to pull off the old one and managed to fit one arm, then her head and the other arm into the clean one.

Her thoughts skittered around as she struggled to pull the hem down over her skinny buttocks. Her body felt brittle.

No one sees me naked. Only Xan.

'Shall I sit with you?' Meroula asked.

Olivia nodded and drifted into sleep again.

The two men and the two boys are in the kitchen when I come back from the shop. They must have been there all the time I was working. I have restocked the shelves, dusted the windows, done everything I can think of to fill in the time, but even so it was a long afternoon to spend sitting in Helen's chair beside the till. It was quiet. Either Panagiotis or the cousin has pinned a Polaroid photograph to the nearest shelf. It shows Helen sitting up with her baby in her arms. The little crimson face is hardly visible in a swathe of lemon-yellow hand-knitting but in any case I can still remember exactly how she looked.

Sitting in her chair gave me an odd feeling of almost being Helen. I have watched her for so long, knitting, waiting. I laced my hands experimentally over my stomach. I am fat, I know, but it feels like dead flesh. Nothing like pregnant.

The thought made me double over with the pain. It is as bad as one of Helen's contractions. No future, Max said. No life like Halemni for us, free of history. Just nothing.

The pain tightens again now as I survey the men and the children and the kitchen of the potter's house. And then anger sweeps after it.

'How is she?' I ask.

'Meroula sat with her until she fell asleep,' Xan says. Max doesn't look up. He won't meet my eyes. He is pained and embarrassed, of course.

'Can I do anything?'

Xan hunches one shoulder. He looks helpless. 'Some supper, maybe.'

So I take off my jacket and wash my hands at the stone sink. I set to work with onions and tomatoes. The boys creep to my end of the table and sit on either side of me, as if I am near enough to being Olivia to be a comfort. They don't talk much. Uncertainty has subdued them.

Olivia woke up as Meroula tiptoed out of the door. The light had faded beyond the shutters, so it must be evening now. Which day? Ferry day, that's right, that's what Christopher had said. And she had heard the hooter as it sailed out of the bay.

There were voices downstairs. She could pick out Xan's low rumble and Max's more clipped tones with the turned-up ends of sentences, and the boys occasionally chipping in, and then the light voice of a woman who didn't speak as often as the others.

It wasn't Meroula, it was Kitty.

As she listened Olivia felt that she wasn't in the bed – there was someone under the covers but it was not her. She was down in the kitchen, although not quite there either because she couldn't see Xan and the boys and Max, or work out what they were saying, even though they were all talking to each other as if it were any ordinary happy evening.

It gave her the most melancholy feeling, sadness darkening like a bruise, to think that she was there but cut off from them. The ordinariness had become anything but. Their happiness had been so fragile and she never knew it.

Kitty said something and then laughed.

Olivia opened her hands on the sheets and remembered that she was in bed, and ill. She clenched her fists at the sound of Kitty's laughter and a wash of anger swept away the sadness. Kitty shouldn't be here, not in the place that belonged to her. She sat up in bed. Somehow she swung her legs to the floor and stamped her feet on the boards.

'Xan,' she shouted. 'Xan.'

He was with her in seconds. He sat down on the edge of the bed, and wrapped her in his arms and tried to calm her.

'It's only a dream,' he said, as she had often said to Theo. He stroked her hair and rocked her like a child.

'I told her to go,' Olivia hotly insisted. 'The ferry did come today, didn't it?'

'Who? Yes, the ferry came.'

'Why didn't she leave on it? I told her she couldn't stay here any more. I told her when I went to see her.'

'Is this *Kitty*?'

'Yes.' Olivia shivered. 'I want her to go away. I'm frightened of her.'

Xan continued his stroking. 'No, you aren't. It's because you're ill. She's just cooked supper for us all. She came straight from the shop to ask after you.'

'No,' Olivia shouted. She pushed him away, trying to make

342

him understand that this was important. 'Tell her. She has to *leave*. Right now.'

'Olivia. Hush now. It's eight o'clock at night. Where is she to go? We can't tell anyone anything of the kind, not under this roof. And listen ...'

Her hands rested on his like burning claws. Her eyes were wide and far too bright.

'... I think Max has told her that he's going back to Hattie. I think that's enough for her to deal with for now. Let's leave her in peace for a day or so, until you're better. Then we can all talk about it. I'm sure she understands that she can't stay here for ever. And why would she want to?'

That's just what she does want, she wants to burrow under the surface, to make everything hers that never belonged to her ...

But his voice soothed her. She stopped trying to take in what he was saying and to insist that it was all wrong, and just listened to the sound of it. Her anger broke up and vented itself in feverish shivers.

Max was going back to Hattie.

Kitty would leave, in the end, she would see to that.

Everything would be well in the potter's house.

The island's doctor came the next day with the local ferry. He was a short, thickset man with a pronounced cleft in his chin. Olivia smelled soap on his hands as he bent over her. His forearms looked dark against his white short-sleeved shirt. He frowned and nodded while she looked up into his face, noticing the pores around the wings of his nose. He warmed the stethoscope in the cup of his hand before placing it on her chest and she felt weakly grateful for this consideration.

Xan was waiting outside the door. She could even hear the faint creak of floorboards as he transferred his weight from one foot to the other. All her senses were heightened; even ordinary things loomed like hallucinations. The doctor's fingers on her neck and under her arms were like steel, as though they might sink into her cloudy flesh. The weave of the pillow scraped against her cheek. He took the dressing off her arm and inspected the wound, then dabbed it with antiseptic and covered it up again.

When he had finished with her, at last, the doctor patted her hand and arranged it to lie across her chest. He drew the sheet up to her chin and smoothed it flat. It was like being laid out. I am not dead, she wanted to say.

Xan came back into the room. He sat down awkwardly on a chair that was piled with clothes, tipping himself to the edge of it so as not to disarrange anything. The doctor put on his coat and clicked open his bag.

Olivia picked out some of the words they exchanged. It was a bad bout. Temperature. Some antibiotics. Rest and fluid. Another visit next week.

Xan nodded and then smiled at her. The doctor was counting pills into a brown vial.

'You'll be fine in a day or two,' he reassured her.

'That's right,' Xan said.

When he came back from showing the man out Olivia held out her hand and Xan took it, sitting down on the bed beside her. He laced his fingers through hers and leaned over to stroke the hair back from her face.

'Sorry,' she said. She felt as though a door was closing and it was becoming important to talk through the diminishing gap. *Sorry* was the faintest whisper of the loss and darkness that swelled on the wrong side of the door.

'Hm? There's nothing to be sorry about. Listen. Do you remember the Darbys?'

The name was familiar. She listened to the echo of it in her mind, without having the strength to pursue the sound.

'They were that couple in the last group, this season. Yannis hit him on the nose. She seemed not to mind too much. You must remember.'

'Yes.'

'They came into my head on Christmas night, when you were angry with me. I don't want us to be like them.' His hand tightened on hers, squeezing the bones. 'I don't ever want to be locked in like that. With anger stuck all around us and hard faces instead of laughing. I love you too much. If you stop loving me, will you tell me instead of making a pretence?'

'I won't,' Olivia said with an effort. 'Stop, I mean.'

When everything in the house was right again, without Kitty, she would prove it.

'Take your medicine now,' Xan said. He shook two tablets out of the brown vial and put them on to her dry tongue. She sipped at the water he held for her and they scraped down her throat.

'Very good,' he said, stroking her hair again.

I meet the doctor walking away from Panagiotis's house. At least, I assume he is the doctor because he has his medical bag with him, although he is not an impressive figure. He is small and plump, with a slightly furtive look. I see him staring at me in surprise but I edge past him, murmuring *kali mera*, and slip under the shelter of Panagiotis's porch.

Panagiotis, I know, will have to go to the shop in a minute. I have deliberately chosen to visit now because I want to see Helen and the baby without him being there.

He opens the door to my knock and makes a show of pleasure at the sight of me.

'Mother and baby very good.' He smiles widely. 'Please, welcome.'

The room opposite the kitchen, the best room, is stuffed with shiny furniture and stiff drapes. It is made even smaller by the addition of an enormous shiny pram. Helen is wedged in a corner, dressed in a wide-collared blue blouse for the doctor's visit, with the baby in her arms. She smiles at me, nervously, and immediately ducks her head over the baby.

'We are grateful, Kyria Kitty, for your help on the night of the birth,' Panagiotis says. Formally he offers me coffee and *kourabiethes*, sweet shortbread made for the New Year, but I beg him not to trouble. After a few more words he leaves us alone together.

'How are you?' I ask. Helen's mouth looks fuller and the shadow of hair above it seems to have darkened. The blouse is taut across her breasts, gaping between the buttons. She is older and riper, having made the transition into motherhood.

'Thank you,' she whispers. *Efharistó*. She is embarrassed to remember what I saw and heard: her modesty has been assaulted. I can see now, too late, that this is a problem.

I sit down beside her on the slippery sofa, although she hasn't invited me to.

'Do you have a name?' I ask in my fumbling Greek.

'Demetria. For my mother.'

'That's lovely.'

Our conversations have never extended beyond a few words, and the placid routines of the shop filled in the spaces. I want to tell her that I was pleased and proud she had asked me to be with her, and that I thought she had been brave, and how I had been moved by the birth as much as by anything else in my life. But, of course, I can't convey any of this. I try a sentence or two and she keeps her head bent in incomprehension and her eyes on the baby's face. My voice falters and I stop.

'Can I hold her?' I ask.

She does understand this. She hesitates, but then she puts the lemon-yellow bundle into my outstretched hands. I can tell that she doesn't want to, but she does it.

I hold the baby against me, cupping the tiny head with one hand. My fatness gives me the illusion that I have full breasts and Demetria seems to understand this because she turns her head and her mouth opens, searching for milk.

The longing for connection burns through me like an electric shock. I hold her tighter, as if the force alone will make a difference, and the baby opens her black, fathomless eyes and stares at me.

I can see reality reflected in them. I am an outsider.

I am not a mother and I never will be a link in the chain of mothers and daughters. I am not a Halemniot, just an English guest who has been made welcome. Helen's embarrassment at seeing me today and the lack of words between us make this all too clear. And above all Max with his carefully poised regret has told me that he is going home. There is no island future for the two of us. And, therefore, none for me.

Olivia has given voice to it – *you have to leave.*

However much I long for it, I don't belong here, Kitty Fisher, Cary Stafford, whoever I am.

The baby doesn't find the smell that will reassure her or the milk that will comfort her. Her fists come up to her face and she begins a tiny, catlike crying.

At once, in relief, Helen holds out her arms for her.

I know that she won't feed her baby in front of me, a stranger. So I stand up, too big for the overcrowded space.

'She is so beautiful,' I blurt out to Helen.

The crying only gets louder and more insistent. So I back away, out of the room and down the chilly hallway, out of the front door and into the whitish winter light. I stand blinking, seeing the dazzle of light off the moving water, wondering what to do now and where to go next.

Another day passes, into the last of the year.

The potter's house is quiet and so am I. I sit and read in

my studio room and then, in the afternoon, unable to bear the four walls any longer, I go out and walk. Without thinking about it, I take the zigzag path up the hill to the old village.

The fallen roofs lie open to the sky and to the jackdaws that loop overhead. The blank doors and windows look inward, on to sour earth floors and ruined bread ovens and shards of broken pottery. I pick out a glazed remnant from a crust of dirt and wonder if it was made and fired by the old potter in Xan's house. This afternoon the ruins are deserted.

In ones and twos, most of the old people who migrated up to Arhea Chorio have retreated down to sea level again. Kyria Elena and a handful of others are still living in their patched-up houses but today, New Year's Eve, they have made the walk down to visit their families in Megalo Chorio. The Halemni wives have made *vasilopita*, the special New Year's cake with a coin baked in it that will bring a year's good luck to the finder, and on the stroke of midnight the men of the houses will cut the first slice. It will be an evening of celebration everywhere, with *kourabiethes* and special songs, and for the men a little gambling over the cards. Everywhere: except this year in the potter's house.

I am making my way up the uneven stones of the main street, heading for the old church and the view over the bay. I want to look at it in the fading light of the short day and to fix it in my mind. I am walking with my head down, watching where to place my feet among the loose rocks, when I hear the singing.

I stop to listen. It is uphill, among the houses that look down over disused crop terraces to the sea; noisy, exuberant singing that is almost a chant. Now I hear running and scrambling footsteps, and I catch sight of a bobbing head above the line of broken stone walls. Another head appears behind it, then another.

It is a group of boys, singing at the tops of their voices as they fly downhill. As soon as they see me they change direction and stream across the narrow street. They are all laughing, and they make a circle round me and start clapping and stamping to the rhythm of the song. I don't know the words but the tune goes straight into my head. I find that I am singing too, and laughing as the biggest boy links his arm through mine and swings me almost off my feet. I know all the village children now, at least by sight, but I don't recognise any of these boys. One of them takes my other arm and for a minute we make a swaying chain, gasping with laughter and with the determination not to be pulled off our feet as we gallop downhill.

I want to run with them and piece together the words of this insistent song. But first one of my links breaks away and then the boy on the other side pulls his arm free too and the whole group tears past me and dives away between the ruins. I can hear the singing for a minute or two longer, but then that is swallowed up by the old stones and I am left standing alone.

Silence falls around me in thick folds. I lift my hands and stare at them, as if in the creases and whorls of skin I can find evidence of my own physical being.

I start walking again, retracing my steps up the hill between the deserted houses. I come out into the square where we had Aghios Pandelios's feast and dancing. *I can't kiss you now*, Max said. *But I will.*

I felt so vital then. Now I am more brittle and faded than the dead leaves drifted against the church wall. I move silently along the wall, my fingertips trailing over the crusts of lichen. I turn the corner at the eastern end and come out to a ledge overlooking the terraces and the bay.

I am not alone, after all. There is a man sitting at the other end of the ledge.

Christopher has a sketch pad on his lap and he is intent on his work. I watch him for a full minute as he works over the paper with thick charcoal strokes. I can't see what he is drawing but he never even glances at the view.

Then his head jerks up. He catches sight of me and the shock makes him start so violently that the pad flies off his lap and he has to dive forward to catch it. It looks as if he is going to topple off the ledge and pitch forward down the steep slope, but he grabs the rock with one hand and just manages to keep his balance. He flops back against the wall, briefly closing his eyes while the shock subsides. The knuckles of the other hand grip the sketch pad so tightly that they turn white.

'I didn't mean to scare you,' I murmur.

'But you did anyway.'

'I'm sorry.'

I walk along the ledge and sit down, back against the wall and knees drawn up, my posture exactly reflecting his. Gently I take the sketch pad from his hand. He has been drawing a woman's face in three-quarters profile. Christopher's work is usually subtle, even too careful, but this is a mass of black lines and vicious shading.

'Is this Olivia? Or me?'

There is a tobacco tin on a stone beside him and he opens it now and pinches shreds of tobacco on to a thin paper. He licks the edge and completes the roll-up, then makes a shelter with hunched shoulders and a cupped hand to strike a match. He lights up and inhales deeply before he answers.

'A hybrid.'

'Why?'

He takes another draw on his cigarette. The wind makes the ragged tip flare scarlet.

'Your similarities trouble me. Ever since the night you made her up to look like you. Since you began putting on weight, changing yourself.'

I look away from him. 'It's the differences that trouble me.'

'So you set out to cancel them?'

'It was a game, Christopher. Making faces.' I twitch the sketch pad that I am still holding. 'You are an artist, you know about surface and depth. You can't blot out anything true with lipstick and a different hairstyle.'

'No. I didn't say that you could. Olivia is happy. She is – or maybe I have to say was – the happiest and most perfectly contented person I have ever encountered. You can't mimic that.' He leans forward, pulling at his knees, as if this will bring him closer to where she is lying.

I say humbly, 'I would like to have a shadow of it. I thought maybe by copying Olivia.'

'Copying? The sincerest flattery? Let me tell you what I think. I think it is more threatening than that.'

His voice has gone cold and I can hear a vibration of apprehension as well as a rebuke in it. I don't want Christopher Cruickshank to be afraid of me. As if I am looking down a long tunnel to a bright little tableau I see our dining room in London, well-fed and confident people sitting round a table, with his brother among them. It is a very long way from our ledge of rock; so far that it makes me shiver.

I can see Peter's good paintings, candles glimmering on polished wood, the crisp lines of folded linen. Lisa Kirk's voluptuous little handbag.

What has happened and where have I come to?

And what would Christopher say if I casually remark now, by the way, I think I know your brother Dan the portrait painter. Or is he perhaps your cousin?

The idea makes my mouth crimp in a smile. But I have cast off Cary Stafford. I wanted to leave her behind because I thought I could outreach history.

'No. I am not a threat to anybody. Not even to Max.'

'You are jealous, Kitty. You are jealous to the point where you want to *be* Olivia.'

'You don't know. You don't see straight either because you are in love with her.' I make it a statement and there is no attempt to contradict me. Christopher is concentrating on the view and his cigarette.

'What are you going to do?' I needle him.

'Nothing.' The resignation in his voice is profoundly melancholy. It makes me think of closed-up rooms and dust, and making do because there is nothing better to be done.

It also makes me think something else.

I have had passion – even grief is a kind of passion. Peter and I loved each other for many years and I would have given him children if only my body had done what I longed for it to do. When that ended, as everything ends, Andreas brought me to Halemni. And here, in Max and Olivia, I saw what was ordinary and the breadth of happiness that can exist within the plain walls of it.

I fell in love with it and them.

I have never felt ordinary after we were stricken on that summer's afternoon long ago, and the scent and the easiness and the opportunities to be ordinary on Halemni seduced me into the shell of Kitty Fisher. Even my anger at Max's and Olivia's rejection of me, and the disappointment I feel now, are vividly passionate.

I would rather know this, with the cold rock under my backside and the wind in my face and the cold glitter of the sea beneath me, I would rather have known it than go on living in a version of Christopher Cruickshank's pale resignation.

I lean my head back and I am laughing. The release of it makes my shoulders shake, makes my hands loosen so the sketch pad drops and bangs against my knees.

Christopher turns to look at me.

'What's funny?'

'How can you live and yet do *nothing*?'

He stares and I feel the laughter congeal at the corners of my mouth. I can see that Christopher thinks I am strange, strange enough to disconcert him because fear flickers in his eyes. He takes the sketch block out of my hand and tears off the hybrid drawing, then savagely crumples it in his fist. He pushes the ball of paper into the pocket of his coat.

'Did you meet the boys, the singers?' I demand. This suddenly seems an urgent question.

'Where?'

'Just down there.' I point the way I came. The light is fading, draining the ochre and turquoise and amber tones out of the landscape, and leaving the silvery chill monochrome of a winter's evening. My breath condenses in the air.

Christopher shrugs, gathering up his tobacco tin and charcoals, stowing them in various pockets.

'There were about nine of them. Older than Georgi and Theo, maybe eleven or twelve. They were singing, a very catchy song.' I hum a few notes.

'It's a custom, I believe. Boys from the village run from house to house, singing New Year's songs. They bring luck to the householders.'

'I didn't recognise any of them. I thought I knew all the village children.'

I have seen children up here at other times, too. And an old man with a donkey. This doesn't worry me. I am comfortable with the idea of present and past inhabitants, with the way that Halemni lies in the blurred margin between what can be explained and what cannot.

'It's a holiday. Maybe they are visiting, or they're older kids who go to school in Rhodos Town.'

Christopher is not comfortable. He is unsettled and

suspicious, and anxious to be gone. He scrambles to his feet and the box of charcoal sticks falls out of his pocket. I rescue it and hand it up to him, and he pushes it out of sight again.

'I'm going. I'm worried about Olivia, something's happening. I can feel it.'

'Xan and Max are with her.'

Christopher is already moving. His breath clouds between us as he calls back over his shoulder, 'You ask how I can do *nothing*. I can do this much, make sure she's looked after. She's really sick. She ought to be in hospital.'

He wants to get away from me. He negotiates the corner but I follow him, in front of the dark bulk of the ruined church and across the cobbled square to the road downhill.

I call after his hurrying figure, 'I'll come with you. There must be something I can do.'

Christopher's pace slows and he swings round. He holds his hands up to ward me off and then shouts, 'Leave her alone. Keep away from her.'

The words echo between the dead black houses. I stand until the last whisper has faded and until I can no longer hear the sound of Christopher's running, receding footsteps.

Olivia woke up from what seemed to have been a long sleep in a shadowy gallery full of people who moved past her in a steady unseeing stream. She couldn't tell what time of day or night it might be because the shutters were closed and there was a lamp beside her bed with a scarf draped over the shade to dim the light. She turned her head, wincing at the pain the movement caused her, and saw that there was a man sitting in the chair in the corner of the room.

At first she thought it was Max. She opened her mouth to say *help me*, but then she realised that it was not him at all. This man was wearing a pale shirt and loose linen trousers, and she had never seen him before.

Are you there?' the man asked. He was at ease, smiling as if he was a friend.

Olivia recoiled from him.

'I can hear singing,' she said.

It was a traditional New Year's song and she remembered the words because the boys had learned them last year.

The New Tear brings blessings, the New Tear brings life.
The old one is passing. We honour its age.

The tune was insistent. It took up residence in the pain-filled chambers of her skull. She was about to close her eyes when she heard a door slam and voices calling out. The hot insistence of people and present concerns and love flooded through her.

'... fetch Anna Efemia,' the voice was saying. This was Xan. That's right. He had left the room just for a minute, to send Max somewhere. Why did it seem so long ago?

There were feet coming upstairs.

The door opened and Christopher was there. He came to the side of the bed, took her hand, smiled at her.

'You are going to be fine,' he told her. She wondered why it was necessary for him to say this, but the thought slipped out of her grasp almost as soon as it had formed.

When Olivia looked again the chair in the corner of the room was empty.

SEVENTEEN

It must be nearly midnight.

The potter's house is a honeycomb of light, but so is almost every other house in the village because this is New Year's Eve. I have chosen a place out here in the dark where I can see in through the terrace windows. If it is cold, I don't feel it.

The kitchen is deserted.

Max lit the fire hours ago, I watched him do it, but no one has built it up and now the hearth is a mound of grey ash. The boys ate a listless supper and let Max shepherd them up to bed. There are cups and plates on the table, the litter of an abandoned meal. I saw Xan standing up to eat, carelessly pushing food into his mouth while Max was upstairs. A few minutes later Xan went and Max came down. I watched him too – he buttered a slab of bread, layered tinned meat and pickle on top of it, then sat at the table and stared out of the window as he ate. The darkness is a shroud. I knew that he couldn't see me, but it was as if he was looking into my eyes. His face was sad.

Christopher Cruickshank came and went, and then came back again. Everyone has gone upstairs now, where I can't look in.

The last few minutes of the year are sliding away.

While I wait for what is going to happen I stand up and move under the bare struts of the pergola. I put the flat of my hand against one of the panes of window glass and look in at the room. The furniture is familiar, and the books on the shelf, even the faint ridges in the stone flags. Then my breath clouds the glass and my view is obscured.

I have to stand back quickly. Christopher and Xan come in together. They are talking urgently. I could hear the words if I edged closer to the foggy glass.

Christopher goes straight to the telephone and picks up the receiver. He is hunting for something among the papers by the telephone: a number. Xan is beside him now, pushing him aside in the search. He finds what he is looking for, grabs the receiver and holds the paper while he stabs out a string of numbers. His mouth moves as he waits, prayers or imprecations.

Someone answers because Xan begins with a flood of words, Christopher making slow-down signals with his hands. They stand close together in the yellow light, looking at each other. They are both scared. I can read disbelief and distress in their faces.

I reach for the door handle and slowly, slowly, soundlessly turn it to the right.

The terrace door swings outwards and I feel warm air on my face. From the way they jump with fright when I slide into the kitchen I know that Xan and Christopher Cruickshank had forgotten all about me.

Christopher puts a sharp finger to his mouth, silencing me before I might speak, and Xan goes on talking into the telephone. Meekly I edge further into the room, forgotten again.

Xan speaks more calmly now. He is answering questions, then giving directions. Christopher stands, watching and waiting, with his arms wrapped round himself as if he is cold.

At last Xan puts down the receiver.

'They are coming,' he says to Christopher.

'How long?'

'Half an hour, maybe an hour.'

'Thank God. I'm going to get Anna Efemia. Until they get here. And we'll need Yannis and Michaelis with lights for the helicopter.'

Xan puts his hand to his face. He has to steady himself against the edge of the table as if he is drunk. Christopher is already out of the room.

'I'm going with her,' Xan says. 'To the hospital.' He looks around the kitchen, desperately searching for help. But Olivia isn't here.

'I will stay here with the boys,' I say softly.

'No.' His response is automatic. I don't belong here. 'No, wait, they'll need my mother. I'm going to run and get her.' He is half a child himself, needing his mother's presence in this crisis.

'I will stay here,' I say again, but he doesn't hear me. He is on his way to Meroula's.

The Christmas tree with the candle lanterns is still glittering in the hallway. I brush the glossy fake needles with the tips of my fingers as I pass by and make my quiet way up the stairs.

Max is sitting beside her bed. His eyes shift from her face to mine but only briefly. All his attention is for Olivia but I go to him anyway and lean down and touch my mouth to the exposed nape of his neck. His skin feels hot, or else my lips are as cold as ice.

I whisper to him, 'Xan says, go and find Yannis and the others. Get them to come with lights so the helicopter can land.'

358

His fingers are laced in Olivia's and his head is still bent. 'Go on,' I order him.

He is my little brother. He always does what I tell him to do. He hesitates a second longer, unwilling to leave her, then lurches to his feet. He tucks her limp hand to her side.

'Quickly.'

He goes, without looking back at me, and I listen to his steps on the stairs. And now we are alone together.

Olivia lies on her back. The sight of her is disturbing. Her neck and spine are so rigid that her body seems to arch off the bed. Her swollen purple eyelids are barely closed over her eyes. Her skin is pale and sheened with sweat, and she is breathing through her parted lips in short, painful gasps. There are cracks in the soft tissue at each side of her mouth and a mottled rash covers her neck and shoulders. Very gently, tenderly, I take the sheet between the tips of my fingers and fold it back. She makes no reaction. She is either asleep or unconscious.

Under the sheet Olivia is naked.

I look down and I could be looking at myself, my old self. The one that Peter Stafford once found so beautiful. Her hip bones stand up as two silvery curves and her pale belly is a taut hollow. Close to the left hip bone there is the whitish half-moon of an ancient chickenpox scar. There is a tuft of pale public hair and long, abnormally long, thigh bones. I take her hand, lacing my fingers with hers just as Max did. Her palm feels dry and very hot.

I know that I don't have very long. I look over my shoulder to the door, then I lie down next to her. Our shoulders, hips and hands are touching. We are close, almost at the same point. Our paths diverged that day in the garden when the statue fell, but our separate lives have finally come together, to here and now. Only the thinnest membrane divides us. I find that I too am breathing in short, agonised gasps.

A bell begins clanging, near at hand, just beyond the closed shutters. I jerk almost to a sitting position and then remember that it must be midnight. The church bell is ringing the change of the year. A second later I hear the zip and splutter of a rocket going off and the faintest echo of shouting.

I lie down again and now we are face to face. The bell has stirred her and she has half turned on to her side. Her eyes are open, staring into mine.

I could be you.

If I didn't say the words aloud, somehow she still heard them. Her eyes widen. I can feel the heat of her breath and the smell of it becomes the smell of myself.

I don't know what disease has overtaken her, but Olivia is ill enough to die and I feel more than strong enough to live instead of her. The possibility beckons me.

Anger at my exclusion from Halemni and Max's rejection, longing for love and a place to belong, and a passion for life – Olivia's life, not my own disabled version of it – all come together in a grand surge of strength. I have never felt strong like this, not since the statue toppled.

I shall be you.

Olivia is laid low. It would be so easy now to muffle the flickering spark out of her. With the thought my hands come obediently up to her throat, crossing like a prayer over her trachea, thumbs pressing to the flutter of her arteries. Our bodies match all along their joined lengths. My hooked thumbs dig into her neck and the flesh yields under my iron hands.

Now you know. Clear and precise understanding of who and what I am slices through me, deadly as a rapier blade.

I know that it must be her or me, not both of us.

If she were dead, instead of me, then I could live.

And then a softening begins in the knot that has always twisted behind my breastbone. Strands unravel and whip free, and the softness travels down through my arm muscles, loosening my wrists, buckling my fingers and thumbs until they are as useless as warm wax.

My thumbs lift and I can see the white pressure points in Olivia's neck flushing as the blood flows back. The tip of her tongue slides out between her teeth and she gratefully moistens her lips. She takes a shallow breath and I watch the ribs rise and fall under her discoloured skin.

Compassion and tenderness make me lift my hand from her neck to her hair. I stroke a thick hank back from her forehead, where there are beads of sweat standing out like seed pearls.

'Help me,' Olivia whispers and she closes her eyes.

'I will.'

I sit up now. Swing my legs back to the floor. Release her hand. I find I am standing at the bedside and looking down into my own face. Up here, this is another part of me, blissfully set free and lightened so that I am ready to float away.

Olivia sighs and stirs, and her eyes move under the closed lids as if she is watching a drama. I have to lean over to catch the words she breathes.

'I am sorry for you.' And then, 'Thank you.'

There is a mess of medicine bottles and cups and tissues on the chair at her bedside, and a clean folded handkerchief. Tenderly I dip a corner of the linen into a glass of clean water and moisten her lips with it.

I hear the front door of the potter's house slam open. The church bell has abruptly stopped ringing. Two people rush into the room and find me wiping Olivia's mouth. They are Anna Efemia, stout and breathless in an alarming bronze gown, and faithful Christopher. I back away.

Anna Efemia bends over the bed. The urgency of what needs to be done and the currents of other people's anxiety wash me to the margins of the room.

361

Xan and Meroula follow. Meroula stands at the end of the bed, excluded by the nurse's business with Olivia's pulse and breathing, but still wanting to be connected to her. She lifts the sheet and with the tips of her fingers gently strokes the pale arch of Olivia's foot. Affection shines out of her and I think, this at least will be better now. Even if I were to stay here, Meroula would not any longer favour me just because I am not Olivia.

Anna Efemia asks Xan a question and he stumbles to a drawer and produces a nightdress. The nurse unfolds it and nods to Meroula as she puts her arms under Olivia's shoulders. The sheet slips off her body as the two women lift her up. Standing invisible in my corner I see the awe in Christopher Cruickshank's face before he turns his back. After the nightdress Meroula and Anna Efemia wrap Olivia in a blanket. Xan still rubs his cheeks with his hands, his eyes fixed on Olivia's mottled face.

'How long are they going to be?'

No one answers. We stand watching and listening to her gasping for breath. Just as she is sorry for me, I am sorry for her. The only thing we can do is wait.

Downstairs the telephone starts ringing.

I am wondering how the children have slept through all of this when Theo patters into the room. His face is creased with sleep and his thumb is in his mouth. He goes straight to his mother's bed but Meroula intercepts him and lifts him into her arms. Somehow he understands that this is serious and he makes no fuss.

Xan comes back from the phone. 'They will be here in fifteen minutes. If we can get her down there safely it will save time.'

Max is back too. I hear his step outside the door. The room is too full of people – he looks in and says in a low voice, 'They are laying out the lights down on the landing field. There are people outside to help.'

362

'We are ready,' Anna Efemia says.

Xan tries to lift Olivia in his arms. Her head lolls against his shoulder and he staggers under her weight. Christopher says, 'No. Like this.' He holds up his crossed wrists. They make a seat with their clasped hands and Meroula puts Theo down on the bed so that she and the nurse can lift Olivia and hook her arms round the men's necks. Slowly, precariously, they shuffle out of the room and carry her down the stairs past the brightness of the Christmas tree. Anna Efemia follows them and holds the blanket in place.

Georgi has come out of the children's bedroom. The two children stand at the top of the stairs and watch their mother being carried away. Tears run down Theo's face and his brother holds his hand.

Max squats to bring his face to a level with theirs.

'The hospital will make her better. Pappy is going with her to make sure.'

'Is Mummy going to die?' Georgi asks in a dry little voice.

'No,' Max says. 'I promise.'

I wonder how he is in a position to promise.

Meroula is here too. Her heavy arms come round the boys' shoulders as Xan and Christopher reach the front door of the potter's house. I slip around the little group and descend the stairs, invisible in my unimportance.

In the darkness the cobbled square between the church and the Taverna Irini seems full of people. News travels. Everyone in Halemni must have cut short their New Year's parties and come to see if they could help the Georgiadises.

Michaelis the fisherman is here, Panagiotis's brother, and standing beside him is one of the other fishermen who crewed the boat on the night Andreas brought me to the island. Nobody looks at me. I feel safe now, in any case. What would there be to recognise tonight?

Yannis and Michaelis have brought a lightweight stretcher,

363

a canvas sleeve that fits over aluminium poles. The island has seen other emergencies, of course. By the light of several torches the stretcher is laid out, and Xan and Christopher gently lay Olivia down on it and muffle her in blankets. Her eyes are open again, but they are clouded with pain and confusion. As soon as the men have buckled straps to secure her, several sets of hands reach for the stretcher poles. They hoist it and Olivia is carried away. Max is behind and the bearers are moving so fast that he has to run to catch up. I am here, of course, in their wake.

I have walked this route so many times. The slope of the village street is familiar and the grey outlines of the houses; only the lights showing in all the windows are out of the ordinary. I remember the first time, when I was wet and cold, and Andreas had fallen behind, and I saw Meroula in the flood debris with her photograph albums in her arms. Meroula led me up the hill and there was Olivia, my other self, standing in the doorway of the potter's house.

The column is heading for the field behind the beach road. It is a flat area of bare earth and rough grass, with the line of concrete shells that were summer guest houses separating it from the crescent of shingle and the torn tamarisk trees. I can see powerful lantern lights set out to form the corners of a square and another small knot of people waiting. At the same moment I hear the distant buzz of the helicopter. A gust of wind and the wash of waves drown out the sound and I think I must have imagined it, but then I hear the thud-thud again, much louder. I can see a point of light in the sky to the west of us, bigger and brighter than the powdery stars.

The stretcher-bearers stand still and everyone's face except mine is turned to the sky.

I am watching Olivia's head, the tuft of hair uncovered by the blanket, the pale gleam of her forehead.

This could have been my story, to be surrounded and lifted up with love, to be saved, to be allowed a full life by the kindliness of fate. But it is *not* my story.

So one instant can alter everything to come.

There is a cone of harsh light wobbling and probing over the grass and rocks as the helicopter ambulance circles the landing area. The watchers crowd to one side of the square, making a protective phalanx around the stretcher. The noise of the engines is deafening, and a scything wind flattens the vegetation and sends spirals of dust into our eyes. The squat shape hovers in the air and slowly descends. It touches down, rocking a little, and the engines abruptly cut out. The rotor blades spin slower and slower, and sink to a standstill. The door lifts and slides to one side, and two paramedics in green overalls hatch out into the lights as the stretcher and Olivia and Xan are propelled towards them by a dozen pairs of hands.

I am running foward too, with the grass whispering under my feet. One of the ambulance men has raced to Olivia's side, the other is waiting to receive her at the helicopter's bay. I can see inside it. There are oxygen cylinders, metal cases of tubing and masks, a narrow bed with straps to secure the casualty.

No one looks at me as I reach her. Xan climbs inside the cabin and the paramedics prepare to hoist the stretcher. I squirm between the busy arms, somehow, and press my fingers to her slack mouth. I don't know, even now, if this is a blessing or a warning or just goodbye.

I do know that Olivia will live, as I have not. My life ended in Branc, in the white concrete hotel. Everything that came after that has been Andreas's gift to me.

The stretcher rocks and she moans in pain. There are terse instructions in Greek and she is lifted away from me into the ambulance. The men deftly transfer her from the stretcher to the bed and secure the straps and blankets around her. One of them lifts an oxygen mask and presses it to her face. I can see the pilot in his headset, and the red and green pinpoints of light from the controls.

The crowd moves back and I am carried with it. The door of the helicopter lifts and slides in reverse, and seals itself on Olivia and Xan. Those of us left behind retreat further, beyond the margins of the lights, and once we are clear the engines splutter and kick into life. The wind buffets us again as the machine rocks on its runners and lifts off the ground. A few seconds later it is a black thumbprint haloed in its own light against the night sky and a minute after that it is invisible. The wind swallows the gnat's hum of the engines.

The group of men stand in silence for a moment longer, then the tension breaks and they stick their hands in their pockets and hunch into their coats, talking in low voices as they turn away. They have done everything required of them and there is that swell of subdued, almost furtive elation that always comes at these times. I remember it after the tsunami, when everyone in the village worked together. It was one of the things that made me, the outsider, wish to be an insider here. They cross the ground to the beach road in twos and threes. Yannis has appeared to be sober while there was a job to be done for his friends but now, I realise, he must have been drunk at his New Year's celebration. Drunkenness descends on him again like a curtain falling. He bends down to pick up one of the lights but knocks it over instead and someone else punches his shoulder so he staggers elaborately and lets Michaelis catch him. There are noisy guffaws of relieved laughter. The Halemniots move off past the broken trees and head back to their wives and their fierce card games.

Max and Christopher, the two foreigners, walk more slowly in their wake. I know they are telling each other that

Olivia will be looked after, that she will recover, that the right thing has been done even if it is late in the day.

And I follow behind them, unseen.

We walk up past the little cube houses and into the square where the cream and orange innards of the splintered fig tree are already silvered by wind and weather. The church door is closed and the bell in the tower is silent. Meroula must have gone through the potter's house, turning off the lights. There is only one showing, in the downstairs window.

Max and Christopher go indoors together and I stand outside with my head turned towards the sea, listening and looking for someone to come.

EIGHTEEN

There are goodbyes to be said.

The first day of the year is another of those flat and colourless ones, when the sky and sea are an identical milky grey, and a low mist rubs out the divide between earth and water. I watch the diffuse brightness steadily bleeding from the east until at last it is full daylight.

In the studio room I dress carefully, then I pick up Squeak the mouse by the tail and put him in the pocket of my trousers. I walk around the side of the potter's house and under the pergola to the terrace doors. Max is sitting at the table, with last night's debris still spread on it. I tap on the glass and his head jerks up.

I am used to being cold and in the kitchen it is warm and stuffy, with too many layers of indoor smells. Not cosy any longer but claustrophobic.

'How is she?' I ask.

'Xan called from the hospital. She has septicaemia, blood poisoning. It had spread right through her system, which is why she deteriorated so suddenly last night. But they think they have caught it in time.'

Max is unshaven, with reddened eyes and gummy white

deposits at the corners of his mouth. His eyes slide towards mine and then skid away again.

'Where did you get to last night?' he asks. He won't remember seeing me with the stretcher, down at the landing place.

'I thought I should keep out of the way.'

He nods at this.

'It will be a day or so, apparently, before they are quite certain Olivia is out of danger. A massive infection like that puts a big strain on the heart. But once we know for sure, I will have to head home again. I've already stayed longer than I meant to.'

He is embarrassed, of course, as well as fearing and expecting that I am going to make demands he will not want to meet. Olivia's sudden illness has put a different gloss on everything for him. He will be thinking that life is a more fragile entity than he has properly understood. Anything could happen to Hattie and his girls; any random tragedy could upend the ordinariness of his taken-for-granted life and make it seem in retrospect more precious than he could have reckoned on.

I know this last thing. Sometimes it has seemed that it is the only thing I do know.

'Of course,' I say softly. 'Just in case.'

'Are you angry with me?' He puts his hands, heavy hands, on my shoulders. I know something else as well – he still desires me, with an awkward, urgent itch that makes him despise himself.

'No. I'm not angry.'

Relief lights up the blank space behind his eyes and he produces a lopsided smile. He is glad to escape so lightly, with only the inconvenience of the physical urge to taunt him. He shrugs his shoulders under his plaid shirt, eyeing me to make sure that I am telling the truth and that there isn't some sting in the tail of my meekness. His utter transparency, the fumbling, adolescent, would-be charming, rueful disengagement of him, makes me smile. It is a dismissive smile, I know, and it diminishes my resemblance to Olivia. His hands drop to his sides.

'Would you like some?'

He indicates the coffee pot on the stove.

'Yes. Thank you.'

He busies himself with the cups.

'It's so early,' he says. 'I didn't sleep much. I don't want to wake Meroula and the kids.'

I have not slept at all. It has seemed a long wait, but it is nearly over.

'I am leaving, too,' I tell him. 'I know I can't stay here.'

'When?'

'Oh. Soon.'

I don't ask if we could travel to the airport together. I don't say anything else at all and he relaxes slightly. He passes me the cup of coffee and we sit down together on the same side of the big table, looking out through the terrace doors to the bare branches of the pergola vine, the slope of the hill and the pale wedge of sea. Silence seeps and then swells between us.

I am thinking about Olivia last night, lying upstairs in bed, and the battle we have fought that was not over Max, although this seemed to be the way it was.

When I look obliquely at him he seems to have shrunk to a smaller size and years seem to have rolled off him, and I know exactly who he is. In Max's silence there seems to be a need for me to reassure or to exonerate him. I am the leader and he is the faithful lieutenant, again, all over again, and memory floods through the cells of my brain like a haemorrhage.

I can see my feet in red sandals and smell mown grass,

and there are dappled shadows and a stone gryphon, and my brother's motionless body.

Last night Olivia and I fought for our identity and I conceded to her.

But if I could have been her, were it not for a split second of history, Max and I would be closer in this loop of space and time than I have fully considered. He was, might have been, even *is* my brother.

Now you know.

I put my cup down with unsteady hands.

He is still waiting to take his direction from me.

A shock current of combined revulsion and extreme longing passes through the marrow of my bones. I want to get away and at the same time I want to submerge myself in him.

'I am sorry,' he says.

'Don't be. You don't need to be. I couldn't have stayed here or offered you any more than you can offer me.'

We both stand up at the same time and I steady myself with my fingertips to the table. Then I close the space between us. My mouth finds his and our tongues meet. While I feel the melt-hot current through my legs and down my spine, I am already standing apart and watching two people standing kissing in an untidy kitchen. It is me in reality who stands back first. I am breathing hard, as though I have been running.

Max sighs, then he shrugs his shoulders again, this time in acceptance.

'Right,' he says. I know that Max is a simple soul, not like Olivia and me. He wants this to be over and he wants to be exonerated, and this is what he shall have. He is like Olivia in one thing: luck smiles on him.

'Goodbye Max,' I say quietly.

'What?' He asks some question about the ferry, about which route I will be taking from Halemni.

'I'll find a way.'

I push my chair neatly back to tuck under the table and turn away and keep on walking out through the terrace doors and into the clear air. It is much easier than I thought it would be.

Christopher opens his door with four fingers cupped round the edge, ready to pull it shut again. The slice of his face that is revealed to me asks sharply, 'Is there more news?' Olivia is his first thought, of course.

'No. Not that I have heard. Can I come in?'

He hesitates, weighing up his unwillingness. Then the door opens only just wide enough to admit me. When I slip into the room he moves quickly backwards, with a complicated reverse step that almost causes him to trip.

Christopher is afraid of me, I understand. I don't know why this hasn't dawned on me before.

The room is tidier than it was the only other time I have seen it. His drawings are stacked up in neat sheaves and the clothes are folded in piles. He stands in the middle of the room with his hands at his sides, doing nothing to make me welcome, just waiting to see what I will do.

'I have come to say goodbye.'

He rakes his hair back off his face now, in the old gesture. He is relieved and doesn't try to conceal it. Olivia will be safer when I am gone – whatever or whoever I am, he knows that I have brought confusion and threat into Halemni's sweet, settled world.

'I see. Are you going back to England?'

Without answering I move to the table to inspect one of the sheaves of drawings. They are all of Olivia. All of them, unmistakably. There are no shades of Kitty here.

'You look as if you might be upping sticks too.'

He steps forward to put himself between me and the drawings.

There was a time when I might have been her substitute. He may even have tried to ease his longing for her by trying to want me instead. But I never came close to matching her, however hard he tried to superimpose my image over hers. It is Christopher, in love, and out of all the little group of us on Halemni, therefore, the one who has studied Olivia and me most carefully. He is the one who sees the differences most clearly.

Maybe he even knows what is wrong about me.

If so, no wonder he is afraid.

There is a little cold wind stirring in the tidy room. I suppose that I have brought it.

'It is time for a move,' he acknowledges at length.

Christopher is accepting defeat. The bleakness of his words fills me with sympathy and I want to console him. Forgetting everything else for a moment, I reflect that we're both disappointed in love. I put my hands out, intending maybe to drop my arm round his shoulder and kiss the corner of his mouth, as a gesture of fellow feeling and a goodbye.

His hands shoot up too. He is protecting himself, warding me off. He steps back so fast that he kicks a stool and it falls over, spilling books on to the floor.

I stop, frozen in my impulsive gesture, and now I can feel the biting cold and see the questions and fear of the answers reflected in his eyes. Christopher is shivering. I let my arms drop to my sides.

'Olivia will recover,' I assure him.

He inclines his head, watchful and with his hands still drawn up against his chest.

'I only came to say goodbye,' I repeat.

He stares at me, waiting for what I am going to do.

I take one step backwards. Two more bring me to the door and I grope behind me for the latch, lift it, pull the door open. As soon as I am outside I hear him moving a chair, wedging the back of it under the latch. Christopher is barricading his door against me, as if I might break back inside.

I walk briskly across the street, cutting between the houses opposite and down a little concreted alleyway haunted by cats. It takes me past the back of the shop and from a vent in the storeroom wall I catch a brief whiff of brine and oil and hessian sacking. Down another alleyway there is a view of the harbour wall and the sea, and then the short cut delivers me to Panagiotis's front door. I know every inch of Megalo Chorio now, even the irregular staves of telephone cables pencilled against the sky and the patterns made by cracks in the whitewashed house walls. The place holds happiness, mine too, like stones hold the sun's heat.

Helen opens the door to me. She is wearing flat fluffy slippers and thick stockings, and a cardigan hastily buttoned across her front. Her hair is uncombed and she looks tired and absorbed, and she blinks at me as if she can hardly remember who I am.

'I have come to say that I can't work in the shop any more.'

There is no sign of comprehension. From behind her a small cry turns into a wail and she immediately turns back into the house. I follow her broad hips and shuffling feet down the corridor to the kitchen, where the baby is laid out under a meringue of lace covers in her shiny pram. Helen extracts her and cups the spiky black head with one hand as she settles her against her shoulder. She walks up and down, humming in the base of her throat and the wailing gently tails off. When Helen turns round she seems surprised to realise that I have followed her.

There are baby clothes drying on a pulley airer and a feeding bottle stands in a pan beside the sink. The room smells dense and milky.

I have been happy in the shop, in Helen's quiet company, and I am grateful for the refuge that it provided. And even though Helen is embarrassed to recall it, after seeing Demetria's birth I feel intensely linked to them both. It would be unthinkable to melt away from Halemni without saying goodbye to them.

'I'm sorry. I don't want to let you down. One of Panagiotis's cousins will be able to help you instead, maybe.'

Helen smiles up at me through her thick black eyelashes.

'Okay, okay,' she says softly. And with her free hand she takes mine and squeezes it. She does understand what I am telling her, then.

I am touched, and I put my arms in a circle to enclose her and the baby. Their combined scent is of warm, oily hair and talcum powder, laced with a faint sourness. I hold them tight, looking down on the tops of their two dark heads, and for a moment, dry as I am, I am linked into the chain of mothers and daughters. I came nowhere close to crying with Christopher, even Max, but I have to squeeze back the tears now.

'*Yia sou*,' I say, the open-ended Greek hello and goodbye.

'*Yia sou*.' Helen is stroking her baby's head and rocking gently on her feet. She is completely self-contained and I know that this absorption in mothering is elemental, beyond happiness.

I wish, for the last time, that I could have known it.

I smile at her once more.

'Good luck,' I say, bizarrely.

Fate, history, luck. Call it what you like.

The cobbled square bounded by the church, Taverna Irini and the potter's house is noisy with children. Goal posts are marked out with discarded jerseys. I pick out Theo at once, running near the broken fig tree in a game within a game of his own devising. Georgi has the football, with Stavros's son Petros launching himself into a tackle. There are six others, girls as well as boys, running and shouting and waving their arms. Their clothes seem to bleed colour into the pale air.

I stand against the papered-up windows of the taverna to watch. It is midday and even though the sun's angle is low there will be heat in it, just for an hour or so, before the mists collect once more.

I know all these children. I can name them and their parents, and I know which houses they live in and what their fathers do, and their position in the subtle social hierarchy of Halemni. It pleases me to realise this. I am only an outsider, the English woman taken in after the wave, but still, I know some things.

Meroula and her friend Evangelina, poor Manolis's mother, are sitting on the stone bench next to the church gate. The blue-painted railings behind their heads are peeling, with rust under the flakes like dirt beneath cracked fingernails. I am too far away to see, but I know even this detail. Meroula is knitting but Evangelina just sits with her hands folded over her stomach. Their heads have turned in my direction but I don't move yet. I am still watching Georgi and Theo, remembering how they were on the first day I saw them, and how much they have grown and altered in the short months since the tsunami. I am glad to have seen it – it is another tiny connection to the present links in the unbroken chain, not mine but Helen's and Demetria's and Olivia's and Xan's.

I find that I am smiling, sunlit in the square.

With my hands in my pockets I stroll round the fig tree and the outskirts of the football game to the church gate. My shadow falls across the two women on the bench and Meroula lifts her square head up to meet my eyes.

'Olivia may be well, please God,' she says.

'I know. I heard. It's very good.'

Meroula continues knitting with clicks of the steel needles. Her mouth is in a firm line. I am the unfavoured now, not Olivia any more, and that is also satisfactory.

I'm not going to say goodbye. Instead, I move back round the margins of the shapeless game. Theo sees me and walks straight through the skein of players. He puts his head against my leg.

'Mummy is ill in the hospital.'

I crouch down to bring my face level with his. He has Xan's dark eyebrows and wide jaw but Olivia's eyes, Olivia's and mine.

'She will get better soon and then she'll come home.'

Georgi detaches himself from the game too and comes to see what Theo is doing. He takes his brother's arm, pretending to twist it but in fact just holding him. Theo doesn't resist. I notice that they draw supportively close to each other.

'Look.'

I take the felt mouse out of my pocket and hold it up by the tail. The boys eye me, where they would once have tried to grab it.

'You can look after him,' I say.

Someone makes a mis-kick. The ball sails over our heads and lands on the other side of the railings. A pair of children pound past and shin over into the church enclosure.

'Here, to me,' Stavros's boy is yelling. Part of my mind registers that I understand a lot of Greek words now. The ball flies back and bounces on the cobbles.

'Will she?' Theo has been turning my assurance over in his head.

'Yes.'

Georgi takes the mouse and lets it sit in the palm of his hand.

'He can live with the others, the ones you gave us for Christmas.' His fingers are dirty.

While they are occupied with the mouse I look at their eyelashes and their ears under tufts of roughly cut hair, and the way that Georgi's top front teeth seem too big for his face while Theo's are still small white seeds.

'Look after him, then.'

Georgi's attention turns back to the game. His head twists to see what Petros and the others are doing.

'I want to take him,' Theo pipes and Georgi drops it into his cupped hands.

'Good.'

I stand up and put my hands in my pockets. The boys run back across the cobbles and I watch until they are absorbed into the game again. Fifteen feet away Meroula is still knitting.

I don't look back. I walk past the potter's house where the sun is shining full into the windows. In a few weeks there will be flowers all over the hillside and the first guests of a new season will be arriving at the studios. I take the track that leads up the hill, walking slowly, enjoying the sun on my head and the distant cries of the gulls over the bay.

Beyond the graveyard, just before the point where the track narrows to a path and zigzags upwards much more steeply – where Olivia fell and cut her arm on the night of Saint Pandelios's feast – a truck is parked. I peer inside the cab as I pass, noticing the key in the ignition and the yellowed newspaper on the bench seat.

There are the white folded wings of tiny wild cyclamen flowers in sheltered hollows and the scent of thyme rises as my ankles stroke the bushes sprawling over the path. On the grey furry leaf of another bush I see a surprising sulphur-yellow butterfly. I would love to have seen all this in spring-time, but the knowledge that I won't doesn't cause me a

378

particular pang. The island seems complete enough now in my mind, with more cold and salt winds still to come before the real heat invades it.

On the shallower incline before the old village a pair of grey-backed crows are pecking at the earth. They lift their heads as I pass, regarding me with hard black eyes, but they don't spread their wings.

I walk between the clumps of thistle and nettle, and climb broken steps past the first houses. The windows and empty doorways frame darkness. But now I can hear something other than the wind and I stop to listen more carefully.

There are footsteps coming, clopping on the stones, and loud voices. The maze of alleys and blind corners makes it hard to judge from which direction and I tilt my head, straining to catch the sound. I am full of a sudden greedy anticipation, poised and ready to run forward in greeting.

Then a man comes round the corner above me. He is carrying a pair of overstaffed torn blue plastic bags, one in each hand, and a pile of bedclothes pinned by one arm against his ribcage. A much older man follows him, leaning on a stick to walk and testing each step before he makes it. It is Kyrie Yannis and the man with the laundry bags is his son. A second later, following his father and grandfather, Yannis himself appears. He is carrying an upholstered chair, his head pressing into the inverted seat cushion and his hands gripping the wooden arms. He has a rucksack slung low on his back and from his belt hang a frying pan and a couple of saucepans.

I stand back to make room, laughing at the sight of this cavalcade.

'*Kali mera, Kyria Kitty*,' Yannis's father says politely. The older man's mouth is hanging open and he is too breathless with the effort of walking to speak. He nods and the folds of his neck wobble. He has a posy of cyclamen flowers in his buttonhole.

'Oof,' says Yannis himself from under the chair. He swings it off his head as the other two plod on downhill, sets it down on a slab and seats himself with a flourish.

'Olivia?' he asks. I answer with an optimistic gesture. Yannis's teeth look very white and his lips are red in a mask of black stubble. 'Good. Very good.' He jerks one thumb back over his shoulder. 'No people now.'

His grandfather must be the last, almost three months after the earthquake and the wave, finally to surrender occupancy of the old village. None of the old people will come back, even the most stubborn, after going down to the sea and their families for New Year. It was only a matter of time, I suppose, before expediency and comfort won out over fear and superstition. I am sorry to think of the life slowly ebbing out of the old place all over again, but then it is cold and remote, and melancholy and full of ghosts. Who would choose to stay here, once the memory of immediate danger has faded?

'Big carry.' Yannis sighs. He stands up and hoists the chair back on to his head with one swing of his huge arms. He walks a few steps, then turns round to look at me from under the cushion. His grandfather's saucepans clink together.

'See you,' he calls.

I raise one arm and hold it aloft in a salute as he trudges off. *Yia sou.*

I climb onwards in the opposite direction, past rank gardens and terraces clogged with brambles. The narrow stone passage opens out into the little square below the church and I kick through the dead leaves that the wind drives into drifts up here. Kyria Elena's old house is empty and cold. There are no chairs drawn up against the walls in the sun, no washing pegged to the makeshift washing lines or blue smoke drifting over the caved-in roofs.

I cross in front of the church and turn the corner to the

vantage point, the ledge that last time was occupied by Christopher Cruickshank.

There is a man there, looking out to sea.

I walk along the ledge and he looks up, calm-faced, before he makes room for me beside him.

I am so happy to see him. I am smiling, a huge wide smile that threatens to split my face. When we are sitting together with the shimmering bay and Megalo Chorio spread out beneath us he puts his arm round my shoulders and I rest my head against him. I am tired, I realise.

'It is about what might have been,' I say to Andreas.

'Yes.'

'That's why you brought me here?'

He inclines his head smoothly.

Now you know. This, I think, is what rightness feels like – the answer to the riddle I have been trying to work out for almost the whole of my life.

Halemni contains what I might have been and what Marcus might have been, Olivia and Max instead of the two of us, and all of this place spread out in front of us is present while I am in parallel.

Andreas has borrowed me from fate, if you like, and given me a chance to see the other side of a tossed coin.

I turn to him, resting my head on my knees to look at his face. He meets my gaze. Then he says, 'You can't undo history. You are what it makes you.'

'Meaning?' Although I more or less know the answer.

'Your life changed the day the statue toppled on your little brother. You became the person that tragedy had befallen.'

'And if it had not, I would have been someone else?'

'A partial else. Of course.'

I wait for a minute, listening to the rattle of dead leaves against dry stone walls. The wind is getting up.

'Who are you?'

His eyes are full of comedy and mockery.

'Your guardian angel, if you like. If you will buy that.'

Maybe I do.

The light of the short day is already fading. The sky to the west of us is streaked with pink.

'Are you ready?' Andreas asks. We stand up and walk back along the ledge and out into the square. The church bell starts to ring, a clear uncracked note.

The square is different again. The roofs of the houses are intact and there are pots of kitchen herbs beside the swept and whitened steps. Two old women in black are sitting on stools in the shade of an olive tree that crooks its branches over two tiny gardens and there is a baby in a basket on the cobbles beside them. The wind stirs washing on a line and a pair of grey cats tussle at the corner of an alley. I can smell frying fish and woodsmoke.

Andreas and I walk across the square and descend into the main street. The windows reflect light and the house doors are painted blue and green. There are rose bushes in one or two of the gardens and others have fig trees and painted tins with woody stemmed geraniums sprawling out of them.

I look around in pure enchantment. Arhea Chorio is alive.

A string of children bursts out from one of the side alleys and they dodge across the street a step or two in front of us before sliding over the wall of one of the gardens. I recognise them; they are the New Year's singers. A big woman in a thick sacking apron appears in the house doorway and she grabs the nearest boy by the collar and hauls him into the house. I can hear her harsh shouting and the child's wail of complaint.

We walk the length of the main street and I see another woman with a rough wooden paddle taking hot loaves out of a bread oven. There are piles of sawn logs stacked against a wall with a timber roof to shelter them, and a coarse rake and a hoe are propped in a corner. Beyond the houses lower down the hill the old terraces fan out in descending plateaux. The low stone enclosing walls are intact now and the ground is dug and raked ready for the spring planting.

'Where are the men?' I ask Andreas.

'Fishing. Farming.'

Life was hard in the old village, of course. Time rubbed out that life and the place itself as soon as there was an easier living to be made from the tourists down on the beach.

As we pass the last pair of houses on the hill we meet an old man and a donkey coming up the path. The donkey's load of wood towers almost as high as itself and the old man walks at its shoulder, encouraging the beast with low murmurs and whistles. His hand pats the donkey's side as they tread slowly past us. I have seen these two as well, down on the beach road.

When we have left the village behind, I realise that it is almost sunset. The sun seems to rest on the lip of the sea, with thick bars of grey and lavender cloud drawn up in front of it.

'I am so happy to have seen the village like that, alive.'

'It's always alive,' Andreas says. And I suppose it is, in the way that he and I are. It is in that parallel place, where I have been – on loan – since the night of the earthquake.

The loan is being called in now but I am happy. No: I am beyond happiness. I am at peace.

The lights are on in the potter's house as we slip by. The main street of Megalo Chorio is deserted except for the cats prowling in the dusk. There is a last wash of luminous grey over the sea to the west of Halemni and a thin white mist is rising off the flat water of the bay.

Andreas takes my hand and we walk down the crescent of shingle.

The water is surprisingly warm. The mist drifts up around my knees and then my hips, and I comb my fingers through it.

NINETEEN

Olivia shifted her position under the hospital sheet. She had been lying in the ward for only two days since they had brought her out of the intensive care unit, but the view was already too familiar. The polished floor reflected bed legs and screens and over-bright rectangles from the tall windows. There were curtains of a murky grey colour. When she turned her head she could see the woman in the next bed who lay propped on pillows with a plastic tube taped in her nose. She was Meroula's age or older and her hands fidgeted constantly with the bedclothes.

I want to go home. The words had been running in Olivia's head ever since she woke up with tubes in her arms and a mask over her mouth and nose, and a thirst like fire burning her throat. Blurred faces loomed over her when she tried to speak and held her arms when she fought to rip the mask off. Then Xan's face swam into focus and the first thing she saw with full consciousness was the tears in his eyes.

'You are going to be all right,' he told her. 'I love you.'

Olivia knew that both these statements were true.

After a day she was able to sip water and then drink some soup.

After another day they took the tubes out of her arms. A doctor in a short-sleeved blue overall came and sat beside her. He told her that she had been brought in with maybe only a few hours to live. Her life had been saved by the helicopter ambulance. In the hospital they had pumped her full of antibiotics and, after twenty-four critical hours, she had begun to rally against the infection.

'It was remarkable to see you come back.' The doctor smiled. 'You are very determined.'

'I want to go home. When can I go home?'

'You are still weak, we will need to watch you for a little longer.'

She was certainly weak, because she didn't argue yet.

Xan sat beside her bed and held her hand. They didn't talk much, because they knew that there would be plenty of time for that. Olivia liked just to lie and look at his face and learn the contours of it all over again. Watching the pull of tiny muscles and the flicker of his expressions made her remember the days when they were new to each other and the first voyage that they had made together to Halemni. She tightened her grip on his hand and the pressure would stir him out of his thoughts and make him lean over her.

'Do you want a drink of water? Is the light too bright?'

She shook her head. It was enough that he was taking care of her. Contentment seeped through her body and fuelled her recovery.

After three days the nurses came with a mirror and toilet articles, and laid them out for her. With eyes made sharp by her illness Olivia looked at the pink whorl of face cream and the glinting teeth of the steel comb as if they had just been invented. She picked up the hand mirror and examined her reflection.

Her hair had grown back into its accustomed tufts and she hadn't shaped her eyebrows since before Christmas. Her lips were chapped. Apart from her hollow cheeks and shadowed eyes the face that looked back at her was her own.

After another day the doctor told her that she would be moving down to the ordinary ward.

'When can I go home?'

'In a few more days, probably.'

Xan and she finally agreed that now the danger was past he would go back to the island and look after the boys until she was ready to come home. Before he left he lifted her up in his arms and held her as if he was afraid she might break.

'I am still me,' she told him, laughing a little.

'Thank God,' he answered, not laughing at all.

Down in the women's ward Olivia sat up abruptly and pushed back the covers. She swung her feet to the floor and stood up, only swaying a little. The woman in the next bed briefly opened her eyes.

The window nearest to Olivia gave a view of a segment of the old town. She could see a Gothic gateway flanked by twin crenellated towers and a short length of city wall. In the other direction lay blue harbour water and the ferry port. There was the massive stone jetty, guarded by a lighthouse, from which the Halemni ferries sailed. Olivia pressed the palms of her hands against the window and cooled her forehead. The glass clouded and she rubbed it clear with her thumb. She stared across at the water as if by force of will she could propel herself to the harbour and up the ramp to the rocking ship bound for home. The island drew her, and the people there, with an intensity honed by illness and the nearness of death.

'Ovvy.'

She turned and saw Max.

He was holding a bunch of wild anemones, purple-blue with a boss of black stamens, and she knew he had picked them in a sheltered hollow on the hillside above the potter's house. He put the cool sappy stems into her hand.

'Brought them over on the boat with some beers, in the eskie,' he said.

They poured water from her bedside jug into a cup and arranged the little flowers. Olivia touched the petals with their faint silky veining.

'Thank you.'

'Is there anywhere we can go and sit?' Max looked at the woman with the tube in her nose and another with parchment-yellow skin whose teeth looked too big for her shrunken face. He had a fear of hospitals and illness.

'A sort of waiting room, across there.'

He put his hand under her arm and they walked slowly.

'You look okay. Surprisingly all right,' he told her, with a shaky note in his usually steady voice. 'Back there, when we had to get the chopper over, I was beginning to worry.'

'I don't remember much about it,' Olivia said.

There was one memory, though, that rolled constantly like a submerged log in the current of her thoughts.

She remembered Kitty lying next to her, with her wide eyes unblinking. Kitty's hands caressed her neck, feeling cool to her heat. There was a struggle going on between them, a terrible and unfathomable battle, and it would have been easy for Olivia just to close her eyes. Help me, she had begged. And Kitty answered, with an effort to bring out the words, I will.

After that had come a great wash of relief.

The day room had high metal-framed windows and a row of red chairs. There was a water cooler, a television showing rolling pictures of a football game and a low table with a battered tin ashtray. Olivia smiled. This was a Greek hospital.

Max drew a chair to face hers and they sat together knee to knee.

'Is Kitty here?' she asked.

Max looked startled, then relieved. He had wanted to talk to her about Kitty but he had been uncertain how to begin – and Olivia understood this because they knew each other so well. They hurt or angered each other sometimes, she thought, but their capacity to do so was part of their closeness.

'No. She's gone,' Max said.

'What? Gone where?'

Olivia couldn't immediately interpret what he was saying, although at some deeper level she knew exactly what he meant.

'I don't know. None of us knows. The morning after you were brought here.' Max rubbed the corner of his mouth. 'She said goodbye to Panagiotis's wife. And to me and Christopher, in a way. And she gave that toy mouse to Georgi and Theo.'

They looked into each other's eyes.

'Did she take a boat?'

'No. Not that we know of.'

'What did she take with her?'

'Nothing, by the look of it. Her room looked the same as it always did. Xan and I didn't want to rummage around too much.'

'She came with nothing, too,' Olivia said.

Kitty Fisher had fleshed herself out with the daily routines of Halemni. Now, as Olivia thought of her, the shape and form that she had taken on seemed to peel away and then dissolve, until there was nothing of it left. She could remember clothes, conversations, walks that they had taken together and meals they had shared, but that was all colouring. All she could find to identify at the core of the recollections was herself: her own jealousy and fear. Kitty had apparently threatened to come between Max and her, but Olivia realised today that there *was* nothing separating the two of them. She had never felt closer to her brother than she did now.

Kitty faded, faster and faster. Had she been there? Had she really come to lie beside her, on New Year's Eve, or had it all been the distortion of fever?

Max stood up and went to the water cooler. He bent down and fiddled with the little tap, then filled two paper cones and brought them back. Olivia took hers and drank some.

'Will you miss her?' she asked.

He nodded his head slowly. 'Yes.'

She considered. 'I won't, you know. I'm glad she's gone. I don't suppose she'll come back, do you?'

If Max thought she was callous or careless, he didn't say as much.

'No, I don't think she'll come back.'

They talked about other things, deliberately, to make a space for their difference about Kitty.

'I'm on my way to England,' Max said. 'To spend a few days with them, before I go home.'

He meant their parents, of course, in their quiet house in the country.

'Yes, I think that's a good idea,' Olivia said softly. She put down her empty cup and held her hands out to her brother. They laced their fingers together, both staring down at the twined fingers.

Later she asked, 'What time's your flight?'

He looked at his watch. 'In three hours.'

'Don't stay here too long, then. You need plenty of time to check in at the airport here.'

He laughed. She always had and always would tell him what to do and when. She was the leader, he was the lieutenant.

'Okay, Ovvy.'

'Will you and Hattie be all right?'

'I don't know. I hope so. Will you and Xan?'

'Oh yes.' Her face broke into a smile. 'Yes, I'm sure we will.'

'I suppose I'd better go soon. Don't frighten me by getting ill like that again, will you?'

'I shouldn't think so.'

They both stood up and he folded his arms round her.

They kissed, a little awkwardly now that the moment of separation had come, patted each other's shoulders and then stood apart.

'I took some of the photographs,' Max said. 'They were there in my room, the darkroom.' He slid a manila envelope out of his flight bag and showed it to her. There were some of the pictures of Kitty in the striped jersey and with the painted moustache, and the others, the ones with her face painted over Olivia's bones. She stared blankly at them. Looks were deceptive. You could change what you looked like, but not who you were.

'Do you mind?' he asked.

Olivia shrugged. 'No, not at all. You could have had them all. I don't want them.'

At the door of the ward they hugged each other again.

'I'm so glad I've got you,' Olivia told him. 'I can't imagine what the world would be like without you in it.'

'A sadder place. A much, much sadder place,' Max laughed.

When the doctor came to see her that afternoon Olivia told him, 'I want to go home.'

He was writing in her notes. 'In a day or so.'

'It's Wednesday tomorrow, isn't it?'

'That's right.'

'It's the local ferry day. I am going home on the Halemni boat tomorrow.'

The woman with the tube in her nose turned her head tiredly on the pillow.

'You are right,' she said. 'You go home. It is best.' Twenty-four hours later Halemni was in sight, a familiar donkey-brown outline rising out of the sea.

A sister of Stefania's and two other Megalo Chorio women happened to be on the boat too, and they had seized on Olivia with cries of surprise and concern. They nursed her through the journey, making her lie across three seats in the saloon, bringing her bottled water and shooing away anyone who came too close. But as Halemni came nearer Olivia told her protectors that she felt dizzy and wanted to go up on the deck for some fresh air. She pushed open the heavy doors that led to the forward deck. There were wooden slatted seats out here and a handful of pasengers wrapped up against the salt wind. Olivia leaned over the rail to watch, exactly where she and Xan had stood when she first came home with him. It was cold and she did feel weak and giddy, but she stood her ground. As the ship came round the headland, the village and the hillside crowned with the Knights' castle were laid out in front of her. In the fading light she could just see the pale-blue front of the potter's house. She rubbed the tears out of her eyes with the back of her hand.

As the ship performed its reverse manoeuvre to bring its stern to the jetty, with its propellors churning the water and gulls planing over the harbour debris, she watched the little crowd of people waiting to greet it. She knew every one of them: Yannis, Michaelis, Stavros; the reclusive egg man, waiting to ship out his boxes of fresh eggs.

As soon as the stern door connected with the jetty, Stefania's sister was striding out.

'Panagiotis! Here!' she yelled. The other two women shepherded Olivia with them and Panagiotis saw her and leapt into his pick-up. He reversed and Olivia was gently handed through the crowd to the passenger seat.

'You are here? Already?'

'I wanted to come home. Enough hospital,' she said.

Xan wasn't watching for the ferry, of course. He was at home with their children. Her longing to see them all made her wrap her arms around herself and hunch forward in the sagging seat of the pick-up truck.

Panagiotis, loving his central role in the drama of her surprise arrival, rammed his thumb on the horn button and stuck his head out of the window to shout for a clear path. The little group parted and someone clapped their hands, and then everyone was suddenly clapping, applauding Olivia's homecoming. The pick-up bucked and skidded up the main street to the potter's house. Panagiotis helped her out, then tactfully climbed back into the driver's seat and left her alone. She walked slowly round to the side of the house and without glancing across at the door of the studio she stood at the edge of the terrace, looking in through the windows at the kitchen.

The room was tidy and swept. Meroula was sitting in the chair by the fire with sewing on her lap, but she was dozing now with her head fallen sideways against the cushion. Theo was sitting at the table intent on his drawing and at the other end of the room Georgi and his father were standing at the sink. The child was holding up a dripping bunch of cutlery that he must have fished out of the washing-up water and Xan was elaborately choosing a fork or a spoon at a time and drying it before putting it away in the drawer. They were looking at each other and laughing, making a game of this mundane job. Xan was wearing his old blue jersey with the unravelling hem and he looked as though he hadn't shaved or combed his hair since leaving her in the hospital.

Olivia balanced on the little wave of rough turf that edged

the terrace stones, almost unable to breathe in case some new shock wave struck the potter's house and broke up the picture before she could make herself part of it once more.

She needed to tell them how much she loved them all.

Xan took the last remaining spoon and polished it. Georgi dried his hands on the back of his jeans and called something to Theo who put down his crayon and trotted round to help him put saucepans on a shelf. It touched her deeply, this sight of the three of them managing in her absence. It made her want to laugh, too. Meroula woke up and as she always did immediately peered at her sewing to make it look as if she hadn't been asleep at all. When she had put in a few stitches she glanced out of the window towards the terrace.

Olivia shrank back. She didn't want to be seen looking in on her family as if she were spying on them. It took a moment longer for her to realise that standing out here, watching the tableau in the light, made her feel like Kitty. Poor Kitty, who must have seen them all often enough, framed in the warmth of the house while she hovered alone on the other side of the glass.

The gathering darkness shielded Olivia as it must have done for Kitty. Meroula rubbed her eyes, pinched the bridge of her nose and went on sewing.

This is mine, Olivia thought. I can walk in now, and let all this love and happiness lap around me. Nothing will come to wash it away, because Xan and I won't allow it to.

She stepped back off the ridge of grass and slipped round to the front door of the house. She lifted the latch, perfectly familiar with the shape and the shiny feel of it under her fingers, and pushed the door open. The voices coming from the kitchen stopped at the sound of the door. The Christmas tree had been taken down, she saw, and the candlelights stored away for another year.

Theo was the first to come running. He looked to where

she stood with the grey-blue evening behind her and cold air blowing into the house.

'Mum,' he shrieked. 'Mum's here.'

He ran, his hands out and his face stretched in a wide startled smile. He buried his face against her thigh and she cupped the back of his head, holding him close.

Georgi came next and she drew him to her in the same way with her fingers meshed in their thick hair.

'How?' Xan asked in amazement as he came and wrapped the three of them in his arms. The boys squirmed between them, pressing their faces into the shelter of their parents' warmth, relief making babies of them all over again. They stood all four together, letting Xan rock them, letting happiness make them dizzy.

'I'll tell you.' Olivia laughed.

'But you won't get ill again?' Theo demanded, reminding her of Max. Georgi, that much older, left his anxiety unvoiced but it showed clearly in his eyes when he looked up at her.

'No, I won't,' she said.

Meroula came, with her sewing scissors clipped to her cardigan and her face still with sleep in it.

'Close the door, Xan, close it right now. Don't let her stand there in this cold.'

Later, Olivia lay in the shuttered bedroom with her head on Xan's shoulder. The scent of the pillows, the denser darkness of furniture against the bare walls, the rhythm of her husband's breathing, were intensely familiar. All of this was ordinary and therefore precious. Her memories of New Year's Eve, of Kitty lying here in Xan's place, the dim picture of a man who wasn't Max sitting on the chair in the corner, these were all distortions or phantasms of fever. She had had septicaemia, originating from the night of Saint Pandelios's feast when she fell and cut her arm. The wound hadn't healed cleanly and then it had become infected, the doctors told her. Their medical terminology was precise. Everything that had happened was explicable. She had imagined herself to be in danger of being taken over by Kitty, but that was all it was – imagination. Kitty was a vivid creature with a sad past and Olivia assumed that her own tranquil existence had probably seemed ripe for colonisation.

But Kitty was gone now. Maybe, after all, Halemni and the Georgiadises hadn't turned out to be as interesting as she had hoped. That was Kitty's affair. All that really mattered, Olivia thought, was that she was gone and would not come back again. She had taken a season of catastrophe away with her.

Xan's hand slid over Olivia's hip and the hollow of her waist. He traced the ribcage with the tips of his fingers, tentatively, as if he was trying to coax her old, fuller shape out of the bones.

With her mouth touching his she smiled.

'I'm back to the size I was when we first met.'

The dusty street, clamouring Thai children, the big dark bear of a man watching her.

'I like it better when there's more of you.'

'You want me to get fat?'

He nodded sleepily. 'Yes please.'

She took it at face value, that he wanted her and no one else, that he made no comparisons, that he loved her for her strength and happiness, and ease with herself.

She said, with a pretence at grudgingness, 'I'll have to see what I can do.'

It was three more days before she ventured across to the studio room.

Even though it was the middle of the afternoon she clicked on the bright overhead light as soon as the door was open.

Everything revealed itself at a glance. It had been windy, and there was a layer of sandy dust on the table and the tiled floor. Kitty's few clothes, which were not really hers but Olivia's or charity handouts, hung on hooks behind the door. Max's Christmas bouquet sat beside the bed, with dust in the loops of red ribbon. Christopher's cartoon was propped against the wall, Greek history and language books sat in a neat pile. There was no one here, not a breath of Kitty in the old pea-coat or the folds of the bedclothes. She was absolutely gone. It was hard to remember that this tiny collection of borrowed or scrimped belongings had once seemed threatening.

On top of the books was a notebook, the cheap ruled kind with red covers that Helen sold in the shop. Olivia flipped it open and glanced at the pages. There was the Greek alphabet with phonetic pronunciations written alongside and a vocabulary list, *bread, honey, tea, boy, mother*. Nothing else. Not a note, not a personal observation or diary jotting to clothe the memory of Kitty Fisher.

Olivia shook out the black refuse sack that she had brought with her. She dropped the notebook into it and bundled in the clothes with the bouquet and Christopher's drawing. She didn't think he would be asking for it back. The books she put aside, to be returned to their places on her own shelves or on Christopher's. In the tiny tiled bathroom she took a bar of toilet soap out of the dish and a comb from the white plastic shelf that hung under the mirror. There wasn't a hair clinging to the comb or embedded in the soap.

When every trace of the room's occupant was inside the plastic sack and she had tied a knot in the top, Olivia stripped the bed. She folded the blankets ready to go back with all the others into winter storage, then scooped the sheets up into her arms. She hadn't meant to, but she buried her face in the folds and breathed in hard. There was the faintest scent, but it stirred no sense of otherness in her.

She lifted her head and looked out of the window towards the narrow slice of sea. Whatever this residual longing or curiosity was that made her smell another woman's bedclothes, it was not important any more. Kitty was gone.

It was time for the boys to be back from school. Olivia dropped the sheets outside the door and put the sack beside them. She took the books under her arm and looked around once more. There was nothing left, only pale dust smeared with her own movements. In the spring, when the summer season lay around the corner, she would come back and make everything ready again for the Darbys and their kind.

There were keys for all the studios because the summer visitors required them. No one on Halemni ever locked up their house in wintertime, but Olivia turned the key in the lock now and twisted the handle to make sure that it was secure. She couldn't have said whether she was putting up a barrier against intruders or shutting away a memory.

There was a big communal wheelie bin in an alley beside the Taverna Irini. Olivia prised off the lid and dropped the black bag inside. Among all the others it was instantly anonymous. She closed the lid securely again.

Xan was in the kitchen of the potter's house. He spent less time now down at the men's bar.

'I cleared the studio,' Olivia told him. *The* studio, not hers or Kitty's.

'I could have done that.' He took the pile of books and sheets out of her arms.

'I wanted to,' she said composedly.

That evening Christopher looked at the spines of the remaining books.

'Yes, these are mine. Wouldn't you like to keep them?'

They were sitting at the table, Xan at the head and Olivia on one side and Christopher on the other, as they had done countless times. It was a cold night and they were wearing layers of jumpers to save lighting the fire. Georgi and Theo were asleep upstairs. Xan and Christopher were passing the Metaxas bottle between them for added insulation.

'Why?' Xan asked lazily 'Haven't you got room in that den of yours?'

Christopher squared his tobacco tin with the wood grain of the table. His hair bisected his face, leaving only one eye visible. He didn't glance in Olivia's direction.

'I'm going back to England.'

Once it was said, she knew that she had been expecting it.

'Your stuff will still be here when you come out again for the summer,' Xan remarked.

'I mean, I'm going back for good.' The lines of graining didn't run parallel. He edged the tin to and fro, trying to find a satisfying alignment. 'I'm sorry to leave you without a teacher, but I don't think you'll have too much trouble finding another. Dabblers in watercolours are two a penny.'

Xan sat back, hooking his long arms over the chair.

'Not like you, they aren't. Why? After all this time?'

'That's one reason. I can't go on for ever, can I, living here?'

He's right, Olivia thought. He couldn't stay here for ever. That was for Xan and herself, who were knitted into Halemni by their children, their commitment to one another. Christopher should go home, kick-start his life again. His brother was a painter, a very successful one, he had told her. Perhaps ambition would belatedly touch him too.

Xan looked startled. 'What will you do?'

'Get a teaching job. Maybe residential, in a school. Do some painting for myself as well.'

Olivia stood up. She went round to Christopher's chair and rested her cheek on the top of his head. When she locked her arms round his shoulders he sat rigid, as if he was afraid that a movement might break something. She understood as clearly as she had ever done that he loved her and that he would gain nothing from it, and it would be selfish to wish for him to stay.

'We'll miss you,' she said, knowing that *I'll miss you* was what he wanted to hear.

'Likewise.'

'I don't understand. Why now?' Xan persisted. 'After the tsunami and everything you did to help us put the place to rights. You and Kitty. And then you both disappear.'

'Xan,' she warned him.

'It's the right thing, that's all.' Christopher's mouth closed in a firm line after the words. Olivia unwrapped her arms and moved away. *Don't go*, he wanted to cry after her.

She uncorked the brandy bottle and refilled their glasses, with one for herself.

'Toast. Here's to you, Christopher, and the future.'

He looked from one to the other. Olivia's face was rounding out again after her illness. She was newly beautiful, with happiness in her eyes. Kitty did this, he thought. Wherever she had come from, whether the terrible eeriness that had veiled her at the end was a figment of his lonely imagination, whoever she was and wherever she had finally gone, they owed her this much. Olivia had what she wanted and perhaps seeing it through Kitty's eyes had doubled its value. He did not have what he wanted but he had seen the futility of hoping, either for Olivia or some doppelgänger. Maybe back in England he could learn to put all this in the past. Maybe he could learn to be slick and impervious, in himself as well as in his painting, just like Dan.

Whatever Xan and Olivia chose to believe about Kitty, whatever explanation they had agreed upon, needed no added commentary from him.

Christopher picked up his glass and drained it.

'The future,' he echoed.

'When are you thinking of leaving?' Xan asked morosely, wiping his mouth with the back of his hand.

'In a couple of weeks. Maybe three.' Nothing happened quickly on Halemni in wintertime.

'Tell you what, then. Why don't you take Olivia back with you? She needs a change of scenery and a rest.' He turned to look at his wife. 'Go and spend a few days with your mother and father. The boys and I will be quite happy here. Christopher will look after you on the way and you can come back when you're ready. Isn't that right, Christopher?'

'I'd be glad to.'

Olivia bent her head. England, she was thinking. Not home, but England.

'It's a long time since I've seen them.'

'There you are, then,' Xan said. He was smiling, pleased with his idea and with the effortlessness of his generosity.

TWENTY

Christopher and Olivia took the cheapest flight from Rhodes to London. They sat at the back of the plane, not talking very much. Christopher read a novel and Olivia sat with the in-flight magazine on her lap because she had packed her book in her suitcase. After all her years of flying around the world, she realised, she had completely forgotten how to travel. The thought didn't worry her in the least. The glossy magazine ads for watches and whisky looked lurid rather than desirable. In the end she stared out at the blue sky and watched the fleece of clouds far below them steadily thickening as they flew northwards.

From Gatwick she had hoped to catch a train direct to Dorset, but there were no connections. With Christopher and his pile of shabby string-tied baggage she boarded a London train. They sat knee to knee in the grimy seats, looking at the houses and bare trees and gardens that backed on to the line. It was more than six years since she had last been here, when Georgi was a baby. This real England felt like a foreign country that she had visited long ago and subsequently more or less forgotten. The thin grey light and the drizzle and the hotchpotch of houses were dingy and unwelcoming.

'Don't measure it by the view from a train on a wet afternoon,' Christopher warned. He was longing to smoke, she could tell from the way he tapped his tobacco tin on his thigh in the rhythm of the train's jolting. Olivia smiled at him, but she was thinking that it was she who should be consoling him, because he was here to stay.

At Victoria Station she tried to persuade him to leave her to make her own way.

'I'll be fine. You go on to your brother's. Where is his apartment?'

'Not until you're on your way home. He's out in the East End. It's smart nowadays. You watch the bags; I'll go and find out about a train for you.'

It was already getting dark. While she waited beside their suitcases the vast glass roof turned briefly and luminously navy-blue and then went black, as if a blanket had been dropped over it. The noise of train announcements washed over her. There was too much to see, the windows of the station concourse, W. H. Smith and Boots were too full of coloured things, the florist's stall looked like a barricade of oversized and improbable blooms, and a multitude of people rushed towards her over the shiny floors. She had completely forgotten that there were so many people and so many choices to be made.

Christopher loped towards her. He was wearing his ancient straw hat and a blue overall jacket, and among the city commuters he looked as outlandish as she felt.

'Five fifteen, platform seven,' he told her. She was glad of his help and amused to realise that she needed it.

There was time to telephone her parents and ask them to meet her at the local station.

'Your dad would have come to the airport if you'd only let us know,' her mother protested.

'It's all right,' Olivia reassured her, raising her voice against the station noise.

She put down the receiver and went back to Christopher. He had taken off his hat and was holding it by the brim with two hands. He looked as if he was about to propose, or to break some momentous piece of news. They hesitated while the crowds swept past on the way to their trains. Then they took one step closer to each other. Christopher put his hat down on top of the pile of baggage. Very carefully he lifted his hand and touched the side of her throat just beneath her jawline.

Olivia leaned forward and kissed him on the mouth, gently and deliberately. His fingers slid round to the nape of her neck and rested there. Then he moved his head a fraction to one side so their cheeks just touched.

'I will miss you,' she said.

Christopher nodded. He straightened himself up and stood back. He examined her face, memorising it, comparing it in his mind with the memory of Kitty's. The two sets of features blurred, swam together and once more became a composite image.

He had been fearful for Olivia. The other creature might have done her harm: his imagination had bred a dozen over-heated horrors. But he understood that it was over and there was nothing to be afraid of; Kitty was gone. His face cleared and he smiled at her.

'I'll be seeing you,' he said. He pointed across to the platform where her train had drawn in. A surge of people moved towards it. 'Go on,' he advised. He wanted the moment of parting to be over.

Olivia hesitated. 'See you,' she echoed uncertainly. She picked up her single holdall and began walking, moving with quick steps. His eyes followed her height through the crowds, watching her all the way until she passed out of his sight.

When she stepped off the train once more the air smelled of smoke and damp. The platform and the cars lined up beyond a fence glittered with rain, and there were foggy haloes round the street lights. Olivia walked slowly, feeling the weight of her bag as the commuters streamed ahead of her. When the crowd thinned she saw her father waiting by the exit. He was smaller than the man she had been looking out for, standing defensively with his hands in the pockets of his green padded jacket. His chin lifted in relief when he saw her.

'So here you are,' he said, when she reached him. It was a shock for Olivia to realise, as they hugged each other, that she was now half a head taller than her once-towering father. Denis was in his late seventies and bowed with age. He had a fringe of grey hair round a bald cranium and the faintest remaining suggestion of spectacular good looks.

'Here I am.'

He made to take her bag, but she wouldn't let him. They walked side by side to the car park.

'Your mother's making dinner. She thought you'd be hungry.'

Olivia smiled. 'Of course.' It had been a family joke, her appetite.

There seemed to be more traffic in the streets, and two raw new estates infilled some of the open country between the town and her parents' village.

'Yes, it's all changing,' Denis sighed.

The square old house stood secluded in its big garden. As they walked up the path Olivia heard rain dripping in the evergreens, the hum of cars in the distance and wind in the bare trees. It sounded foreign rather than homely. This place wasn't home.

The front door opened and a wedge of yellow light slanted across the paving.

'Bye-bye, Mrs Flint, dear,' a big woman in a headscarf called as she came out. 'Oh, now, here's your hubby and daughter already.'

404

Denis introduced her as a neighbour, so kind, always looking in to see if they needed anything. They are old people now, Olivia thought. Left above the high-water mark, exposed to the variable winds of neighbourliness, after the tide has carried their children out of reach.

'Hello,' she said lamely.

'It's lovely to meet you. In you go, don't stand out in the cold.'

It was cold, Olivia thought. The damp chill seemed already to have sunk into her bones.

Maddie was wearing a coral-pink jumper and lipstick to match. Her hair was freshly shampooed and set. Maybe the neighbour came in to do it for her.

'We were so worried about you. Xan would hardly tell us anything. And you look terribly thin.'

Olivia kissed her mother and breathed in Arpège and face powder. 'It's nothing to worry about. I'm as strong as a horse, you know that.'

In the drawing room there was a gas-coal fire. The curtains were drawn and bottles and glasses stood on a tray. Olivia had never lived in this house but the room was full of furniture and pictures and framed photographs that stirred memories. Max and she had played caves under that sideboard, Max had made those bookends in school carpentry classes. There was a choice of sherry or gin and tonic. A clock was ticking.

They had family news to exchange, drawings and presents from Georgi and Theo to be handed over, a top-up of everyone's glasses before dinner. The room was warm and Olivia felt her edginess dissolving as gin trickled through her. Xan's instinct had been correct. Even though it cost such a lot of money, it was right to have come.

They ate dinner in the dining room. Grilled lamb, carrots and potatoes. Denis obediently ferried dishes to the table from the hatch that opened into the kitchen. He waited with his head slightly on one side, listening for the next instruction.

'Don't drop that,' Maddie told him sharply. 'And put a mat underneath it.'

Olivia remembered the evenings when her mother had waited and waited for her handsome, critical, cruelly impatient husband to come home from work or wherever it was that he had been. It was true. Everything had changed.

They talked about the earthquake and the tsunami and their aftermath, and about Max's visit. Olivia waited for Kitty's name to come up, but it didn't. She didn't mention it either. How would she explain about her, if she did?

'We thought it was strange, Max leaving Hattie and the girls on their own over Christmas like that. Are there problems, do you think?' Maddie asked.

'Nothing serious, as far as I know.'

Denis rolled his napkin and slipped it into the ring. 'Young people have their upheavals, Maddie. You should leave them to work it out. Don't keep on about it.'

'Keeping on, is that what you call asking one question?'

He said he was going to turn on the news. Maddie watched him to the door with her mouth tucked in and her fingers tapping a soundless rhythm on the polished table. Afterwards the two women went into the kitchen to do the washing-up together.

'Your father's getting forgetful. He repeats himself.'

Olivia nodded. He was tentative and somehow apologetic, as well as physically smaller. After so many years the balance of power had shifted from husband to wife. Maddie was the strong one now. This is how it happens, she thought. But it won't with Xan and me. The certainty flared up in her as hot and bright as the gas-coal flames.

Xan and I have always been equal, because we were both strong when we came together, and we'll stay that way because everything we do is together and that tightens the

406

bond instead of fraying it. Max and I must have absorbed what was wrong between Maddie and Denis when we were children, even though we couldn't have put it into words, and we instinctively backed away from the possibility of living in a marriage like this ourselves. We needed to get away out into the world and establish our independence.

Maybe it's a coincidence, she thought, that when we did settle it was a long way from here, whatever version of home this place represents. But it's no coincidence that both our marriages are different from our parents'. They're full of difficulties and cracks, like everyone else's, but they're dynamic. They're still alive.

Maddie hung her tea towel to dry and took off her apron.

'Don't let's worry about the pans. Joyce will do them in the morning. She's very good like that.' Joyce must be the woman in the headscarf.

'She sounds it,' Olivia said.

Her mother followed her upstairs to the spare bedroom. A little grid of wooden shelves on the wall above the bed held china animal figures that Olivia had been given as a child. She had acquired a reputation as a collector, without actually caring in the least for china kittens with bows round their necks or Disney creatures. It struck her now that the premise of entire families might be just as inaccurate: the strong one who was really a coward, the leader who might have preferred to be led. She picked up a china Bambi.

'Look at these. Do you know, I never really liked them.'

Maddie started to laugh. She reached up and scooped a handful off the top shelf and dumped them in the floral waste bin that stood beside the dressing table.

'I'm not surprised. They're hideous. I must have been trying to make a little girl out of you, instead of a wild creature.'

Olivia aimed the Bambi after its companions. It made a satisfying crack. 'Is that what I was?'

'Oh God, yes.'

They were both laughing now.

'I'm glad you're here,' Maddie added. 'It sometimes feels as though I haven't got any children at all.'

'You have. Me and Max.'

'I remember. Tell me, have I made a mess of it all?'

Maddie had drunk two glasses of sherry and half a bottle of wine.

'No, you haven't.'

Olivia looked at her mother's neat hair and lipstick. The way Maddie had chosen didn't amount to a mess, did it? Making the best of things, that's how her parents' generation would describe it. This house harboured melancholy in its corners, but it wasn't tragic. Kitty's childhood, her parents' story, that was a real tragedy. Olivia found herself wondering how Maddie and Denis would have survived if the axe blade of real grief had fallen between them, if she or Max had died like Kitty's brother had done. They wouldn't be together now, she thought. Making the best of things didn't cover an eventuality like that.

And stop being so morbid, she rebuked herself. None of it did happen, and here they are bickering about the small details of life as they will be to the end of their days. She put her arms round Maddie and held her tight.

'Goodnight, Mum. You've done everything well, no one could have done better. Tell Dad goodnight for me.'

'Goodnight, my daughter.'

There was an electric blanket warming the fitted sheets. As she lay in the darkness waiting to go to sleep, Olivia thought how much she loved Xan and her children. A sense of good fortune glowed inside her.

The days with Denis and Maddie were a matter of fitting into their minutely measured routine. They ate breakfast

408

– grapefruit, halved and segmented the night before, and toast with Maddie's own marmalade – at half past eight every morning. Afterwards Maddie did the dusting and laundry, and Joyce came in to look after the heavier house-work. Denis flitted ahead of them, an awkward shadow, trying to keep out of their way. Coffee was made at eleven and after Joyce had gone home there was lunch, soup or salad, over which they did the crossword. Maddie was quicker to solve the clues now, whereas in the past her husband had always hurried on and left her frowning. When the lunch was cleared Denis took the newspaper and went upstairs for a sleep. Maddie liked to go out for a walk and Olivia went with her.

'Such a treat to have you here,' Maddie said as they set out in their thick boots, with hats and gloves to counter the late-January cold. Wind lashed the hedges and flurries of rain prickled their faces.

'I'm enjoying it too,' Olivia would say. 'Maybe you should get a dog, to keep you company when I'm not here?'

'Your father takes enough looking after, thank you very much.'

They walked down mud-furrowed lanes or climbed stiles to follow footpaths across the fields. Maddie talked and talked, and Olivia understood that she and Denis didn't talk much any more because there had been too many years and their dialogue had long ago settled into grooves that allowed no deviating or improvising. Yet there was no one else for her mother to confide in, and as she listened while they skirted dripping woods and breathed in wet leaf mould Olivia felt her growing admiration for this small, brisk woman. She had once seemed vulnerable and even pathetic but now she had acquired a stature all of her own. Her independence, late in the day, was a prize.

'Do you think I've wasted my time?' Maddie asked her once. Like the question about whether she had made a mess of everything, it came out with eager anxiety. Maddie had never asked such things before, never even hinted at them. It indicated, Olivia thought, that her mother was giving herself the right to a life of her own, even if only in retrospect.

'Only you can answer that. Would you do it differently, if you had your time over again?'

'Let me think. Not you and Max, of course. You were always more important to me than anything else. You can understand that.'

It was a statement, not a question. And Olivia did understand it.

'More important than Dad?'

'Yes.'

That was the difference. For Olivia, Xan and the boys were knotted all together, the three of them, in a thick web of love. No one was less important than anyone else. Nor could she imagine life without one of them, or away from Halemni, and she suppressed a shiver of superstition as dark as a bat's wing. It was only a few weeks ago, when Kitty had fully insinuated herself into their lives, that she had dreamed of an England composed of laburnum tunnels and mothers in Volvos. Today's reality was much closer to the truth – bare branches whipping against a gunmetal sky, the swish of traffic down a country road, sparse field grass pasted over heavy mud. She recognised all this and accepted its familiarity, but it would never again be home. It was just Kitty who had come in and threatened the perspectives, and forced Olivia to look at her world in a different light.

Halemni was a harsh place, and Xan and she would never live in reasonable comfort, let alone luxury, in their travel-brochure paradise. But she had seen almost everywhere and there was nowhere else on earth she wanted to be.

Maddie's knitted hat was bobbing at her shoulder.

410

'I might have done some things differently. I might have had a job. Doctor's receptionist, maybe.'

'Something in a bank.'

'Maybe a uniform. Traffic warden.'

They were walking up the lane that led towards the house and they stopped because they were laughing so much. Olivia saw her mother's face suddenly bright with amusement and she thought, maybe for the first time since her childhood, she's all right. She's hung on and she does have the power now. Dad needs her and her impatience with him has a triumphant edge. It's not ideal, but it's better than nothing, better than what might have been.

She put her hand out and took hold of her mother's, and their gloved fingers locked together. Coming round the bend a grey Jaguar, travelling too fast, had to brake and swerve to miss them. The driver's horn blared shockingly and they jumped aside.

'Why is everyone in such a hurry?' Maddie shouted.

'Actually, I think that was our fault.'

Olivia took her mother's arm and steered her towards home. There was the remainder of the day's routine to be negotiated. There would be a cup of tea, a quiet interval with a book, preparations for dinner, an aperitif and then dinner itself, and the day winding down towards bedtime. The sameness was soothing, in a way. Just for a week.

In a parallel place and a couple of miles further on, the Jaguar indicated and turned into the driveway of a country house hotel. Peter Stafford parked the car on the gravel sweep and walked quickly round to open the passenger door. Lisa unfurled her legs and he helped her out.

She flicked a glance up at the windows and the thick veins of wisteria that netted the façade.

'Looks nice,' she said. A porter in a striped waistcoat was coming to greet them.

The flats in Dunollie Mansions had both been sold and they had just bought a good house in Fulham not far from where Clive and Sally Marr lived. Lisa would have preferred to stay at home and have friends over, especially now, but Peter still liked to get out of London for weekends. He kept an up-to-date library of guidebooks and enjoyed picking the hotels he thought she would like. But on the way down this afternoon he had seemed tired and distracted. *I'm* the one who should be tired, Lisa thought, as the bellboy led the way up to their room.

The suite had corner windows overlooking beech and oak trees in the grounds. The bare branches of the trees were diamond-tipped with moisture. There was a sofa in the windows and the usual armchairs and little side tables and chintz cushions with crimson frills and piping, as well as an eight-foot bed. Peter ordered tea and the bellboy withdrew. Lisa wandered into the bathroom and turned on the bath taps. She emptied miniature bottles at random into the water, undressed and got in. She could hear from the bedroom that Peter was on the telephone, making a business call. She lay back under the hot water with her hands folded over her stomach.

When she opened her eyes again he was bringing her a cup of tea. He put it down on the bath side, then lowered the lavatory lid and sat down. Steam condensed on his glasses so he took them off and rubbed the silvered lenses with a corner of fluffy towel.

'Shall I stay?' he asked.

'If you want.' Lisa didn't like it when he was meek. She preferred him to be authoritative in looking after her. She sat up and began to soap herself, turning sideways to him so he could admire her fullness.

'Who was on the phone?'

He sighed and pinched his nose. 'Sullivans.' He began to tell her about the problem, but she didn't listen. She had only asked out of politeness.

'Come on,' he said in the end. 'Don't lie in there too long and get dizzy.' He unfolded a towel and held it out for her, and she stepped into it so that he could wrap her up. He lifted her and carried her through to the bed. When they started making love he stroked her stomach.

'Thirteen weeks,' he whispered. 'Twenty-seven to go.'

Lisa smiled lazily. This was what she liked. To be adored was no less than her due. But after a little while she propped herself up on one elbow. Peter lay flat on his back, looking beyond her.

'Is something wrong?' she murmured.

'No. I'm tired, that's all.'

'You were very quiet on the way down. There is something, darling, isn't there?'

Peter rolled away and sat up with his back to her. He was in good shape for his age, but there were little ears of flesh at the sides of his waist. He stood up and opened cupboard doors until he found the bar and a whisky miniature.

'Do you want anything?'

'I'm not supposed to drink, am I? Is there a Coke?'

'I don't think so. It's her birthday, actually.'

'What? Whose?'

'Catherine's. Cary's,' he said very carefully.

'Oh. I see. Why didn't you say? We should have stayed at home.'

Save me, Lisa thought, from grief and remorse. She's *dead*, isn't she? Gone, although never forgotten, it seemed. She was beginning to understand that Peter's first wife would always be present in the memories of her husband and their friends, coming between Peter and herself, in a way that she could never eradicate.

'Being there or here wouldn't have made any difference.' Peter drank his whisky.

Lisa rallied herself. She didn't like to think of anyone

413

getting the better of her, alive or dead. She stood up, and found that he had unpacked her clothes and hung them up for her. She rolled stockings up her thighs and took a black knitted dress off a hanger. She made sure that Peter was watching as she wriggled into the tight tube and smoothed it over her belly.

'If Cary hadn't died in the earthquake, do you think you would have gone back to her?'

His eyes were on her, with an imploring light that she hated. He wanted to be told that everything was all right, that he would be forgiven. Men were all the same. They were weak, except in the cast iron of their selfishness.

'No,' he confessed. 'It's strange. It's the fact that she's dead, finally out of my reach, that keeps her in my mind.'

That was honest, at least. She went and stood in front of him, and drew his head to rest against where the baby lay.

'Poor Peter. Poor you. It was a terrible earthquake. Cary died. Nobody could have changed anything. Not you, not anyone.'

He nodded, with half of his face crumpled against her. Lisa stroked his head until he sat up again.

'Let's go downstairs,' she cajoled him and he nodded. She knew that he would drink another whisky or two and wine with his dinner, and then he would sleep heavily, twitching a little in his dreams. She picked up her handbag. It was black velvet, in the shape of a tulip, opening in petals lined with rose-pink silk.

Instead of sherry or gin before dinner, there was champagne. Denis produced the bottle and made a flourish of uncorking it with the aid of a dinner napkin. He wanted to search for an ice bucket but Maddie told him that the bottle would be empty long before he could manage to find and fill it.

They drank a toast to Olivia.

'And here's another,' Olivia responded. 'Mothers and daughters.'

Maddie flushed with pleasure.

She had cooked a special dinner and Denis poured burgundy into the best glasses.

'Do you remember?' she said when she lifted hers. 'You and Max bought us these for our silver wedding?'

The reminiscences carried them through the pheasant with cranberries, and the crème brûlée that Maddie claimed had always been Olivia's favourite pudding. They remembered the Christmas when Olivia and Max both had chickenpox, several summer holidays on the Norfolk Broads, weekends with Denis's grand cousins in their big house in the country. That these memories were so selective, Olivia thought, was hardly surprising. It was like looking through family photograph albums. Every day appeared to have been lived out on picnics or at weddings or on sunny beaches. The bright times were all there, captured for everyone to see, while the dark ones were locked separately within each individual. Secret histories were unique, but public celebrations were common to all. Perhaps in the end, in old age like Denis and Maddie and even Meroula had achieved, the two faces of history became blurred again. For her parents, at this distance, the good memories seemed almost the whole truth.

It was not a bad point to reach, she thought.

Alcohol brought out a red flush across her father's nose and cheekbones. Denis grew jovial and then sentimental.

'You and Max,' he murmured. 'Do you know how proud your mother and I are?'

Maddie gave him a sharp look, then raised her eyebrows at Olivia.

'We should get the old projector out, you know.' Denis had owned a cine camera before camcorders became universal, and birthdays and Christmases always signalled its appearance.

'Not tonight,' Maddie protested.

Denis grinned at her. 'Where have I heard that before?'

'I'd like to see some of the old movies,' Olivia said quickly. At once, her father was on his feet and hunting in cupboards.

'Don't turn everything upside down. I'll get them, if you really must,' Maddie sighed. Olivia followed her upstairs, while Denis moved furniture aside to leave a space of white wall. In the close-carpeted space of her mother's bedroom Olivia stood with her arms held out while Maddie piled boxes into them. The old reels of film were labelled with dates and events in her father's handwriting and they stacked up into a public monument to family life.

'Look at it all. Celebration by omission,' Maddie said.

'Just what I was thinking.'

They smiled at each other, complicit smiles with a wealth of acknowledgement in them.

'Are you still angry with him?' Olivia asked. She was looking past her mother's shoulder at the photographs on her chest of drawers.

'What good would that do?'

'None, I suppose.'

'He stayed, didn't he? In his way. I wonder sometimes what my life would have been like if he'd gone.'

Olivia dragged her eyes away from the pictures. 'Yes. The one thing that happens or doesn't happen and changes the course of everything that comes after.'

Maddie briskly closed the cupboard doors. 'It doesn't matter now. You and Xan and Max and Hattie are what's important. Should I worry about you and your marriages, do you think?'

Olivia gave the question proper consideration. 'There was a time when things might have been going wrong for us. Not very long ago. But we're straight again now. I don't know for sure about Max and Hattie, how could I? We only

416

know about our own marriages and our own perspective within them.'

'I know that much,' Maddie said.

'I hope they'll make it.'

Denis shouted up the stairs, 'Are you going to be up there all night?'

He had set three chairs in a row and a table with the projector on it.

'Choose a film, any film,' he ordered Olivia. She picked one, from the year when she was seven and Max was five. He threaded the film through the spools. 'Marvellous piece of kit this, you know. Solid as a rock. Don't know why anyone bothers with all this video stuff.' A grey speckled rectangle steadied itself on the dining-room wall.

There were two children astride an old-fashioned rocking horse. The horse's head filled the picture with flaring nostrils and a horsehair mane above a mouth full of wooden teeth, and then the camera panned upwards to the children's faces. The girl was a huge child with pale hair that stood out in a stiff halo. One arm waved a sword as she rocked the horse into a gallop. Her brother sat in front of her, smaller and frailer, clinging on to the horse's mane. They were in the playroom at Denis's cousins' house. Olivia could remember the lino and oilcloth smell of the room, and the deep cupboards stacked with wooden jigsaws and Meccano and a Hornby trainset.

'I was scared of that horse's teeth,' Olivia said.

'You were never scared of anything' Denis laughed.

Another figure moved into the frame. It was a girl of about sixteen. She had wavy hair down to her shoulders and long arms, and she slapped the horse playfully on its painted rump. The huge child tipped her head back and shouted with laughter while the boy clung on even harder.

'Big Olivia,' Olivia said wonderingly.

She was the daughter of the house, and the focus of all Olivia's envy and admiration and love for the whole of her early childhood. Olivia's devotion to her had been such that she had even taken her name, and wouldn't answer to anything else. Big Olivia had become a nurse. She had never married and had finished her long career as senior nursing officer at a hospital in Sheffield.

The telephone rang and Maddie went to answer it. 'It's Xan,' she said when she came back. Xan never used the phone in the potter's house.

Olivia ran to pick up the receiver.

'Is everything all right? Georgi and Theo?'

'Yes, yes.' His lazy voice struck into her bones. 'I just wanted to say happy birthday. And to tell you to come home soon.'

'Two days,' she said. 'I will be there in two days' time.'

'That's good. I love you.'

'I know you do.'

When she came back to the dining room, Maddie was still watching the flickering film. Two children ran through a grand garden ornamented with stone statues. Denis's head had fallen forward on to his chest.

'I knew he'd be asleep within five minutes,' Maddie remarked.

Olivia did her packing, such as there was of it. When she had finished Maddie called her into her bedroom. Her mother was sitting on her bed with the films and a pile of photograph albums on the cover beside her. The house was quiet. Denis had gone into his own bedroom with the newspaper to have a sleep.

'Would you like to take these?' Maddie pointed to the public monument.

Sharp in her mind's eye, Olivia saw Kitty walking up the

main street of Megalo Chorio through the wreckage of the tsunami morning. She was soaked, like a shipwreck survivor, and she was carrying Meroula's family memories in her arms.

Gently Olivia said, 'No. You hold on to them. They're yours and Dad's.' Her eyes travelled to the chest of drawers again and two pictures among the framed ranks. Her own face twice over, one with a painted moustache, the other theatrically made up.

'Max gave them to me. You were born with it, one of those faces that the camera loves. You should have made your living in front instead of behind it.'

'No. I wouldn't have enjoyed that.' Any more than Kitty did.

'Who took them? Xan?'

'No. It was a woman who stayed with us for a few weeks, after the tsunami. She came and went. Didn't Max mention her?'

Maddie looked surprised. 'No. What was her name?'

'Kitty.'

There was a little click of breath in Maddie's throat. 'That was my baby name for you, Catherine Kitty Cat. Before you told the world you had to be called Olivia after your big cousin.'

A second's silence shivered in Olivia's head. Time lost its linearity and became a maze, an optical illusion of parallel planes. She might have felt shock or fear, but what seized her was love. Affection and gratitude flowed out of her for what and who was not, but might have been.

Poor Kitty, so beautiful and so damaged.

No wonder she wanted to take over my life. No wonder I feared her power to do so. It was her life too and I might have been her, but for a second out of time on a summer's afternoon. One second was all it took to end a life and set all the others diverging.

419

Now I understand. Now I know.

I needn't fear her any longer. Wherever she came from and however she slipped into my world and out of it again, in this place and time Kitty doesn't exist.

And so I believe she is at peace.

Maddie was looking curiously at her. When she could speak again Olivia murmured, 'It's a nice name. A bit old-fashioned. I never asked Kitty where hers came from.'

Maddie gathered up the photograph albums and began to put them away in their cupboard.

'I wish I'd had a daughter,' Olivia said.

Her mother turned round. 'Is it too late?'

'Oh yes, I think so. Much too late.'

Denis and Maddie both came to the station to see her off on the London train. Olivia watched them from the window as the train pulled out. They were standing side by side, not touching, not looking at each other, but they held up their arms in an identical wave. Their figures were small and fragile against the backdrop of the railings and the crowded sweep of the car park.

When she couldn't see them any longer she turned away.

Going home, she told herself. Home to Xan. She rested her head back against the dusty seat cushions and closed her eyes to see the picture more clearly, the harbour wall and the crescent beach and the slope of hill up to the potter's house. Xan and Georgi and Theo.

Halemni bound.

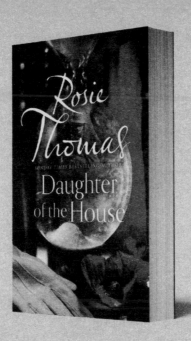

LONDON 1919

The Great War is over and London lies on the brink of an uncertain future. With the misery and horror of war in the past, the men who fought and survived the trenches believe the future is theirs by right, and any woman who has celebrated her freedom must now redouble her efforts to keep it.

Nancy Wix is just such a woman. Born into a down-at-heel family, Nancy has always known that the visions she has seen since she was a child will set her apart from her peers and when a chance encounter reveals a way in which she might take hold of her future, she grasps the opportunity with a desperate intensity.

As the roaring twenties dawn, Nancy strives to break free from the rigid bonds of society and find her own place. The only thing that could hold her back is her love for an unattainable man…

Out now, turn the page to read an extract

CHAPTER ONE

Kent, 1910

Mr and Mrs Devil Wix and their three children made a vivid picture as they strolled towards the steamer jetty. Devil wore a loose blue flannel coat with patch pockets, and a straw hat that he tipped to the other holidaymakers. His wife Eliza's short steps were dictated by the fashionably narrow hem of her rose-pink and dove-grey hobble skirt. She had dressed her hair under a grey turban with a matching pink feather cockade.

Arthur, the youngest child, dashed ahead in his enthusiasm to get aboard the pleasure boat before doubling back to chivvy his family. Cornelius and Nancy trailed behind with Phyllis, their paid companion. Cornelius's slumped shoulders revealed how much he would have preferred to spend the morning out on the heathland with his butterfly net. He was gloomily asserting to Nancy that with the swell that was running out in the bay they would certainly all be seasick. It was very like him to adopt nautical terms without having ever ventured out to sea.

Nancy only half-listened. She was watching the little

procession of guests strolling from their hotel towards the sea, and to her dismay she saw that the Clares and Mr Feather were also planning to take the excursion. Her mother, Eliza, had chatted to Mrs Clare on the hotel terrace, and on one or two evenings Mrs Clare had invited Eliza to sit with her after dinner in the drawing room. Once the two men had enjoyed their cigars they had joined them too. Devil had not been present to keep Eliza company, of course. He was almost always in London, because of the theatre. He was only here with his family now because it was a Sunday afternoon and there would be no stage show until tomorrow evening.

Nancy and Cornelius and Arthur had been introduced to Mrs Clare and to her husband and brother, and they had endured the usual polite conversations. Arthur and Mr Clare talked about cricket while Mrs Clare's pale blue eyes assessed Nancy's clothes. Nancy knew she was dressed too brightly. Her cerise coat marked her out, instead of concealing her in mouse-grey or mole-brown folds like the daughter of a conventional family. She tried not to mind about this, noticing on her own part that Mrs Clare looked quite prim and colourless next to Eliza's abundant glamour.

Mr Feather was Mrs Clare's brother, and it was his presence more than the others' that made Nancy feel uncomfortable. Mrs Clare was always anxiously glancing at him, almost as if she suspected he might be angry and she was obliged to soothe him, but whenever Nancy looked in his direction he was staring at *her*. She couldn't help returning his look even though she tried very hard not to. His dark eyes seemed to drill into her temple or the back of her head. Whenever he spoke to her it was always in a low voice and with a sympathetic half-smile, as though she had already confided something incriminating to him. His manner seemed to suggest they held an experience in common, and Nancy particularly hated this because she did have a secret. But she held it so deep within herself that she had never told a soul, and certainly not Mr Feather. How could the man know about her Uncanny? And if he didn't know, why did he watch her with such close interest?

His presence was like one of her father's hidden stage magnets, dragging her closer and weighing her down, and now he was coming on the steamer trip with them. Was she never to take a step in any direction without the man's unwelcome concern reaching out for her, like the tentacles of an octopus? She could feel the tickle of one on the back of her neck right at this moment. She wanted to slap it away.

'Come along, dear,' Phyllis said.

The companion was clutching the frame of her bag in two hands and looking as if she was already seasick. Poor thing, Nancy thought. Why must her father always sweep them all along with his enthusiasms? The steamer trip had been his idea and Eliza had taken some persuasion before she agreed to it.

The Wixes joined the short queue to board the steamer. Arthur struck up a talk about the Eton versus Harrow cricket match with two boys of his own age. Devil had promised to take his sons to Lord's for the Schools' Day in a month's time and Arthur was already working himself into a froth of excitement.

'Half a crown's on Eton,' one boy taunted and Arthur feinted a punch at him. The three of them chased up the short gangway and sprang down into the launch.

When it was Nancy's turn a seaman with a full beard took her hand and called her 'miss' as she stepped down to the rocking deck. She hesitated. Although she couldn't see anything out of the ordinary the smells of engine oil and seawater and boat varnish were overpowering, and that was always a sign. All her instincts were to leap back to safety on dry land.

The man's grasp tightened.

'I won't let you fall, missy. Step this way.'

Salt-caked sisal matting was laid on the deck in case any of the ladies should lose her footing. Nancy felt she had no choice but to take the seat that was offered to her. Hampered by her fashionable skirt Eliza needed a helping hand on either side before she could step down. Devil escorted her to a cushioned bench under the awning and Phyllis nervously sat further along towards the rail.

Nancy watched the boatmen making their preparations for departure. Heavy ropes dragging swags of weed were hauled through the water and thick-legged boys in ragged trousers applied their backs to the capstan. The air was thick with more layers of stink, of tar and brass polish and coal smoke. Nancy had to swallow hard.

Devil chose a seat in the open nearer to the bow. He beckoned to some of the younger children and they sidled towards him. He winked at his little audience, making a show of flexing his fingers and pushing back the cuffs of his coat. One of Arthur's new friends was playing with a cricket ball and as soon as he spotted it Devil held out his hand. The boy was reluctant but at a stern nod from his father he passed it over. He watched apprehensively as Devil tossed the ball high in the air. Even though the boat was rocking he caught it without an upward glance, as Nancy knew he would. With a casual flick of the wrist he threw the ball a second time, higher still. A big wave slammed the boat against the jetty, causing a gentleman to stumble as he squeezed between the crowded benches, but again the ball was drawn back to Devil's hand as if magnetised. Three more times he threw and caught, defying the boat's pitching. The owner of the ball had relaxed enough to smile as the ball flew upwards one more time.

There was a beat, stretched by the breeze and the shriek of a gull gliding overhead. This time there was no satisfying slap from the leather dropping into Devil's cupped palm.

Devil took off his straw hat and peered inside it, scratching his head in astonishment. Several children looked down to the deck and others peered over the side, but there was no clatter or splash.

'It's gone,' the owner wailed.

Devil replaced his hat.

'Sorry about this, old chap,' he murmured to the boy. 'I'll make it up to you somehow.'

Peering around, he noticed a girl with a posy basket set on her lap.

'May I perhaps have a look in your basket, miss?'

Seated a little to one side Mrs Clare raised her eyebrows at her brother and almost imperceptibly pursed her lips. No one else was meant to see, but Nancy did. She hated it when her father chose to be conspicuous in this way – even though he had always been the same – and she turned her head in anguish. A yard away, on the jetty, the bearded captain and one of the other sailors spoke urgently together. They had been considering the wind and the sky but the bearded man indicated the full boat and the jaunty pennants snapping in the breeze. With his big sea boot he kicked the boat away from the moorings, leaping inboard over the widening gap at the very last moment. There was a roar from the engine and a churn of green water, a sailor snatched up the last end of rope and dropped it into a loop, and the steamer's bow swung out into the bay. Nancy sneaked a look towards her father and saw that – of course – he had produced the cricket ball from the little girl's basket. The boy grabbed it back and stowed it inside his coat as Devil bowed over his doffed hat.

Please, no more, Nancy prayed with a twelve-year-old's disloyal fervour.

It seemed that she was heard because Devil came back to sit beside Eliza under the awning.

Arthur and his companions were gamely ragging each other and Cornelius had never looked up from his book. The steamer ploughed the length of the pier and then drove out into the stiff wind. Spume flew and Phyllis's hands tightened on the cane handles of her bag. In trying not to look longingly at the pier amusements Nancy made the mistake of meeting Mr Feather's eye again. Beadily he held her gaze and she thought there was a glimmer of superior amusement, as if the pleasure craft and the crew and the benches lined with ladies and gentlemen in their holiday outfits had all been placed there for just the two of them to observe, and enjoy.

It was intolerable.

The prow reared upwards. The view of the houses clustered at the side of the bay vanished behind a wall of green as a huge wave lifted the steamer. Spray scattered over the laughing gentlemen and bolder boys in the forward seats, sending them scurrying for the shelter of the awning even though a crewman shouted that they were to hold tight and keep their places. A second later the boat pitched down – and down – into the wave trough. Phyllis let out a mouse's squeak of alarm. Nancy wondered if the budding apprehension she was experiencing inside her ribcage, like a dark flower beginning to unfurl, might be the beginning of seasickness. It was *not*, she told herself firmly. At least Mr Feather had transferred his attention to Mrs Clare. He was patting his sister's hand and reassuring her.

Cornelius raised his head. Another huge wave lifted and tossed the boat down again. Eliza was the only one of the ladies who did not show any sign of dismay. She sat upright, seeming quite ready to meet the salt wind and the flung diamonds of spray.

The land dropped further behind them. After a few minutes Nancy grew used to the motion. It was even quite exhilarating to watch the glassy rollers with their curling lips of white foam as they swept towards them, and to feel the sharp upwards swing and then the answering downwards plunge as the boat cleaved through the water. The beat of the engine was steady, and her bearded sailor stood squarely in the wheelhouse with his pipe between his teeth and his eyes on the horizon. He looked just like a hero in a book.

'I say!' Arthur sang out. His childish grin split his face. Arthur loved all kinds of roughhousing.

Phyllis's face had taken on a sweaty glimmer. She left her seat, treading with exaggerated care, and the gentleman next to her supported her arm and handed her closer to the rail. She sank down, her handkerchief to her mouth.

'Oh dear, poor Phyllis,' Eliza murmured.

She stood up too and took short, swaying steps to the companion's side. Phyllis fended her off, clearly indicating that she preferred to be left to suffer alone. Eliza returned to her husband. The steamer turned slightly in its circuit of the bay and immediately pitched even more threateningly as the waves caught it broadside. Mrs Clare got unsteadily to her feet and joined Phyllis. One of the gentlemen had to make the same move and Nancy became aware that the talk and laughter had faded. Most of the passengers were sitting in silence. The stink of smoke and hot oil was not helping matters. Nancy uneasily scanned the faces, and black petals further unfurled in her chest. Two sailors passed down the twin gangways, moving with easy confidence. One of them ducked into the wheelhouse and conferred with the captain.

'Pappy?' Nancy said. His nod reassured her.

Mrs Clare leaned miserably over the rail. As if she set the proper example in this and in all other social matters, some others followed suit.

The bearded captain surrendered the wheel and took a megaphone from its cabinet. Bracing himself at the wheel-house door he announced, 'Ladies and gentlemen, the sea is not going to be our friend this morning. We'll make an early turn about. We don't want any of our passengers to feel uncomfortable aboard *Queen Mab*.'

The engine laboured as they swung round in an arc, the churn of water at the stern swallowed by a wave that broke over the gunwale as it surged past them. The steamer bobbed and rolled, seeming for the first time unequal to the job of keeping afloat.

Devil said merrily, 'Will we get our shillings back, do you think?'

At least the waves now swept them towards the welcome shore. Phyllis laid her forehead against the rail. Within quite a short time they were nearing the seaward end of the pier, where the strollers and fishermen were clearly visible. Cornelius's book was closed in his lap but he held his place with his forefinger.

There came a lurch and a shriek of protesting machinery, and then a rending noise like metal plates being crunched up and pitched on a metal floor. When this din stopped the engine had stopped too, and in the strange quiet the buffet of wind and the waves churning beneath the pier sounded even louder.

From Cornelius's expression Nancy knew that something must have gone seriously wrong.

The steamer rolled heavily as its prow turned through the water, unable to make headway without engine power. Two sailors dashed to the rail, pushing aside the passengers in their hurry. One of them grabbed a fender and the other took a boathook. Turning to her hero, Nancy saw that the pipe was gone. He fought with the wheel, trying to bring his boat round, but wind and current swept it towards the pier supports.

A woman pressed her hand to her mouth, stifling a scream.

The male passengers began shouting and dashing to the seaward side, propelling their children and womenfolk away from the looming pier. The people on the walkways were now far above them and at the lower level yawned an underworld of heaving water and dripping iron stanchions.

Devil caught Eliza tightly at his side. Arthur was trapped in the press of people who had fled to the far rail.

'For God's sake hold on,' Devil bellowed to his family.

The sailor made a stab with his boathook, but the sturdy pole splintered as the *Queen Mab* smashed into the pier.

The force of the impact threw the steamer sideways. The outer rail dipped and water flowed over it before the vessel sluggishly rolled in the opposite direction, sending bodies tumbling across the decks and falling against the benches. Cornelius lunged towards his sister and caught her by the arm to stop her skidding down the crazily angled gangway. A confusion of shouts and screams tore the air. Water poured everywhere, covering the decks and the seats and flooding into the wheelhouse.

Devil supported his wife as the water rose past his knees. She was trapped by the weight of her sodden skirt. A barnacled ladder on the nearest pier support rose to an opening that was already jammed with shocked faces. An arm reached down with a dangling lifebelt and Devil somehow hoisted Eliza up the lowest metal rungs. She grasped the lifebelt and men began to haul her up from above. Only when she was safe did Devil turn to look for his children.

Nancy saw all this, as if from the depths of the Uncanny.

Cornelius shouted her name as icy water sucked round her knees. A wave slammed into her chest; she was torn away and thrown against the submerged rail. All around there were people in the water, splashing and flailing as the *Queen Mab* went down.

To her horror she saw Arthur amongst them. His blond head was darkened with the hair plastered against his skull. Nancy let the next wave lift her free of the sinking vessel. Her skirt caught between her legs as she tried to kick out. She was submerged, sinking into bubbling depths with her hair fanning out like seaweed. Somehow she freed her limbs and frantically fought her way upwards. Her face broke the surface and she gulped for air.

There were boats approaching, and at the same time men with ropes came swarming down the pier stanchions. A half-submerged dark shape was bobbing close at hand and she recognised it as one of the boat's wooden benches, the green seat cushion still attached. She launched herself at it and somehow caught hold. She took a sobbing breath, trying to remember where she had seen Arthur in the water. Clawing back the hair that clogged her eyes and mouth she yelled his name.

The waves were dotted with hats and cushions and a dark floating web that had been a woman's shawl. Rotating as far as she could without losing her hold on the seat she caught sight of him. He had torn off his coat and his shirt billowed in the swell. When she glimpsed his face it was dead white, frighteningly like a corpse.

But Arthur knew how to *swim*.

She screamed again, 'Arthur. Here, Arthur. Swim to me.'

He caught sight of her and tried to reach out, a splashy scramble that brought him no closer. He was already exhausted by his efforts to stay afloat. His head seemed to sink lower in the water.

Powered by desperation Nancy kicked towards him, towing her makeshift raft. Arthur's shirt ballooned as another wave caught and released them. They were only a yard apart now. Filling her lungs with a huge breath Nancy let go of the bench. She splashed frantically to her brother and at last caught hold of him. They clung together and there was a long, suffocating and terrible moment when it seemed certain they were going to drag each other down. But then Arthur seemed to revive a little. He struck out with his free arm and Nancy followed suit and somehow they propelled themselves through the water to reach the floating bench. They grabbed it at the same instant. The seat wallowed and sank deeper but it was just buoyant enough to support them both.

A rowing boat swayed on the crest of the next wave.

'Two children here,' a man at the prow shouted.

Nancy's layers of clothes were dragging her down. It took every ounce of her strength to keep her head above the waves, but somehow she managed also to watch Arthur and make sure his grip was secure. He shuddered and coughed as the waves tipped their raft up and down.

Water sluiced over his head and she screamed at him to hold on.

An oar thrust past Nancy's ear and then a grappling hook caught the slats of the bench. A man's hand reached for and snatched the collar of her coat. She felt herself being towed in to the side of the rowing boat where more sturdy arms supported her. The boat rocked fiercely and she howled at her rescuers, 'Save my brother.'

'Your brother'll be right enough,' someone shouted back.

A man in a jersey leaned right down into the waves and tried to lift her, but it took another fellow to help him and they hauled on her wrists and arms and then her heavy body until her hips cleared the side and she tumbled into the bottom of the boat. Her petticoats and even her drawers were all on show but she didn't give it a thought.

'Arthur!'

She fought to sit upright and her rescuers steadied her.

'We've got 'im. You'm a brave girl, ain't you?'

A sodden, inert mass was hoisted and deposited beside her.

Sobbing and spitting up water she half-crawled to him. His shirt was twisted up to his armpits and his exposed skin was mottled but his eyes opened, startlingly blue in his blanched face. Two of the boatmen bent at the oars and Nancy glimpsed the looming corner of the pier as they swung away from the wreck. The third wrapped a coat around the shuddering boy, and then did the same for Nancy.

'You'll be good as new,' their rescuer said.

The grim faces of the three men told Nancy that they were the fortunate ones.

Arthur lay half in her lap with his eyes fixed on her face. His breath came in shallow gulps but he was clearly reviving. Through chattering teeth he gasped, 'Mama? Where's Mama?'

Nancy stretched upright to look back at the pier. Eliza

had reached the ladder and the lifebelt, and must have been saved.

But where was Cornelius? Phyllis? And their father?

The water was dotted with floating debris and rescue boats that had made the short trip out from the beach. She saw some steamer passengers in the other boats, and others being helped up to the pier walkway, but she recognised none of them. The *Queen Mab* was almost submerged. The funnel and the wheelhouse tilted at a crazy angle, and the jaunty awning had been torn to tatters by the force of the waves.

The black flower grew so big that it filled her whole chest.

Their boat rode a wave close in to the beach and a man in big rubber waders strode out to them. He swept Nancy into his arms and carried her to the shingly rim, where she was passed along a chain of hands and finally set down on the sand where a blanket immediately enveloped her. Arthur was given the same treatment, and the boat pushed out again.

'My father,' Nancy screamed. 'Where is he?'

Her legs gave way beneath her. A woman in an apron knelt to take her in her arms and wrap the blanket tighter. Nancy thought she recognised her from the cockle stall on the beach corner.

'There you are, my love. You'm all right now. Don't you worry.'

'*My father.*'

She was shuddering now like Arthur, great uncontrollable waves of cold and panic sweeping over her. 'My other brother. I have to find them. Phyllis was with us too. Where are they?'

'Your daddy will be here, I'm sure. Where are you staying, my darling?'

Someone else was trying to make her drink warm milk out of a thick white cup. The smell of it was unbearable. Her teeth rattled on the rim before she managed to turn her face away. Arthur drank his although his head was hanging and he seemed too shocked to speak.

'Terrible,' a voice said nearby. 'I seen one drowned at least.'

'Not now, Mary,' another reprimanded.

The little boats straggled back to the beach with the last of the rescued passengers. Women and children were passed ashore as Nancy and Arthur had been, to be immediately swaddled in makeshift coverings. Arthur's friend with the cricket ball was amongst them. He was crying and trying to hide his tears. Nancy sat with her arms wrapped round her knees in an attempt to control her shivers. Her eyes stung from the salt and the effort of scanning the beach for her family.

A shadow fell across her. Mr Feather loomed tall and black like the gnomon of a sundial. One of the rescuers had draped a rough blanket over his wet clothes, giving him the look of an Old Testament prophet. The resemblance was strengthened when he raised one hand and brought it to rest on the top of her head. The uneasy sense of being weighted down that she felt in his presence now became real. She tried to duck away but his hand pinned her beneath it like one of Cornelius's butterflies in a case. In the shingle beside her feet she saw a pink shell, the size and shape of a child's fingernail.

In a hoarse voice he begged, 'She slipped away from me. Where is she now? Tell me what you see. Is she here or has she passed?'

'I can't see anything.' Nancy was close to sobbing. The man did know her secret, her way of seeing with her inside eyes, into places no one else saw. Ever since she was a little girl she had possessed the ability. When she was small she linked the waking dreams with her sleeping dreams, and she assumed that everyone had the two different kinds. She was almost thirteen now, and as she grew away from childhood she understood – because no else ever mentioned such a thing – that the wakeful dreams were somehow hers alone.

He crouched to bring his mouth closer to her ear. 'Yes, you can. As soon as I set eyes on you, I knew you were a seer. Where is my Helena?'

She tried to shake off his hand, but she was paralysed. It seemed that her head was no longer made of bone and skin because it was softening and lightening to the point where it threatened to float off her shoulders. The blood noisily surged in her veins.

The beach and the rescuers melted away. Instead of the sand and a slice of busy sea she saw billows of mud with the skeletons of trees poking up like crooked fingers. At the same time a foul smell wrapped round her. She coughed in disgust and tried to pull away, but Feather still restrained her.

The smell became overpowering, nauseating. She blinked and the mud churned and there were broken men lying in it. Dozens of them were strewn as far as the eye could see, dying and already dead, with smirched or shattered faces gazing up at the white sky.

She had no idea where this horrifying place could be. All she knew was that this inside vision was made somehow sharper and more real by the man's hand resting on the top of her head.

She screwed her eyes shut. Tears burned the inner lids. She whispered, 'Please. Please make it stop.'

Mercifully the scene was already fading. It had been no more than a glimpse. As swiftly as it had come the smell ebbed away, carrying the mud and the wounded and dead with it. Her head grew heavy once more and wobbled on her neck, and the man's hand lifted at last.

He murmured, 'Don't be frightened. You are a seer. You might even think of your ability as a gift. Some of us do.'

She didn't want to be any sort of *us*, not in a company with this man who excluded her father and mother and even Neelie and Arthur.

Then to her joy she saw Devil. He was searching the knots of people lined up on the beach. She scrambled to her feet and now Feather did not try to hold her back.

'Pappy! We're here.'

She ran at him and pressed her face against his soaked clothes as he hugged her. Neither of them could find words. Arthur came more slowly, white with shock, and Devil bent his head over his two children.

'Thank God,' he murmured.

'Mama?' Arthur managed to ask.

'She is safe. Cornelius is with her.'

'And Phyllis?'

Nancy's question was not answered. Devil thanked the cockle seller and her helpers and shepherded his children away from the rescue scene. At the pier entrance Eliza and Cornelius had been searching amongst the passengers who had been brought in that way. As soon as she saw them Eliza ran, tripping up in the constricting skirt. Tears were running down her face, her smart turban was gone and her hair had come down in thick hanks. Nancy had never seen her composed mother in such a way and the sight was deeply shocking.

Devil hustled them away from the beach. Nancy didn't look back to see if Mr Feather was still searching for his sister. Devil said they must get back to the hotel immediately, to warmth and dry clothing. Some of the townspeople had brought drays and fish wagons down to the promenade to ferry survivors, but these had now set off and it seemed that the Wixes must either walk or take the little pleasure tram that ran to their hotel from the pier. Its driver looked incongruous in his smart braided uniform as he tried to hurry their shivering group towards it.

'But where is Phyllis?' Nancy demanded. Eliza was trying to massage some warmth into Arthur's blanketed body. Cornelius took Nancy's hand and tucked it under his arm.

'We don't know,' he said.

'*Where is she?*'

'The men are looking for her,' Devil answered.

'We can't go without her,' Nancy flamed.

Her father's face darkened. 'There's nothing you can do here, Nancy. Do as you are told.'

The toy tram trundled towards the hotel, leaving behind the rescue scene and the stricken steamer. It was wrong to be perched like carefree holidaymakers under the little canopy. In Nancy's head the wind seemed to chivvy the fragments of the day, briefly pasting lurid, disjointed images of the steamer and their escape from it over the innocent seaside landscape.

Arthur had still barely spoken.

Eliza told him, 'You're safe now. You did very well, you know, to take care of your sister. Papa and I are proud of you.'

The tram rocked around the curve of track. Arthur turned his coin-bright profile towards Nancy. There was a tick of silence during which she prepared to accept whatever he would say. He was younger than her by fifteen months, but she was only a girl. Cornelius was watching her too from beneath his heavy eyelids. Cornelius often saw more than he would afterwards admit to.

'I didn't take care of her,' Arthur said.

It must have been the salt in his throat and chest that made his treble voice crack and emerge an octave lower.

'Nancy saved *me*. She was safe but she let go and came for me. The boatman told her she was a brave girl.' There was another silence before he added, 'So you see, actually I was rather useless.'

The last words came out in a boy's piping voice once more.

Nancy noticed that her skirt was beginning to dry, leaving wavy tidemarks of salt. She was thinking that from today – or from the day before yesterday, really – everything would be different. You could never un-see what you had seen; that much was clear without any intervention from the Uncanny or Mr Feather.

'No, Arthur, you weren't useless at all,' she mumbled.

Eliza cupped Nancy's chin and lifted it so their eyes met. Her fingers were icy cold and the grey in her matted hair was revealed. With the blanket over her shoulders she could have been one of the cockle women, but still she commanded attention. Nancy yearned for the warmth of her approval.

Eliza asked, 'Is that what happened?'

Arthur's honesty was brave because it had cost him something. Nancy had done what she did without thinking, and therefore she hadn't really and truly been brave at all. So she reluctantly nodded because to claim any more would have felt like an untruth.

'Good girl,' Eliza said, and Nancy stored up this praise like treasure.

'Well done, Zenobia.'

At her father's insistence Nancy had been named after the queen of the Asian desert kingdom of Palmyra, and Devil invariably used her formal name on significant occasions. But there had never been a day like this one. Nancy shifted closer to him on the narrow seat, he put his arm round her and she nestled against him.

At the hotel Eliza took charge of running a hot bath in the clanking bathroom at the end of the corridor. Usually it was Phyllis who filled baths and laid out nightclothes and brought hot-water bottles when they were needed. Her absence shouted at every turn.

When Nancy was dressed Cornelius and Arthur came to her room. Cornelius settled himself at the foot of his sister's bed and Nancy rested her feet against his solid thigh. Of all of them he seemed the best survivor – he told her that after he had lost sight of her and Arthur he had paddled to the pier ladder and clung on to the lowest rung until all the women and children had climbed to safety. Devil had swum several times between the pier and the stricken steamer, desperately searching the water for the two of them.

Arthur remained silent, standing with his back to them and apparently staring out at the heathland. Finally he spun round.

'*I* want to be a brave man,' he blurted out.

The possibility that he might not be, that bravery was not the automatic right of boys of his sort, was deeply disturbing to him.

Cornelius blinked behind his glasses. Nancy said quickly, 'Of course you will be.'

Arthur's mouth quivered. He was on the point of tears. 'And I want Phyllis to come back.'

*　　*　　*

Late that afternoon Devil and Eliza broke the news to their children that the companion's body had been recovered from the sea.

Four of the forty people aboard the *Queen Mab* had lost their lives. The others were Mr and Mrs Clare and the youngest passenger, the little girl with the posy basket. Nancy couldn't put out of her mind how Devil's first thought had been for Eliza, and she imagined how Mr Clare must also have struggled to save his wife, never giving up until the waves claimed him too. That evening, the Clares' usual table in the dining room was covered with a cloth but left unlaid.

In her bed, after the strange dinner where almost no one in the room spoke or ate much and the rattle of cutlery seemed too loud to bear, Nancy was unable to sleep. For the last year Phyllis had been with her to make sure she brushed her hair and placed her shoes side by side under her chair. Now the gaunt little hotel bedroom was full of strange shadows, and although she forced herself to lie still her head seethed with unwelcome images.

She lay awake for so long that sleep seemed impossibly remote. The procession of images through her mind led her to the Palmyra, to one of the theatre's private boxes. She was watching a performance but she wasn't enjoying the stage spectacle because Devil was in danger, and she was the only one in the audience who knew it. When she tried to call a warning no sound came because her voice was stuck in her throat. Nor could she run to save him because her legs and arms were frozen. The audience was shouting, black mouths flapping open as waves of noise crashed over the stage. Nancy sweated and gasped as she struggled to break out of her paralysis.

Her father grinned straight at her and then glanced up

into the shadowed recess above the stage where scenery and mirrors were suspended out of sight. He swept off his silk hat and began to make a bow.

There came a terrible rush of air and a black pit opened at his feet. Nancy had once been shown the dark realm of machinery and pulleys and ladders that lay beneath the stage. Devil tipped forwards, slowly, like a giant puppet, and disappeared into the darkness. Too late, her voice tore out of her throat. The roaring filled her mouth with scarlet noise and she thrashed in the coils of her clothing that had now become slippery and voluminous.

Phyllis appeared in the audience, her face white and round as the full moon, and then she was gone and Nancy's face was pressed up against the cold bars of the box. To her relief she found that the metal bars belonged to the hotel bedstead, not a box at the Palmyra. She was tangled up in the bedcovers and she writhed to set herself free.

She had fallen asleep after all and it had only been a nightmare, nothing more.

She had no idea of the time, but the depth of darkness suggested that it was the lowest hour of the night. She was sweating and shivering and her mouth was parched. Her water glass was empty. Phyllis had not filled it up for her.

Phyllis was dead.

Nancy slid out of bed and haphazardly drew on some clothes. She set out for the distant bathroom but in her confused state she remembered there were windows on the half-landing just beyond it. She was taken with the idea of looking out of one of the windows at the shifting sea. It wouldn't be soothing, but it might be something like looking the enemy in the eye. Feeling her way along the wall she shuffled through the darkness. In an angle of the stairs a little triangular bay jutted out towards the sea. She sank down on a window seat and pressed her forehead to the cold glass.

There were bobbing lights out on the water but she thought at first that the beach below the terrace was deserted.

Then, looking harder, she saw that there was someone out there. A figure like a black stone pillar stood alone, staring in the direction of the pier. From the set of his shoulders, the angle of his head, Nancy knew it was Mr Feather.

She watched him for a long time but he didn't move. The black flower was withering in her chest, its petals falling into soft dust.

ALSO BY ROSIE THOMAS

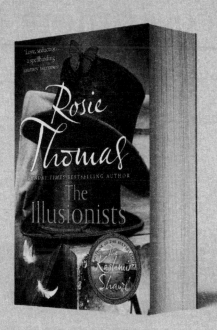

LONDON 1885

As a turbulent and change-filled century draws to a close, there has never been a better time to alter your fortune. But for a beautiful young woman of limited means, Eliza's choices appear to lie between the stifling domesticity of marriage or a downwards spiral to the streets — no matter how determined she is to forge her own path.

One night at a run-down theatre, she meets the charismatic Devil Wix — showman, master of illusion, fickle friend. Drawn into his circle, Eliza becomes the catalyst of change for his colleagues — a dwarf, an eccentric engineer, and an artist — as well as Devil himself. And as Eliza embarks on a dangerous adventure, she must decide which path to choose, and how far she should go when she holds all their lives in her hands.

Out now

Discover more from

'Rosie Thomas is one of the best storytellers around'
Daily Express

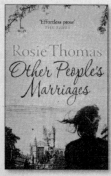

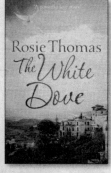

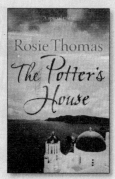

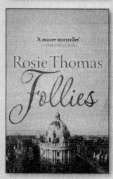

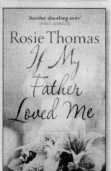

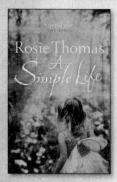

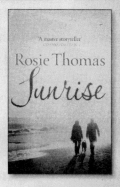

Rosie Thomas

'Beautiful, effortless prose'
The Times

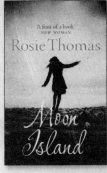

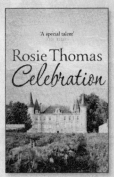

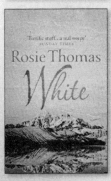

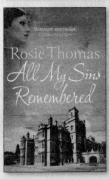

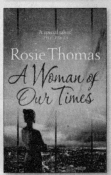